SHADOWS

WARRIOR SERIES

Also by Melanie P. Smith

<u>Warrior Series</u>

Dusk

After Dark

Serendipity (Anthology)

Dawn

<u>Novels</u>

Hidden Lakes

SHADOWS

Warrior Series

Book Four

by:
Melanie P. Smith

MPSmith Publishing

Dedication:

To my sister Heidi...

Who always speaks her mind but has a big heart

There's no better friend than a sister.

Chapter One

Thomas walked into the elegant hotel and casually glanced around. He knew she wouldn't be here yet. Diana Martingale enjoyed making an entrance. She mistakenly believed it gave her an edge. It didn't, not with Thomas anyway. He slid up to the counter and ordered a glass of wine. He really didn't have time for this, but Diana had sounded so desperate. At least the wine would help settle his nerves. He'd had such a terrible day at the office, he deserved a relaxing dinner out. Thomas sighed, chances were low that dinner with Diana would be relaxing.

Out of the corner of his eye, Thomas noticed the hotel manager hurrying his way. He'd hoped to remain anonymous tonight but since his father's death, that rarely happened. "Sir," the impeccably dressed man called. "Let me get that for you. Over here." He quickly took Thomas' drink and headed for a private booth. "Will you be dining alone tonight or shall I watch for a guest?" he queried.

Shadows

Thomas smiled at the man. What was his name again? Parker? No...Porter. That was it, Martin Porter. "Thank you, Martin," Thomas paused. The man beamed at the acknowledgment. "I am waiting for a guest tonight. It's a woman by the name of Diana Martingale. I believe she is staying here, in the hotel."

"Awe...yes," Mr. Porter acknowledged. "Ms. Martingale is in room 514. Is she a good friend of yours, sir? I wasn't aware the two of you were acquainted. I apologize. Had I known, we would have done something special when she arrived. We had that fruit art come in today, would you like me to have one sent up to her room?"

"That won't be necessary. I don't believe she'll be staying much longer. Apparently she's leaving town," Thomas paused. "Did she happen to say why she was staying in the hotel in the first place? A few weeks ago, she had an apartment of her own."

"Not to my knowledge," the man mused. "I believe she's booked into next week though. That's strange. We haven't been notified of her departure," Porter paused. "Oh, well. I guess plans change. If there is anything I can do for you, just let me know. Pete can take care of your needs at the restaurant." Porter signaled for a young teenager. The kid sauntered up to the table waiting for direction.

"Pete, this is Mr. Thomas Deveraux. If he needs anything, anything at all, please make sure you take care of it immediately."

"Will do," Pete nodded in Thomas' direction.

"Hey Pete," Thomas grinned, keeping things informal usually minimized tension and lightened the mood. He still wasn't used to the reaction he always got from lower level employees. Too bad the upper level didn't take notes. "I'm expecting a guest tonight. I'd like to hang out here in the bar until she arrives. Once Ms. Martingale shows up, she'll expect to be seated immediately. I'll apologize in advance for her impatience. She can also come across as rude at times. Could you have our table prepared and ready? She should be arriving any minute now. Maybe we can head off a scene."

"I'll get right on it." The kid rushed off to prepare a table.

"Pete is very reliable. I assure you, he'll give you his complete attention throughout the entire evening." Martin scowled at something in the lobby. "If you will excuse me, sir. It looks like there may be a problem at the front desk."

"Of course," Thomas said in understanding. He took another sip of his wine as he watched the man rush off to handle an upset customer. Martin paused just an instant at the check-in counter. Thomas assumed he was telling the greeter what to do with Diana once she arrived.

Thomas settled back into the comfortable booth. He was thankful to finally have a minute alone, it had been such a horrible day. Running so many businesses was hectic enough, he didn't need the insubordination and constant nagging he was getting from his managers. Luke had been grooming his children to take over the business for years. Well actually, all their lives if he was completely honest. Thomas and Alex knew each branch of the organization inside and out. They had since they were ten years old. As children, Luke and Marlena would quiz them. It was a game their parents developed to see which child knew the most about current business operations. The one thing their parents hadn't prepared them for, was the constant chaos. Luke, like Thomas, believed his managers would accept the change in ownership when Luke was gone. They all believed Deveraux Industries would run just as smoothly as it always had. That was not the case. One by one top level managers were testing the waters. They were attempting things they knew they'd never get away with under Luke's control.

It was obvious the executive managers of Deveraux Industries believed he and Alex were weak. Many of them also thought the two siblings were oblivious when it came to day to day operations. Thomas had been forced to fire one of his top men this afternoon for embezzlement and lying. He would not tolerate dishonesty in his company. The man had the gall to look him in the eye and tell an out and out lie. Not just a little white lie either. It was a whopper. As if Thomas wouldn't notice forty thousand dollars was missing from operating expenses. It didn't take a lot of investigating to track the money. Phil Burton had used his budget to finance a competitor. It still amazed Thomas that anyone would believe they'd get away with such a betrayal. To top it all off, the man had been sincerely surprised when he got fired.

Burton actually had to be escorted off the premises by security. He'd been very vocal about his intent to sue the company over his termination. Thomas wasn't worried about legal problems. He had called Tom immediately and was assured it would be taken care of before the end of the day. Tom Elliott Knox was the best legal counsel in the industry, that's why Luke had hired him. Tom dealt with legal issues involving the company, Jake handled personal business as well as the supernatural. Thomas had been surprised and a bit curious when Knox insisted he and Alex needed to attend a ten o'clock meeting the following morning, no excuses. Clearly something important was brewing. Tom wouldn't even give a hint what the meeting was for. That was unusual and not like

Knox at all. Thomas just hoped it wasn't bad news. Lately, he and Alex had dealt with enough bad news to last a lifetime.

Thomas took another sip of his wine. It was almost gone now. If Diana didn't show soon, he was going to leave. He had too many fires to put out. He couldn't waste an entire evening waiting for a woman he really didn't want to see in the first place. Thomas thought back to his earlier conversation. He hadn't talked to Diana for several months. Hooking up with her had been a mistake. She was beautiful and sophisticated, but she was cold. He'd realized that after their first excruciating date. To be honest, he hadn't planned on ever seeing her again. Which is why he was more than a little surprised when she tracked him down a few weeks later. In a moment of weakness he'd agreed to a second date. They'd gone to an expensive restaurant and during dinner he questioned his original assessment of her. She'd been charming and flirtatious. When she invited him up to her apartment, he hesitantly agreed. At the time, he wanted to avoid returning home to a house full of warriors. Big mistake. Sleeping with her had been an eye opener. She was the most distant, frigid woman he had ever encountered. He promised himself that night he'd never see her again. And he hadn't.

Thomas had confided in Jake, describing the awful experience to his friend. Jake insisted on hiring a private investigator to look into Diana's background. Thomas was even more set on avoiding her when he found out she'd been married three times and had walked away with a large settlement at the conclusion of each one. If she thought he was going to be husband number four, she was sadly mistaken.

Now here he was, sitting in a dark booth waiting to find out why she was so upset. Why was this woman who was completely

5

void of emotion in such a panic? Had she somehow gotten herself into trouble? It wouldn't be the first time he'd broken things off with a woman only to hear from her again down the road. They usually wanted money. Just enough to give them a new start. It was difficult to say no, but he knew he didn't have a choice. Once he started down that path and gave the first one money, women would come out of the woodwork asking for a hand out. Luke and Marlena had taught him that lesson long before he even went on his first date. He wouldn't allow anyone to take advantage of him, or his families' reputation that way. He glanced at his watch again. Five more minutes and he was out of here. Diana should know better. Her incessant games were going to backfire this time.

Diana sat in the luxurious room waiting for the call. The bell boy would come through, she'd tipped him generously. As an added incentive, she'd flashed him a seductive smile and lingered just a minute to flirt a little. The kid was smitten. Men were so easy to manipulate. She sighed. Too bad things hadn't worked out with Thomas. He would have been just the challenge she was looking for. This time suffering through the intimacy would have been worth it. She hated that part. Pretending to be affectionate with someone she despised was always so difficult. Unfortunately it was part of the package. What was that saying about no gain without sacrifice? If Luke hadn't died and ruined everything, she was sure this could have been the last time. A payout from the Deveraux's would have been enough to last a lifetime.

Diana wondered what secret Thomas had. All men had one, especially rich men. The wealthy thought they were above the rules. If only his father hadn't died so unexpectedly. The police were still trying to solve Luke Deveraux's murder. That was another problem with the exceptionally wealthy. It was the reason she never went after the big fish. If something went wrong and she had to kill them, it would be too difficult to get away with it. The police wouldn't stop searching until they found their man. Or in her case, woman.

Diana had definitely learned her lesson with her first husband. She'd been so worried throughout that entire investigation. The police had come too close to discovering the truth. That experience taught her one thing, she couldn't kill her targets when she was finished with them. If all of her husbands died mysteriously, she'd immediately come under suspicion. Eventually one of the cops would figure it out. She would not go to prison for killing a man. Her body shuddered in revulsion. The very idea was ridiculous.

Then there was the added delay, which was even worse than the risk of discovery. Once she disposed of her first husband, she wanted out. She needed to move on. After two long years of marriage the town was stifling. Instead, she had to stick around for a couple more months. If she had packed up and left immediately, it would have looked suspicious. Once Diana finally escaped, she landed in a fairly small town. This time she changed tactics. She had to admit she'd made a mistake with husband number two. Mayor Edwards wasn't as wealthy as he led everyone to believe. After a few bad investments and several years of lavish living, his family fortune was almost depleted. It had been such a relief to find his dirty secret so early on in their marriage. The rest had been child's play. She didn't even have to fake her disgust. Diana smiled at her performance. Edwards thought she was disgusted and horrified over his fondness for teenage porn. In reality, she just found the moron revolting. He'd been more than happy to give her a quick divorce to save his political career. Unfortunately she'd only gotten a couple million out of him.

That's when Diana headed to California. Husband number three was a wealthy lawyer. His secret was more difficult to find.

Shadows

She'd almost given up when she stumbled onto it by accident. The sly lawyer was smarter than she thought. He had a hefty nest egg tucked away for a rainy day. A nest egg he'd acquired by over billing and creative book keeping. She'd walked away with a large chunk of that particular retirement package. He was more than happy to share in exchange for her signature on that ridiculous gag order and a promise to leave town immediately. That's how she ended up in New York where she had set her sights on Thomas Deveraux.

Diana figured Thomas was a spoiled rich kid, living off his father's success. She'd underestimated him. He was more involved in the company than she'd given him credit for. But, by the time she realized it, she had invested too much into the scam. There was no way she would walk away empty handed. Now that he was running the entire enterprise, he didn't have time for her. Well, she was going to change that tonight. She casually reached into her purse and fingered the glass bottle. Once she slipped him the sleeping powder, she'd still need to coerce him up to her room. According to the website she would have approximately twenty minutes to get him into bed before he passed out.

Diana wasn't looking forward to carrying a child for nine months, but the payout would be worth it. She'd done her homework this time. The Deveraux's were loaded. At least she wouldn't have to sleep with him again. With Thomas unconscious, she could get what she needed and let science do the rest. She was positive he would take the bait. Her research had revealed Thomas was a family man. There was no way he would let her sell his child to strangers. Strangers that didn't qualify to adopt a kid through legitimate means because of their criminal history. He'd pay anything if it meant saving his brat. She planned to ask for a bundle. Oh, he'd scoff at first. She knew he'd try to play hard ball, but she'd win in the end. Diana squirmed in anticipation. She was so engrossed in her thoughts she almost fell off the chair when her phone rang. She rushed to the door, anxious to get this night behind her.

* * * *

Abby sat with her friends at their usual table. They'd been coming here for years. Tonight's outing was a welcome distraction. It was nice to get away from the house for a few hours. Her family was always so serious these days. They were sure the vampires were going to attack again. Unfortunately, no one knew how. All the shifters were on edge. They had been since her kidnaping, but it was far worse after their community had been bombed. Abby assumed the fae and the warriors were preoccupied with the vampire problem as well.

She was shocked back to the present when Thomas Deveraux casually walked through the door with a gorgeous blonde on his arm. Apparently he wasn't on edge worrying about the vampires. He was clearly on a date. She inhaled sharply as the young waiter began to lead the couple to a nearby table. Thomas was always handsome and sexy, but tonight he looked exceptional in his tailor made suit. It accentuated all the right places. Just thinking about that man always took her breath away. Watching him stroll in with another woman was painful. She'd been thinking about him more frequently lately. Well, to be honest she hadn't been able to get him off her mind since her rescue from that cave. For just an instant, she hated the woman draped on his arm.

What was wrong with her? Thomas wasn't interested in her. He'd had plenty of opportunity on their long journey back through

Shadows

the forest. He'd been friendly but clearly unimpressed. Abby had never been jealous before in her life, but she was extremely jealous right now. She wanted to be the one on his arm. She wanted Thomas to invite her to dinner. She wished she were beautiful like his date. Maybe then he'd notice her. Abby's thoughts drifted back to the cave. Thomas had been so fierce as he battled Hector. She'd stood there mesmerized by his strength and his passion. Did he have that much passion for his women?

Abby snapped out of her thoughts immediately as the two passed feet from her table. It was obvious Thomas hadn't seen her. Or maybe he had forgotten her already. Abby studied his date closely. The woman was giving off an unmistakable odor. The blonde was on the hunt. Abby could almost feel the adrenaline pulsing through her veins. This woman may be beautiful and sophisticated, but she was clearly up to something. The smell of a predator ready to pounce permeated the entire room. Abby glanced at Thomas. He was completely oblivious to the danger.

She continued to watch as the couple was seated at a nearby table. The woman was brisk as she said something to the waiter but Abby wasn't close enough to hear the conversation. The boy hurried off and returned moments later with a bottle of champagne. He poured them each a glass, provided menu's, then hurried off. Thomas immediately picked up the menu and began to study his options. Abby watched horrified as the woman slipped something from her purse and dumped it into Thomas' glass. She didn't think, she excused herself and rushed toward the couple's table. Abby's heart sank when she realized she wouldn't make it in time. Thomas absently reached for his glass and took a long drink of the toxic champagne as he continued to study his dinner choices. His eyes never left the menu.

Abby pretended to trip as she reached her destination. Thomas' glass immediately tipped on its side. The contents crept across the table, seeping into the elegant white tablecloth. Thomas' date glared at Abby, obviously furious. Abby forced herself to look ashamed. Inwardly she was grateful she'd hit her mark.

Thomas didn't notice Abby until she fell against the table. He looked down and realized she must have tripped on the uneven floor board. He made a mental note to have that fixed. He barely noticed when Diana jumped from her chair in a huff. Thomas stood and helped Abby to her feet then smiled warmly. "It was nice of you to drop in," he teased. He glanced around wondering where she'd come from.

"I'm so sorry," she apologized. "I was just having dinner with some friends when I saw you come in." She motioned toward the table where she'd been dining. "I'm sorry I was such a klutz. I just wanted to say hello." She focused her attention on Thomas' suit. "I didn't get any on you did I?" she asked sincerely.

"Huh?" Thomas asked, "Oh, no. I think it went in the other direction." Thomas noticed Diana frantically brushing at her dress. He was surprised at the amusement he found in that. Maybe she'd go away. He still didn't know what she wanted, but he was beyond bored with her antics. He'd only spent five minutes with her and she was already grating on his last nerve.

Diana shot a venomous look towards the clumsy woman. She'd ruined everything. Thomas hadn't ingested enough of that sleeping powder to put him out. Now what? She didn't have any extra, not even at home. Her plans were ruined. She wanted to lash out at the bimbo. Why had she interrupted them anyway? "Thomas, I need you to walk me to my room." She tried to remain civil but it

Shadows

was difficult. She would not walk away empty handed. If she could get Thomas to her room, she'd see what she could get from his wallet. Someone as rich as Thomas would carry several credit cards with him. If she took one from the back, he may not notice it was missing for days. With any luck, she might even have a few weeks.

Thomas studied Diana. He didn't want to go to her room. "Actually, I need to take off. I have some pressing issues to deal with at work. Maybe we can talk some other time." Fat chance. He wasn't going near this woman ever again.

"Thomas," Diana pouted trying to sound desperate. "I really need to talk to you before you go. Please, just walk me to the door. I don't have much time and I need to get out of this wet dress." She held her breath. Would he take the bait? She was counting on his compassion. If he turned her down, the pesky intruder would pay dearly. She might pay anyway. Diana could barely look at the woman without strangling her. The unwelcome girl had ruined everything.

Thomas glanced at Abby and sighed. He'd rather have dinner with her. He shifted his gaze back to Diana. She looked so desperate. What did she want anyway? Thomas decided to get it over with. If he blew her off tonight she'd just call him again tomorrow. He wanted to be done with this. "Alright," he finally said quietly. He refocused his attention on Abby. "It was nice to see you again. Tell your family hello," he paused then gave her a friendly hug. "I'm sorry we don't have time to catch up. Apparently Diana has something pressing she needs to talk to me about." He rolled his eyes. "And she thinks she needs to change." He smiled at Abby as he slipped past her and headed for the elevator,

Diana breathed a sigh of relief. Nice guys were easy targets. She followed Thomas toward the elevator. Once she had him in her room, she'd keep him there until he became drowsy. She didn't think he'd pass out completely, but with any luck he'd be incapacitated enough to get to his wallet and disappear. She didn't notice the small mouse slip into the corner just before the heavy doors slid closed.

Abby caught her breath. Being that close to Thomas was electrifying. She wished she could enjoy the moment, but she was worried. The woman, Diana, was angry and obviously up to no good. Abby could feel it. She studied Thomas as he walked away. There was no way to know what Diana had slipped into his drink. Abby also had no idea how the human drug would impact a warrior. From what she understood, any kind of chemical made warriors extremely ill. She rushed down the hall and looked around, grateful it was empty. She quickly shifted on the fly and slipped through the doors just in time.

Thomas felt dizzy. What was going on? He'd felt fine just a few minutes ago. He swung his glance to Diana then grabbed the railing. He was going to pass out. He fought the darkness with everything he had. What was happening? It didn't make any sense. Was Diana somehow responsible for this? Was that why she insisted he walk her to her room? What game was she playing? At this point it really didn't matter. He was going to black out. Whatever she wanted, he was too weak to stop her. She was going to win.

Diana studied Thomas. He looked ill, like he could pass out any second. Why was he so white and clammy? Was he having some kind of allergic reaction to the drug? She was sure he hadn't ingested enough to knock him out. Maybe luck was on her side

Shadows

tonight. She smiled an evil, triumphant grin. This was better than she'd hoped. If Thomas had a serious allergic reaction, that would give her more time. It might take days before anyone found him. By that time she'd max out the cards and disappear. She'd need to make sure she covered her tracks well. If he ended up dying, everyone would be looking for her. She might have to take care of the girl too, just to be safe. The elevator door slowly slid open. Diana placed an arm around Thomas' waist and awkwardly stumbled to her room.

Abby hesitated for the slightest instant then shifted again. A mouse would draw more attention up here than a pet on the loose. She glanced at Thomas. He was in trouble. He looked like he was about to black out. Abby wasn't sure how to help him, but she was determined to find a way somehow. Diana didn't notice the orange tabby slip through the door as she entered her room. The cat quietly darted under the bed, a silent observer for the moment. She knew she couldn't help Thomas until Diana left, or her family secret would be discovered. But the instant the woman was gone, Abby would be ready. She continued to watch as Diana unhooked Thomas' watch and slipped it into her bag. The woman then began to hum gleefully as she rummage through his pockets until she found his wallet. After sliding out two credit cards, Diana rushed through the door, shutting it tightly behind her.

Chapter Two

The instant the door closed, Abby shifted back and rushed to Thomas. He was having a hard time breathing and seemed to be unconscious. She pulled out her cellphone and began to dial Morrigan when Thomas' phone chimed loudly. Abby grabbed it and looked at the display. She felt relief flood over her as she read the large name flashing across the screen. "Alex!" She exclaimed as she answered the phone. "It's Abby. Thomas is in trouble. I need your help."

"Abby?" Alex answered confused. Why was Abby with her brother? "What's wrong with Thomas? Dimitri is going nuts here and to be honest, so am I."

"Some woman named Diana slipped something into his drink. I...well, this is going to sound strange, but I could smell she was up to no good so I followed them. She brought him up to a hotel room, stole his watch and a couple credit cards and left in a hurry. I suspect she's on her way to go shopping," Abby paused. "Thomas' breathing is strange and I'm worried about him. What should I do?"

"I'm on my way," Alex assured her. "What hotel and what room?"

Abby relayed the information then paused abruptly. "Didn't I hear something about a big social event tonight for D-Tech? Are you and Dimitri missing something important because of this?" she asked.

"Yes, but Thomas is more important," Alex insisted. "We're just pulling in, we'll be there in a minute." She hung up as Dimitri stopped next to the curb, not caring he was currently parked in a red zone. Alex stopped to address the doorman before rushing inside. Dimitri followed close behind.

Abby hurried to the door and opened it wide. Alex and Dimitri were practically running up the hallway. She stepped aside as the two of them entered the dimly lit room.

Alex inhaled sharply. Thomas looked bad. She rushed to his side and immediately dropped to her knees, closing her eyes as she concentrated on Thomas. Alex instantly realized she couldn't save him. He wasn't injured. Her eyes darted up to collide with Dimitri's. "I can't help. He doesn't have any injuries for me to heal." A tear slid down her cheek.

Dimitri moved to the bed and pulled a large metal container from a bag. "Hold his head up, I need to get this blood into him." He put an arm around Alex. "He's going to be okay. He just needs more blood to cleanse his system."

Abby moved to the other side of the bed and rushed to stuff as many pillows as possible under Thomas' head. Once he was propped up, she took a step back. She felt helpless, but there was nothing else she could do here.

Dimitri slowly slid a feeding tube down Thomas' throat. He gradually poured the entire contents of the container into the tube. Then he fed him a second bag. Within minutes, Thomas' color looked better.

Alex turned to Abby. "I'm so glad you were here to help him. If you hadn't answered the phone, we never would have found him. We were on our way to systematically check every business we own. It would have taken hours," she paused. "Uh...why are you here anyway?"

"Oh yeah," Abby began. "I forgot I didn't explain that. Well, my friends and I have a regular standing dinner date in the restaurant downstairs. I was actually just getting ready to leave when Thomas and the blonde walked in. The woman smelled like a predator on the hunt." She cleared her throat a little embarrassed. "I guess it's a shifter thing."

"I understand," Alex prompted.

"Anyway, I couldn't ignore the smell or the feeling she was up to no good. I kept my eye on the woman as the waiter escorted them to their table. I was shocked when she pulled a small vile from her purse and dumped some kind of powder into Thomas' drink. Thomas was still studying the menu so he didn't see her, and it all happened so quickly. I jumped up to intervene, but was too late. Thomas took a long drink of his champagne. I pretended to trip over an uneven floor board and dumped the remaining contents of the glass onto the table. The woman was livid. She jumped up and

17

Shadows

began this over exaggerated display, claiming her dress was all wet and she needed to change. At first I didn't think Thomas was going to go. He said he was busy and had to leave. She whined and pouted and said she needed to talk to him. Thomas said goodbye and left with the woman." Abby was a little embarrassed but continued, hoping her honesty about Diana hadn't revealed her interest in Thomas. "I was still worried so I shifted into a mouse and slipped into the elevator. Thomas was clearly in trouble. The woman had to help him to the room. I shifted into a cat and was able to slip through the door and hide under the bed," Abby paused. "Diana stole Thomas' watch and then rummaged through his wallet and stole some credit cards. I was just dialing Morrigan for help when you called." She turned to Alex. That's when she noticed the couple was in fancy evening wear. They were going to miss something important over this.

Alex noticed Abby was studying their attire. "Don't worry about it. This is more important," she assured her and sighed. "I'm sure Thomas and I will have to deal with the fallout later, but I can't leave him alone like this. That woman had to be Diana Martingale. She's been after Thomas for months. Jake told me a little bit about her, she's bad news."

Abby considered their options. "What if you don't have to miss it? Maybe you could just be a little late."

"I think the whole night is a bust," Alex sighed. "I can't heal him, so I won't leave him."

"The blood seems to be helping. If Dimitri can get him into my car. I can have Morrigan meet me at Thomas' house and unload him. You guys can go to your event and I'll stay with Thomas tonight. I do have some nursing skills. I've helped mamma for years when our pack has been injured," she paused. "You can come by first thing in the morning. That way Thomas isn't alone and you and Dimitri won't have to miss the event. It sounded important."

"I don't know," Alex said as she looked at Thomas again. He did look a lot better after the blood.

Dimitri turned Alex to face him. "I think it's a good idea. We both know how important it is for you to make an appearance at this event." He glanced at Thomas. "He's doing better. Abby can hook up an IV when they get back to the house and continue the blood all night." He turned to Abby. "Right? You know how to set up an IV?"

"Oh yes," she answered. "I've done it a million times, not with blood but the concept is the same." She turned to Alex. "I promise, I'll call you if there are any problems. He's already improving. I'll make sure he has blood all night and I'm sure he'll be better in the morning," she urged. "Go. Let me help out here. I owe you guys my life. I owe Thomas my life. Let me do this to help repay him for the sacrifices he made for me."

Alex studied Abby, she seemed to really want to help. She turned her attention back to Thomas. They were right, he was doing better already. "Okay. If you promise to call if he takes a turn for the worse," she finally agreed.

"I promise," Abby assured her. "Let me call Morrigan and have him meet me at the house. What's the address?" she inquired.

Once Thomas was settled into the car Alex and Dimitri turned to leave.

Shadows

"Oh," Abby stopped them. "Do I need to call the police or something to report the theft?"

"No," Alex answered. "I've called the bank, they've put an alert on the cards. Diana can't use them without getting arrested."

"Good," Abby said relieved.

* * * *

Radek sat in the large chair trying to relax, but he was so excited about his new plan. He glanced up as Lilith walked into the room. "Well?" he asked. She was doing much better. Her stomach wound was almost completely healed and her focus was back where it needed to be. On him and his plans. Radek never understood how a simple human had gotten the best of her in the first place. He was just glad the human was dead and Lilith was focused on the war again.

"It's all taken care of," she assured him. "I just left him. He's going to get started tonight. Nobody will ever link his activities to us. This is brilliant!" Lilith exclaimed, excited. "Our secret weapon will wreak havoc while we focus on building an army. How is that phase of the plan coming along?" she asked casually.

Radek stood and walked to the desk. He returned with a stack of papers and handed them to Lilith. "I've already organized the teams and I'm almost finished coordinating destinations. For now I can't risk another visit from those three pesky kings. As much as I don't care what they think, I don't have the resources to fight more than one war. So, all of our men will have to be split into teams and disbursed throughout the country. I'm even sending a couple groups into Canada. I also thought we'd send one team to Mexico, although Mexico is more dangerous. Our people are active while the Mexican drug lords are active. We tend to lose more vampires in populated cities down there, but I'm willing to sacrifice a few to propagate my army."

Lilith studied the plan. It was good. Radek's teams were carefully thought out. He distributed the men for effectiveness. Each team had men that could easily control the new vamps. This was going to work, she could feel it. She looked at Radek and smiled. They proceeded to engage in a lengthy discussion about destinations and strategy. This, the two of them did well together. They worked throughout the entire night, organizing teams and developing a time line. Radek still didn't trust Lilith with personal issues, but he did know she was devoted to winning this war.

* * * *

Rand McBride groggily reached for the annoying device that was screaming at him from the night stand. He searched blindly through the darkness until his fingertips found the incessant phone. The seasoned detective slid his legs off the bed and sat, pressing the button to stop the alarm and casually switching on the lamp. "Why couldn't people die at a decent hour?" he grumbled as he glanced at the clock; four twenty three. He scrolled through the tiny display reading the information, then stood. Today was going to be a very long day.

Twenty minutes later, Rand pulled the black Ford up to the curb. Police cruisers speckled the area making it easy to find the crime scene. Beat cops had already taped off the area to keep out curious onlookers and the press for now. A formal statement would be given later in the day, probably in time for the morning news. Rand was grateful he wouldn't be handling that particular duty. He hated the constant barrage of questions, each reporter trying to trick the cops out of information that was supposed to be kept confidential. It never ended. Public Information Officer for New York's finest was not in his career path. He smiled. No worries there, his superiors would be horrified at the prospect of him acting as PIO.

McBride slid under the yellow tape and headed for the body. His shield prominently displayed on his belt was the only identification the uniforms needed. Nobody would obstruct his path. The beat cops were always anxious to turn the situation over to someone else. Once a detective arrived on scene, the uniforms could relax and just focus on containment. Rand stopped to study the woman lying motionless on the dirty sidewalk. A small spider crawled over the placid gray skin stretched across the back of her right hand. He shifted his gaze to her face. Her dull, glazed eyes stared blankly into the darkness. The first thing he noticed was the lack of blood.

McBride turned to the uniformed officer standing by his side. "Do you see anything out of place here?" he asked, taking advantage of the opportunity to teach the rookie.

"Yes sir," the kid said enthusiastically. "I've been wondering where all the blood is."

"Very good. Is someone from the Crime Scene Unit on their way?" McBride asked.

"They were called at the same time as you were. I expect them any minute." The enthusiastic uniform replied.

"Good, what's your name?" McBride asked.

"Garcia," he answered.

"Once CSU is finished, the ME will take the corpse and tell me everything I need to know. I'd lay odds this body's been moved. She was killed somewhere else, then dumped here on the street. I don't suppose we have any witnesses?" He was sure he knew the answer but asked anyway.

"Not that we've found so far. My partner's been canvassing the area, but last I heard nobody saw a thing," Garcia supplied.

McBride laughed. "Welcome to New York, kid." He glanced behind him as a Crime Scene Unit parked behind his vehicle. "Millions of people milling around all hours of the day and nobody ever sees anything." The group continued to process the scene well into the morning.

* * * *

Foster sauntered down the stairs and entered the kitchen, anxious for a cup of coffee. He stopped abruptly at the sight of his brother sitting at the table with his mother. Lawson casually slid a check into his front pocket. Foster scowled. So, his mother was giving the bum money again. He closed his eyes and prepared for the altercation.

"Good morning, son," Patricia Dillinger greeted her youngest child.

Shadows

"Good morning, mother," Foster returned as he walked to the counter and poured himself a cup of coffee. He dumped in a teaspoon of sugar and poured in some cream.

"Uh," Lawson said clearing his throat. "I need to head out," he stood, leaned over and gently kissed his mother's cheek.

"Don't leave on my account," Foster told him. "I have work to do. I realize you don't know what that's like...actually working for a living, but it typically requires an early morning."

"Don't start," Lawson warned. "I'm not in the mood for this today." Lawson strolled out of the room, then continued out the front door.

"I'm going to need you to replenish my funds early this month," Patricia said innocently.

"Sorry mother," Foster answered. "I told you what would happen if you gave your money to Lawson again." He took a sip of his coffee. "You're just going to have to make do until your regular payday."

Patricia glared, furious with her son. She was the head of this family. If she wanted more money, she would have more money. "Are you forgetting who the head of this household is?" she said trying to sound civil, but failing.

"No," Foster said unmoved. "You are the head of the family. I am the head of the company. Which means, I get to disperse the funds as I see fit. Until you and Lawson help with the work, you get what I decide to give you when it comes to financial support."

"I'm not going to argue with you about this Foster," Patricia said behind gritted teeth. She was more than tired of begging her son for money.

"Neither am I," Foster agreed. "You will get paid in one week, the same as always," he paused and grinned. "If you're short, maybe Lawson will give you a loan. He seems to have come into some money this morning." He turned and left the room, then headed out the front door. He was proud of himself. In the past, he'd felt sorry for his mother and eventually had given in. Not anymore. Lawson was a huge drain on their finances. Foster was tired of his brother. Lawson thought he was too good to help with the family business. Instead, he sold explosives to the human underground, partied all night and even experimented with human drugs. Foster was sick of it. He would not finance such a reckless, selfish lifestyle.

Lawson watched as Foster entered the garage, slid into his car and exited the underground parking area. He wasn't finished with his mother. They had plans to finalize. He'd be surprised if Foster gave the old lady more money today. Foster was livid the last time his mother wrote him a check and had vowed she was on her own if she ever did it again. Foster might think he was going to keep the family fortune from his older brother, but he was mistaken. Lawson was in charge of this family. He was the oldest son. He should be the fae king. If it wasn't for those damn warriors he would be. Well, in time the warriors would be extinct and a new protector would take their place. Then he'd be worshiped by all the fae just as he should be. Lawson yawned as he pushed the penthouse button on the elevator panel. He'd been up all night, he needed a few hours of sleep but this couldn't wait. He had an idea he wanted to run by his mother. If she agreed, they would soon have all the money they needed for their experiments.

Shadows

* * * *

Rand McBride pulled up the long, elaborate drive toward the large mansion. Just his luck. After such a pleasant morning, he got to deal with the wealthy as an encore. He parked his dark sedan in front of the house and strolled to the front door. The bell had barely stopped ringing when the door slowly slid open. A young, fairly attractive girl stood in the doorway.

McBride handed her his card. "I'm Detective Rand McBride. I need to speak with Thomas Deveraux," he demanded.

"Oh?" Abby asked, studying the card. Why did a homicide detective need to speak to Thomas? "I'm sorry, Thomas is not available this morning. He's ill."

McBride took a step forward. "I don't think you understand ma'am. I'm not asking."

Abby raised an eyebrow. Did this cop really think with a little intimidation she'd just open the door and let him in? Not a chance. She stared at him, unmoved.

What an obstinate brat. Who was this woman anyway? He'd had Garcia pull information on the family and this girl was not in the packet. "Well, then maybe I could ask you a few questions while I'm here?" he pressed.

Abby didn't budge. What was this guy up to?

"Look," McBride softened. "I think we got off to a bad start. I'm in the middle of an investigation and I've been up for hours. I only have a few questions. Can I come in and talk to you for just a moment?" he asked trying to sound sincere. What he really wanted to do was strangle the girl.

Abby hesitated only a moment then pushed the door open in invitation. She casually leaned her back against the wall and waited. She wasn't about to invite him into the library. This was clearly an interrogation, not a social call.

Okay, so they were going to talk in the foyer. She might think that bothered him, but McBride actually preferred it. "What is your name?" he asked.

"Abby," she supplied.

"Abby...?" he paused. No answer. "I assume you have a last name, Abby. What is it?"

Abby hesitated, would he make the connection to her father this soon? Oh well, it couldn't be helped. "Cooper," she said casually.

"Okay, Abby Cooper. How are you related or associated with the Deveraux's?" Rand asked.

The detective hadn't reacted, maybe he didn't realize her father and his Chief were good friends. Or maybe he was just good at his job. "I'm not related. I'm a friend of the family," she supplied.

"So what brought you to their home this morning?" he asked.

"As I said, Thomas is ill. I didn't arrive this morning. I've been with him all night," she supplied.

Well, that put a kink in his theory. If Thomas was at home sick all evening, how had he killed the woman? But he hadn't been

Shadows

ill all evening, McBride spoke to three people that placed Thomas at the hotel, in the restaurant and at the bar last night. Three people that could place Thomas with his victim. Maybe Thomas was trying to arrange an alibi.

"What time did you arrive last evening?" he asked, then paused when the front door flew open.

Alex took in the room, she was annoyed. Why was a police officer standing in Thomas' foyer so early this morning? It was inappropriate for him to be questioning Abby. Abby was their guest, it was rude. Her mind was searching for an explanation, she hadn't reported the missing items or the poisoning to the police. Wait, had Diana been arrested already? But wouldn't they be dealing with the bank, not Thomas? She turned her gaze to Abby and softened. The shifter was a lifesaver. Once Alex arrived at the social last night she realized her absence would have been catastrophic. When would these management games end? "Good morning, Abby." She leaned in and gave the woman a hug. "I'm sorry I wasn't here to deal with this, but I had no idea an officer would be paying us a visit this morning." She turned to McBride. "Can I help you with something?"

McBride wasn't sure if he was grateful for the interruption or annoyed at it. He didn't feel like he was getting anywhere with Abby, but he wasn't sure teaming her up with Thomas' sister was going to improve the situation. "As I've been trying to explain to Abby here," he shifted his gaze to Abby then back to Alex. "I need to speak with Thomas."

"I'm sure Abby has informed you that's not possible." She saw a slight nod from Abby then continued. "Thomas is sick."

"Yes. Ms. Cooper did mention that," Rand took a deep breath. Okay, back to square one. "However, I'm not asking, I'm telling." He knew she wouldn't like that, but he was tired and not in the mood to play games. He was going to get answers.

"Hum," Alex pondered. What an arrogant buffoon. Before she could respond, her phone rang. She glanced down and saw it was Dimitri. "Hi hon," she answered catching the annoyed look on the officers face as she brushed him off.

"Did you speak to Thomas yet? You didn't call," Dimitri asked. He was certain she had forgotten him and was a little annoyed at that, although he was trying to pretend it didn't matter. Alex had been worried about her brother all night. He knew she had barely slept.

"Actually, I haven't seen Thomas," she admitted.

"Why not? Did something happen? Were you in an accident?" He was worried now.

"No," she cut him off. "I'm at the house. When I arrived, an officer was questioning Abby. He's being evasive and demanding right now so I haven't had a chance to check on Thomas yet," Alex told him, exasperation evident in her tone.

"An officer? Why?" he asked.

"I don't know," she paused. "Why are you here?" she asked, glaring at McBride.

McBride handed her his card. "There was a homicide last night. I need to talk to Thomas about his involvement." He decided to be direct.

Shadows

Alex studied the detective coldly. "Thomas wasn't involved in a homicide last night," she stated flatly. "As I told you, he's been ill."

"Alex," Dimitri spoke into the phone. "I'm coming over. I'll be there as soon as I can."

"That's not necessary," Alex informed Dimitri. "You have an important meeting this morning. You can't miss it. I'll be fine."

Alex was right, he couldn't miss the meeting. "Okay. Call me when he leaves and you've talked to Thomas," he finally agreed.

"Okay, I love you," she softened.

"I love you too," he said, smiling. "If you need me, just call." Dimitri disconnected the line and pondered the situation then he scrolled through his numbers and dialed Jake.

Alex turned her attention back to the detective. How could he possibly think Thomas was involved in a murder? In reality, Thomas had almost been murdered himself last night. He'd spent the evening fighting for his life. He was not going to spend the morning defending himself against a bully.

"I assume you are Alex Deveraux," McBride began. He knew she was, she looked exactly like her photo.

"I am," Alex said without emotion.

"May I call you Alex?" he asked.

Alex considered the request then shrugged. "If you like," she finally answered.

"Thank you," Rand said hoping he sounded sincere. "Alex, I need to talk to Thomas. The longer you stall, the more suspicious the two of you appear. If Thomas really is ill, that might change things. Right now I'm wondering what you're hiding."

Alex wasn't moved. "As I told you, Thomas is very sick." She paused. "If you will wait in the library, I'll check on him. If I decide he's up for it, I'll grant you a few minutes with him but no more." She turned to leave.

"I'm afraid I can't allow that," he said forcefully.

Alex stopped and turned to face the detective again. "I'm sorry?" she said coolly. "You can't allow what, exactly?"

"This is not a meaningless social call, it's an investigation. A woman was murdered last night," Rand told her angrily. "For the last time, I'm not asking for permission. I will talk to Thomas immediately. If you think I'm going to allow you to warn him I'm coming, or collaborate on a story, you are mistaken. Where is Thomas?" he demanded. "If you don't point me in the right direction in the next five seconds, I'll tear this place apart until I find him myself."

Alex wasn't intimidated by this man. His overbearing bullheaded approach might work with some, but not her. "I didn't realize you had a search warrant for our home," she said coolly. "We could have avoided all of this if you had just produced it immediately upon my arrival. Once I see the actual signed document, feel free to search your heart away," she countered.

Rand was taken by surprise by that one. He hadn't said anything about a warrant. Now what?

Shadows

"I see," Alex continued. "So you don't have a search warrant to...what was it you said?" she paused. "Oh yes, I believe it was tear this place apart?" she waited. No answer. "Then unless you have a warrant of arrest or some kind of subpoena for Thomas as a material witness in a crime, I'm afraid I'm going to have to ask you to leave my home immediately."

Rand didn't budge. He was not leaving. Sure, he was on shaky ground, but this woman was not going to thwart his investigation. Clearly this family was responsible for the murder. He was sure of it now. There was no other reason the sister would be so protective of her brother. He was about to change strategies when the door opened and a man walked in. Seriously? What was this, Grand Central Station?

Jake surveyed the room and sighed. Tensions were high. He was afraid that might happen. The Deveraux's did not handle attacks on their family well. He thought of Luke and smiled. Now there was a man that went berserk when his family was threatened. He walked to Alex and kissed her softly on the forehead. Then he placed an arm around her shoulders and guided her into the library. "I think we should take this conversation somewhere a little more comfortable," he said gently as he walked through the large doors and settled Alex into a large lounge chair. He turned to see the detective standing in the doorway.

Jake knew that stance. The detective was out of patience and about to forcibly take control. Jake hoped the man had at least a little tolerance left in him. This was all a big misunderstanding. Most cops weren't used to resistance. Clearly this one was no exception. He casually walked towards the man and held out his hand. "Hello," he waited for the cop to shake it. "My name is Jake Wilder, legal counsel for the Deveraux's."

"Funny, I don't recall Alex calling an attorney." He narrowed his eyes. "Any particular reason you just happened to show up this morning?" Rand asked skeptically.

"Dimitri called," Jake said simply. "He's quite protective of his fiancé. I guess he thought I might be of use. Oh, I know Alex can handle things on her own, but Dimitri was under the impression you were being a bit too forceful with the woman he loves. Of course I agreed to head over and see what I could do." Jake turned his attention to Alex for the slightest instant. "Alex is loved by many. None of us take kindly to someone trying to bully her," he added for effect.

"Fine," Rand pushed himself from the door jamb and walked casually into the room. "I'll deal with you for now." He hesitated as Abby joined them, sinking into a chair next to Alex. Jake leaned against the large desk and waited. When the room remained completely silent, he nodded at the detective as a sign for him to continue.

"Last night a woman was murdered. A woman that was seen earlier in the evening with Thomas. I arrived this morning to have a civil conversation with Mr. Deveraux about his activities last night. I wanted to get his side of the story so to speak. So far I've gotten the run around. First from Abby over there," he pointed a thumb in her direction. "Then from Alex," he shifted a hard glare her way. "So, once again let me start from the beginning, Jake Wilder. Where is Thomas?"

"Well, since Thomas was poisoned last night and has been fighting for his very life I can only assume he's still in his bed resting," Jake said flatly. So, Dimitri hadn't been over exaggerating. This man truly believed Thomas was involved in a murder.

Shadows

Huh, that was a new twist. This might be interesting after all. "Any reason he's not in the hospital if his condition is that serious?" McBride inquired.

Abby interjected. "There was no need for him to go to the hospital. I agreed to stay with him and monitor his condition throughout the night."

"Are you a nurse?" Rand asked.

"No," Abby said honestly.

"A doctor maybe?" Rand pressed.

"No," Abby said shaking her head a little.

"So, exactly what makes you qualified to tend to the medical needs of a man who was supposedly poisoned and is fighting for his life?" McBride sneered.

"I'm not a certified nurse or a registered doctor but I could be if I wanted. I don't. I've helped my mother since I was five. I have more experience than most when it comes to dealing with the sick or injured," she told him. "And Thomas wasn't supposedly poisoned. He was poisoned. I witnessed it personally."

"So you were an accomplice?" Rand asked.

"Not at all," Abby replied.

"Okay look," Rand sighed. "I can see I've offended both of you somehow. That was not my intention. I'm here to do a job, that's all. Stop with the yes and no's and actually explain what is going on here. It would be extremely helpful."

Nobody spoke. The room was uncomfortably silent.

Rand turned to the lawyer. "Let's start with you," he decided. "How do you know Thomas was poisoned last night?"

"Alex called me," he said. "She was worried, but said Abby was with him and he seemed to be improving."

"Why didn't you stay with him?" he asked Alex.

"I had an engagement I couldn't miss. It was important for the company. Initially I planned to ditch but Abby convinced me she could handle it and would call if Thomas took a turn for the worse," Alex answered. "I trusted her, so I fulfilled my obligation then came here first thing this morning to take over," she scowled. She still hadn't seen Thomas. She needed to know he was okay.

McBride really wasn't getting anywhere. Maybe if he shocked them, if he showed them the brutality of the murder, they might open up. He pulled a snapshot from his pocket and set it on the table in front of the two women. "This is my victim. Do either of you recognize her?" he asked.

Alex and Abby looked down at the photo then studied it more closely. "Diana Martingale," they both said softly. Some mistakes came with a high price. What exactly had she been involved in? Now they would never know.

Rand was waiting for a gasp or some sign of revulsion. Nothing. The two women studied the photo as if it were a serene landscape or a flowery garden. What kind of family was this?

Jake moved to stand behind the two women, curious about the photo. "A little inappropriate don't you think?" he asked as he too

Shadows

studied the picture. The woman was clearly dead, her throat had been slashed from ear to ear. Her color was gray and clammy. Her eyes cold and dead. It was impossible to determine cause of death from this one photo. Oh, the assumption would be she'd been killed when her throat was cut, but Jake wasn't about to take that for granted. He leaned in closer to see if there were any marks on her neck. This could have been a vampire attack. It would be unusual for them to cover their feeding by slashing her throat, but Radek and his followers had been unpredictable lately. Maybe the scare they'd caused throughout the city was catching up to them. Maybe someone had ordered them to be more subtle. The lack of blood surrounding the body told him something was definitely off.

"I don't know," Rand commented. "They don't seem to mind." He was still annoyed by that. He'd wanted to shock them into submission.

Alex looked up at the cop. "I live in New York detective," she paused. "I've seen violence before. If you thought this was going to shock me, you were mistaken. Nothing shocks me anymore." She picked up the picture and held it out for McBride.

Abby's mind was reeling. Of course this man assumed Thomas was the killer. Diana had absconded with his credit cards. People had seen them together at the restaurant. She needed to clear this up. "Uh," she cleared her throat to get their attention. "I assume you are here because Thomas was seen in public with this woman, Diana, last night. Was it the stolen credit cards? Did she still have them when you found her?" Abby asked.

Rand narrowed his eyes. Clearly Abby knew something about Thomas and Diana and their date. "She still had the cards," Rand admitted. "That's one reason we can rule out robbery as a motive." He wasn't going to explain the other reasons. "Why don't you tell me what you know, Abby. It would certainly help me and it might help Thomas." He took a chance and continued. "If you are withholding evidence, I'm going to have to charge you with obstruction. It would be better all-around if you just cooperated."

Abby rolled her eyes. Clearly this guy hadn't made the connection between her and her father. Once her identity was known, most cops tiptoed around her. How would this guy react once he knew his career was on the line? She'd hold that one in reserve for now.

"I'm not going to allow you to threaten and harass Abby this way," Jake interjected.

"I thought you were council for the Deveraux's. Are you now representing Abby as well?" McBride asked.

"No. He's not," Abby said quickly. "My family attorney will represent me if she needs to."

"Abby," Alex turned to her. "It's my fault you are even here. Let Jake handle this for you."

"Nope," Abby said stubbornly. "I know Jake's good, but so is Nancy. I'd be more comfortable if we didn't muddy the waters here. Let Jake handle things for your family and I can handle things on my end. This guy doesn't scare me. I haven't obstructed anything."

Rand frowned, apparently the whole group was familiar with the law. He really hated rich people. "Abby," he said trying to sound soothing. "Talk to me," he pushed. "Will you tell me what

Shadows

you know about last night? About Thomas and Diana and the credit cards?"

"Sure," Abby replied. "I was sitting in the restaurant last night having dinner when I saw Thomas walk in. Diana was with him. They were being escorted to a nearby table," she began.

"Were you eating alone?" Rand asked, pulling his notepad from his pocket.

"No," Abby admitted. "But I'm not going to tell you who I was with unless it becomes absolutely necessary. I'm not going to have you harassing my friends the way you've been browbeating the rest of us this morning."

Rand wanted to argue, but let it drop for now. He'd get the names before he left today. "Go on."

Abby studied him. The man wasn't going to lose that easily. He'd bring it up again. "So Thomas walks in and I realized he didn't see me. It took me a minute to excuse myself. I was finished eating anyway and I thought I'd chat with Thomas for a minute, you know…catch up. I haven't seen him for weeks. Anyway, that's when I saw Diana slip some kind of powder substance into Thomas' drink. I tried to get to the table before he drank any, but I wasn't quick enough," she said regretfully.

"Why didn't Thomas see this happen himself?" he asked.

"He was concentrating on the menu at the time. It was blocking his view. Anyway, I rushed over to their table and pretended to trip on a board. As my hand hit the table, I knocked over the glass of champagne," Abby provided.

"Then what happened?" Rand asked. So far, the story was pretty close to the one he got from the kid. The waiter hadn't known who the mystery girl was, but he'd described basically the same events minus the poison.

"Diana jumped up and began to frantically brush at her dress. She was pretending it was ruined. Her acting skills leave a lot to be desired," Abby silently added and glanced at Alex. "I doubt even a drop of that liquid touched her dress. I was suspicious. Diana asked Thomas to walk her to her room. At first he refused. He said he had company business to handle and he didn't have time. Diana insisted and actually began pouting. It was really over the top," she looked back to the detective.

"Sounds like you didn't like her much," he observed.

"I didn't know her, but no. From this first encounter I didn't like her," she said honestly. She didn't have anything to hide. "Anyway, the two of them left. I continued to watch as they entered the elevator," Abby paused. Now she had to wing it. How did she get to the right floor? A thought struck her. "After the powder in the drink, I didn't trust Diana. It seemed like she was up to something. Plus, I had no idea what Thomas had ingested. I had to check on him," she paused. "I watched the elevator and saw it stopped on the fifth floor. Then I punched the up arrow and waited. It was the longest few minutes of my life. I was nervous and terrified. I didn't have a clue how I was going to help. I just knew I couldn't leave Thomas alone with her. He didn't even know he'd been poisoned." She glanced at the detective to see if he was buying it. So far, so good it seemed.

"Once on the fifth floor, I didn't know what way to go," Abby continued. "I had no idea who the woman was other than Thomas

Shadows

had introduced her as Diana. I certainly didn't know what direction she went. I got lucky. I headed down a long hallway. Once it split into a T-like intersection, I paused. I was trying to determine which way to go when a door opened and Diana slipped out. She was glancing around, you know, like you see in the movies when someone is trying to escape unseen. I quickly slid into the shadows of the doorway and waited. She disappeared the other way. I ran to the door and barely caught it before it latched," she took a long breath.

"That's when I saw Thomas. He was white as a ghost and was having a hard time breathing. His wallet was thrown on the bed haphazardly. I couldn't tell if anything was missing. To be honest I didn't care at the moment. My focus was on Thomas. I needed to get him some help. I started to call mom, she's a nurse, but then Thomas' phone rang. When I saw it was Alex on the display I answered and explained the situation to her."

"Thomas was supposed to call me and let me know if he would be attending the social that evening," Alex explained. "It was time to leave and I hadn't heard from him. We've had a few issues to deal with at work lately. I just assumed he'd gotten tied up with something and hadn't had a chance to call. I thought I'd convince him to ditch for the night. Dimitri and I could handle the social alone."

"What was the social?" Rand asked.

"It was important. An annual fundraiser D-Tech sponsors for MS research. Top management from all of Deveraux Industries are expected to attend. We put a lot of pressure on them, so if neither Thomas nor I showed it would have caused problems," she

40

admitted. "That was the only reason I agreed to go once I found out how sick Thomas was."

"Okay, so what happened next?" Rand asked Abby.

"Alex and Dimitri arrived at the hotel and we were able to get Thomas into the car," Abby continued with her story. So far it seemed they were doing okay. "Dimitri and Alex headed to the social. I called home and my brother met me here. He helped me get Thomas to his room. I was able to get enough ipecac syrup into him to make him vomit. I then hooked him to an IV. He seemed to be doing a lot better at that point."

"You just happen to carry ipecac syrup in your handbag?" Rand said sarcastically.

"No, Morrigan brought it with him," Abby said. "Mom suggested it."

Morrigan Cooper, that name sounded familiar. "As I recall, doctors do not use ipecac anymore. I believe I heard it is ineffective and in fact causes problems with legitimate forms of treatment. Why would a nurse tell you to use such a hazardous and outdated treatment?" he quizzed.

"Typically ipecac is not used on patients any more, even those who have been poisoned. It does reduce the effectiveness of other treatments," Abby agreed. "However, Thomas was different. He had ingested such a small portion of the powder but had a significant reaction. Mom felt it was necessary to remove as much of the substance as possible before it infiltrated his blood system," she paused. She'd need to get to her mother before this detective did. Their stories would have to match.

Shadows

"Okay, so you make him throw up, hook up an IV and then what?" he paused. "What was in the IV?"

"A saline solution," Abby answered quickly.

"That's it? That's all you did for him?" Rand asked skeptically.

"No," Abby replied. "I also administered an active carbon to clean his system of any additional toxins."

Okay so the girl did know what she was doing. Rand had to admit that. Maybe Thomas had been in good hands with this one after all. "And?"

"And nothing," Abby said. "Thomas has been out all night, but his color is better and he seems to be doing well." She was grateful she knew about the medications she'd been describing. The detective seemed to be satisfied with her explanation.

"So I assume if I make contact with your mother and your brother they can confirm your story?" he asked.

"Of course," Abby said confidently.

"Would you mind giving me their names and numbers as well as an address where they can be reached?" he inquired.

So, here it comes. Abby thought. "Sure, my brother's name is Morrigan as I said." Abby provided her home phone number and address. "My mother is Jackie Cooper." Abby waited, there seemed to be something but not the recognition she'd been expecting. "Her number and address are the same," Abby added.

"No cellphones?" he asked.

"Morrigan has a cellphone, but he is usually pretty busy during the day. I'll give it to you, but don't expect an answer." She grinned as she provided the number to the detective. She'd call Morrigan and get him to call their mother. "Mom can't have a phone in the ER where she's volunteering this month. You won't be able to reach her until this evening unless you head over to the hospital."

"Which hospital?" Rand asked.

"Bellevue," Abby responded.

"Okay, so you stayed with Thomas all night? Anything else?" he asked her.

"Nope," she replied.

"Alex, do you want to tell me about the credit cards?" He shifted his gaze to her. "And maybe why you didn't report the missing property or the poisoning last night."

"Sure," Alex answered. "I did report the missing credit cards last night."

"I looked. There's no report," he disagreed.

"I didn't report them to the police," she said simply. "Why would I? When I got to the room I went through Thomas' wallet. I realized he was missing two cards. I immediately called my contact at the bank and reported the theft. They assured me the cards had not been used yet and they would immediately put an alert on them. If Diana tried to use one, the police would be notified. It seemed redundant to make a police report last evening. I understand that Thomas is not the victim if someone uses those cards, the bank is. I didn't see the point in reporting them simply for a paper trail."

Her explanation made sense, for the rich that is. "And the poisoning?" he asked.

"That wasn't my place," she said casually. "I knew Abby was a witness and Diana had probably run off. There was no urgency. If Thomas wanted to file a complaint once he recovered, that was up to him. It wasn't my place, nor my concern. My attention was focused on Thomas and his recovery."

"Are you finished with me for now?" Abby interrupted.

"Uh, yeah. I guess," McBride answered a little suspicious.

"Do you mind if I excuse myself to go to the bathroom then?" she asked.

"Where is the bathroom?" he demanded.

"Right around the corner," Alex assured him.

"Okay, yeah. Go ahead," he shifted his attention back to Alex, then to Jake.

Abby slipped out of the room and into the bathroom. Once inside she quickly slid open the window then shifted. She needed to get far enough from the house her voice would not be detected. Once she was sure no one could hear her, she shifted back and hid behind a tree. Then, she pulled out her phone and dialed Morrigan. Her brother promised he wouldn't answer the phone for any strange numbers and he would relay the information to their mother. "Should I call dad?" he asked. "You know he's not going to be happy about this."

Abby laughed. "Not yet. If I need him, I'll call. Even after I told him my name, your name and mom's name he still hasn't put it all together. I think he's going to freak when he realizes who dad is."

"Good," Morrigan told her still annoyed. He had forced himself to listen silently. But as Abby casually described her encounter with the detective, he had grown more and more furious with each passing minute. The man was a bully. It was inexcusable to treat women in such a manner.

"I've gotta go," Abby said abruptly. "I think his next step was to insist on seeing Thomas again. I need to sneak into the room and switch out the IV."

"Right," Morrigan agreed. "You better hurry and don't get caught!"

"Fat chance," she countered.

"I've got everything on this end, sis. Don't worry about a thing," Morrigan promised before he disconnected the call.

Abby shifted into a hawk this time and rushed back to the house. She circled the perimeter twice before she saw it, a small window near the rear of the house was slightly ajar. Luckily it didn't have a screen attached. She flew through the small opening and shifted midair planting her small Yorkie feet on the tile floor. She casually walked past the library making sure Alex saw her before pouncing up the stairs.

Alex smiled inwardly. If Abby took care of the IV they could let this persistent detective see Thomas. He had no idea Abby wasn't still in the bathroom. She turned her attention back to Detective McBride who was discussing protocol with Jake. Well, actually he was giving Jake a lecture on how all this could have been avoided if Alex had simply made a police report in the first place and taken Thomas directly to the hospital. Jake was handling it well. Better than Alex was in fact. She'd been about to interrupt when she spotted Abby, in the form of a small Yorkshire terrier, pouncing up the stairs. Now Alex relaxed. Abby needed more time. A few more minutes and they could get this over with and she could finally see Thomas for herself. She refocused her attention on the conversation between Jake and the annoying cop.

"I realize Thomas is sick," Rand persisted. "However, that is even more reason for me to see him now. I need to verify for myself that he was in fact poisoned. Well, that he is down in bed as a result of whatever Diana placed in his drink. At this point it would be impossible to determine if it was poison or some other chemical." Rand was trying to be cooperative but he was going to see Thomas before he left.

Jake glanced at Alex and then looked back at the detective. "Okay," he agreed. "But if Thomas isn't up to being questioned, you are going to have to postpone the interrogation until a later date. Are you okay with that Alex?" Jake asked.

"I am," she agreed, anxious to see how Thomas was for herself.

The group headed for the stairs. Rand stopped. "Should we wait a minute for Ms. Cooper?" He was wondering where the girl was. He glanced at the bathroom, a light was still shining beneath the door.

"No," Alex answered. "I'm sure when she's finished she'll return to the library and realize we're gone. It will be obvious we've gone to check Thomas."

Abby was frantically trying to change the IV bag from blood to a clear saline solution. She'd secretly placed a clog in the tube to prevent the liquid from entering Thomas' blood stream. The last thing he needed was another foreign substance his blood would have to change. Thomas was awake, but still groggy. She wasn't sure he understood what was going on or even who she was. Once the IV was in place she returned to his bed with a large glass of blood. He needed to drink it quickly.

Thomas took the glass and began to sip. He still felt off. What had happened to him? How did he get home? He didn't remember anything after getting into the elevator. He glanced back at Abby and a part of him realized that was strange. Why was Abby in his bedroom?

"No," Abby took control of the glass. "You need to gulp it. Detective McBride will be here any minute."

Thomas wasn't exactly registering what Abby was saying, but he took the glass and gulped the contents.

Abby grabbed the empty container, rushed to the bathroom and rinsed out the blood. That would have to be good enough for now. She quickly returned to the closet and placed the empty glass back into the mini fridge, closed the secret compartment and rushed back into the room. She heard voices at the top of the stairs. She was running out of time. She frantically searched the room and spotted the sliding glass doors that led to a balcony. She had just slid the door closed when she saw the bedroom door begin to open. She shifted back into a hawk and flew to the open bathroom window. She flushed the toilet, ran the water a little longer than necessary then rushed up the stairs.

Chapter Three

Rand studied Thomas. He appeared to be sick. Was he faking or were these people telling him the truth? He still didn't believe them. They were all acting too mysterious and uncooperative. They were hiding something. He knew it in his gut. But the IV threw him. If Thomas wasn't sick, he wouldn't be hooked to an IV. He'd have to think on that one.

"Hello Thomas," Rand began. "I'm Detective McBride and I need to ask you some questions about last night," he paused. "Are you willing to talk to me?"

Thomas slowly pushed himself up until he was sitting against the large headboard. He rested his weight against the pillows and gazed at the officer. He was so weak and exhausted and he wished he knew what this was all about. He turned his gaze to Alex. "I'm so weak. Why am I weak?" Then he stopped himself. Maybe she couldn't answer with a detective in the room. It was at that moment he noticed Jake standing in the doorway. Why was Jake here?

Alex rushed to Thomas' side and sat down on the edge of the bed. "Thomas, what do you remember about last night?"

"Not much," he admitted. Alex was looking him straight in the eye. He could tell she was trying to comfort him, assure him it was okay to talk. "It was a bad day at the office. I had to fire Phil," he told her. "He was pretty upset, ultimately security had to escort him out."

"Tom Knox told me," she assured him. "We'll deal with it later."

"Knox!" Thomas just remembered. "What time is it? We were supposed to be in his office at ten this morning for a meeting."

"Don't worry about that," Alex said softly. "We need to handle this situation first. Tom said it could be postponed for a while. He'll meet with us another day."

"Good," Thomas said relieved. "Anyway, Diana Martingale called just before I went in with Phil. She wanted to have dinner. Initially I told her no, I didn't have time. She wouldn't accept no for an answer though. She sounded desperate. She begged me to meet her. She said she was leaving town and needed my help before she left. Eventually I gave in. If I'd known how ugly the situation with Phil was going to be, I never would have agreed to meet with her. I really wasn't up for another confrontation."

Rand moved closer and addressed Thomas. "How long had you and Diana been dating?"

Thomas studied the detective trying to focus on what was happening. Why was a detective asking him about Diana? "We weren't dating," Thomas answered, spotting Abby as she silently slipped into the room. He furrowed his brow in confusion, wasn't Abby already here?

"You met for drinks, then dinner and ended up in her room. I'd call that a date." Rand disagreed.

"It wasn't a date," Thomas began, refocusing on the detective. "Wait, I ended up in Diana's room?"

"Yes," Alex assured him. She looked at McBride. "If you continue your interrogation in this manner, I'm afraid I'm going to have to ask you to leave. Thomas needs time, I can see he's still suffering from the effects of that drug."

"What drug?" Thomas demanded.

Abby stepped forward. "Diana slipped something into your drink at dinner, Thomas. I saw her, that's why I pretended to trip on the board and tipped over your glass."

Thomas focused on Abby. Now it was coming back to him. "Diana arrived late. I'd had such a bad day. When I got to the hotel, I immediately went to the bar for a glass of wine. I knew she'd be late, she always liked a dramatic entrance."

"I thought you said you weren't dating," Rand interjected.

"Diana and I had gone on two dates prior to meeting her last night. I do not consider dinner last night a date," he continued when he saw the detective was going to object. "Diana insisted she needed to talk to me. She said something was going on and she needed help. She said she'd left her apartment and was staying at the hotel. She also told me she was leaving town. I assumed this was just another attempt to get money out of me."

"Meaning?" Rand asked.

"Meaning this has happened before. Diana's phone call sounded all too familiar. I assumed she was in some kind of trouble and decided to leave town but didn't have the funds. So, who better to hit up than a Deveraux? It wouldn't have been the first time a former acquaintance tried to get money out of me."

"Then why did you agree to meet her?" Rand asked.

"She sounded desperate. They all do. I guess I thought she deserved the chance to give her pitch before I shot her down," Thomas supplied.

"Before last night, when was the last time you saw Diana?" Rand pressed.

"Months. Like I said we only had two dates. It was obvious after the first one that she wasn't my type," Thomas said casually.

"And what is your type?" Rand asked skeptically. She'd looked awful in death, but the woman had been a strikingly attractive lady. She seemed like a perfect match for a wealthy man like Thomas.

"I haven't figured that out yet, I guess that's why I'm still single." Thomas was starting to feel a little better. It must have been the large glass of blood Abby had forced into him before the group arrived. That had seemed like a dream, had Abby really been here before?

"What exactly about Diana did you dislike then?" Rand persisted.

Shadows

"She was cold, distant. I guess she seemed fake," Thomas admitted. "I like my women to be warm and friendly I guess. Diana wasn't either."

"That's an understatement," Jake mumbled.

Rand turned to the lawyer. "I wasn't aware you knew Diana Martingale."

"I didn't," Jake admitted. "Not personally anyway. I know the type and I have met her. That's why Luke and I decided to have Paul conduct a thorough investigation on her after Thomas' first date."

Thomas shot a look Jake's way. "You what!" he demanded. "You and dad investigated her?" He knew there had been an investigation but he thought it was just a cursory check and that it hadn't been initiated until he had agreed to it. Knowing his father and Jake had taken it upon themselves to check out a woman he had dated infuriated him. Then another thought struck him. "How many women have you done that with behind my back?"

"A few," Jake admitted. "Calm down Thomas. I eventually gave you the information. You know she was bad news and just after your money. Why are you so upset?"

"Gee, I don't know. Maybe I'll hire someone to investigate Marta and see how you like it." Thomas shot back.

Jake wasn't so casual now. Nobody was going to look into Marta's background. Anyway, the idea was ludicrous. Thomas already knew everything there was to know about his wife. She'd lived with the Deveraux's since before Thomas was born. "Okay, point taken. I'm sorry," Jake finally relinquished.

"How long ago did this investigation occur?" Rand asked. He was actually getting more information than he had dared hope for.

"Before Luke died," Jake offered. "Maybe a few weeks before that. Why?"

McBride ignored the question. "What did this Paul person find out?"

"I guess if you want to know that, you can either investigate the woman yourself or serve Paul with a subpoena to produce his records," Jake said narrowing his eyes. This detective was getting on his nerves. Nobody ignored Jake. McBride didn't know who he was dealing with.

"Any particular reason you want to make this difficult?" Rand asked.

"Sure," Jake said casually. "It's called tit for tat. You are the one making this difficult. You set the tone, I'm just following your lead. You don't want to treat this family with dignity and respect, we'll return the favor. You can do this the hard way. I don't have anything to hide, neither does Thomas. The only one hiding something was Diana."

"But you're not going to elaborate on that?" Rand asked.

"No," Jake said. "In fact, I think now is a good time to end this conversation. If you have any additional questions you can contact me later. Thomas is tired."

Thomas could see something was up. "Jake, I'd actually like to finish this now if you don't mind."

Shadows

Jake didn't like it, but he waved a hand for Thomas to continue.

Thomas looked at the detective. "I'm not sure what it is you want to know. Like I said, Diana and I dated a couple times months ago. Then, out of the blue, she called me yesterday and needed to meet. I wasn't interested in a relationship with her, but I thought she deserved to hear it from me. In person. I really don't know any more than that. Abby interrupted our dinner and Diana and I didn't have a chance to talk."

"So on these two dates, were the two of you intimate?" McBride asked.

"What does that have to do with anything?" Abby asked. She really didn't want to hear about Thomas and Diana having sex.

"It's okay," Thomas assured her. "We were intimate on the second date. That was the clincher. I was second guessing my original assessment that she was cold and distant. The second date was going well until we went back to her apartment. In fact, I wouldn't call it being intimate with her. It was sex, that's it. There was nothing compassionate or loving about the entire experience."

"And did you plan to have sex again last night?" Rand persisted.

"No," Thomas assured him. "Like I said, I planned to have dinner at which time I assumed I'd have to break the news to Diana that she wasn't going to get any money from me. Then we'd go our separate ways and never see each other again."

"So you sat down to dinner, then what happened?" McBride asked.

"Like I said, Diana was late. I sat in the bar and had a glass of wine. When Diana arrived we were escorted to our table. I was reading the menu when Abby dropped in." He flashed a charming smile Abby's way. "Literally," Thomas watched Abby for just a minute before he continued. "We had a quick, casual greeting and then Diana began throwing a fit saying she needed to change and I had to follow her up to her room so she could talk to me. The last thing I remember is getting into the elevator and feeling off. I felt dizzy, like I was going to pass out." Thomas looked at Abby again and then Alex.

"That's it?" McBride asked. "You don't remember anything else? Nothing at all?"

"No," Thomas said narrowing his eyes at the detective. What exactly was he looking for?

"Do you want children, Thomas?" Rand asked casually.

"Someday, what does that have to do with anything?" Thomas asked.

"Did you and Diana talk about having children together?" he persisted.

"Of course not," Thomas said immediately. "What exactly did Diana tell you?"

"Diana isn't saying anything," Rand said coldly. "Diana is dead."

Thomas glared at Detective McBride, wide eyed. He was in shock. What had Diana been involved in? Was she really in trouble and needed his help? "What happened?" he finally asked silently.

Shadows

McBride wanted to see Thomas' reaction. He pulled the photo from his pocket and laid it on the bed.

Thomas picked up the photo, studied it for a moment then closed his eyes. Diana was a snake, but she didn't deserve this. Then it hit him. His eyes flung open and he glared at the detective angrily. "You don't think I had anything to do with this, do you?" he demanded.

"I don't know. Did you?" Rand asked. Thomas hadn't reacted the way he believed he would. He'd gotten more emotion from Thomas than the two women in the room. He was still confused about the whole situation. Could Thomas be innocent? Were Alex and Abby the killers? Who knew, stranger things had happened.

"Absolutely not," Thomas said immediately. "Why would I? What would be my motive for killing Diana?"

McBride shrugged. "You said she was after your money. Maybe you decided she was too much of a nuisance and knocking her off would be easier to deal with than paying her."

"That's ridiculous!" Alex defended Thomas. "Now it is time for you to leave Mr. McBride." She walked to the door and held it wide open. "If you have any further questions you will need to go through Jake. You are not welcome in my home any longer."

"I was under the impression you lived with Dimitri Montgomery," Rand said as he stood.

Alex took a deep breath. "I do," she admitted. "However, this house was left to both me and Thomas; jointly. Legally, it's my house and I'm asking you to leave."

McBride strolled out the door, down the stairs and casually pulled out of the drive. He wanted them to worry. He was going to watch this family very closely. He had conflicting feelings about Thomas, but there was something off with the entire clan. His first stop, the courthouse for a warrant then off to the Deveraux's private eye. He needed to know what they knew about his victim.

"Okay, spill" Thomas said once the front door closed. "What don't I know?"

The group proceeded to fill Thomas in on the rest of the night's events. Each one taking turns, adding parts the others missed.

When they were finished Thomas immediately looked toward Abby. "Thank you," he said sincerely. "Thank you for everything. You saved my life last night and then saved our secret again this morning," he paused. "I'm sorry you got pulled into this. The reward for all your kindness is probably going to be constant harassment from the police. I'm sorry we've caused problems for you," he told her.

"I'm not worried about that detective," Abby said confidently.

"I wouldn't underestimate him," Jake told her. "I've seen his kind before. They are ruthless. We've gotten under his skin. He's going to be very focused on our family and unfortunately on you Abby for the next while."

Abby shook her head. "Actually, he won't. I'm afraid that might make him angry though. And he may be even more focused on you guys once he finds out who I am."

"Oh?" Alex asked. "What does that mean?"

Shadows

"My family is very close to his Chief," Abby admitted. "Almost everyone on the force knows it. I kept waiting for him to make the connection, but he never did. I guarantee he'll know before long. I told Morrigan not to contact dad, but I'm sure he told mom. Travis Monroe will get an earful if he hasn't already, about how one of his detectives treated Mason Cooper's daughter," she smiled. "I am quite confident that detective will get back a little of his own before the day is through."

The group laughed then Abby sobered. "I'm just worried he might take that out on you guys. Specifically you, Thomas. It's going to make him angry when he gets challenged by his boss over his behavior. He can't come at me and he certainly can't take it out on his boss. That leaves the three of you. I'm going to stick close for a while if that's okay. I can help if the harassment gets too bad."

"Maybe you should distance yourself from this family for now Abby," Jake suggested. "If you stick close, he may pull you in anyway in spite of the connection to your family."

"Thomas didn't kill that woman," Abby said. "We need to find out who did. Once the murder is solved, the detective will go away. I can help with that."

"Then at least let me help you with any legal issues that arise out of this. There's no need to pay a family attorney when I'm already involved," Jake argued.

"Nope," Abby refused the help. "I meant what I said. I think it muddies the waters to have you represent these two and me. Plus, Nancy is under retainer. It's not going to cost me a thing. It comes out of the family trust. I'm in good hands already if I need an attorney. Anyway she always loves a challenge. She'll be disappointed if she can't take on the local police on my behalf," Abby finished with a smile.

"Can I assume you're talking about Nancy Williams?" Jake asked.

"I am," she affirmed.

"Is she good?" Thomas asked Jake. "I want Abby to have the best if she needs to defend herself against this."

"Oh, she's good," Jake assured him. "She may be better than me."

Abby laughed. "Not from what I've heard," she said smiling at him. "I'd guess you're about sixes." She turned to Alex. "I'm going to head out. I have some things I need to take care of this morning." She turned back to Thomas. "I'm really glad you're feeling better. I'll see you guys soon," she said airily as she headed for the door.

Alex followed. "I think you're up to something Abby," she said quietly. "Please, don't get into more trouble on our behalf. We can handle this."

"Don't worry about me," she said confidently. "I have special talents that you don't. I'm not worried about avoiding detection by a human." She pulled open the front door and headed to her car.

Alex stood in the doorway watching her go. She was grateful for the help, but Abby worried her. This wasn't a game. That detective was serious. He sincerely believed Thomas, or maybe all of them, was responsible for Diana's murder. She pulled her phone out of her purse and dialed Dimitri.

Shadows

Rand entered the foyer of the small office and approached the receptionist. She was a middle aged woman, with bright red lipstick and short blonde hair. It had dark black streaks running through at regular intervals. McBride thought it made her look like a zebra. Things women did for vanity baffled him.

"Can I help you?" she asked professionally.

Rand produced a copy of the warrant. He hadn't had any trouble getting it. Now he was anxious to see if he would get the run around or if Paul would produce the records willingly.

"I see," she said as she studied the document. "One moment please," she pushed back from the desk and disappeared into a small office.

Moments later a man in his fifties entered the room. "So you want the dirt on Diana Martingale?" he inquired. "May I ask why?"

"She's been murdered," Rand answered directly. "I spoke to the Deveraux's this morning and learned they hired you to investigate her a while back. They hinted she had a few secrets."

"Pissed them off did you?" Paul laughed then shook his head. "Some cops love to do things the hard way." He gave the receptionist a slight nod. The woman moved to a filing cabinet and began shuffling through papers.

"What makes you think I pissed them off?" Rand asked a little defensively.

"Because they made you get this," Paul pointed to the warrant. "The Deveraux's are good people. If you asked for the info, they would have simply picked up the phone and called me. Within minutes you would have had everything you wanted. Unless you pissed them off. Then they would have made you go this route," he shrugged. "So what'd you do?"

Rand narrowed his eyes at the man. "You're pretty cocky for a PI," he observed.

Paul sobered. "Now you're trying to piss me off." He moved a little closer to McBride. "I did my time and got out. You might think about doing the same. I don't know, it may already be too late for you. Drop the tough guy act. I've used it a million times myself," he paused. "Of course, I do it better," he let the words fade.

The receptionist pulled a file from the drawer and handed it to Paul. Paul scanned his notes then handed it back to the woman. "Copy everything," he told her. "If the woman's dead there's no need for privacy." The secretary left the room.

"So, what does a dead woman and the Deveraux's have in common?" Paul asked.

Rand studied the man. He vaguely remembered the name Paul Jackson from the force. If this was the same guy, he could be trusted. "When did you leave the job?" Rand asked.

"Awe, I see. You want to quiz me. See if I deserve to know the real scoop. That's okay. I'd do the same. I left six years ago," he paused. "Retired as a Lieutenant. I could have stuck around and made Captain, but my heart wasn't in it anymore. I got tired of the politics," he looked around the room. "No politics here. Just me and Candice. This place may not look like much, but compared to the precinct its paradise. I make my own hours, do what I want, turn away those I don't want to deal with. It's much better for my health. All around I'd say it was the best move I ever made."

So this was Lt. Jackson. He'd been a good cop from what McBride heard. After six years the guys still referred back to the good old days working for Jackson. That was unusual. So why was he tied up with a murderer?

Paul sobered. Detective McBride was working something out. Always on the job. He didn't miss that part either. "What's troubling you?" he finally asked.

"You have a good rep at the office," Rand admitted. "I'm just wondering why you're tied up with the Deveraux's."

Paul raised his eyebrows at that. He didn't know what business the NYPD had with the kids, but Detective McBride must have really gotten off to a very bad start. Paul had never met a better group of people in his life. He'd been tainted after leaving the force. Working with Luke and getting to know his family had been therapeutic for Paul. He'd been relieved to find a family as loaded as Luke's still had values. They were good decent people, which had come as a huge surprise after thirty years of dealing with criminals. "I'm tied up with the Deveraux's as you put it because I like them and I respect them. Yeah, they can play hard ball," he glanced down at the warrant, "but somehow I suspect you deserved that."

Rand wasn't in the mood for this. "Thomas Deveraux is the prime suspect in a homicide. The murder of Diana Martingale. Personally, I don't find that a quality I respect in a man."

Paul laughed out loud. "You've got to be kidding. Thomas? Murder Diana?" he sighed deeply. "You couldn't be further off base," he studied McBride. "Let me give you some advice. Stop looking at Thomas simply because he's wealthy. No wonder they made you jump through hoops. Please tell me you didn't just show up on their doorstep and accuse Thomas of murder."

"That's exactly what I did," Rand said defensively, then shrugged. "I'm not going to tip toe around the obvious just because the family has money."

"I can see there's no reasoning with you," Paul shook his head. "You're going to have to learn the hard way." He looked over as Candice entered the room. He took the stack of paper she offered and pushed it towards McBride. "Good luck, man. You're definitely going to need it. I hope you come to your senses soon and start looking for the real killer. I'd hate to see the Deveraux's harassed by a bullheaded detective for too long just because you refuse to see the truth." Paul turned and headed back to his office. He silently shut the door. Once he saw McBride climb into his car he picked up the phone and called Jake.

Rand sat at his desk seething. He was furious. So the guy had been a good cop. So he retired with rank. That didn't give him the right to act all superior and condescending. Couldn't see the truth my ass. It was staring right at him. He glanced back at the murder board he'd assembled. Thomas and Abby were sitting prominently on top. For now they were his two prime suspects. Alex was alibied. Rand checked. Alex and Dimitri Montgomery were at the social from eight o'clock until after midnight. There's no way they could have committed the murder. The ME would narrow the window, but McBride estimated time of death right around ten

Shadows

o'clock. Alex had about a dozen witnesses that could alibi her for the time of the murder. Thomas and Abby only had each other.

McBride turned his attention back to the file. Jackson had been thorough. He had to admit it was interesting. Diana had been married three times. The first one had lasted almost two years. How had a relatively healthy man suddenly died? The small town hadn't even conducted an autopsy. Could Diana have been involved in his death? That would have been a leap if it weren't for the records on husband number two and husband number three. He pulled out the information on Mayor Edwards and began to read the material in its totality.

Chief Travis Monroe rounded the corner and stopped abruptly. Seeing Abby's face plastered to the murder board as one of the primary suspects was a little shocking. So, Mason hadn't been exaggerating. Monroe took a deep breath and approached the cubical. He studied the board, reading McBride's notes carefully. His gaze shifted to the photo of the dead woman. Was it possible she'd been killed by a vampire? He couldn't tell from the photo. If so, slashing her throat was a good cover-up. There would be no way to detect the bite marks that way. "I'm curious," Chief Monroe finally began. "Why is Abigail Cooper your prime suspect? Well, one of them anyway?"

Detective McBride jerked to attention and stood. "What?" he asked, not sure what the Chief was after.

"Abby?" he said again. "Why is Mason Cooper's daughter prominently tacked to your murder board as the prime suspect in a homicide?" he asked again.

"Mason Cooper?" Rand asked.

"Yes, Mason. You know the Clinical Psychologist our members are sent to after they're involved in a traumatic incident. The man countless family members go see to help them deal with the stress our officers bring home as a matter of routine. Mason Cooper, the man the NYPD contracts with to profile serial killers and rapists. Mason Cooper who gives countless hours of his personal time to study forensic evidence for our department. Mason Cooper, who has never once hesitated to put his paying clients second to help stop a madman or profile a sadistic sexual deviant. Why is his daughter's picture taped to that board, on display for all to see, as your prime suspect in a homicide? The murder of a woman she didn't even know?" Monroe asked clearly annoyed at the display.

Rand pulled the picture off the board. "I'm sorry sir," he apologized. "I had no idea she was related to Dr. Cooper." How had he been so stupid? Lack of sleep maybe. But that was no excuse. He should have made the connection immediately when the girl had mentioned her mother was Jackie and her brother was Morrigan. Rand groaned inwardly. Yet another roadblock he was going to have to overcome in this investigation. It struck him almost immediately. Abby knew he'd be hassled over this. She'd withheld her connection on purpose. What else had that manipulative imp withheld?

"I spoke with Mason earlier today," Monroe admitted. "He is not happy about the way his daughter was treated this morning. Nor is he happy that his friend's, the Deveraux's, were accosted in that manner."

Rand narrowed his eyes. "Are you telling me to back off an investigation, sir?" he asked.

Shadows

Monroe had encountered McBride once before. That's when the man had caught his attention. He'd handled the drowning of that woman very quickly and professionally. There was something about Rand McBride that intrigued Monroe. At first, Travis had believed McBride was one of them. But after watching him for several weeks, he realized Rand must just be a human with some kind of special sixth sense. Now, he was just pissing him off. Relentlessly focusing on the Deveraux's was short sighted. Of course a warrior wouldn't murder a human. They protected them. The very idea was ridiculous. Chief Monroe took a deep breath, "Don't push your luck, McBride. I like you, but that could change very quickly."

That was a surprise. Rand hadn't had many encounters with the Chief. He was a little shocked to hear the man liked him. "I'm not trying to push my luck, sir. Right now Thomas and Abby are my only suspects. It just sounded like you were ordering me to back away from two people that, in my opinion, are guilty of murder."

"Well, your opinion doesn't mean shit," Monroe said calmly. "You have absolutely no evidence to support your theory. Investigate all you want, any way you want." He let that sink in. "What I'm telling you, is that you will not contact Abby Cooper again without notifying me in advance. The Coopers have asked that all communication goes through their attorney. Here is the information, Monroe handed McBride a card. The Deveraux's also wish any further contact with Thomas or Alex to go through Jake Wilder. Do you understand?"

"Of course," McBride agreed, glancing at the card. He closed his eyes, could this get any worse? In addition to everything else, now he had to deal with Nancy Williams. He definitely needed a vacation.

Chief Monroe looked back at the board. "I realize my opinion doesn't mean shit in this investigation either, but for what it's worth I think you're focusing on the wrong man. Thomas is an acquaintance of mine. I do not believe he is capable of killing this woman. Not for passion, revenge or inconvenience as you so bluntly put it. I suggest you broaden your investigation, McBride. I suspect with very little effort you will find Ms. Martingale had a few skeletons in her closet. Skeletons that might be out for revenge." He turned and walked out of the room.

Detective Lloyd pushed up over the cubicle wall. "Watch your step man, he's not happy with you right now."

"Really? You think?" Rand said sarcastically as he plopped back into his chair. Why did he have to get stuck with this particular case? He ran his fingers through his hair and laid his head against the back of the chair.

Lloyd moved around the wall and studied the board. "He's right. You've got nothing. Well, less than nothing. Sure, they can't be ruled out altogether, but why such the hard-on for the Deveraux's?"

"Just a feeling," Rand admitted. "They're hiding something."

"And Abby?" Lloyd persisted.

"I don't know. She was evasive from the moment I saw her. It just struck me as wrong somehow. Like there was more to the story," Rand mused. What was it about Abby that had pushed her to the top of the board? He couldn't quite put a finger on it.

"Well, watch it with that one," Lloyd warned. "Mason Cooper is very tight with the Chief. Everyone around here respects

Shadows

him. One wrong move and your career could be on the line. I'm guessing you don't want to go back to the beat?" Lloyd asked, grinning.

Rand settled in and decided to focus on Diana and her past for now. He'd figure out the rest later. Why was he so put off by a family that everyone else seemed to love and admire? He just didn't get it.

"So what's the kit for?" Lloyd asked a few minutes later.

"Huh?" McBride said pulling his attention away from the PI's file.

"The kit?" he asked again. "Why did the victim have a fertility preservation kit in her bag? I'm not an expert, but I don't think that's a common item. Makeup, comb, birth control maybe, but not that kit. It's got to be relevant. You have it mentioned as a side note, but I'd look into that if I were you," Detective Lloyd suggested. "Even if nothing comes of it, Monroe can't say you weren't checking out other avenues."

"I suppose," Rand agreed.

"Well, I'm outta here," Lloyd said moments later. "I get to go interview the mother of a three time loser. The kid that stabbed his dealer because he refused to supply him for free. I can hardly wait to hear how her son is such a good kid, he's just misunderstood," Lloyd mimicked, then grabbed his keys and headed down the hall.

Abby's mind was reeling. A fertilization kit? Had Diana been planning on getting pregnant? Was that her scam? She needed to talk to Alex about this, and Thomas. He'd know for sure, but Abby was confident she'd just figured out Diana's scheme. The reason she'd tried to poison Thomas. Knock him out, get his sperm and then implant it at a later date. Better yet, go invetro and eliminate the risk. Abby was so deep in thought she hadn't realized she'd been spotted. She looked up just as a large cop threw a bowl in her direction. She scurried off and hid behind a garbage can, barely escaping. She'd thought a mouse was her best bet inside the office. All old buildings had them. The men should be used to mice by now. Out of the corner of her eye she saw another cop pull his gun. Was he serious? He was going to try to shoot a mouse with a .40 caliber handgun? These guys were nuts. A third guy started shoving furniture out of the way. He looked determined as he barreled toward her. The guy with the gun kept pace directly behind the furniture throwing madman. She had to get out of here.

Abby knew she would have to make a run for it. Her heart was pounding in her chest and she couldn't breathe. She was literally risking her life to escape a police station of all things. She darted behind a cabinet then quickly slipped through the small opening of the wall where she had entered the room, immediately shifting again just in case. The small bird would be able to fly through the panels effortlessly and hopefully nobody would shoot her on the way out. She just needed to find that opening again and she'd be free.

Abby followed Alex into the library and realized Dimitri and Thomas were also present. The two men were casually drinking cokes and visiting about something. The conversation cut short as soon as Abby stepped through the door. She smiled at the men and walked to a large chair and sat down. Once Alex positioned herself on the couch next to Dimitri, Abby began. "After I left here this morning I went to the police station. I wanted to spy on that detective and see if I could get some answers. I also wanted to know what he knew. You know, what he hadn't told us."

"Oh Abby," Alex sighed. "You could have gotten caught. I'm going to ask you again, please don't pursue this. I would never forgive myself if, in an effort to help us, you caused more problems for you or your family."

Abby smiled. "I'm not going to get caught," she insisted. "Anyway, how could a stray bird in the wall or a tiny mouse cause problems for my family?" She shuddered at the memory of the large detective chasing her with his handgun.

"Please be careful," Dimitri added. "We really appreciate your efforts, but please don't get yourself injured on our account."

"I won't," Abby promised. "Anyway, I was right about Travis. Chief Monroe was not happy about Detective McBride's visit this morning. Apparently dad has already called him. I'm confident our not so friendly detective will be a little more behaved next time any of us encounter him."

"I realize your father's concern was for you. But I don't like dragging so many shifters into this mess. Jake's going to have his hands full protecting our secret from the police already. Now your family is at risk as well," Thomas said concerned.

"Not really," Abby disagreed. "I may have forgotten to mention that Chief Monroe is also a shifter."

"Really?" Alex exclaimed in surprise. "Well, that does come in handy doesn't it?"

"It does," Abby agreed. "Anyway, I saw the direction McBride is going with this investigation. He got the information from your PI but he still believes that Thomas and I are his prime suspects."

"What?" Thomas said outraged. "Why you?"

Abby's stomach did a little flip. She knew it didn't mean anything, but it felt good to see Thomas upset at the accusation. "Because I was there," Abby said simply. "Don't get too upset about that. Travis warned him about pursuing me any further. I'm really not worried about it. You guys shouldn't be either."

The small group of three scowled. None of them liked the direction this investigation was headed.

"Anyway, that's not the reason I'm here." She paused until she was sure she had their full attention. "It seems McBride forgot to mention Diana had a fertilization preservation kit in her purse that night."

"A what?" Thomas and Dimitri asked together.

"It's a kit to preserve a man's sperm," Alex answered. "Why?"

"They don't know. One of the other detectives encouraged McBride to check it out. He thought it was relevant. I do to," Abby admitted.

"How?" Dimitri asked.

Thomas' mind was reeling. Was that what Diana was up to?

Shadows

"I think Diana was planning on getting pregnant. Here's my theory but I need to know if you guys think it's possible. I didn't know her, you did," she paused as she looked at Thomas. "So she doesn't know Thomas is a warrior. She just sees him as this mega rich bachelor and she wants his money. I'm guessing here, but I think the powder was probably sleeping powder or some other kind of drug to make him pass out. She thought she could knock Thomas out, have her way with him..." Abby blushed a little but then continued. "Then take the proceeds and get herself pregnant," she looked around the room. "Do you remember McBride asking Thomas if he and Diana had talked about children?"

"That's right!" Alex exclaimed.

"So she gets pregnant then advises Thomas he's the father. Of course Thomas would have insisted on a DNA test. But it would have been his. Then the games begin. She wants money, you have it. She has your kid. I'm sure she thought she could get quite a windfall from your family. If she was successful this scam would have put her on easy street for the rest of her life," Abby concluded.

A very long silence followed. Thomas finally spoke quietly. "It would have worked," he admitted. "I would have paid her whatever she wanted for my child." He was horrified by what might have happened.

"We would have," Alex corrected. "There is no way I would have let any niece or nephew of mine remain in that woman's care. There's no way you would allow your child to be subjected to that, either. We would have paid her anything she wanted."

"True," Thomas agreed. "I would have gone to any length to take my child away from such a cold, heartless woman. I would have done it if I were human as she believed, but can you imagine the nightmare if Diana was around my child as it grew up. If Diana discovered our secret? She would have blackmailed all of us just for fun." Realizing the possibility of what could have happened if Diana had been successful, made Thomas sick. He was disappointed in himself. He'd put them all in danger.

"We would have handled it," Dimitri assured him. He knew Thomas was upset about what had almost happened. "Keep this in perspective, Thomas. Sure, it could have been a problem but it wasn't. Abby saved all of us last night," he turned his attention to her. "Thank you again, we owe you a great debt."

"I owe you a great debt," Thomas corrected. "This was my doing. I got us into this, I will get us out of it," he promised.

"Thomas," Dimitri said gently. "You know this could have happened to any one of us. She was a predator. Diana Martingale could have targeted any one of the warriors. We all have money. We've all enjoyed meaningless nights with various women. You couldn't have known what she was up to," he sobered. "Snap out of it. Now. It's over. It's time to focus on the murder. Forget what might have been and focus on what is." Dimitri was giving an order as a leader now. They couldn't afford to lose Thomas to his guilt.

Thomas studied Dimitri. He wanted to be angry, but Dimitri was right. Things could have been disastrous but Abby's intervention had saved him. She had saved their entire community. Diana was dead. She couldn't harm them now. Instead of worrying about what might have been, they needed to solve her murder. They needed to get this detective off their back. That would be his focus now.

After a few moments of silence Abby stood. "I need to get home. It's been a long day and I need to talk to my parents about this morning's events." She quickly hugged Alex then headed for the door. "I'll be in touch," she told them as she left the room.

Chapter Four

Abby heard voices in the sitting room. She casually strolled through the door then stopped abruptly. Travis Monroe was the first to notice her. "Abby," he said with a smile. "I was hoping I'd have a chance to talk to you before we left." He stood and walked to her, pulling her into his arms for a hug. "Sorry about your ordeal this morning. It seems you've made quite an impression on Detective McBride."

"Not much on charm is he?" she said with a smile.

"I guess not," Monroe agreed.

Katherine Monroe stood and approached her husband. "Travis," she said softly. "It's getting late. Abby's had a difficult day. Let's go home."

"Give me just a moment dear," Travis smiled warmly at his wife. "I need to speak to Abby alone. Then we can go."

Shadows

"Alright," Katherine moved back to sit across from Jackie. "We can entertain ourselves with girl talk while you speak to Abby," she smiled at her husband. "Hurry back."

Travis Monroe took Abby by the arm and guided her out the large door. "Where to?" he asked her.

"Uh, how about the kitchen. I could use a Coke," she suggested.

"The kitchen it is," he said turning in that direction. "Don't worry. I just wanted to make sure you were okay. I know Rand can be a bit overbearing."

"Oh. Well yes, but I'm fine," she assured him. "He was a bit rude, but nothing I couldn't handle. Anyway, I'm sure you took care of everything," she smiled.

"Be careful Abby," Monroe warned. "My detectives weren't bluffing today. They hate mice. Richard shot one last month. I had to write him up for discharging his firearm in the building, but I'm confident he'll do it again in an instant. He's deathly afraid of the things. It seems he's terrified of the diseases they carry."

"I thought you may have realized I was there. But since you didn't give any indication, I kind of hoped I'd gotten away with it," Abby confessed. "I just needed to know where we stood. Are you angry with me?" she asked.

"No Abby," he assured her. "I'm worried about you." He slowly lowered himself into one of the sturdy kitchen chairs.

Abby walked to the fridge and pulled out a Coke. "You want one?" she asked.

"Sure," he nodded.

Abby grabbed a second can and joined him at the table. "Don't worry. Everything is going to work out fine."

"McBride's good. He's set his sights on you and Thomas because he could tell you were keeping secrets. We both know the secrets didn't have anything to do with Diana, but McBride doesn't. McBride believes your evasiveness makes you guilty. If a vampire did this, to be honest, we're in trouble. McBride needs closure. He won't stop until he has it. I'll do my best to intervene but this could end badly. Thomas may have to go into hiding for a while."

"We'll figure it out," Abby assured him. "Somehow we will get through this. Nobody is going to escape into hiding."

"I hope so," Monroe sighed. "I hope so."

The two sat in silence as they drank their Cokes. Finally Monroe rose. "I need to get my lovely wife home." He gently brushed his hand over Abby's head. "Promise me you'll be careful. Don't do anything that will get you injured," he smiled. "And if you're going to sneak into my precinct again, change into something other than a mouse."

"I promise," Abby smiled. "Your detectives are nuts. I had no idea they'd have such an aversion to an innocent little mouse." She watched as Chief Monroe left the room.

* * * *

Foster entered the large penthouse, silently closing the door behind him. He didn't want to argue with his mother again, but he

Shadows

knew it was inevitable. He'd only taken a couple of steps when he smelled it. If mother thought she could charm him with dinner, she was mistaken. He would not give her more money. He'd thought a lot about this. Actually he'd thought of little else today. It was difficult to stand up to Patricia Dillinger, but Foster knew he didn't have a choice.

He slowly entered the kitchen and froze. Lawson was here. Foster could smell the strong odor of cigarettes. He narrowed his eyes at his mother. What exactly was she up to? Patricia was sitting at the far end of the table.

"Oh good," she said enthusiastically. "You're home."

"I am," Foster still hadn't moved.

"Well come in and have something to eat," she insisted as she raised her arm and motioned to an empty chair.

"What is this about mother?" he asked.

"I know you've had a long day. We both know I upset you this morning. I thought we'd have an enjoyable dinner together tonight." She rose and handed him a glass of wine.

Foster reached for the glass, but never took his eyes off his mother. He still wasn't sure where Lawson was, but his being here was evidence these two were up to something. Just as his hand touched the stem he saw it. His mother had a mischievous glimmer in her eye. It was so quick if he had blinked, he would have missed it. But he didn't miss it. He surveyed the room again. That's when he recognized the chair. Now he understood. He casually set the wine in front of the covered plate of food that had been strategically placed at the end of the table. He knew this day was coming, but he really hadn't been prepared for it.

Foster walked to the fridge and pulled out a bottle of water. He took one sip then turned back to face his mother. She was frowning. "I think the wine would have been more relaxing." She was trying to hide her frustration.

"I'm sure you do," Foster said calmly as he leaned against the counter. "So, how was this supposed to work?" he asked. "Is the serum in the food or did you plan to chain me to the chair and forcibly inject the formula into my vein?"

Patricia glared at her youngest son. How had he known? This plan should have worked. Now what? They needed to control him. They needed more money.

Lawson barreled across the room aiming for Foster. He didn't know how his brother discovered their plan, but he would not let him ruin everything. Foster was going to cooperate. Lawson would make sure of it.

Foster waited. Just before Lawson reached him he shifted, pivoted then effortlessly knocked Lawson to the ground. Foster stood over his brother shaking his head. He kicked out the leg of the chair, then reached down and forcibly flung Lawson into the seat. With the flick of his wrist Foster snapped the metal manacles closed, locking Lawson securely to the chair.

Lawson immediately began fighting his restraints. He yanked relentlessly at the metal enclosures trying desperately to get free. "You are going to pay for this brother," he bellowed. "You will regret this every minute for the rest of your life. Granted, it will be a very short life once I get free," Lawson promised.

Shadows

"Somehow I doubt that," Foster said unmoved by the threat. He glanced at his mother then back to Lawson. He shoved the plate towards his older brother. "We're going to be here awhile," he began. "Why don't you have dinner?" He grinned as his mother gasped and watched his brother shrink away from the food. "What's wrong?" Foster asked. "Not hungry? I think you could use the nourishment. Seems you're a little out of shape these days."

"That's enough Foster," Patricia said through gritted teeth.

"What's wrong mother? Not so confident in your potion after all?" Foster was a little hurt, but mostly he was furious. "It's good enough for me, but not for your precious Lawson?"

Patricia sighed. "Foster, we need money. You refuse to be sensible about this. We had no other choice. I didn't want to risk you that way, but what else could I do?"

"Oh, I don't know mother," Foster said angrily. "For starters, one of you could offer to help me run the business. How many times have I asked you to help with the ordering or with payroll? But, no. You're too important to do something so meaningless," he turned to Lawson. "And you," Foster glared at his brother. "Instead of being a lazy no good bum, you could have helped out a little. But apparently it's beneath you to work for a living. Too many parties to attend. Too many drugs to experiment with. There was a reason dad wrote you out of the will. There's a reason you're sitting in that chair instead of me."

"Like I said, you refuse to be reasonable," Patricia repeated.

Foster laughed. "It's unreasonable to expect the two of you to do something, anything for the free ride I'm supplying? Well then, I guess I'm unreasonable."

"You know as well as I do, I earned my station. If it wasn't for me and your father, you wouldn't have the business in the first place. I am simply asking to be compensated for the sacrifices I made for my children," Patricia argued.

Foster rolled his eyes. "What exactly did you sacrifice mother? Father started the hotel chain to fund that stupid project of his. If he'd been as passionate about the business as he was about taking back the crown, you might have an argument. You might actually have a claim to part of the business. Instead, dad worked here and there, making only enough money to fund his next experiment. I always found it ironic that Lawson got his laziness from father, then dad wrote him out of the will completely when he refused to work," Foster shrugged. "I'm not complaining. Lawson's loss was my gain," Foster sighed. "The two of you were sucked in from the very beginning. Dad's dream was a fantasy. You will never create a superior race. You will never develop a new species that can wipe out the warriors. You will never be queen. The monarchy is gone forever. Deal with it."

"This is the very reason we could never include you in the plan. We can't trust you. You don't understand, Foster. You never have. It is regretful. I'm afraid you've gone too far this time. Once Lawson is free he's going to come after you. Lawson will be king one day. I really am sorry you won't live long enough to see us succeed. Somehow I doubt you would appreciate it anyway."

"I think it's time to explain something to both of you," Foster began then he glanced at Lawson. "Before I get into that mother, I wonder if Lawson told you he's been partnering with the vampires."

"That's ridiculous," Patricia refused to believe the accusation. "Lawson hates the vampires as much as I do."

Shadows

"Really?" Foster asked. He looked at his brother again and knew he was right. Lawson's discomfort told him everything he needed to know. "Then maybe he could explain to both of us how that female vampire acquired several of his bombs."

He studied Lawson, waiting for a response. Lawson remained silent.

"I guess he's speechless," Foster grinned at the shocked look on his mother's face. She wouldn't want to believe Lawson was capable of such a betrayal, but after seeing Lawson's reaction she wouldn't be able to deny it. She knew all about Lawson's experiments with explosives. The evidence was too strong against him.

"So," Foster continued. "Once I realized the bomb that almost killed me that night in the ballroom was made by Lawson, I assumed he was trying to eliminate me for the money. The following day I went to Jake. We all know he's the best in the business. Jake prepared a trust for me," Foster smiled widely. "An unbreakable trust."

"What kind of a trust?" Patricia said, worried now.

"The trust outlines the family assets at the time of father's death. It also clearly demonstrates that without the expansions I have implemented this family would be destitute. Basically, the company owes you nothing mother. When father died, he insisted the small farm in upstate New York belonged to you. As long as you are alive, the farm can never be sold. Father wanted you to have a place to live. I agree. This same stipulation is present in the new trust. Upon my death, if you are still alive, you don't need to worry. You'll still have the farm," Foster was grinning now. He knew how much his mother hated that farm. "I wouldn't want you to be homeless."

"I won't be homeless," Patricia insisted. "This is my home now."

"Oh, it is for now," Foster agreed. "However, without the additional funds you would never be able to afford something this expensive. I'm afraid eventually you'll need to move back to the farm."

Patricia glared at Foster. How could he do this to her? She'd fight it. Her husband had a will. He had stipulated, very clearly, that she would be taken care of. If Foster died, the family business would be hers to do as she pleased. She would not move back to that horrible farm.

"Oh, I know what you're thinking," Foster told her. "The two of you assumed that upon my death the business would transfer to one of you." He shook his head. "Sorry to disappoint you. My trust addresses that as well. In the event of my death, especially if it's an untimely death, my managers will continue to run the day to day operations of the business."

"As your only surviving relatives Lawson and I are entitled to everything," Patricia argued.

"Well, you see that's where you're mistaken." He was enjoying this. "I do have another living relative. The family trust clearly states that in the event I am incapacitated in any way, Victor Keisser becomes executor."

"What!" Patricia and Lawson screamed at the same time.

Shadows

"Yep," Foster assured them. "I thought that might upset you a little."

"A little?" Patricia glared. "How could you do this? How could you betray your own family this way? You put our lives in the hands of a warrior?"

"Oh, I betrayed you did I?" He looked at each of them in turn then at the chair and finally at the plate of food. "What do you call this?"

Patricia brushed the accusation away with a swipe of her hand. "Necessary," she finally answered.

"Well, so was the trust," Foster assured her. "So here are the details. If anything happens to me, anything at all, Victor takes over. Good luck getting money out of him," he smiled. "Mother, you will continue to receive an allowance. Unfortunately, the amount will be up to Victor, as it is up to me. I allow you to live here, where you want. Considering the way you've treated that family I wouldn't expect the same generosity from Victor," he turned to Lawson. "I'm sure you realize you won't be getting a thing."

Patricia was floored. Foster couldn't do this. The money belonged to her. She deserved it. She needed it. How would she ever perfect her formula if Victor Keisser was in charge of their finances? Once again she regretted her past generosity.

"It was only a few days after Jake finished the trust that I realized Lawson wasn't trying to kill me. He'd simply sold explosives to the vampires out of greed and probably vengeance. It was actually pretty easy to figure out. Lawson didn't have a beef with the shifters, but the vamps do. The vamps also despise the fae. It all fell into place rather nicely. Lawson doesn't hate the vampires the way you do mother. He'll do anything for a buck. And like father, he'll risk anything to do away with the queen. I decided to leave the trust in place. It's kind of an insurance policy you see. I don't have to die for the trust to become active. If I am incapacitated in any way, mentally or physically, Victor immediately takes over. You can try to fight it, but I'm sure by now both of you realize a trust created by Jake is unbreakable. Plus, I've already taken it to the council. It's already been approved and recorded. At this point the only way to reverse it would be to appeal to the queen," Foster paused. "Good luck with that."

"You idiot," Lawson growled. "You've ruined this family."

"No," Foster disagreed. "I've just ruined your plans to use me as a test subject. If I were you, I wouldn't try to sneak any more toxins into my food. In fact, I'd avoid trying to contaminate me by any means Lawson. I don't think any of us want to suffer the consequences." Foster turned to leave the room. "I'm sure mother has the key to that ridiculous chair. Feel free to use it once I'm gone. Oh, and I suggest you don't come after me again. I'm busy, but I still find time to work out every day, especially now that the treaty's been broken. We're all at risk, even you. Anyway, you don't have a chance Lawson. Next time, I won't hold back." Foster turned and left the room.

He was surprised at how liberated he felt. He'd always felt responsible for his mother. He believed it was his job to make sure she had everything she needed since his father's death. Not anymore. She'd chosen Lawson, now she could deal with her choice. The house was almost finished anyway. It was far enough along for him to move in. He'd send a service over for his things in the morning then he'd move on with his life. He wasn't even going

Shadows

to tell them how to reach him. It was over. As far as he was concerned he didn't have a family anymore.

Patricia walked to Lawson and set him free. "Now what?" she asked.

"We move to plan B," Lawson shrugged. "We've got enough formula to begin the experiments. So, we can't use Foster. You wanted women anyway. I'll bring the first one tomorrow night," he assured her. "Don't worry mother. This is going to work. Soon, we will be in charge." He kissed his mother on the cheek. "With a little more time all our dreams will become reality, Queen Dillinger."

The two began to smile. They immediately started discussing their targets. Patricia wanted women. She strongly believed they were stronger and could withstand the dangerous transformation.

* * * *

Ty loaded the last bag into the truck and sighed. He wished they could stay here longer, but with everything going on he and Sam had been lucky to get a whole week together. He turned when he heard the screen door slam shut. Samantha traversed the stairs carrying two mugs. Coffee no doubt. He smiled. She was so beautiful, inside and out. He was still amazed he'd gotten so lucky. Even now it was hard to believe she was actually his wife.

Samantha stopped in front of Ty and handed him a mug as she leaned in and kissed him softly. "Ready?" she asked.

"Almost," he agreed. "Bo, Ace...truck." Ty watched as the two dogs joyfully darted towards the pickup, then leapt into the back mid-stride.

"I'm so glad they're coming with us," Samantha smiled. "I'd miss them terribly if we had to leave them here."

"Me too," Ty agreed, taking one last longing glance around his property. "So then, we're off to New York," Ty was trying to sound enthusiastic, but knew he failed.

Sam nodded, then sighed. "I love it here," she admitted wistfully. "In a way it reminds me of my childhood, only much bigger." She grinned. "Can we come back soon?"

"I hope so," Ty agreed. "With everything going on, I haven't been able to spend as much time at home as I used to. Pete's got it covered. I don't worry about the day to day operations. But I have to warn you, I get a little grumpy when I can't get away on a regular basis." Ty opened the passenger door and held it for Sam.

Sam climbed into the truck then grabbed Ty's belt and pulled him forward. "I know how much you love it here." She leaned in and kissed him. "I hope we can find a place in New York that gives us both the peace we need between visits. I want to spend a lot of time out here, but I know realistically we're going to be living in New York most of the time. Until the vampire threat has subsided, we can't just pack up and leave for the weekend anytime we want."

"I know," Ty agreed. He hated the city but before he'd met Sam he'd finally admitted he was going to have to buy a condo downtown. They'd talked about their situation a lot over the past week and finally agreed to purchase a home instead. After studying the area, they'd settled on Staten Island. It was close enough to

Shadows

allow an easy commute, but would also provide plenty of space and solitude. Ty smiled as he closed the door and headed for the driver's seat. Sam was still uncomfortable about the price. He knew if they were going to get something they both liked it would cost several million. Sam wasn't exactly being realistic about the budget, but he was confident she'd come around eventually. Once they started looking he knew she'd give in. They had plenty. Ty wanted to use it to find a place they both loved. He refused to settle just to save a few bucks.

The two traveled in silence for a long while. They were both lost in thought, watching the ranch fade into the distance. The honeymoon was over. It was time to get back to work. It was time to focus their energy on the vampire problem and the fort.

"I've arranged for an apartment in the interim," Ty told her. "I hope that's okay with you." He glanced her way.

"Sure," Sam agreed. "We can't live in my apartment and I'm not comfortable moving in with Thomas. Will we be stuck with a lease?" She was worried about that. She didn't want to be trapped in an apartment if they found a house, and she didn't want to pay someone for an apartment they weren't using.

"No," Ty grinned. "I never charge myself rent. It's a personal policy of mine."

"What? You own an apartment complex?" She narrowed her eyes at him. "Why didn't I know that already? And more to the point, is there anything else you haven't told me?"

"Not exactly. I co-own an apartment complex with my cousin. I don't have the time to manage it so I'm basically a silent partner. I keep it for my employees. In fact, it's mandatory for them to live there while they're attending training. I guess I should have warned you about that, too. No wild acrobatics after ten," he smiled at her. He knew she understood the implication.

"That's too bad," Sam laughed. "I was hoping we could consummate each room before we moved out."

"Oh, we will," he assured her. "We just have to do it before ten." Ty lifted her hand to his lips and gently kissed her palm. "I am the luckiest man in the world," he told her sincerely.

Samantha felt tingles flow through her entire body. She had come to appreciate the connection she shared with Ty. It no longer scared her. She was starting to rely on it.

"I'm glad the anxiety you used to feel about our special bond is finally gone," Ty told her. "It's nice that you now recognize it as a blessing, not something to regret or fear."

Samantha smiled. "I didn't realize how amazing it would be to actually experience the extent of your love. It's impossible to be insecure about our relationship when I can feel your emotions," Samantha paused. "It's too bad everyone doesn't have what we do. If I had the power, I'd give this gift to everyone I know."

"I agree," Ty told her softly. "I know Dimitri loves Alex and they share a special bond of their own. Victor and Ariel also have a special connection. But somehow I feel like I have more," he grinned at her. "Well, first I have you. That in itself is amazing. I still don't know how it's possible that you fell for me. But, we have something more. We never have to doubt the other's love. You and I will always know our spouse is totally and completely devoted to the relationship," he paused then laughed. "You will be devoted to me forever. I'll make sure of it," he assured her.

Shadows

"I was actually wondering why you would be devoted to me for that long," Samantha admitted.

"Because I love you, silly woman," Ty told her simply. "And I always will," he assured her.

"Do you have any idea how strange it is for me that I actually believe that?" Samantha asked. "I was alone so long, now I will never be alone again. It's strange and wonderful and amazing," she said. They rode in silence for several miles. Then Samantha flipped on the radio, reclined her seat and relaxed, enjoying the ride back to the city.

* * * *

Samantha paused before she slid the key into the lock. "Are you sure you won't let me do this alone?" she pled. "It's not a pretty sight. I'm embarrassed for you to see my old place. Especially after leaving the ranch where it's so relaxing and homey. My apartment is impersonal and a little disgusting."

Ty took the key from Samantha and slid it into the lock. He gently pushed the door open and reached around to flip on the light. Samantha stepped inside and closed her eyes. She was concentrating on Ty. She wanted to feel what he felt. She wanted to know the truth.

Ty pushed her a little. "Stop probing me and go pack. Of course I don't like knowing you actually lived here for years. It's beneath you," he grimaced as he studied the couch. There was no way he was going to actually sit on that thing. He swung around, relieved when he spotted the wooden kitchen chairs. "Please tell me we don't have to take the furniture," he begged, lowering himself onto one of small seats and resting his elbow on the table. "I'm not sure I could handle actually touching that couch, let alone bring it within miles of my apartment complex. I'm sure it has termites or something, not to mention the fact that it's the ugliest thing I've ever seen in my life."

Samantha laughed. "You don't like my taste? I was thinking about decorating our new home myself," she paused. "If I can't have the couch, can I at least take my favorite chair?"

Thank goodness Ty knew she was joking. Her furniture was awful. "What exactly do you need from here? I think we'd be doing the world a favor if we just torched the place."

Samantha sobered. She glanced around the tiny space and realized there wasn't much she actually wanted. Mostly she just wanted to leave her whole life behind. "Actually all I need are a few clothes and a couple things I was able to recover from mom. Everything else can stay."

Ty stood and walked to Samantha. "Bring whatever you want." He glanced back at the couch. "Except that," he grinned. "You absolutely cannot have the couch." He took her hand and led her to the bedroom. He was struck by the lack of personal touch. Samantha had lived here for several years, but he couldn't find one thing that hinted at her personality. Nothing that demonstrated who Samantha Reed really was.

Samantha strolled to the closet and began packing her bag. Once that was empty she moved to the night stand and removed what looked like a jewelry box and a few additional items.

Shadows

Ty sat on the edge of the bed, watching. He grinned when she glanced his way. Once she had finished, he reached for her hand but missed. Samantha placed her belongings on the floor and walked to the bed. Ty immediately pulled her on top of him. "I think it's my duty to make sure you have one memorable experience in this apartment." He grinned as she continued to watch him intently. "I love you Sam," Ty whispered in her ear as he gently rubbed the palm of his hand over her back. "I want you, right now."

"You've got to be kidding," she said in disbelief. "How could being in this disgusting, overpriced, dirty apartment put you in the mood?"

Ty tucked Sam's hair behind her ear. "This is where you lived for a very long time," he paused pulling her head down to kiss her, hoping she would read his emotions. "I doubt you have any pleasant memories here." He smiled as he looked around the room. "I want to give you one," he studied her. "If we ever walk down this street again, which is something I actually can't imagine happening in the near future, but if we do..." he kissed her again. "I want you to look up at that dirty, hazy window and think of us. I want you to think of me. Okay, I know that's selfish but I want you to have one good, well great really, memory of us in this apartment." Ty rolled over, trapping her body beneath his. "Will you give me this one small pleasure, Sam?" he asked as he leaned down and skillfully kissed her neck. She could never resist him and he knew it.

Sam hesitated for only a moment. The thought of making love to Ty in this apartment actually appealed to her. It made sense in a strange sort of way. She liked the thought of having one extremely memorable moment in this awful place before she walked away and never looked back. Samantha relaxed and gave in to her husband and the moment.

* * * *

Tala stopped the rented jeep in front of the small cabin. She was amazed she'd actually found the place. She wasn't that familiar with Utah. Cornelia had brought her here once just before they'd left for an extended trip to California on a case. She wondered if Cornelia's mother, Shaylee would remember her. She hoped Cornelia was still here. Tala had searched for weeks in Moab. She'd almost given up and headed to Seneca to begin the investigation on her own when she'd run into the man. Unlike her daughter, she never hesitated to push her way into someone's mind. Megan thought it was tacky or rude. Tala thought it was practical. Why waste time trying to convince someone to answer your questions when you could just waltz in and find out on your own. However, in Moab she didn't have to force her way in. The man's emotions were almost shouting at her. The guy was in love with Cornelia. He was depressed and fighting with himself. He wanted to chase after her, but Cornelia had told him she needed time away. The guy had decided to give her whatever she needed. He hoped his willingness to let her go would convince her they were meant for each other.

After thoroughly picking his brain, Tala immediately flew to Salt Lake and rented a jeep. Shaylee's cabin was deep in the Uintah Mountains. The place had so many dirt and gravel roads taking off in all directions, Tala had been sure she'd get lost out in the wilderness, never to be seen or heard from again. She sighed, beyond relieved that she had found the place as she gently knocked on the front door. Shaylee was very antisocial. If Cornelia wasn't here, her mother may panic at the intrusion. Tala needed to be prepared for an adverse reaction. Shaylee didn't like unexpected

Shadows

guests. She didn't like people at all. Tala waited. Come on Cornelia, open the door. She was just about to venture around the back of the cabin when the door swung open and Cornelia appeared. Her look of annoyance immediately turned to a large smile.

"Tala!" she exclaimed. "How in the world did you find me?"

"I knew you were in Moab," Tala began. "Once I got there it was pure luck. Still leaving heartsick men in your wake I see," she teased.

"Oh! You ran into Trent," Cornelia sighed. "I had to escape. The man would not take no for an answer," she shook her head. "You know how I feel about relationships. I'm afraid I can't go back there now. Not for at least ten or twenty years anyway. It's a shame. I love the beautiful red rocks and the relaxed tourist atmosphere."

"Sounds like you're a little displaced," Tala observed.

Cornelia narrowed her eyes. "Can I assume you're here because you have a job offer?" she asked cutting to the chase.

"Actually I am," Tala admitted.

"Well, come on in and you can tell me all about it." Cornelia turned and headed into the cabin. "I was just cooking dinner. We have plenty. Do you have time to stay and eat? If you're not in a hurry maybe you could spend the night and if I'm interested we could head out in the morning. We still have the guest room," Cornelia offered.

"That sounds wonderful," Tala agreed. She spotted Shaylee. "Hello," Tala said gently hoping the woman remembered her.

Shaylee smiled and stood, holding out her hand. "It's Tala isn't it?" she asked. "It's so good to see you again."

Tala breathed a sigh of relief. Cornelia had explained the situation involving her mother prior to Tala's first visit. Corni had warned her that Shaylee didn't always handle company well. Sometimes the nicest, gentlest person could set her mother off. If Shaylee became agitated she was prone to mental breakdowns. That could range anywhere from locking herself in her room to violent attacks. Cornelia felt living in solitude in the mountain cabin calmed her mother. Not many people could, or would, visit her up here. Winters were tough, but the summers were magnificent.

Tala walked to Shaylee and took her hand. "It's wonderful to see you again, Shaylee." She paused, looking towards Cornelia. "I'm afraid I need Cornelia to help me with another case. Will you forgive me if I take her away for a while?"

Shaylee smiled. "Of course." She sat back down in the comfortable chair. "Corni's been here a few weeks now. I think she's going stir crazy," Shaylee confided. "She doesn't love the solitude as much as I do. I'd be grateful if you gave my girl something to do. I understand the two of you make quite a team."

Tala smiled. She'd won over the mother, now for the daughter. "I think so," Tala smiled. "Maybe I'll go help Cornelia in the kitchen. I need to schmooze her and see if I can convince her to head out of town in the morning. I have an important case and I don't think I can handle it on my own."

Shaylee nodded and went back to her needlework. She was perfectly content to sit in front of the fire and work on her new project. Cornelia needed people. Shaylee hated them. She knew her daughter would never come back to her for good. The solitude

Shadows

drove Cornelia crazy. The hustle of the city was too much for Shaylee to handle. Their lifestyles were too different, opposite ends of the spectrum really. Shaylee was just grateful her daughter loved her enough to pay regular and frequent visits. But she'd been here too long this time and the solitude was driving her daughter crazy. Tala's unexpected visit was just what Cornelia needed.

Tala and Cornelia sat in the kitchen discussing the new case and the possibility of Cornelia joining Tala in New York. The idea made Cornelia nervous. Could she actually go to New York City? She'd never planned to set foot anywhere near that place. But, they wouldn't actually be confined to the big apple. Unfortunately, it was clear they would have to spend some time there. What if she encountered her father? Would he know? How would he react? Then there was the other problem. How would she handle her uh...medical needs in New York? She was going to have to think about this overnight. She wanted to help Tala, but New York? The idea made her more than a little nervous.

"Why don't you sleep on it?" Tala proposed. "I'll need to leave first thing in the morning but we can talk about it again over coffee," Tala suggested. "If you can't help, I understand. It would just be a little easier with two of us."

Cornelia took a deep breath. "I do need a little time to think about it," she paused. "I'm sorry, I wish I could give you an enthusiastic yes, but I just don't know. Let me think about it tonight and I promise I'll let you know first thing in the morning."

"Deal," Tala agreed. They spent the rest of the night catching up and visiting with Shaylee. All in all it was a wonderful evening.

* * * *

Tala pulled the rental up to the farmhouse and shut off the engine. "Touchdown," she said with relief. It had been a long trip. Once she collected Cornelia, they'd returned to Denver to clean out the office then packed her stuff and shipped most of it here separately. Tala had kept a few personal items with her but most of her stuff had been sent ahead days ago. Hopefully she'd find it stacked in the apartment she would now call home. She didn't know how long she'd be here, but she did know it was going to be awhile. She smiled and turned to Cornelia. "You ready?" she asked.

"As ready as I'll ever be," Cornelia was beyond nervous. There were very few fae in Utah and she rarely saw a vampire. Of course, no warriors lived there. It was too far from home and the queen. She wasn't sure what to expect from this crowd. She hoped they would accept her but she couldn't count on it. Then there was her condition. She was starting to get desperate. Tala had kept her so busy she hadn't had a minute to herself. She needed medication. Tonight, she promised herself. Last night at the hotel she'd googled the fort and was happy to discover a hospital nearby. She would finally have access to what she needed. Once introductions were made, she'd excuse herself and then head over to the hospital before bed. By morning, all would be okay again.

* * * *

Cornelia waited under the cover of darkness. She felt a lot better about the situation now. Everyone had been very kind and nobody seemed to notice she was different. That had been her

Shadows

biggest worry. Would they know about her past? About her condition or what she called her medication? But no one seemed to notice. Maybe this wouldn't be so bad after all. She straightened as a group of nurses exited the large doors. Finally, shift change. That was the best time for her to gather what she needed and head back to the apartment. Once the women disappeared around the corner, Cornelia darted for the door. She caught it just in time to slip in unnoticed. The rest was easy.

Within minutes she was sitting back in the apartment, mission accomplished. Thank goodness she only needed a boost once every week to ten days depending on her activity. It had been nearly two weeks since her last dose, which was far too long. The only thing that saved her was the long car ride. She couldn't let that happen again. Now that she was living around the others, somebody would notice if she allowed herself to get that weak again. She inhaled a long, relaxing breath and settled further into the couch. She felt so much better now that she'd taken the medication. She knew what she'd gathered tonight would only last a few weeks. Then she'd have to improvise all over again. But by that time, she should be in downtown New York. Getting what she needed in such a big city should be easy, right? She certainly hoped so. She flipped on the television and relaxed for the first time in days.

* * * *

The killer leaned casually against the wall of the old building. He knew he was well hidden. The shadows would protect him until his target came out. The streets were almost empty now. Those left wouldn't notice the subtle abduction, he was a professional after all. His heartbeat quickened ever so slightly, it was almost time. He could feel it. A smile crept across his face as adrenaline pumped through his toned body. Any second now his unsuspecting prey would appear.

The side door of the building flew open. The killer straightened, beyond ready for the game to begin. He knew tonight was going to be a success. It had to be. The first woman had gotten the ball rolling but in all honesty she'd been a bore, no fun at all. It had ended too quickly. Tonight would be different. Tonight was a capture, not a kill. That would come later. He continued to watch as the bubbly young girl closed down the business for the night.

Susan Jones turned and locked up the theater. She loved everything about her job. Right now their current act was a musical. It would be running for a couple more weeks, then that popular dance group would move in. She could never remember their name. Anyway, that show was extremely popular with the young crowd. The performance was going to last eight weeks and six of them were already sold out completely. She was always so busy these days, but she absolutely loved working here. It was a dream come true. She'd only met Thomas a few weeks ago but instantly knew he was just like his father. Her thoughts turned back to Luke Deveraux, he had been wonderful to work for, so was his wife. Susan had really enjoyed it when Marlena stopped by. She frowned. Those memories always made her a little sad. She often wondered how a young, energetic woman like Marlena had suddenly died of a heart attack. It just didn't make any sense.

Susan exited the alley and strolled down Broadway. She was definitely a New Yorker through and through. She loved the bright city lights and even the crowds. Some people thought that was strange, but she couldn't imagine herself anywhere else. She was so deep in thought she didn't notice the man slide in behind her. Susan continued toward the subway, oblivious to the danger. Just as she was about to head underground she was yanked to the left. She tried to pull away, but the man covered her mouth with a dirty glove and continued dragging her into the dark alley ahead. Susan wanted to scream, but it was impossible with the gloved hand covering her face. She struggled, trying her hardest to pull away, but he was so strong. She tried to take a deep breath, but the glove was partially covering her nose as well. Between the fear and lack of oxygen she was sure she was going to pass out. Susan began to cry as reality set in. She was going to die tonight. That too was part of New York. In contrast to all the good, New York definitely bred the bad.

* * * *

Tala arose early the next morning. She'd gotten a good night's rest and was anxious to begin her investigation. She sat at the kitchen table reviewing her file. There wasn't much in it so far. The case seemed pretty clear cut. There had been the incident with Victor years ago where Atticus had killed Dannica Dillinger, or Keisser at the time of her death. Foster had pressured the council to punish Atticus for the murder. Typical of a family member, especially one that was close to his sister. She'd need to find out where Dannica's parents were. And the other brother, Lawson was it? It seemed the group had ruled out Foster because of the explosion at the ballroom. Granted, that moved him to the bottom of her list but she wasn't ready to rule him out completely. The attacks on Atticus could be a family affair. They could have planned to have Foster in the room to shift suspicion elsewhere.

Tala scribbled on a blank sheet of paper. What tied the bombings together? First there was the shifter camps. Then the ballroom, then Atticus' farm. Lawson was the obvious choice, but why would he want to harm the shifters? She was going to have to dig deep into Lawson's background. Not just the obvious stuff, the dirty little secrets as well. She wasn't going to get what she needed from a computer or other legitimate means. That kind of dirt was something only a shadow could find. Once again her gift was going to pay off. She felt sorry for humans, they always had to play by the book.

Tala jumped at the abrupt knocking coming from outside her door. She slowly stood and looked out the peephole. She grinned as she flung the door open and pulled her daughter into her arms. "Megan!" she exclaimed. "I didn't know you were going to be here. I thought you were going to Pennsylvania."

"We were. But we got delayed, so we thought we'd wait for you and then we could all go together," she paused. Her mother looked good. "You seem rested. How was your trip?"

"Long," Tala answered walking back to the table and picking up her coffee. "Oh, do you want some?" she asked. "I have plenty."

"No, thanks. We already ate." Megan was thrilled to have her mother here. She thought maybe she could help her with the case, the way she used to when she was young. "So are you going to block me out of this one or can I help?" she asked.

Tala studied her daughter. She wished she could let her participate, but she was too close to the victim. Tala knew the connection. Megan's husband Tony was best friends with Atticus' son, Victor. Megan would talk to Tony, she wouldn't be able to stop herself. Then, Tony would talk to Victor and Victor would tell Atticus.

Shadows

"Oh alright," Megan said after watching her mother squirm uncomfortably for a minute. "I'll stay out of it. I just thought it sounded like fun to be your faithful assistant again." Megan remembered Cornelia. "Speaking of assistants, did you bring one with you?" she asked.

"I did," Tala said obviously thrilled. "It was harder than I originally thought it would be to track her down, but once I found her she agreed to help. She's across the hall. Probably still sleeping. We had a pretty long trip from Utah to Denver, then New York."

"I really am glad you could make it mom. When we left Denver I assumed it would be months before we could get together again. Then Charles called and Tony insisted we had to head straight here," she smiled. "These guys are great. You're going to love them," then she paused. "Will you please try to keep your curiosity in check though?"

"Whatever do you mean?" Tala grinned.

"Mother," Megan pressed. "I like these guys. They're warm and friendly and don't deserve to have you picking around in their brains."

"I'll try," Tala finally said. No way would she promise her daughter anything. "So, on a different topic, just how many people are living out here anyway? I woke early this morning and looked out my window to see about six kids wandering around the field."

"Oh that," Megan brushed it away. "It's just the students."

Tala furrowed her brows in confusion. "What students? I thought you said the academy wasn't open yet."

"It's not," Megan assured her. "But about a dozen kids have arrived to help with set up. We've all been so busy there hasn't been much time to paint all the bunkers or even set out the furniture. The kids are painting one row at a time. After they go up one row and down the other, the paint is dry enough to outfit the rooms. Then they move on to the next row. I'm told there are about three hundred bunkers so the kids have their work cut out for them."

"Too bad I didn't have a project like this when you were a kid," Tala thought out loud. "It might have kept you out of trouble."

Megan laughed. "Nothing would have kept me out of trouble. It's in my genes."

"I can't wait until you have a child of your own. Then you'll know how nerve wracking it is. I'm just glad you found Tony when you did," Tala smiled. She liked Megan's husband. "He'll keep you in line from now on."

"Oh, yeah?" Megan countered. "Wait until you hear some of the harrowing stories I've heard over the past few weeks. Victor and Tony are not allowed to be alone together for more than twenty four hours, tops. They turn into maniacs after that." The two women turned when they heard the door slide open.

"I've never been a maniac in my life," Tony disagreed.

"Ditto," Victor agreed following Tony into the room. Atticus brought up the tail.

Megan moved to stand next to Tony. She'd thought the euphoria would wear off soon after the wedding, but they'd been married almost four years now and it was still there. She loved her husband and lit up whenever he walked into a room.

Shadows

Tala smiled at her daughter. She was so glad Megan had found such happiness. For just an instant Tala's mind shifted back to her past. She immediately stopped the memories. She wouldn't let Megan's father spoil her mood. She'd just be grateful for the love her daughter shared with such a wonderful man. Tala froze as soon as she noticed the final guest enter her room. He was the most handsome man she'd ever seen. Oh, he was rugged and worn but striking. She continued to study him as Victor and Tony plopped down on the couch.

Tala walked to the man and held out her hand. "I'm sorry, I don't think we've met. My name is Tala Fitzgerald."

Atticus took the dainty hand and shook it gently. Tala was gorgeous. Not in a super model sort of way, but she was a beautiful woman that seemed down to earth and sophisticated yet lovely. She had an air of confidence Atticus had not encountered before. That self-assurance made her even more attractive somehow. Atticus was surprised at his reaction to her. He was considering the implications when he felt the first nudge. He hadn't been prepared for the intrusion, so it initially took him by surprise. Then it annoyed him. No wonder she was over confident. She was apparently in the habit of reading the minds of everyone in the room. Over the centuries he'd encountered shadows before. It was easy enough to block them. All the warriors could, but their attempts to penetrate his thoughts always annoyed him. He continued to study Tala as she again tried to force her way into his mind. He didn't need mind reading skills to understand her emotions. She went from confident to surprised, then he saw a look of determination, then frustration and annoyance. It didn't matter how long or hard she tried, she wouldn't get in.

Tala was shocked. The only time this had happened before was with Cornelia. Nobody else had ever thwarted her attempts to get inside their head before. She pushed harder, nothing. She slowly began to circle with her mind, looking for holes or weaknesses. Tala suddenly realized the room had gone quiet. She pulled her hand away and tried to regain control. "I'll need a list of possible suspects," she turned back to the complex man standing before her. "Atticus, I presume?" she asked realizing he hadn't told her his name.

"Yes," he said flatly.

"Then that request is for you. I'll need you to separate the list into two categories." The surrounding silence was awkward so she continued to focus on business. "The first will be those who know you well. Anyone that may know your routine, your characteristics, the intimate details of your life. Those people go in one column. Acquaintances go in the other column. Those people you've just met, or casually greet but don't share your life details with. The grocery clerks or the mailman for instance." Atticus wasn't giving anything away. She needed a reading on him. Did he suspect anyone he hadn't mentioned, what was his relationship like with his son. If she couldn't get in, how was she supposed to get the answers she needed?

Tala strolled to the kitchen table and pulled out a notepad. She casually walked toward Tony as she once again tried to penetrate Atticus' mind. Nothing.

Atticus wasn't surprised when he felt the pressure again. The woman was persistent. He'd let it drop the first time but she needed to be put in her place. Her constant attempts were a nuisance at best, but if she was going to stick around for long she needed to be

Shadows

stopped. He was not going to live his life on guard, constantly anticipating her next attack on his system. He stood and walked her way.

Victor was watching his father. He could tell the man was annoyed, he just didn't know why. Then it hit him. Tala was a shadow. Had she tried to read his father's mind? He studied his father closely as Atticus stood and walked toward Megan's mother. Yep, he was pissed. Victor straightened. He didn't want to interfere with his father but he liked Megan. If her mother needed help, he'd step in.

Tala turned, surprised to see Atticus standing directly in front of her. She straightened and side stepped to walk around him. Atticus also took a step to the side. At the same time, he moved slightly closer, crowding her personal space. She didn't like it. The closeness was uncomfortable. Tala took a large step backwards. Atticus took a slightly larger step. He was being rude on purpose. What was his game? She took a deep breath then stepped back again. At the same time she held her hand out in front of her. "Please stop," she said before he could move forward again. "You are invading my space. I'd appreciate it if you did not come any closer."

Atticus didn't move. He continued to watch her with an amused grin on his face.

Victor relaxed and sunk back into the couch. He should have trusted his father. Dad was pissed, but he was still a gentleman. He would handle this his way. Victor smiled, it was nice to see dad interacting so well again. He'd forgotten how much he enjoyed watching his father in action.

Tala was livid. The man thought this was funny? Well, it wasn't. "Mr. Keisser," Tala paused as she held out her arms in front of her. "This is my space. I would appreciate it very much if you did not invade that space in the future. It makes me uncomfortable and it's just, I don't know...rude and..."

Atticus raised one eyebrow. "Invasive?" he offered.

"Well yes," she agreed then froze. She understood his meaning and she didn't like it. How had he known? Nobody ever knew when she tried to read them. Not even Cornelia, her one and only failure until today. She studied him intently. Maybe she was mistaken. No, he was warning her to stay out of his space all right.

"I'd be happy to respect your space Ms. Fitzgerald as long as you respect mine." He didn't move. He just continued to study her, waiting for a response.

"Fine," Tala finally agreed. She turned to face her daughter and saw the anger.

"Mother, how could you!" Megan exclaimed. "I asked you not to do that. How could you disrespect my friends that way? How could you disrespect me like that?"

"Megan, you're over reacting," she sighed. "Just drop it. We need to move on. I have a lot to do. I want to interview everyone here at the fort first. Then we can move to the others in New York City and on to Pennsylvania." Tala's gaze left Megan and landed on Tony. Not him too. She didn't have to try to read his mind, it was practically screaming at her. She'd never seen Tony this angry before. What was the big deal? So she tried to read the man's mind. She glanced at the son, Victor, expecting more of the same. She was surprised to see he too was grinning just like his father. Maybe

Shadows

she'd take one little peek. If she couldn't read the father, she'd get her answers from the son. She gave his mind a little push then glared at him in amazement. Was it genetic? She wondered. Over the centuries she'd only had one person thwart her efforts. Now in a matter of minutes it had happened twice.

Victor pushed himself off the couch and walked towards Tala. "Ms. Fitzgerald," he began. "I'm afraid I did not inherit my father's skill with subtlety. I tend to be much more direct."

"Mother!" Megan bellowed in frustration.

Victor momentarily glanced at Megan then returned his attention to her mother. "I am going to ask you nicely not to do that again," he paused. "Next time I will simply tell you to leave. If you try to force your way into my mind, my father's mind or the mind of anyone else here at the fort again, I'm afraid you will not be welcome here."

"What exactly does your group have to hide, Victor?" Tala said coolly.

"Nothing," Victor answered just as coldly. "It's a matter of respect. It seems that's a concept you do not understand," he paused. "Your efforts will be futile anyway. The rest of us can block you just as easily as my father and I just did. We simply find it rude and a bit tacky."

The room was quiet for a moment then Megan spoke. "Mother apologize to Atticus and Victor."

"I have nothing to apologize for," Tala insisted.

Megan walked to Atticus fighting back tears. Her mother had humiliated her. She'd been getting along so well with everyone here. Would they isolate and reject her too because of her mom's bad behavior? For the first time in her life she was sorry she'd invited her mother into her new world.

Atticus took Megan's chin in his large hand. "Megan," he soothed. "Don't you fret about this."

"I am so sorry," she whispered.

Atticus pulled her in for a large hug. He had come to think of Megan as family the same as he did Tony. Her mother's actions wouldn't change that. Atticus gently kissed the side of Megan's head. Then pushed her back so he could talk to her. "There is nothing for you to be sorry about." Atticus gently draped his arm around her shoulder and walked toward her husband. "Tony, I think your wife needs a little TLC," he smiled at Tony. "You two go take a break for a few minutes." Tony was about to argue when Atticus shook his head slightly. "Go, I've got this."

Tony took Megan's hand and began to lead her to the door. Megan jerked free and ran to Victor. "I want to apologize to you, too. I'm sorry my mother behaved so badly."

Victor smiled then placed his hands on her shoulders and turned her back around to face Tony. He gently leaned down and whispered in her ear. "Nobody's angry with you Megan. Go spend some time with Tony. It will make you feel better. There's no hay at the fort, but maybe you two could go romp in the forest." A grin spread across his face as he gently gave her shoulders a shove towards his friend.

Shadows

Tony loved his mother-in-law, but she was way out of line here. He was furious. He watched as Victor whispered something in Megan's ear then as Megan relaxed a little and smiled. He was grateful to his friend. Victor always knew how to put people at ease. He continued to watch as Victor gave him a wink and lifted his chin as a sign for Tony to escort his wife out of the room. Tony put an arm around Megan and headed for the door.

Megan paused and turned to her mother. "I'd like to speak to you in private later. This conversation is not over." She proceeded out the door with Tony by her side.

Tala was shocked. Her daughter had never behaved that way before. Oh sure, she'd been upset when she thought Tala was invading someone's privacy without cause, but Megan was actually angry with her over this. She shifted her attention back to Atticus. That had shocked her, too. He'd been so gentle and caring towards her daughter. The only word Tala could think of to describe his connection with Megan was fatherly. She needed to get her daughter away from these people immediately. Megan was setting herself up for disappointment. Tala worried it was already too late. She looked at the two men who remained in the room. "As far as I'm concerned we're finished here. The sooner you get me that list, the sooner I can get started."

Victor spoke before his father could. "I'm no longer sure you are the right person for this job." He paused to allow time for his father to object. When nobody said a word Victor continued. "I realize you are new to our community and so I'm willing to excuse your behavior this morning. However, you clearly believe you are justified in pushing your way into any mind you see fit, anytime you want. We don't work that way here. Stay and visit with Megan and

Tony as long as you like, but I'm afraid we're going to find another PI to investigate the threats against dad."

"There's no one that can protect your father as well as I can," Tala argued. She was dumbfounded. She was getting fired? She'd never been fired in her life.

Again Victor answered before his father, who looked like he was about to explode. "It seems you have been given some bad information Ms. Fitzgerald," Victor paused. "My father does not need anyone to protect him. He is more than capable of protecting himself. Far more capable than you, or even I am. We are simply looking for an investigator to identify the individual or individuals that have been threatening his life. We also need evidence collected against said individuals so they can be properly punished for their crimes."

Tala watched Victor silently. She couldn't decide if she liked him or hated him. He certainly had character and was very protective of his father.

"We'll just have to find someone else to do the job. Don't worry, I will make sure you are fully compensated for your troubles." Victor turned to leave the room.

"Just like that?" Tala asked. "I have no say in the matter? I have no recourse? There is no person other than yourself for me to appeal to? I have pulled up stakes in Denver, not to mention the fact that I convinced Cornelia to drop everything she was doing, to travel to New York only to be fired for no reason." She paused at the look on both men's faces. "Okay fine, you think you have a reason. But regardless, I think the situation should be discussed more completely with Megan and Tony and certainly Cornelia present before you make a rash decision based on emotion."

Shadows

Atticus could see his son wasn't about to budge on this. Maybe they had been a little too rash. What would be the harm in giving her a chance? "As far as having a recourse, no you do not. We are talking about my life and I have the final say," Atticus began. He continued on when Tala was about to argue. "However, to be fair I would be willing to have a meeting later this evening to discuss the situation with those individual's present that you mentioned."

Tala relaxed. She couldn't really say why, but she wanted this investigation. She was determined to stay. That would give her the rest of the day to develop a strategy to win them over. Somehow she would help them to see she was the best person for this job.

"In the meantime," Victor interrupted Tala's thoughts, "I need to speak to the others. I need to know how they feel about keeping Tala on, knowing she will attempt to invade their thoughts at any moment." He immediately left the room before she could argue.

Tala turned to Atticus. "I guess he doesn't like me much," she sighed. She needed time to think.

"I'll get started on that list," Atticus said turning to leave as well. "Regardless of who conducts the investigation, I think that list might be helpful." With that he also turned and left the room.

* * * *

Thomas sat behind the large desk in his home library concentrating on the double screens. He'd be spending another night going over spreadsheets instead of fighting. Dante and Nick would be here any minute but he couldn't leave this. Something was off. He'd already found several discrepancies in the records. What he needed to determine, was whether they were honest mistakes or if someone was skimming on purpose. Why had so many of his top people become dishonest after Luke's death? It was baffling to Thomas. Good, reliable family men were doing stupid and reckless things. Alex was having the same problems with her side of the house. Were there no honest people out there anymore?

He stood and walked to the door when he heard the knock. Right on time. They were not going to be happy about his decision to stay home tonight. He pulled open the elaborate wooden door and grinned. He'd missed his two best friends. He wanted to go out and fight with them. Actually he needed it. He knew just spending time with them would relieve some of his stress.

"Nu-huh," Dante said immediately. "No way. You are not bailing on us again."

"I wish I didn't have to," Thomas started.

"No way," Dante said again. He looked to Nick for support.

Nick shook his head. "I have to agree with Dante," then he groaned. "Please never tell anyone those words came out of my mouth," he smiled.

Dante punched Nick in the shoulder. "You're not helping, man."

"Really, I have too much work. I'll catch you two tomorrow," Thomas said without conviction.

"Sorry," Nick apologized. "You're outnumbered. We're not taking no for an answer tonight. You need to get out, Thomas. We can barely stand you these days. Take a break until morning. The distraction will do you good."

"Always the diplomat," Dante added rolling his eyes. "How 'bout you try this on for size, we're not leaving until you join us. So, it's your call. A night of you trying to concentrate on some boring document, scrolling through numbers while I do my very best to distract and confuse you. Or a night out hunting vamps," he paused, "What's it gonna be, bro?" He casually shrugged like he didn't care either way.

Thomas knew better. His friend cared, but the thought of Dante spending the evening tormenting him while he tried to work did not appeal to him in the least. "Okay, a few hours," he paused. "But that's all I can give you."

Dante turned to Nick and gave him a high five. "I knew we'd get him. Where are we going to eat?" he asked his two friends.

"Italian," Nick insisted.

"Works for me," Thomas agreed. He realized he was starved.

"Just like old times," Dante observed. "Now we just need to find a vamp. They've been kind of scarce lately."

"What do you mean?" Thomas asked. The vampires were usually easy to find. Especially this time of year. Humans stayed out longer in the fall, he assumed it was in anticipation of the cold winter. They wanted to enjoy the good weather outside before the snow began to fly.

"I realize we've had several battles with large numbers of vampires getting killed lately," Nick told him. "But it just seems like there should be more vampires on the streets. Radek has to be increasing his army. Just a few weeks ago disappearances were splattered across every human newspaper in the area. I heard it was even making international news."

"They're gone?" Thomas asked.

"Yeah," Dante put in. "We think they've headed out of town to hunt and create an army. They were getting too much attention here in New York."

"Does Dimitri know?" Thomas asked.

"Sure," Dante frowned. "That's not something we'd keep to ourselves."

Thomas walked to the computer and shut down the system. He'd get back to that later. He needed to see what was going on in the city for himself. The trio left the comfort of the mansion and headed for the streets of New York.

* * * *

Tala had been gone all day. She'd spent most of it on the beach thinking. Megan returned to the apartment shortly after Victor and Atticus left. She didn't understand her daughter. They had a huge fight. Megan was still mad about the mind reading thing. They'd never fought like that before. Not even when Megan was young and trying to assert her independence. The argument ended badly. Tala was confused and frustrated so she decided to go to the beach. She needed time alone. It hadn't helped, so eventually she'd decided to head back.

Shadows

It would be dark soon. She wanted to get back to her room and change before her meeting with the group. Tala stopped abruptly at the edge of the forest. Megan was interacting playfully with Victor, Ariel and Tony. The kids were clearly having a blast.

Victor and Tony were wrestling, boxing, whatever move struck their fancy at the moment. Victor ducked just in time to miss a right hook from Tony then pivoted and plowed into Tony's stomach knocking him to the ground. Megan jumped on Victor's back wrapping her arms around his neck. "Don't worry honey," she called. "I'll rescue you."

Victor skillfully maneuvered Megan off his back and pinned her to the ground. He immediately began tickling her mercilessly. Megan was laughing hysterically as she tried unsuccessfully to get away. Tony was up in an instant. He tackled Ariel, who was casually sitting on the lawn watching the group.

"Hey, what did I do?" she protested.

"I have your woman Victor," Tony taunted. "Surrender or she's going to pay for your mutiny," Tony called.

Victor glanced over at Ariel and smiled. She was grinning from ear to ear. He knew what was coming. He continued to pin Megan to the ground while he waited for Ariel to take the offense.

Tony tried to make a slight adjustment to his grip. That was the moment Ariel had been waiting for. She quickly grabbed Tony's hands and concentrated. Her hands heated at once. Tony instantly let go, jumping back in surprise.

Ariel didn't hesitate. She knocked Tony to the ground and sat on his stomach. "What shall I do with him Victor?" Ariel asked.

"Hey, no fair. You cheated," Tony protested.

"We win," Victor told them pulling Megan to her feet. "You are now our prisoners for life." He grinned at Megan. "How are you at full body massages?" he teased.

Ariel narrowed her eyes at Victor then turned back to Tony. "That's a good idea. I get one from Tony. It's been a long time since I've had a full body massage."

Victor sobered. "Never mind," he said flashing a warning glare at Tony. "Don't get any ideas. You're not touching my future wife."

Tony laughed as he reached Megan and pulled her to him. "I think we just got off easy babe."

Tala watched in amazement as the four friends sauntered toward the farmhouse. She'd never seen her daughter so happy. Megan wasn't carefree and playful like this. As a child, Tala had to order Megan to go out and play with the neighborhood kids. She liked seeing this side of her daughter but what had changed? Tony? That was only part of it. Tala looked around. People were everywhere. There were about a dozen kids working on the bunkers yet Tony, Victor and Ariel were willing to let loose and enjoy a lighthearted evening together. They didn't seem to care what anyone thought of their playfulness. And Megan had joined in. How was that possible?

"They really aren't that difficult to figure out, Tala." Atticus spoke from her right.

Tala jumped. She hadn't seen him approach. "What do you mean?" she asked casually.

Shadows

"Why are you so perplexed about what you just witnessed?" he persisted. "They're just kids having fun. They enjoy each other's company."

Tala took a deep breath. If she was going to fix this, she might as well start with Atticus. She might as well start by being honest. "I've never seen Megan interact with anyone that way," she admitted. "Not even as a child. I knew Tony was good for her. He brings out a side in Megan that she's never shown to anyone else. Not even me," she paused waiting to see what Atticus would think about her. He didn't speak, so she continued. "Megan's childhood wasn't all that pleasant. As a result, she was always quiet and reserved. I saw her open up when she met Tony. He's so good for her. I'm just surprised she's been able to open up so completely to Victor and Ariel as well. I guess I'm just shocked by the drastic change that has occurred in my daughter so quickly," she smiled at Atticus, "Shocked, but proud. I'm glad my girl is finally enjoying life."

"Did you get anything to eat while you were out?" Atticus changed the subject.

"Uh...no," Tala said a little confused. She'd just opened up to this man and he completely ignored it. Clearly he didn't know how monumental that was for her.

"Well then, let's head back to the house. I'm starving and I think it would be good for you to spend some time getting to know us," Atticus paused then grinned at her. "The old fashioned way. I've decided to keep you on the case," he paused. "For now anyway."

Tala understood. Atticus still didn't trust her. Well, she couldn't blame him. They hadn't gotten off to the best start.

Atticus gave her a little push. "Don't close up on me now. I was almost starting to like you." He began walking towards the gravel path that led to the farmhouse.

Tala hesitated only a minute then hustled to catch up. The two walked to the old farm in silence, each lost in their own thoughts. Little did they know, they were thinking almost the exact same thing.

* * * *

Abby was antsy. She wanted to check on Thomas. She even tried to convince herself it was for his safety, not just because she wanted to see him. She just couldn't get the man out of her mind. She glanced down at the large puzzle, then up at the clock. It was late. She might as well go to bed. The puzzle was boring her and there was no way she was going to drop in on Thomas after midnight. Abby gathered up the pieces and placed them back in the box then slowly climbed the stairs. She wondered what he was doing. Was he alone or out hunting or working on some project left over from earlier today? She had to stop this. She was driving herself insane.

Abby had kept herself occupied the last few days trailing McBride. As far as she could tell he hadn't made any more progress on the murder case than they had. She talked to Alex yesterday. They didn't know anything either. It seemed that particular homicide was a mystery to everyone. They were all worried it had been committed by a vampire. She entered her room, changed then climbed into bed. Tomorrow she was going to find a new project. Maybe she'd take care of her father's books. Boring, she thought to herself, but at least she wouldn't spend her entire day dreaming

Shadows

about Thomas or what life might be like if he miraculously noticed she existed. She sighed. Eventually she would drift off to sleep.

Thomas moaned at the incessant buzzing. What was that noise? He pulled his pillow over his head and tried to get back to sleep. There it was again. This had better be important. He climbed out of bed and marched to the door. As he flung it open, he noticed the car. What time was it anyway? "Detective McBride," Thomas said coldly noticing the sun was just coming up. "What exactly can I do for you this morning? Isn't there some kind of nuisance law or something about bothering people before seven?"

"May I come in?" McBride asked ignoring the question.

Thomas studied him. "What now?" he finally asked.

"I think this would be better if we handled it inside," McBride repeated.

"Fine," Thomas pushed open the door and took a step backwards.

"Do you want to do this here or in the library?" McBride asked.

Thomas slowly headed for the library. He needed coffee. There was no way he was going to get any sleep now.

McBride followed Thomas into the large room and watched as the man walked to the corner and prepared coffee. Once the pot was started Thomas settled into a large chair. "Can you tell me where you were last night?" McBride began.

"Here. Asleep," Thomas answered immediately. He was on alert now. He couldn't be a suspect in another crime.

"Was anyone here with you?" he asked.

"Why?" Thomas asked.

McBride didn't respond. He studied Thomas, waiting for an answer.

Thomas didn't move. He wasn't one to fill a silence just because it was out there. "I believe my family asked you to contact Jake Wilder prior to any additional questioning. Can I assume Jake is on his way?" Thomas asked smugly.

McBride studied Thomas. So they were going to have to do this the hard way. "Fine. You want your lawyer present, we can do this at the precinct." He stood and headed for the door. "Make sure you're available all morning. Your attorney can contact you with the time."

Thomas watched him go. If the man thought he was going to chase after him, he was sadly mistaken. A Deveraux never chased after anyone, especially a cop. Thomas was curious though. What exactly was going on here? That didn't sound like news about Diana. Thomas leaned back in his chair and waited for his liquid energy to brew. He was going to need about a gallon of it to get him through the day. He glanced at the clock, it was too early to call Jake. Hopefully after he had his coffee he could get some answers.

Thomas had just finished his second cup when Jake called. "Morning Jake," Thomas said as he picked up the receiver. "Can I assume you received a wake-up call from our not so friendly detective?"

"I have," Jake confirmed.

Shadows

"Any idea what this is about?" Thomas asked.

"He said there's been another murder," Jake told him. "He also said he's going to get a warrant for your security system. He wants to know if you went out last night and what time you got back."

"Uh…that could be a problem," Thomas responded. "I went out hunting with Dante and Nick last night. We didn't get back until around three."

"Can Samantha fix it?" Jake asked, knowing Luke's system was one of D-Tech's.

"Maybe. I'll call Ty," Thomas assured him. "Am I seriously a suspect Jake? Who died?"

"You are a suspect, but he won't tell me who she is. At first he wouldn't even say if it was a man or a woman. He slipped and I picked up on it. We have to be in his office at ten. See what Sam can do and meet me there. Don't be late," Jake ordered.

"Don't get testy with me, Jake. You know I didn't kill anyone," Thomas said defensively.

"I know," Jake sighed. "I'm tired, and this is getting sticky. We're going to have to be on our toes and I don't think you should be alone at night anymore."

"No way," Thomas argued. "I just got rid of the warriors. They are not moving back in."

"What did you tell McBride?" Jake said ignoring Thomas' protest.

"Nothing. He asked where I was last night I told him here asleep. He wanted to know if I was alone and I asked him why, I think. Then I asked if he'd gone through you and he left."

"Can we use Dante or Nick as an alibi?" Jake asked.

"I'd rather not," Thomas told him. "I don't want them to be added to his watch list. We still need the freedom to hunt."

"True," Jake agreed. "Call Ty and we'll go from there. If Sam can rig the system so it looks like you didn't leave, we're fine. Let me know what she says."

* * * *

Ty sat in the large library with Thomas. Samantha was messing with the security system, erasing all evidence that Thomas had left the night before. His phone rang. Ty looked at the display and sighed. "Sam it's for you," he said a little annoyed.

"You answer it and tell Dimitri I'm busy," she snapped.

"Hello Dimitri," Ty said casually.

"I forgot to remind Samantha to check..."

"Hold on," Ty interrupted and switched the phone to speaker. "Okay, you're on speaker now go ahead."

"Samantha I forgot to remind you to check the front..." Dimitri began.

Shadows

"Dimitri," Sam interrupted. "I realize you are the warrior leader and I am expected to follow you, obey you and just stand in awe of you at all times. However, this is not my first rodeo and you are seriously getting on my nerves," she paused.

"But..." Dimitri started.

"I already finished the front gate, I've checked the main box and the panels individually. I know what I'm doing here. Please just let me do my job," she pled. "I know the police, they're going to be here any minute. In fact, I suspect they're already sitting down the street waiting for Thomas to head to his appointment. I'm running out of time and your constant phone calls are not helping. And yeah, I realize I'm probably being insubordinate. Maybe you can deal with that when I'm done. I'm not going to forget anything. I don't think Thomas would look good behind bars," she smiled over at Thomas.

"Okay," Dimitri sighed. "I'm just worried about Thomas. I won't call again."

"I've got this," Sam assured him. "Don't worry. I'm very familiar with this system. I helped design it. I know how to rig it so nobody will know Thomas left. Maybe you could have a little faith in the rookie." She turned back to the system and continued working.

Ty clicked off speaker and walked into the other room. "I know you're worried Dimitri, but don't. Sam knows what she's doing. I think she's almost done. She'd never let anything happen to Thomas. She's thorough," Ty said with conviction.

"I do trust Sam," Dimitri admitted. "It's just driving me crazy that I can't be there myself. Security is my specialty. It's hard to trust someone else with it."

"I know," Ty agreed. "I'm the same with explosives but we've got this. Go back to work. We talked about this. You can't be seen anywhere near here today. It's not exactly a secret what you do for a living. They won't trust what they find if they see you on the premises. Sam and I are going to stay here after Thomas leaves. We don't want it to look too suspicious. That way we'll also be around when the cops do the search. I'm confident they won't find anything, but this way we'll know."

"I'm worried about the sink in his bathroom," Dimitri admitted. "If they test for blood, they're going to find some."

"I know," Ty answered. "But we'll know if they do and we'll deal with it. This is an inconvenience, but it's not serious. Worst case Thomas goes to the fort and hides out for a while. We may have to do some shuffling, but everything is going to be fine."

"You're right," Dimitri agreed. "I'll take a step back for now. I never have liked a micro manager. Call me when the cops leave and we'll decide what we need to do."

Ty laughed. "You are definitely not a micro manager, Dimitri. You've had a lot dumped on you in a short time. We all think you're doing great. I'll call in a few. Gotta go. It sounds like Thomas is leaving."

Dimitri ended the call and stared out the window. There were too many things demanding his attention. He wished Luke were here. Luke was much better at managing several problems at once. Luke would know exactly how to get Thomas out of trouble with the police. Dimitri sighed again and thought of Jake. That's how Luke would handle the police. He'd leave it up to Jake. That's exactly what Dimitri was going to do. Jake could handle this. He'd done it a million times before.

* * * *

Thomas and Jake sat in the small, dirty interrogation room. A uniformed cop escorted them inside then left. Apparently they thought he and Jake would sit in the room and chat about how he was a serial killer. Thomas had thought a lot about his encounter with McBride this morning. Another murder was the only explanation he could come up with for the detective's evasive questions and the slip he'd made with Jake. McBride couldn't have been there about Diana or he wouldn't have asked where Thomas was all night. Clearly somebody else had been killed and the guy wanted to pin that one on Thomas, too. Probably out of convenience. He didn't have time for this nonsense.

Thomas looked up as McBride entered the room. Another man dressed in a suit followed close behind. The two cops sat at the desk across from Thomas. McBride set a file on the table. He addressed Jake. "So, now does your client want to tell me where he was last night?"

"I believe my client has already informed you that he was home in bed last night," Jake said coolly.

"He did. But I thought he might want to reconsider his answer." McBride raised his eyebrow and looked at Thomas. "Would you like to amend your statement Mr. Deveraux?"

"No," Thomas said confidently.

"What time did you arrive home last evening?" McBride asked.

Thomas knew exactly what his answer would be on that one. He and Sam had gone over it a million times. "About eight," he told McBride.

"And when did you leave again?" McBride asked.

"About..." Thomas casually looked at his watch then frowned. He wondered when he would get the watch his father had given him back from the police. "About an hour ago," he answered.

McBride stared at Thomas. He hoped the silence would make him squirm. After a few seconds he continued. "You do realize I have a warrant for your security system. Once we analyze the contents I'm going to know exactly what time you arrived and when you left again. It would be a lot better for you if you were straight with me. Once the results come back from that system all bets are off. I'll have no need or desire to work with you any further."

"Detective McBride," Jake interrupted. "My client has answered your question. Could you please tell us why we are here today? Otherwise, we're leaving. We both have a busy day ahead of us and I think you've wasted enough of our time."

McBride glared at his partner. Matthews didn't like the attorney any better than McBride did. They both knew they wouldn't get anywhere with Thomas when his lawyer was present. He continued to study the lawyer, debating. Why not lay it out on the table, literally and figuratively. They were going to find out as soon as they left anyway. "You are here because there's been another murder," he told Jake. "Another woman was killed by the same person that killed Diana." He reached into the file and pulled out a photo, slamming it on the desk in front of Thomas.

"Do you know this woman, Thomas?" McBride asked. Thomas had to know her, she worked for him.

Thomas studied the picture in shock. What possible connection could Susan Jones have to Diana? "I do," he finally choked out.

McBride was studying Thomas. Again, not the response he had expected. Thomas acted as if he didn't know the woman was dead, but McBride knew better. The only connection between the two women was Thomas. He'd run everything backwards and forwards, nothing. Just Thomas Deveraux.

"Who is she?" Jake asked, studying Thomas with concern.

"Susan Jones," Thomas said looking over at Jake. "She ran the theater on Broadway. She worked for me." He was studying Jake for answers. What was going on here?

"So Thomas," McBride began. "How intimate was your connection to Susan Jones?"

Thomas looked over at McBride. He was really beginning to dislike the man. "Not intimate at all," he replied. "She worked for me."

"Did you ever date her?" he asked, then decided to amend that. "Wait, I remember you have an unusual idea of what a date is. So let's just cut to the chase shall we? Did you ever sleep with this one?"

"No," Thomas answered shortly.

"Never?" McBride asked. "I also remember you had an aversion to the word intimate. So, did you and Susan ever have sex?"

"No," Thomas said coldly.

"Are you sure?" McBride taunted. "Keep in mind someone always notices. The smallest thing to you could be monumental to a waiter or a bellboy. If you had an intimate encounter with Susan, someone is going to remember you. Especially a rich, powerful man like yourself. Save us both a lot of work Thomas and tell me about Susan."

"As I said, Susan worked for me. She ran the theater on Broadway. She was good at her job." One of the few managers he wasn't currently having trouble with, Thomas thought to himself. "Things have been busy lately, so I only met her a few weeks ago. We have a new show starting and I wanted to make sure she had everything she needed to take care of so many dancers. Susan was competent and seemed enthusiastic about her job. That's really all I know about her. Like I said, I just met her a few weeks ago and the encounter was brief," Thomas paused. "Her people seemed to like her. She's going to be missed," he added softly.

"When exactly did this meeting take place and where?" McBride asked.

"I can't remember the exact date. I'd have to check my calendar. It was shortly after the group signed on with us. We currently have a show running so it wasn't pressing. Just something I wanted to check on. Three weeks ago, maybe. I went to the theater. Like I said, we still have a show running so I wasn't about to pull her away to come to me. I drove out just before lunch, introduced myself and we talked a little about the shows. Both the current show and the upcoming dancing group. Like I said, she was competent. The conversation lasted maybe fifteen, twenty minutes tops. She said she didn't need anything and she was fully staffed so they could handle the crowds. I gave her my card and told her to call me if anything came up. That was my first and last encounter with Ms. Jones."

McBride's phone beeped. He glanced down then excused himself.

Thomas, Jake and the other detective waited silently in the room for McBride to return.

McBride stepped into the hallway and dialed Brown, the precincts' computer security specialist. "What do you have for me?" McBride asked shortly.

"Nothing," Brown answered annoyed.

"What do you mean nothing?" McBride bellowed. "I thought you were the best."

"I am the best," Brown said flatly. "There was nothing to find. Mr. Deveraux's system shows security was turned on around nine o'clock yesterday morning. It was active until eight thirteen when the system was shut off. It remained down until ten twenty three when it was activated and remained on until five forty two this morning."

"What does that mean exactly?" McBride asked annoyed with the information.

"It means Thomas Deveraux set his alarm at precisely ten twenty three last night and remained inside the home until at least five forty two this morning," Brown said in a condescending tone.

"That's impossible," McBride argued. "Dig deeper."

Brown rolled his eyes and tried to remain patient. "I have dug as deep as it is possible to dig Detective McBride. The evidence does not support your theory. Do not bite my head off simply because you are harassing the wrong man."

McBride disconnected the call then slammed his phone into the pocket of his suit coat and stewed. What now? He had to let Thomas go. But he was going to watch the man like a hawk. Thomas was a killer. He was not going to get away with murder. Not in his city. He flung the door open and walked back to the table.

"Is there anything else Detective McBride?" Jake asked.

McBride narrowed his eyes at the lawyer. "You're free to leave for now," McBride continued to glare. "I'll notify you if I have any further questions."

Thomas and Jake stood and left the room. Once they reached the sidewalk they paused then continued walking away from the station. "Why don't we stop in here and have some coffee," Jake said pointing to a small café.

The two men sauntered to a table and sat in silence as the waitress poured coffee. Jake studied Thomas. He'd been shaken by the news that one of his employees had been killed. "Thomas, don't take this personally. I don't think it has anything to do with you. Deveraux Industries employs thousands of employees in New York alone. If there's a killer on the loose, I'd be more surprised if some of the victims didn't work for you. I'm surprised it hasn't hit this close to home before now. Especially with Radek taking so many people over the past few months."

"She was so happy and full of life," Thomas said sadly. "It's inexcusable for someone that exuberant to be killed so young. She had so much ahead of her. Do you think it's human or them?" Thomas asked Jake seriously. "Because if it's them, I'm going to make them pay."

Jake took a sip of his coffee. He wished he could help Thomas sort this out, but the boy was too much like his father. Luke would have taken the news just as hard. And, he would have been just as pissed. It always amazed him how Luke could have so many employees and still consider them his own. Luke knew the names of almost every man and woman that worked for him from his top execs to his janitors. He considered them his extended family and was very protective of every one of them. Thomas was following in his father's footsteps. They were both very good men. Jake hoped things settled down for Thomas soon. Of course the execs would test the kids a little but enough was enough. The warriors and Alex had too many supernatural problems on their plate. They didn't need trouble with the humans. "We are all going to make them pay if they are responsible for this, Thomas. We primarily protect Alex and her people, but we've come to believe it's our duty to protect all of New York." Jake was talking in code just in case someone was listening.

"I know. But they were mine," Thomas argued. "Well, not Diana. She certainly wasn't innocent and I don't owe her anything, but somehow I still feel responsible for her. Susan..." Thomas paused. "Susan was a young, innocent woman with her whole life ahead of her. It just seems so unfair." Thomas was depressed. For some reason Susan's murder hit him hard. Once he left Jake he was going to head to her parents' house and speak to them personally. He'd insist on paying for the funeral and helping them out in any other way he possibly could. He'd also need to stop by the theater and speak to the employees. They would have counseling available if anyone wanted it. He had a lot to do today. He really needed to get started.

Jake was watching Thomas, reading him. He smiled to himself, it was Luke all over again. "I'm going with you to talk to her parents," he finally told Thomas. "Don't argue. I've done this before. Plus, having an attorney there will put them at ease."

"Fat chance," Thomas laughed. "Having an attorney there will make them think we're hiding something and trying to head off a lawsuit. I need to do this by myself."

"Fine, how about a friend? Can I accompany you as a friend?" Jake persisted.

Thomas studied Jake trying to find a motive. After a moment he realized there wasn't one. Jake was just worried and wanted to accompany him to the parents' home. "Do you promise not to tell them you're a lawyer?" Thomas finally asked.

"You have my word," Jake said with relief. There was no way he would let Thomas visit Susan's parents alone. The detective would try to charge him with witness tampering. Thomas was new to this, Jake was not. He would protect Thomas whether he wanted it or not. Not just for Luke, but because Thomas and Alex were like his own kids. Nobody would harm his kids, especially not a human detective with the NYPD.

Shadows

Radek sat in his large chair glowing. So far their plan was working. Several vampires had checked in. His numbers were growing, quickly. Soon he'd have hundreds of vampires ready to battle Alex and her defiant followers. He still hadn't decided what the punishment would be for their betrayal. Alex of course would die, as would all the warriors and those obstinate council members. But would that be enough? He couldn't decide. Of course he'd also have to find those responsible for his father's death. His face hardened. Anyone that participated in that raid would suffer greatly for their crime. That might be enough, he'd have to think about it. Once he finished with the fae, he'd focus on the shifters. First, he'd have to know who killed Hector. Anyone that assisted with the rescue of those two women would also have to die. Both pack leaders would be included in that group. But once the trouble makers were gone, the rest would fall into line.

He couldn't wait. Things would be so different once his son was born. The possibilities were limitless. The idea had actually come from a human. That was ironic. Radek had ventured past the cages one day and overheard a conversation two of the women were having about Dracula. Radek had never heard of a vampire king named Dracula so he listened intently. If there was a new leader, he needed to know everything he could about him. The women started to discuss his vampires and wondered aloud if vampire guards could really change into bats. Radek was immediately captivated. A vampire that could change into an animal seemed impossible.

Once back in his chambers Radek began to worry. If such a vampire existed his monarchy might be in danger. He promptly sent several of his sycophants on a mission to find this Dracula. His relief was palpable when he discovered Dracula was fictitious. A vampire created by a human's active imagination. But the idea stuck. Over the years a plan began to formulate. Now he was ready to put the plan into action. Soon his dream would become a reality. Once his kingdom was under control he'd have hundreds of shifters begging him to let them carry his child. Somehow kidnapping and imprisoning a fae had worked for his father. But Radek hadn't had the same success. He'd captured two separate women, well three if you counted the panther, and all of them had escaped before he could impregnate them. Radek wasn't worried. Once he had total control, the women would come to him.

Chapter Five

The killer stood in the cover of darkness hidden by the large trees. He marveled at the fact that so many women traveled through Central Park at night with all the recent activity in the area. Only two women had been killed so far but prior to his involvement, so many New Yorkers had disappeared. People were so dense. They were all in denial. Somehow they had an uncanny ability to convince themselves it would never happen to them. Idiots.

The man smiled a sadistic grin. His target was headed straight for him, just like clockwork. The brunette never missed her evening jog. He stepped closer to the edge of the trail. He'd have to be quick. This woman was faster and stronger than the last one. Two more steps and he'd pounce. Gotcha! He began to laugh softly as the woman tried to fight. She was definitely a wired one. This time was going to be fun.

* * * *

Alex laid her head on the desk in frustration. She was tired and worried and stressed. She needed to work but she was just too worn out. She heard the door open and close, but didn't budge.

Dimitri walked in and saw Alex sitting at the large desk, her head pressed flat against the surface. He walked to her, gently lifted her into his arms and moved to the couch. Once he sat down next to her, he gently shifted her body so he could massage her shoulders. She was so tense. "Talk," he ordered.

Alex sighed, "Any chance you can sit here and do that for the next hour or so?" she asked.

"Only if you tell me what has you so upset," he pressed.

Alex leaned back against Dimitri and took a deep breath. It felt so nice to have someone to lean on, but she was having a hard time fighting back the tears.

Dimitri wrapped his arms around Alex then leaned down to gently kiss the side of her head. "Talk to me," he said again. "I can see you're upset. Tell me what's wrong."

"Everything," she finally said in a whisper. "I'm a failure at everything."

Dimitri pushed Alex forward and turned her body so he could look at her. "You're not a failure at anything. What's this about?"

"I had to fire two more people today," she began. "One was no big deal, he's in Paris and Luke was ready to fire him anyway before he died. I regret passing that on to the execs instead of flying to Paris to do it myself, but there's just no way I could leave right now."

"I agree," Dimitri said without emotion.

"But the other one was so difficult," she told him. "Beth has worked for the company for years. I went to school with her daughter. I just don't understand what's going on. Why are good, decent people suddenly becoming monsters?" she asked.

"Greed?" Dimitri offered. "Maybe power and control. Something they never felt they had under Luke."

"Maybe," Alex consented. "I just don't understand it. Thomas and I are more than willing to let them run their departments the way they always have. We're not being unreasonable or forcing unnecessary changes down their throats. Why are we having so many problems? Why can't we control these people? There are two of us. Luke managed the company all by himself."

"Why did you fire her?" Dimitri asked. She wouldn't be happy with his assessment of the situation. If they were really good, decent people they wouldn't all of a sudden become dishonest and greedy.

Alex studied him. He was so good for her. She knew once she talked to him she'd feel better, but this part was hard. "I guess the official reason will be insubordination," she finally told him. "Beth brought a proposal for an acquisition to me a couple weeks ago. I told her I'd look at it and get back to her."

"I remember, you brought that particular task home with you. Something that's becoming a habit these days," he teased. "You researched that company for days. Didn't you say they were in trouble? As I recall it was irreversible trouble. Something you didn't feel you guys could fix."

"Right," she told him. "The company was failing. They were so far into debt they'd never get out. If we acquired them, we'd have to sink millions into the company right off the bat just to get them out of the red. Then, an additional ten million to get their systems up to date. It's a sinking ship, a black hole. We'd never get half of our investment back out of that company even if they turned around and became a raging success, which is unlikely. I believe they would have gone under within five years."

"So what's the problem?" Dimitri asked.

"I told Beth in no uncertain terms Deveraux Industries would not have anything to do with that company. I ordered her to cease and desist immediately. I even offered to talk to them myself. She said she'd take care of it," Alex paused.

"Let me guess, she didn't?" Dimitri offered.

"Not only did she ignore my order, she called a meeting with the board of directors to sell her idea. Of course, I wasn't invited. The only way I found out about it was because Tom called. He wanted to know what I was thinking. How was he supposed to draft a contract to protect us from something so volatile? I set Tom straight and decided to make a surprise appearance at the board meeting."

Dimitri winced. He was sure that hadn't gone well.

"Initially the board supported Beth. Of course, that made it worse. I was immediately annoyed at all of them. Beth had all these charts and graphs and I could see the board was convinced. There was just one problem, Beth's numbers were flat out lies."

Dimitri raised his eyebrows. That was going a little far.

"Yep. She falsified her reports to get their support. It took me over an hour to convince them my figures were accurate and Beth's were fake. She had the nerve to call for a vote of no confidence and requested the board order me out of the room."

"She deserves to be fired," Dimitri said flatly.

"Of course she does. But it still wasn't easy. I've known her most of my life. I went to school with her daughter. I attended birthday parties in her backyard."

Dimitri studied Alex soberly. "Apparently none of that meant anything to her," he finally concluded. "She clearly wasn't thinking about birthday parties in her yard when she excluded you from the board meeting. She didn't care that you've known each other for years when she asked the board for a vote of no confidence."

"I know," Alex said defeated. "But I still feel like a failure. I was shocked the board didn't follow her suggestion. It seems none of our top level employees have even the slightest degree of confidence in Thomas or me," she admitted.

"Give it time," Dimitri said. "Luke was good to his employees. He paid them well and gave them great benefits, but he also left no doubt who was in charge. They're testing you. Both you and Thomas are going to have to assert yourselves for a while. I think things are going to subside soon. Over the last couple weeks you've fired five people between you. Word is getting around, I have no doubt. Gradually your managers are going to get the message. They'll continue to push for a while, but not so forcefully. I promise. People need their jobs. You might lose a few more. Some you'll have to fire and some will leave on their own. But your employees are starting to realize the two of you know more about operations than they initially believed," he paused. "So what else is up? I know it's not just business."

"No," she agreed. "It's everything. We are all so spread out I just feel like I'm failing at everything. Mom was good at being queen. I suck at it," she confided.

Dimitri laughed.

"It's not funny," Alex said defensively. "Since I became queen look how many people we've lost. Look at how many warriors we've almost lost. Now I have half the warriors at the fort. Then there's the attacks on Atticus. The kidnappings, which victimized the shifters, the attack on Sam. How could our people possibly trust me when I keep messing up?"

"Where's the mess up in any of those things?" Dimitri asked. "Anyway, everything you just mentioned is more my responsibility than yours," he paused. "Thanks for pointing out what a poor job I'm doing."

Alex was horrified. She didn't think Dimitri had messed up at all. "That's not true!" she immediately countered. "I just feel like I'm not handling anything well. Mom clearly handled her responsibilities with ease. So much so, I didn't even know about them."

"You are forgetting one very important thing here," Dimitri said calmly.

"What's that?" she asked hesitantly. Dimitri was just trying to make her feel better.

"The treaty wasn't broken while your mother was alive. She didn't have to deal with constant attacks, coordinating an army or trying to make sure her people were prepared for anything. While you're mother was alive, things were very different. Things were significantly calmer. Her death is what set the chaos in motion." Dimitri pulled Alex back down so she was resting on his shoulder. "You are not failing at anything, baby."

Alex couldn't stop them, the tears began to fall. "What about Thomas?" she asked sniffling. "I've completely failed him. I have no idea what to do about that detective. Thomas can't sneeze without him recording it. He's going crazy locked up in that house like he's a prisoner. That's my fault. He's reluctantly doing what I asked for now, but he won't be able to handle it much longer. Then there's the guilt. He feels responsible somehow for that girl's death," Alex hesitated.

"And..." Dimitri asked.

"And another employee is missing," she finally admitted. "If she ends up dead I don't know what Thomas is going to do. I'm afraid he may do something reckless."

Dimitri was worried now. Another missing girl that worked for Alex and Thomas. This wasn't coincidental. He was afraid it was just a matter of time before another body turned up. He wondered how the detective was going to account for that when he'd been holding surveillance on Thomas the entire time. Somehow, Dimitri was sure the guy would find a way around that. McBride was convinced Thomas was his man. So convinced he wasn't even trying to find the real killer. Dimitri gently rubbed Alex's back.

"We are all failing with Thomas. And he's staying home because I ordered him to, not just because you asked. We'll figure this out," he paused. "Somehow we'll figure this out." The two sat in silence, comforted by their closeness as they worried about the dilemma they were facing.

* * * *

"Enough mother," Lawson demanded. "How exactly is it my fault you killed her?"

"You were supposed to bring me a girl that was strong enough to handle the transformation. You failed and now she's dead. You're going to have to find a way to dispose of that body. And make sure you don't get caught. We can't have this traced back to us. The council would not approve. They can't know we've resumed the experiments."

"I'm very well aware of that," Lawson said impatiently. "Admit it, your potion is not ready. This girl didn't die because she was weak. She died because your magic potion killed her. We need to make an alteration before I take another one."

"The potion is fine. The girls you keep bringing me are weak. If you would find a good, strong woman we would have our first paladin."

Lawson was getting impatient. His mother was so stubborn. "Let me explain this to you as plainly as I can. Work on that potion. I will not bring you another girl until I'm confident you have improved the serum. So unless you plan on venturing out at night on your own, we're at an impasse."

Shadows

Patricia was getting tired of her children. First Foster took off and disappeared, now this. She hadn't seen the youngest Dillinger since that disastrous night in the kitchen. How was she supposed to get more money out of him if she never saw him? "I believe we need more ephedrine but we're already short on money and I still haven't heard from Foster. The formula is not the same since we've had to switch from opium to heroine. How am I supposed to perfect it when everything keeps changing?" Patricia whined.

Lawson considered their problem. "Ephedrine is difficult to get because humans use it to produce meth. What if we tried meth instead?" he suggested. "My contacts in the underground can get me a fairly substantial supply, for a price of course. I'll get the meth, you work on the potion. If nothing else, getting the next woman high will keep her quiet during the process."

"I told you, I'm almost out of money and I can't find Foster," Patricia said impatiently.

Lawson was bored with this. "If you skipped getting your nails done or your hair fluffed once a week we might not be so desperate for funds." He changed tactics when he saw the look on his mother's face. "Don't worry about it. I'll get the stuff and we'll figure out the money later."

Patricia didn't want to know the details of Lawson's underhanded crimes. She just wanted another woman. She wanted a strong, healthy female that could be turned into a paladin. If she could just create one, the rest would be easy. Once she had enough, she could reveal them to the world. The paladin's would completely replace the warriors. She almost salivated in anticipation. Soon, the kingdom would be hers.

* * * *

Abby had been following Detective McBride for weeks. He was so focused on Thomas he wasn't even trying to find the real killer. She had to do something. Thomas looked awful. He rarely left the house unless he was working. The confinement was clearly taking a toll. She watched as the unmarked car pulled away from the curb. Then she pulled out her phone and dialed Chief Monroe.

"Monroe," came a voice on the other end.

"It's Abby," she told him.

"Abby," Travis softened. "What can I do for you? Let me guess, my detective has become a nuisance again?"

"He was a nuisance from the beginning. Now he's escalated to full blown harassment," she accused. "He's not even trying to find the real killer. He's obsessed with Thomas Deveraux."

"I see," Monroe mused. "How does that impact you?"

"I just thought I'd let you know I plan to spend more time with Thomas. The constant surveillance seems to be getting to him and he can't go out and accomplish his other duties if you know what I mean. I intend to give him an alibi," Abby confessed.

"Exactly how do you plan to do that?" Chief Monroe probed, he was concerned now. McBride had set his eyes on Thomas, but he seemed to have forgotten Abby. Monroe didn't want her brought back into this.

Shadows

"I'm going to visit Thomas right now. I just thought you should know my name may surface again. I'd appreciate any help you can give me but I understand if I'm on my own," Abby said casually.

"Abby," Chief Monroe began. "Please stay out of this. McBride is ruthless. As soon as he sees you with Thomas you're going to be bumped back to the top of his list."

"I understand," Abby assured him. "But I can't just sit back and watch Thomas suffer when I believe I can help. Don't worry, I'll be careful."

"Of course I'm worried," Monroe grumbled.

"I've gotta go," Abby said cheerfully. "I'll keep in touch." She quickly hung up the phone and reached out to ring Thomas' doorbell.

"Abby?" Thomas said, relieved as he opened the door. He'd been braced for the worst. There still wasn't any word about Tiffany Petersen. She'd been missing four days now. Every time the doorbell or the phone rang he was sure it was going to be Jake or Detective McBride calling him in for another interview. He couldn't even go out and look for her. The cops were trailing him everywhere he went.

"Can I come in?" Abby asked hesitantly. Was she interrupting something?

"Oh, sorry," Thomas pushed the door open and motioned to the library.

Abby wrinkled her nose. "Do you have anywhere else we can go? That room reminds me of McBride. I'd rather not think about him right now."

Thomas grinned. He thought of little else these days. "Will you be staying long or will this be short and sweet?" he asked. "I don't get many visitors these days. I guess my new sidekicks scare them all away." Thomas glanced back at the front of the house then sobered. "You really shouldn't be here, Abby. Now you're going to be a suspect again."

Abby waved that off. "We need to talk. I think you are spending entirely too much time on your own these days. It's not good for your health."

Thomas studied Abby. What was she up to? He was grateful for the company, but he didn't want her risking her neck for him. "Do you have a remedy?" he asked.

"As a matter of fact I do," she told him. "I thought I'd entertain you for a while."

Thomas raised his eyebrows. "What kind of entertainment?" he asked. "Do you table dance?" he joked.

"Nooo," she answered coyly pushing him up the stairs. "You go change. We're going clubbing."

"Uh… I'm not sure we should do that," Thomas argued. "What if something happens tonight? I won't have an alibi."

"What am I?" she asked defensively. "Plus, those two goons out there are going to follow us. You know they will. Let's give them a challenge," she smiled. "Come on, Thomas. Let's go have a little fun. You are way past due."

Thomas hesitated only an instant. "Maybe you're right," he finally admitted. "Give me a minute and we'll head out."

Thomas thought about going to Bojan Taverns, but Victor was at the fort and he didn't want to draw attention to his friend, or his club. They ended up at a trendy place downtown. The unmarked car followed the cab to the nightclub then parked just outside the door. Could they be any more conspicuous? Thomas and Abby stepped from the cool night air into the loud, stuffy club scene. "I'll try to get us a table. Maybe you could check our jackets," he suggested.

Abby grabbed Thomas' leather coat and rushed over to the large window. Once the coats were checked she casually made her way through the crowd, watching for Thomas. She was just starting to panic when she finally spotted him. She was impressed, he had a large table positioned in the corner of the room. They would have a good view, but also a little privacy. Her heart did a little flip. She'd been so nervous about this. If Thomas had refused to go, she would have been devastated. Now here they were, hanging out in a popular club together. Thomas spotted her and smiled, then stood. What a gentleman, she thought.

Thomas waited until Abby was seated before he sat back down. "I wasn't sure what you wanted, so I told the waitress to come back. Is this table okay?" he asked. She was going to a lot of trouble for him. He wanted her to be comfortable.

"Perfect," she assured him. She glanced up as the waitress returned. The two ordered drinks then Abby surveyed the room. Most of the people were out dancing. She really wasn't big on that sort of thing, but wondered if she should try to convince Thomas to go out on the floor. She hoped he would loosen up and have a good time.

Thomas laughed. The look on Abby's face was priceless. It was obvious she didn't want to dance but was debating whether she should consider it for him. "I don't dance," Thomas said leaning in close so she could hear him.

Abby froze. Thomas' breath in her ear did strange things to her body. She was thankful he didn't dance, but had she been that obvious? "Good," she yelled above the music. "I dodged that one." She smiled.

"So tell me about yourself Abby Cooper," Thomas finally said. He realized he didn't know that much about the woman.

"There's not much to tell," Abby confessed. She immediately found herself relaying stories about her family, helping her mother in medicine and the adventures she'd had with Morrigan growing up. Before she knew it the club was closing. Thomas had barely said a word about himself all night. Not that Abby needed him to. She knew his history. She was just surprised she'd told him so much about herself.

"Looks like that's our queue," Thomas stood. "You have the coat tickets?" he asked holding out his hand.

Abby pulled them from her pocket and placed them in his palm. As her fingers brushed his warm skin, a tingle shot up her arm. If only the attraction was mutual, she sighed. Once they were back out on the street, Abby glanced down the road. "It's a nice night for a walk. Are you game?" she asked, not wanting the evening to end.

Shadows

"Absolutely," Thomas agreed. It had been a long time since he'd been out at night. He missed it. He was surprised at how much. The couple strolled casually down the sidewalk, continuing their conversation. This time Abby made Thomas do the talking. He talked about his father and Alex and what it was like to have a new mother after so many years with just his father. They were nearing Thomas' house when they spotted the car. Abby wanted to scream. Why did McBride have to spoil such a wonderful evening?

"Maybe you should leave me here," Thomas suggested. He didn't want Abby pulled into this again.

"No way," Abby said with conviction. "We're going to deal with him together." The two walked past the dark sedan and headed for the front door.

"Thomas," McBride called. "I need a word with you."

Thomas stopped and turned to McBride not saying a word. Abby also studied the detective. Something was up. She could feel it.

"Do you know a woman by the name of...?" McBride began.

Here it comes, Thomas thought to himself. They've found Tiffany Peterson. Just his luck. The night he spent with Abby would be the night they found the body.

"Regina Parkins?" McBride asked.

"Huh?" Thomas said surprised. "No, I don't believe I do." What was this? Had two women gone missing at the same time? Did this mean that Tiffany was safe? He didn't dare hope.

McBride was now standing directly in front of Thomas. "You're sure?" he asked.

"Pretty sure," Thomas said furrowing his brow in concentration. "I'm almost positive I do not know anyone by that name," he said more confidently.

"She didn't work for you?" McBride asked.

"Not that I know of," Thomas said shaking his head. Unless it was someone Alex employed in one of her departments he didn't think that woman worked for them. Maybe this wasn't about him after all.

"Are you familiar with BBQ Kebabs?" McBride asked.

"With what?" Thomas said perplexed.

"Is that the street vendor that sets up in Manhattan?" Abby inquired.

McBride raised an eyebrow. Abby was returning to the top of his list. "Been there lately?" he asked her.

"Uh...no actually," she said innocently. "But I love their lamb kebabs," she admitted. "Unfortunately I don't get out that way very often," then Abby sobered. "What does that have to do with Thomas?" she asked.

"Regina Parkins' grandmother is the street vendor that owns that particular enterprise. Regina sometimes operated the business for her grandmother to give her a break. She was working a few nights ago but abandoned the cart and disappeared," McBride said watching Thomas for the slightest movement.

Shadows

"And?" Abby asked.

"And her body was discovered this evening," McBride said angrily. "I need to talk to Thomas about his connection to Regina. I'm curious why this one ended up dead," he said coldly. "She didn't work for you Thomas, maybe her grandmother's business was cutting into your profits? Did she threaten the success of one of your numerous enterprises?"

Abby pushed Thomas into the house then turned to look at McBride. "You were previously warned that neither one of us would be talking to you unless you contacted our lawyers first. I assure you, Chief Monroe is going to hear about this. Now, if you're interested in some kind of interview, you have Nancy and Jake's numbers. I suggest you call them." She stepped into the house and shut the door.

"Damn," McBride muttered under his breath. He remembered why he disliked that girl so much. Now what? Now you have to get your butt off the Deveraux property before Chief Monroe arrives and busts you back to 38th. He solemnly walked back to the unmarked car and headed to the office. It was going to be another long night.

"I don't know that woman," Thomas insisted when Abby walked in.

"I believe you," she told him. "That's good, right? The others had a connection, but not this one so that's good I think."

"Maybe," Thomas agreed. "I knew leaving with you tonight was a bad idea. Now you're right back in the middle of this."

Just where she wanted to be, Abby thought. "Nonsense," she disagreed. "I think it was a good idea. At some point Rand McBride is going to have to admit you couldn't have committed these murders. To begin there's no evidence. Plus, when would you have had the time or the opportunity? He's had you watched twenty four hours a day for the past week. He said Regina came up missing four days ago. You were being watched four days ago, right? How did you grab her? He doesn't have a leg to stand on. I plan to make sure the pressure is put on him for a change."

"Abby don't," Thomas begged. "It's going to cause problems for you."

"Nonsense," she told him again. She looked around the house. "Do you mind if I sleep on the couch?" she asked casually, although she felt anything but casual about the request.

"Why?" he asked.

"I think it would be a good idea for me to stay here awhile. You know, someone to give you a constant alibi. We've been making this too easy for Detective McBride. I think we need to start creating obstacles."

"This isn't a game Abby," Thomas warned. "It's your life. What if we can't find who is really doing this? What if it's a vampire? I've accepted the possibility that I may have to go into hiding. Are you prepared for that possibility yourself?"

Abby wanted to ask if they would hide together, but she stopped herself. "Sure," she said honestly. "I don't have a gazillion businesses to run. And as a shifter it would be easy for me to visit my family as often as I wanted. I don't have a problem going into hiding for a while, Thomas. In fact, it would be a lot easier for me than it would be for you."

Thomas stared at her skeptically. She couldn't really be that nonchalant about the possibility she might have to hide out.

"Stop worrying so much. It's all hypothetical and it's not going to happen anyway. Neither one of us is going to run away and hide from McBride. We're going to find the real killer and force the truth down his throat," she said with conviction.

Thomas laughed at her. "Well, nobody can say you're not passionate about the cause," he studied her. "We have enough guest rooms, you're not sleeping on the couch. I don't suppose arguing with you is going to do me any good?" he asked.

"Nope," she affirmed. She may not be able to have him, but she could at least help him. That would have to be enough. She wondered how the other warriors would feel about her staying here. She hoped Thomas wouldn't be harassed by his friends over this. He was getting harassed enough by the cops.

"Well, we better try to get some sleep. I have a feeling we'll be summoned to the principal's office first thing in the morning," Thomas smiled at her.

Abby smiled back. "Point me in the right direction and I'll hit the sack. I have to admit I'm beat."

As soon as Thomas closed his bedroom door, he called Dimitri. He and Alex needed to know about the new developments.

Dimitri sat silently listening to Thomas. He wasn't sure letting Abby get involved was a good idea, but from what Thomas was saying it couldn't be helped. Once he got finished with Thomas he was going to call Mason Cooper. His new ally needed to be aware of what his daughter was up to. "I don't like it," Dimitri finally told Thomas. "Somehow we need to figure out a way to have a meeting. I'm going to talk to Sam and see if she can help with some video conferencing. For now that is going to have to work. We made do with it when the council needed to meet a while back. I guess we'll have to make do now as well."

"I'll call Sam," Alex offered. "Thomas, I know you two are concerned about Abby's involvement, and I agree she's sticking her neck out for us, but I for one find it comforting. For what it's worth, I think it's a good idea. Let her stay for a while. If nothing else, it will throw McBride off a little."

"That's what I'm worried about," Thomas countered. "I don't want him harassing Abby just to save myself."

"I don't see it that way and neither will she. Focus on the important stuff. That's what I'm trying to do. Now, you two can talk about the manly way you're going to fix this while I call Sam," she started to turn away. "I love you, Thomas. Hang in there, we'll fix this."

Before Thomas got off the phone, Alex assured him the conferencing equipment would be up and running before the end of the following day. Thomas knew that with both Alex and Sam on it, the equipment would be tested and ready to go before that. He spread out on the bed and tried to clear his mind. He needed rest. He couldn't get his mind off Abby. Why was she doing this for him? Until tonight, he really hadn't known her very well. Did she think she owed it to him for the rescue? That wasn't his doing, it was

Victor's. He'd make sure she understood that in the morning. He didn't want her sacrificing her future for a debt she didn't owe.

* * * *

McBride stood beside the medical examiner and watched as the autopsy was performed. Dr. Alder was the best. He knew if there was any forensic evidence the man would find it. Alder seemed perplexed by something. He kept making notes and continued to study the thin line running across Regina's neck. "What is it?" McBride finally asked.

"This woman was not killed by the same person as the first two," Alder finally told him.

"Impossible," Rand argued. "She was killed in the same way as Diana and Susan."

"The same way but not by the same person," he said again.

"Explain," Rand ordered, annoyed.

"The first two women were killed by someone that is right handed. He sliced those women from here....to here," he explained running his finger from one ear to the other. "This woman was sliced in the opposite direction. She was killed by someone that is left handed."

"Well..." Rand considered. "That doesn't necessarily mean two different people," he argued. "It may just mean the killer used his other hand."

"No," Dr. Alder disagreed. "The force and precision of this cut could not have been made by someone that was not left handed." He looked at Detective McBride. "I know this is not what you want to hear, but I am certain this woman was killed by a different person than the first two."

"Could the killer be ambidextrous?" he asked hopefully.

"In my professional opinion, no," he disagreed again. "Like I said, the cut is different. The angle is different, the direction is different. There are no similarities between this woman and your first two victims. You have two murderer's McBride. I can't tell you if they are working together or if you have a copycat, but it is definitely not the same person. This one is also missing the circular marks. If it were the same person, I'm confident she would have them. She also didn't suffer the same level of blood loss. Which is another reason I can say with certainty this woman was killed by someone else."

McBride left the ME's office frustrated and confused. Could Abby Cooper be the second killer? Alder couldn't answer that question, but he did not believe a woman had the strength to make the incision. That left him with nothing. He'd been hoping Thomas would leave some evidence this time, instead he'd gotten more questions and no answers. He entered the precinct and headed for his cubicle then stopped abruptly when he saw Chief Monroe sitting in his chair. The man did not look happy. Now what?

"I see you are about as happy to see me as I am to see you, McBride." Monroe stood and offered the man his chair.

McBride leaned against the wall. "I'm fine. How can I help you?"

Shadows

"I thought I made myself clear the last time I was here. Was there something you did not understand about that conversation?" he asked shortly.

"No," McBride answered hesitantly. "I understood you perfectly."

"Then why, may I ask, did you attempt to interrogate Abby Cooper without my knowledge?" he queried softly.

The quiet tone was somehow more threatening than if the man had been yelling. "It wasn't intentional," McBride assured him. "I was there to speak to Thomas and she just happened to be present. It couldn't be avoided."

"Okay, I'll give you that one for now. However, it is my understanding that you did not contact Jake Wilder before showing up on the Deveraux's doorstep. Was I unclear about that part of the conversation?"

McBride grimaced. No, the Chief had not been unclear about that either. McBride just ignored that order. He didn't like Jake Wilder and wanted to avoid him at all cost. He knew he wouldn't get anywhere with him around.

"I didn't think so," Monroe said watching McBride. "I should write you up for that but I'm not going to. Don't let it happen again. You will have absolutely no contact with Thomas Deveraux or Alex Deveraux without going through Jake Wilder first."

"Yes sir," McBride grumbled. Hawaii was looking better and better every day. Why did he get stuck with this case anyway? What was he being punished for? Was it Karma for some bad deed in the past? He must have done something to deserve this, Rand just wasn't sure what that something could be.

Chief Monroe slowly exited the squad room. That should put a cog in his wheel for a while. Jake could give him the run around while the rest of them figured out their next move.

* * * *

Tony hung up the phone and glanced at Megan. He wasn't sure how she'd feel about the request he was about to make. The small group had settled into Victor's apartment complex earlier that evening. Atticus was staying in Victor's old apartment, which according to Victor now belonged to his father. Cornelia was directly below him and Tala was one door down from her. Megan's mother refused to stay anywhere else. She insisted on being as close to Atticus as possible in case there was another attack on his life. Tony and Megan were currently lounging on Tala's comfortable couch. He had initially called Victor to see if there was another vacant room on this floor that he and Megan could occupy for a few days. Instead, he was now going to ask his wife to leave the complex completely. "Victor would like us to head over to Thomas' place. There's plenty of room and he's worried about his friend. He'd like us to check on him and keep him company for a couple days."

"Okay," Megan agreed. She liked Thomas. She didn't know him well, but he'd been at the fort a few days during the ordeal with Sam and then at the wedding. If Thomas was in trouble she wanted to help.

Shadows

"Are you sure it's okay?" he asked. "I know you wanted to be close to your mom, but things are getting kind of complicated here. I think I need to call dad." He wasn't sure if that was a good idea, but it felt right to him. His parents were powerful people. Maybe they could help somehow.

"I think that might be a good idea. Let's head over to Thomas', get settled and then you can call Charles," she agreed.

"Why are you being so amenable tonight?" he asked.

"I don't know. I guess I just have a feeling you're right. For some reason I think we need to be there for Thomas. Maybe I can help in some way, I don't know. Anyway, I agree about your parents because I think they should know what's going on here. They are the ones that asked us to come in the first place. They're going to be upset if we don't keep them appraised."

"Okay. Let's go," Tony said, standing. They explained the situation to Tala then Tony led Megan to the car.

* * * *

Abby flung the door open then hesitated. She didn't know these people. Who were they? Thomas walked up behind her and smiled. "Tony, Megan, I didn't know you were in town."

Abby studied Thomas. He seemed to be happy about the new arrivals. She wasn't. She planned to have a relaxing evening alone with Thomas, building a stronger friendship. She knew she wasn't a raving beauty but she was a good person. Abby hoped that if Thomas spent more time with her, maybe eventually he would be attracted to the inside and not care so much about the outside. It was a long shot but she had to try. Now her plans were ruined.

Thomas moved aside to let the couple enter. "Uh, Victor said you might have a room you could spare," Tony said hesitantly. Maybe Thomas was on a date or something and wanted privacy.

"Sure," Thomas said enthusiastically. "Abby's in the first room, but take your pick of the others." He closed the door and headed for the library. "Once you get settled, join us. We were just about to have a night cap."

The group sat in the library catching up and getting to know each other. Megan studied Abby. She wondered if Thomas realized the girl wasn't only attracted to him, she was completely smitten. He didn't appear to have a clue. She hadn't meant to read the girls mind, but she couldn't help it. Abby practically screamed her disappointment the moment Thomas invited her and Tony inside. Megan smiled when she saw Abby sneak another glance in Thomas' direction. They really would make a lovely couple. Megan hoped everything worked out for the shifter. She was a very caring but fragile woman. That part Megan had read on purpose, since Abby's mind was so open Megan couldn't resist. Thomas could crush Abby if he wasn't careful. Megan was so deep in thought, she actually jumped when Tony linked his hand with hers. She glanced at her husband and smiled knowingly. He was ready to turn in for the night. Or more to the point, anxious for them to be alone so he could call home. Once he spoke to his father, Tony would relax. Charles always knew what to say to make his son feel better. "Tony, I'm a little tired. Would you mind terribly if we headed off to bed?" she asked.

Shadows

"Of course not," he told her and stood. "Thank you again Thomas for the hospitality. We'll see you two in the morning."

Once the door was shut Tony turned to Megan. "Do you think Thomas knows that girl is in love with him?"

Megan smiled. So Tony didn't need her special powers to pick up on the love vibes. "No, I don't think so. I don't know how Thomas feels about Abby, but I got the impression he is too preoccupied to realize she's besotted."

"I agree," Tony smiled then sobered. "I guess it's time to call dad."

Abby settled back into her chair, relieved the couple decided to go to bed so early. Now she would finally get some one on one time with Thomas. Maybe her plan wasn't completely foiled after all.

"So," Thomas said with a smile as he reclined in his chair. "Tell me about your day." He was thankful Abby was staying with him. He knew he should try to encourage her to go home. Dragging her into this mess was unfair, but he liked having someone to talk to at the end of a long, stressful day. Abby helped him relax. So for now, he'd let her stay. Hopefully he wouldn't regret that decision down the road.

* * * *

Ty watched Sam's face glimmer in the candle light. She was beaming as she sipped her champagne. "I'm glad you're happy about this." He was thrilled with the new house and even happier the deal was finally complete. They couldn't move in for another thirty days but less than an hour ago, he and Sam closed on their first home.

"You have no idea how happy I am." she said enthusiastically. "Okay, I guess you do. But I also know you are just as happy. That's what makes this so great," she couldn't stop smiling. The house was perfect. She owned her own pool!

Ty studied her lovingly. "I'm kind of sad it's over," he admitted. "I was having a lot of fun house hunting with you. Now comes the hard part, moving in." He took her hand in his and kissed her fingers gently. "We just bought our first home together. It feels nice," he said lovingly.

"It's better than nice," Sam sobered. "I can't believe we paid more than five million dollars for a house. I can't believe I married a man that can afford to spend five million on a house." She was still a little uncomfortable about the price. "And we didn't even take out a loan."

"Actually you spent five mill on a house. I just went along because you were having so much fun. I don't know though, I might have to get a second job to pay the bills," he teased. "Maybe I could sell my body," he mused.

"I'm not going to ruin this by fretting about the money. I know we have it. It just seems so surreal to actually spend millions of dollars on one purchase," she paused ignoring his jibe. "No regrets. I just bought the house of my dreams."

"We just bought the house of *our* dreams," he corrected. "I can't wait to get out of that apartment. Now I remember why I stopped staying there in the first place," he grinned. "I am so glad those kids have a curfew."

Sam was still thinking about the house. She loved the layout. It was so big and spacious and the back deck was going to be wonderful for parties. As soon as things calmed down they were going to have a big shindig in their back yard. They could BBQ and swim. She had a pool! She gave Ty a coy look. "So, do I get a pool boy?" she asked seductively.

"Absolutely not," he said with finality. "Unless of course he's a ninety year old man."

"Really?" she said enthusiastically. "I wonder if there are any shifters, or single warriors or maybe one of the fae that needs a side job. How old did you say you were?"

"Not funny," Ty warned. "You hire a hot pool boy, I get a sexy maid." He laughed at Sam's sudden change of mood.

"Never mind," she said immediately. "I see your point. No sexy people in our house except you."

"Can I let you in occasionally?" he deadpanned.

"I'm not sexy, I'm your wife," she countered.

"I beg to differ," Ty said casually as the waiter placed two large plates of food in front of them. He waited for the man to leave. "You my dear are the sexiest woman in the world."

"Eat your food," she ordered. "I want to continue the celebration when we get home. You're going to need all the strength you can get, I'm pretty pumped and need an outlet."

Over an hour later, Sam and Ty casually walked out of the restaurant and strolled toward their apartment. It was a nice evening. A little cool, fall was in the air, but not too bad. "We're going to need warmer coats soon," Sam observed.

"I can't believe it's almost winter," Ty agreed, putting an arm around Sam's waist and pulling her close. "I can't wait to spend our first Christmas together. I'm going to spoil you rotten."

Sam smiled, but again she was uncomfortable. It just felt wrong to spend all Ty's money on herself. Plus, she couldn't use his money to buy him a Christmas present. She had her salary, but she'd been using that for new clothes and incidentals.

"Stop it," Ty scolded. "Why can't you think of it as ours?" he asked.

"Because it doesn't feel like ours. You have so much and I have so little in comparison. I feel like you are the one bringing everything into this marriage and I'm just along for the ride."

"Maybe you should spend more time with my mother. I think she'd be able to cure you of this nonsense," Ty suggested.

"It's not nonsense. I'm just being practical and honest." She knew she was upsetting him and she needed to stop. They could deal with the financial gully between them some other day. Sam swung around to face Ty, stopping his movement. She casually placed her arms around his neck and pulled him in for a long, hard kiss. "We just bought a house!" She exclaimed stepping back and twirling around. "I can't believe I bought a house."

Ty smiled. He loved seeing Sam so happy. He just wished she could get past her hang-ups about his money. It didn't matter to him, it shouldn't matter to her. He watched her for several seconds then began to move forward again. It was late and they needed to get home. Sam took Ty's hand and started skipping backwards as she continued to celebrate their purchase. He was so engrossed in Sam's mood he almost didn't see them.

Sam didn't see anything, but she felt Ty's emotions shift from loving and happy to sober and tense. She turned just in time to see him plunge a dagger into a vampire's chest directly behind her. She pulled out her own dagger and prepared for battle. It only took a second for her to realize she was out of her league. She watched Ty, amazed at his speed and skill. How did he do that, she wondered. Out of the corner of her eye she saw a large vampire charging her way. She planted her feet trying to prepare. She could do this. She was a warrior now. Just as he came into reach she plunged her knife into his chest. The vampire dissipated, dust floating everywhere. She didn't see the second one coming at her from the opposite direction. Before she knew what was happening, she was knocked on her butt.

The vampire jumped on her chest and pinned her to the ground. Sam was scared. What was she supposed to do? How could she get out of this? Was she going to die already? She tried to maneuver away, but she couldn't move.

Ty felt Sam's fear and quickly searched for her in the darkness. She was on the ground, a vampire was on top of her pinning her to the concrete. A second vamp was charging her way. Ty didn't hesitate, he abandoned his fight and flew across the expanse. He reached her just in time to plunge his dagger into the approaching vampire as he flung the other vamp off her chest. Sam was shaken. Ty could feel it. She wasn't going to be any help in her condition. "Stay close, we'll get through this. I'm not going to let you get hurt," he promised as he skillfully disposed of the remaining vampires that now encircled them. Once the immediate area was clear, Ty carefully studied his surroundings for any vampires he might have missed.

The instant he was certain they were safe, he turned and pulled Sam into his arms. "We need to get home. I want to get off the streets as soon as possible," he told her as he took her hand and guided her down the sidewalk.

Sam was in shock. She'd been so sure she was about to die and she didn't know what to do about it. Once Ty saved her, she was ashamed. What kind of warrior was she anyway? In all the time she'd been hunting vampires she'd never tried to take them on as a group. She'd never tried to fight face to face. Her talents were from a distance. She could shoot an arrow better than most, but she had no idea how to fight. The few times she'd tried to take one on, she'd always ended up in the ER.

The couple silently entered their apartment. That's when Sam broke down. "You could have gotten seriously injured because of me," she choked out, tears running down her face. "I didn't know what I was doing and I could have gotten both of us killed." She plopped down on the couch covering her face with her hands.

Ty walked to her. He wasn't sure what to say. She had scared him tonight. Those two vampires could have killed her. This was partly his fault. He knew she'd been hunting vampires for years. When they attacked, he'd just assumed she'd know what to do. Ty sat down next to her and pulled her into his arms. "It wasn't all your fault," he told her. "I should have been there to protect you."

Sam's head shot up and she glared at him angrily. "Why? I thought I was supposed to be a warrior. Warriors fight vampires.

Shadows

Why exactly should you have protected me? Does Victor have to protect Ariel? No!" she barked. "Does Dimitri have to protect Alex? No," she said again. "I know, I've seen both of them fight."

"True," Ty agreed. Then smiled at the conflicted look on her face. "You thought I'd disagree with you? Well, I won't. You need to learn to fight. Just like Alex and Ariel learned to fight. Plus, Ariel has an advantage, so that's not a fair comparison."

"What about Alex?" Sam asked. "She doesn't need some guy to shield her from the dangerous vampires."

Ty couldn't help it, he burst out laughing. He just couldn't stop himself. His emotions combined with her emotions were swirling around, and they were on opposite ends of the spectrum. "Sam, don't get mad. You can feel exactly what I'm feeling. You know how strange it is. Take a deep breath and listen to me for a minute."

Sam took a deep breath. She had to admit she felt a little better. "Okay, I'm listening."

"Well to begin, Alex also has an advantage. It's just a different one than Ariel. It's harder to explain. Plus, I suggest you ask Alex and Ariel if Dimitri and Victor try to protect them. Just be prepared for their angry wrath and the egomaniac comments when you do."

Sam smiled in spite of herself. She could only imagine the earful she'd get on that subject. Well, from Alex anyway. Ariel still wasn't really talking to her.

"It's not about me being macho or egotistical. It's my nature. I protect people. Humans, fae, shifters. It's our nature. Once you get used to this, you'll understand. It's in your nature now, too."

Sam already understood. She wanted to protect Ty, but she knew she couldn't.

"I think you will understand this better than Alex or Ariel ever could. I love you. I will always protect you. Not because I think you're weak or need protection, but because the thought of losing you makes me physically ill. I don't know what I would do without you."

Sam took a deep breath. She could feel Ty's emotions. She did understand. She felt the same about him. "I know," Sam assured him. "I'm sorry, Ty. I am so ashamed of myself. I was a liability out there instead of the asset I should have been."

"Which leads me to my second point. Alex and Ariel have been training since they were children. Their parents taught them to fight vampires at a very young age, Sam. Nobody taught you. That's on me. I should have been there to protect you because you haven't learned to protect yourself yet."

Sam studied Ty. Was he serious? He thought this was his fault? Why did Ty always find a way to blame himself for her shortcomings? "I don't agree with you. This is my fault, not yours. I won't let you take this on yourself."

"Instead of arguing about who is to blame, let's decide how to fix this," Ty suggested.

"I need training," Sam said. "How do I get it?"

Shadows

"Would you be comfortable with me as a trainer?" he asked.

"Of course," Sam smiled. "I watched you out there. I realize all the warriors are talented. I saw Victor fight that night in the alley with Ariel, but you are so systematic and fluent," she scowled. "That's not exactly what I mean. It's more than that. When you fight it's like watching a carefully choreographed martial arts scene with a twist. I really don't know how to explain it. You're amazing. Do you think I'll ever be that good?"

Ty pulled Sam into his arms. "I know you will. Knowing you, I'm sure you'll be better than me one day. You have a competitive nature," he sobered. "We'll work on this, Sam. I'm going to make sure you are safe out there no matter who you're with. It's going to take time, but we'll figure this out. Okay?"

"Okay," Sam agreed moving in closer to Ty. She felt so safe and loved in his arms. She believed him. Ty would make sure she could protect herself. Until then, he'd be there to protect her from danger.

Ty stood, took her hand and led her to their room. "You promised me a celebration when we got home," he grinned pulling her onto the bed.

Sam laughed a little. For now they could put the horror behind them and celebrate their new purchase. "We bought a house!" she exclaimed just before Ty pressed his lips to hers.

* * * *

Tony, Megan, Thomas and Abby sat in the library watching the large screen. Abby was impressed. The screen was split. One side had Dimitri, Alex, Ty, Sam, Dante and Nick. Another showed Victor, Ariel, Orin, Breena, Kylee and Bastian. "How do you do that?" she asked Thomas. "I assume each of their screens are adapted to look just like ours?"

Thomas smiled. "You're going to have to ask Alex or Sam the specifics. They're the tech geeks."

"Okay. Let's get started," Dimitri barked. "It looks like most of us are here."

"Uh, mom and Atticus are on their way. They are also bringing Cornelia with them. They're just running a little late. Cornelia wasn't feeling well. We can get started without them if you want," Megan said reluctantly.

"While we're waiting," Bastian spoke up. "Kylee had something she wanted to talk to Alex about," he turned to Kylee and motioned for her to go ahead.

Kylee looked at Bastian nervously. This wasn't exactly how she wanted to have such an important conversation. She took a deep breath and began. "Well, my vacation time is up on Monday. I haven't been missed so far because they all think I'm sitting on a beach drinking margaritas. So, I wanted to make a proposal," she paused to gather her thoughts. "I've talked to the hospital staff here in town and they could use my help. I was thinking maybe I could transfer out here and hopefully continue my work at the fort if you would let me," she studied the screen watching for a response. "Unfortunately I'm not independently wealthy, so I'd have to work full time at the hospital and I'll find an apartment close by. But I could still give you a few hours each week and I'd be close in case of an emergency. I realize you may not trust me yet, but I really think you need me. I came in handy when Ty needed his lung repaired and with Sam. I'd also like to continue working with Breena and Bastian on the fae's difficult pregnancy issue. I really think I could help with that." She was worried she was starting to babble. "Anyway, I guess that's it. If you will let me continue to work with you, I'll call the hospital immediately and give my two weeks' notice. I'd have to return to New York to work for at least a week and secure my house but I could start almost immediately."

Alex studied Kylee. "I see," she finally said. "I don't think that's a decision I can make alone. You know a lot of our secrets and if you continue to work with us, you're going to know more. Would you mind leaving the room for a few minutes while I talk to the group about the situation? I'd like their input before I make a decision on this."

"Of course," Kylee said standing and heading for the door. Bastian stood and walked with her. After a moment he returned to his seat.

"I told her to wait in the kitchen," he announced to the group. "I locked the door so there's no chance she'll interrupt the discussion."

"Okay," Alex took a deep breath. "So far I've been impressed with Kylee. She seems to be dealing with our strange world very well."

"I agree," Dimitri said in support. "However, Alex and I haven't been able to spend a lot of time at the Fort. I'd like input from those of you that have gotten to know her. Ty, Sam, Bastian, Breena and Orin as well as Victor and Ariel. You guys are in a better position to make this decision. Give us your thoughts," he directed.

"I support her one hundred and ten percent," Breena said confidently. "I've been working with her on my pregnancy. She's amazing. We've come up with a treatment that's really working for me. I feel better than I have in weeks."

Ariel looked at her friend in shock. She knew Breena was feeling better. She didn't know she'd been taking some experimental treatment. "What are you thinking?" she demanded. "How could you be so reckless with your life and the life of your baby? What if that treatment has side effects?"

"Ariel," Bastian said calmly. "Do you really think any of us would risk something like that? Do you think Orin would agree to gamble with the life of his wife or his unborn child?"

"You know about this?" she asked Orin.

"Of course," he answered. "And I assure you we're not doing anything risky."

Ariel felt better. If Orin knew, whatever the treatment was, it was safe. He wouldn't allow them to try anything that had the slightest risk. "Okay good," she finally relaxed.

"Kylee also has my vote," Bastian continued. "She's very good in the lab and she's an excellent doctor. I agree with her, we could use her talents. What we do is dangerous. There are frequent injuries. Right now we are so spread out, Alex can't be everywhere. Having a doctor here at the fort is a good idea. Especially now that we have so many children present. I wasn't happy about her involvement at first but I have to admit she came in handy with Ty and Sam." He glowered at the memory of Sam's transformation.

"I say keep her," Victor agreed. "She came in handy with Sam and when Ty's lung needed repair. We have our own ways of healing, but having Kylee here has really helped. I realize she's human and it seems risky, but I honestly don't believe it is. Kylee's not going to betray us."

"I agree," Ariel put in.

"Ty?" Dimitri asked. "Sam? Do either of you have any concerns?"

"I agree with Victor. I think she's solid," Ty looked to Sam.

"I do have a concern," Sam studied Ty, still ashamed of her failure last night. "Our world is dangerous. My experience over the past few weeks is a very clear reminder of that. Kylee is human. If we allow her to stay, she's going to be in constant danger. If Ty hadn't stepped in and changed me, I would be dead. I don't have any concern about Kylee's commitment or her loyalty. I think the fact that she followed me to the fort speaks volumes. I don't know of any other doctor that would go to those extremes to protect a patient. I just worry about her safety. If we allow her to stay, I think there needs to be conditions. We should make her agree not to go out at night for any reason. If there's some kind of emergency, as a group, I believe we should make a commitment to protect her."

The entire group expressed their agreement. Alex watched as Atticus, Tala and Cornelia stepped into the room. "It looks like the last of our group has arrived," she observed. "Welcome and thank you for coming to such an early morning meeting."

"Looks like we may have missed something important," Atticus pointed out.

"Kylee has asked to join us permanently," Alex explained. "We were just discussing our feelings on that matter before I make a decision."

"She has my vote," Atticus said enthusiastically. "If that makes a difference."

"Of course it does," Alex assured him. "You've been spending as much time with her as anyone. I want input from all of you."

"Isn't the girl human?" Tala asked, perplexed. "I've never met her, but I thought Megan said she was human."

"She is," Bastian answered.

"How interesting," Tala mused. "In all my years I've never seen a group of fae quite like you before." She was still surprised they were considering such a phenomenon.

"What do you mean?" Victor asked.

"You just seem very liberal," she began. "This group seems to be accepting of everyone, no matter the species. I just find that very unusual and intriguing."

"We have a very open minded queen," Ty smiled at Alex. He supposed it was a bit unusual, but he personally liked the fact that they welcomed anyone regardless of species, if that individual was trustworthy.

"I'd say that's an understatement," Tala said, still astounded by their acceptance. "Shadows are usually ostracized by the fae. Humans avoided, shifters...I don't know, I guess they are really not even acknowledged. I just find it fascinating that this community welcomes everyone without prejudice. To be honest, it's difficult to understand."

"I guess Alex is an equal opportunity employer," Ariel joked.

They all laughed.

"Okay, back to the issue at hand. We have a lot to discuss this morning," Alex commanded. "Does anyone else have concerns or input they'd like to give before Dimitri and I decide?"

"Actually," Thomas paused. "I do have something to say on the matter."

Alex was surprised. Thomas barely knew Kylee. He'd spent very little time at the fort. "Yes Thomas," she said, curious.

"I'd like to expand on what Sam said," he began. "Our world is very dangerous. Kylee has agreed to uproot her entire life and move out to the fort to help us. She's entering a world that could literally get her killed. I think we owe her something for that. Having her involved is obviously beneficial to us. If you decide to let her stay, I'd like our family to hire her Alex. I want to provide her a generous salary and if we have the space, give her one of the apartments on base. She shouldn't have to work at the hospital to support herself when she is giving up so much already. If we are going to bring her in, I think we should bring her in all the way. Pay her, house her and as Sam said, above all, protect her."

"I agree," Alex told Thomas. She was proud of her brother. He was always so cognizant of people's needs. He had such a natural ability to take care of others. They would definitely take care of Kylee Quintana. It was the least they could do considering the sacrifices she was willing to make for their people. She looked at Dimitri. "I think she should stay, what do you think?"

"I agree," he confirmed.

"Before we call her back in and give her the news, does anyone object to the decision?"

Everyone shook their head at once. It was unanimous. Kylee was now one of them.

"Good," Alex said with relief. "Bastian, do you want to get Kylee so we can give her the news and move on. We have a lot to talk about."

Kylee was subdued as she slowly entered the room. This meant so much to her. She wanted it more than anything. She knew she could do a lot of good in their world and she loved these people. The last few weeks had been the best of her life. She didn't think she could stand it if they turned her away. She stopped and braced herself on the back of the couch, waiting for the verdict.

"We've unanimously decided we would like you to join us," Alex began. "However, the offer comes with strings."

Kylee grinned. She was so relieved. She'd agree to anything if it meant staying.

Shadows

"First, our world is dangerous. I think you know that by now. Sam and Ty are just two examples of how quickly you can get into serious trouble. If we allow you to join us, you will have to make a solid commitment to safety."

"Of course," Kylee agreed.

"That means you cannot go out after dark. Being human, you are an easy target for vampires. I need your solemn promise that you will not go out alone in the evening. If there is some kind of emergency and it's imperative you travel at night, you must promise you will not go alone. No matter what, you must find one of us to go with you. Can you do that?" Alex asked.

"I promise," Kylee agreed. "I do know how dangerous this world is. Believe me, I don't have a reckless bone in my body. I have no desire to take unnecessary risks with my life."

"I'm afraid you are taking a huge risk simply by associating with us," Bastian disagreed.

"Maybe, but it's a calculated risk," Kylee argued.

"I have one other request," Alex continued.

"Okay," Kylee nodded.

"Thomas and I would like you to work for the Deveraux family. We want to hire you as our personal family physician. I promise we will give you a generous salary. If you agree, Jake will draw up the contract immediately. Oh, I forgot to mention Jake was going to join us today, but a problem came up that needed immediate attention. It seems one of the wealthy human families is insisting their child be allowed to attend the academy. He's putting out that fire this morning. I'll fill him in later. Anyway, Kylee we all agree, you are making a significant sacrifice to join our world. It's not fair to expect you to relocate, find an apartment and work full time to support yourself. If you want in, we want you in all the way. You will be provided your own apartment at the fort and I'd like you to continue your work with Breena and Bastian on the pregnancy issue. There are a few other items I also think you can help with. I believe we will keep you busy full time if you are willing to accept the job. In your spare time you can work at the ER locally if you want. I know they can always use volunteers."

Kylee was stunned. This was more than she dared hope for. "I don't want to be an inconvenience or a burden," she began. "I'd love the job but if I take it, I will expect to earn my way. No handouts," she demanded.

Alex smiled. That was part of the reason she had liked this woman immediately. "Deal," she assured her. "Now, on to other business." She turned to Dimitri. "I'll turn things over to you for now."

"As you all know we've been spread pretty thin lately. I feel like we are all going in a million different directions," Dimitri told the group. "Everything is chaotic. It's difficult to keep track of who is where and what they are doing. I'd like to try to tighten that down a bit. I called this meeting because I'd like to get input from all of you," he paused. "When we started the project at the fort we only had two big things to handle. Getting the fort up and running and protecting our people here in the city. We all knew Radek would be a threat on both fronts, but things have changed significantly."

Everyone nodded in agreement.

"I think the fort is coming along very well. In fact, the progress is ahead of schedule. Letting the kids assist with setup is a big help, but also a burden. Their safety is my top priority now. So far that hasn't been a problem," Dimitri continued.

"These are good kids. They understand the risks and have been very diligent in obeying the rules we've set forth," Orin provided.

"I agree," Victor assured them. "It's definitely a risk to have them here, but to be honest it's fairly easy to protect them. The fort is now a controlled environment. I realize their safety is important, but I think it's covered. We can move that one down on the list of priorities, not in importance but in focus because it's already complete."

"Good," Dimitri moved on. "The last thing I want to do is pay a visit to a parent because their child was seriously injured or killed while in our care."

"I agree," Victor and Orin said at once.

"I'd like to continue in the same direction as we've been going with that. Unfortunately, that means some of us are going to have to remain at the fort at all times until I can recruit more permanent instructors," Dimitri continued.

"Breena and I would like to stay on here until the baby is born," Orin spoke up immediately. "We feel safe here and I think the two of us can do a lot of good. I've been working with the kids on fighting techniques and Breena has been working with Kylee and Bastian, when he can get away, on a curriculum for the academy. They've got a lot of good ideas, but coming up with a detailed course plan is going to take time. If you don't need us back in the city we're happy to stay here as long as we can."

"I appreciate that," Dimitri said, truly grateful for their willingness to help. "If you're happy there I don't see any reason for change. Keep doing what you've been doing. You have the conferencing abilities now if something urgent comes up with the council. With Kylee on board, I think it's a good idea for Breena to stay there anyway. They can continue to work together on the pregnancy challenges our people experience as well as academy issues."

"Victor," Alex called.

"Yes," he gave her his full attention.

"I know you've been out there longer than we initially planned. I appreciate everything you are doing and I realize you need to get back to the city to check in at the shelter and your club," Alex paused. "I hate to ask but can you stick around for another week? I know it's a lot to request, but I'm just not comfortable leaving the kids out there alone with Orin and Breena." She turned to the couple. "I hope you don't take that the wrong way, but if something happened, if the vampires decided to attack the fort, I think you would be too vulnerable without additional help. For now I want at least four adults there to protect the kids at all times."

"No offense taken," Orin assured her. "I agree. We're pretty isolated and I believe we're well protected but if the worst happened, I don't think Bree and I could handle it alone. Plus, right now Breena's not a hundred percent. It would be difficult for me to protect her and the baby and all the kids if I was alone. We need the help."

Shadows

Ty thought this would be the perfect time to bring up the subject. He took Sam's hand and spoke up. "Sam and I would like to return to the fort," he requested. "We've taken care of everything we needed to here in the city. I think we'll be of more use out there. Sam wants to check in on Romulus and we still need more droids. We also have a few additional details to finalize with the Sims and we haven't worked out the bugs in the VR goggles and the obstacle course yet. Basically our work is not finished. We still have a lot to do before the academy opens completely."

Sam was touched that Ty was trying to spare her, but she wanted it out on the table. "There's something Ty isn't telling you," she admitted.

All eyes were on her. Alex detected the tone in Sam's voice and was instantly on alert.

"Ty and I were attacked last night on our way home from dinner. It became immediately apparent I can't fight. I almost got us both killed. Ty has agreed to be my trainer but right now I'm a liability," she paused. "So, Ty left out the part about me needing to go back to the fort to learn to fight. I'll be safe there and he can teach me what I need to know," she was embarrassed but knew it was important that everyone understood the situation completely. Right now they could not rely on her for assistance. She needed to be protected like Kylee. Sam had mistakenly believed that being a warrior meant she could immediately help the cause. She wanted to deserve the gift she'd been given, but right now she didn't. She was worried about the impact the news would have on the warriors but it couldn't be helped. They needed to know the truth. No more secrets.

"I see," Alex said calmly. She was concerned for Sam, not because she was inexperienced, but because the incident last night had obviously upset both Sam and Ty. Ty was clearly worried about protecting Sam and Sam was upset because she felt like an outcast again. "Ariel, how long have you been fighting? How long have you been training to prepare yourself for an attack?"

"Basically all my life," Ariel admitted. "So conservatively, over three hundred years."

"And Breena, how did we first meet?" Alex asked.

Breena smiled. "Ariel took me out in the woods to kick your butt," she provided.

"Do you think I was ready to take on a mess of vampires at the time?" she asked.

Breena laughed, "No way," she said honestly. "Ariel and I sent you home begging for mercy for weeks before you got the hang of it."

"I know you're just trying to make me feel better about this, Alex," Sam wasn't buying it. She'd seen Alex fight. She was good, better than good. "Don't patronize me. I'm not exaggerating. I'm horrible at fighting. My talent lies with a bow and arrow. Hand to hand is foreign to me. I have no idea what I'm doing. Ask Ty, I literally almost got both of us killed."

Ty closed his eyes. She did need a lot of work but this wasn't in the plan, nobody else needed to know this.

"I don't have to ask Ty," Alex assured her. "I'm sure you don't have the first clue how to take on a vampire," she said honestly.

"That's not my point though. My point is that you are the only one in the room that expected the impossible."

"Huh?" Sam asked surprised.

"Is there anyone else in attendance that thought Sam could go out on her own and take on a coven of vampires without training and a significant amount of hard work?" she asked.

"Of course not," Dimitri said in support of Alex. "In fact, Alex and I have had numerous conversations about this very topic. Sam, are you forgetting the request I made just before you and Ty left for the ranch?"

"Well, sort of," Sam admitted. She had completely forgotten Dimitri's request to set up a meeting once she and Ty got settled. What did that have to do with anything?

"Well, my request for a meeting was to discuss your training. Alex already brought a droid home for you. It's in the closet waiting to be moved to your place. As soon as the two of you figure out where home is going to be that is," Dimitri said calmly.

"Really?" Sam asked then paused. "I want to pay for that, but I'll take it," she smiled slyly. "The developer is a genius. I hadn't thought of that, duh. How could I have missed something so obvious? The droids would really help me."

"The developer *is* a genius," Alex agreed. "Except when it comes to her own safety. Sam you have always overestimated your abilities. That's what drove me nuts when you were human. I don't know why you thought you could jump in and be the best fighter around, but apparently you did. Dante, can you tell Sam how many warriors have joined the fighting actually prepared for battle on their first day?"

Dante grinned. "Only one that I know of, Thomas."

"Okay, Thomas is an exception because he trained with dad since birth. I think he could fight before he could walk. He doesn't count," she waited for Dante to continue.

"Well, if you don't count Thomas…none. That's why we're opening the academy, isn't it? These kids don't know how to handle vampires. They've been living in a peaceful world all their lives. We decided unless a warrior passed the academy, they couldn't join the fight. Sam, I think the same standard should be applied to you. I agree with Ty. Those two should go back to the fort. They do have a lot of work to finish, but Sam also needs to go through the same training as everyone else if she wants to join us on the streets."

Sam was surprised. She hated knowing she was a liability to these guys. She'd work extra hard to deserve their support. No matter what they said, she was still disappointed in herself.

Alex could see Sam wasn't convinced. "Sam?" she asked.

"Yeah," Sam answered immediately.

"I also have another favor to ask," she waited to make sure she had everyone's full attention.

"Sure, what?" Sam agreed.

"I've seen you with a bow and arrow so I know how good you are. So does Ariel," she paused as Ariel nodded. "I was hoping you could start developing a curriculum on that. It's going to need to be detailed. You seem to have a talent for drawing and preparing diagrams. I don't plan to leave you two out there indefinitely so I want something we can hand out to the kids to teach them the basics. Everyone is not going to be talented in fighting. We're offering the academy to shifters and fae at this point. Some of the girls attending may be better at shooting an arrow than hand to hand combat. The boys too for that matter. We're at war. I intend to use any advantage I can. Also, you treated your arrows with holy water. I'd like to teach them that process as well. Dummy it down, for lack of a better explanation. I want anyone who picks up the instructions to be able to follow them. That particular skill is also something we can teach to the adults. Mothers with young kids, teenagers, the possibilities are limitless. You were able to fight the vampires for years with your skills as a human. I see no reason our weaker members can't use those same skills for their own protection. My ultimate goal is for every member of our community to have a means to fight in an emergency. Clearly the majority of our people are not going to head out to the streets of New York and hunt like the warriors do. But as far as I'm concerned even the weakest member of our community should have at least one skill, one form of protection against vampires in an emergency."

Ariel studied Sam. She wasn't sure she completely forgave her, but Alex was right. Sam had talent. This was a way Sam could contribute to the cause. It might even give her the self-confidence she was lacking. "I agree," Ariel chimed in. "I've seen Sam a couple times. Alex isn't over exaggerating her talent. Sam shot those arrows into a crowd of young vampires and hit her target every time. I'm grateful for that since Alex and I were right in the middle of the mix. At first I thought we were nuts, but Sam never even came close to hitting one of us. She hit the vamp every time." Ariel glanced around the room and saw the group was interested. "There are bound to be members of our community that could use that training. It's a great way for Sam to pull her weight while she learns to fight."

Sam was dumbfounded. The last person she expected to support her was Ariel. She was humbled by the praise and excited to take this new project on. Ariel was right about one thing, this was something she could do to contribute while she got up to speed on the rest. "I'll get started right away," she promised. "When do you want Ty and me to leave?"

"Whenever you can," Dimitri answered. "The sooner you get out there, the sooner Victor can come back and deal with his personal responsibilities." He turned to look at Victor. "I too would like to tell you how much I appreciate all you have done. I know you're businesses here have gone unattended for a lot longer than you originally planned. Your sacrifice hasn't gone unnoticed."

"Actually I've been checking in regularly with Bojan and Tèarmann. Things are running pretty smoothly right now. I think Ariel and I can give you another week anyway. We'll play it by ear from there, but for now we're good."

"So that covers the fort," Dimitri continued. "Bastian, where are you on that tablecloth?"

"I've isolated the substance and narrowed down the distributors. I didn't plan to go any further with that project. We know it came from Diana so what's the point?" he asked.

Thomas perked up. What was all this? "What are you talking about?" he asked.

"I told Nick to retrieve the tablecloth from the restaurant the night Diana poisoned you. It had such a dramatic effect I thought we should know what we were dealing with. Also, I wanted Bastian to start working on an antidote if we needed it."

"Why didn't anyone tell me about that?" Thomas asked, annoyed.

"You got better. There was no need," Dimitri answered flatly.

"I've been able to break down the compound and identify the elements. At this point, I'd like to pass this off to Breena and Kylee. The two of them should be able to work together and come up with an antidote. In fact, I've been thinking. Now that we're bringing Kylee on fulltime we should start the same process on other human drugs. We are always fearful that we'll be injured and end up in the hospital. Human drugs can be deadly to a warrior. If we had an antidote for the most common drugs a physician would administer in the ER it might save someone's life. As an ER doc, Kylee can help with that as well."

"I think that's a great idea," Alex concurred. "Kylee are you willing to get started on that project?"

"Absolutely," she said at once.

"Bastian, I'm afraid that's going to mean constant trips to and from the fort. At this point I don't think we can confine you to one area. We need you in both places. I know it's going to be difficult, but can you manage?" Dimitri asked.

"I'll manage," Bastian assured him. "I think the helicopter is almost ready. Once we have that, it's going to make things a little easier as well." Everyone already knew Bastian was having one of his medical helicopters overhauled to use at the fort. He was donating it to the nonprofit as a tax write-off and purchasing a new one for his company.

"Nick? Dante?" Dimitri called.

"Yeah," they said in unison.

"I realize we've kept you here in the city throughout this whole process. Are you okay with your current assignment?" Dimitri asked. "I don't want you to feel overlooked."

"We're fine," Nick said for both of them.

"Yeah," Dante affirmed. "Actually, with Thomas stuck here we'd rather remain close in case he needs our help."

"Good," Dimitri nodded. "For now, you two and Thomas will stay in New York. Sorry, Thomas. I know it might be easier for you to leave right now, but with the detective on your tail I don't think we should have you traipsing back and forth to the fort. The last thing we need is a search warrant at the base. There's no way we could explain our operations out there."

"I agree and I understand," Thomas said soberly. "With all the issues at the company I doubt I could get away for long anyway."

"I know you want to watch out for Thomas," Dimitri told Dante and Nick, "But I still want you to stay away from the mansion. We can't have the police following you while you're out on patrol. I don't care if you meet up with Thomas as long as you make sure you're not followed or identified in the process. You can also call him as often as you like but use the phones I gave you. They can't be traced back to you. They show as belonging to myself and Alex, which won't be suspicious to McBride if he tries to trace them."

"Abby?" Dimitri called.

"Yes," Abby replied.

"We appreciate all you have done to assist with the situation in New York," Dimitri began. "I've spoken to your father and he thinks it's a good idea for you to remain involved. I have to be honest, I'm a little baffled by that."

"I talked to dad about my plans. He understands and supports what I'm doing. We both know there are risks, but in our estimation they're minimal. Having our family involved is very beneficial. Dad is well respected with the police. Chief Monroe is also a huge asset. We can't keep tabs on McBride if we keep our distance. You're people have helped our community in so many ways over the past few months. Thomas and Victor saved my life. Ariel realized we were in danger and warned us before any of our people were injured by those bombs. Ty and his family rebuilt our homes so quickly it can only be described as miraculous. Ty also risked his life time after time to disarm the multitude of bombs planted throughout our community; as well as the panther's. Thomas and Alex provided temporary housing for displaced families at substantial loss in profit to their companies. In short, we owe you. We owe more than we could ever repay. In comparison my involvement is nothing," she looked around. "So I wish all of you would stop trying to change my mind about this. I'm sticking, you'll just have to deal with that."

"Then we'll deal," Alex told her. "But in my estimation what you are doing is not nothing. I thank you as the fae queen, but even more sincerely I thank you for being there for my brother."

Abby nodded, a little embarrassed.

"So that brings us to the two remaining issues at hand," Dimitri sighed. "The two most difficult. First, the situation with Thomas. Detective McBride is obsessed with Thomas and not likely to back off anytime soon. He is not considering any other possibility. As such, his investigation has basically ended. In other words, we cannot rely on the police to find and stop the killer. It's going to be up to us to solve this particular crime."

"We thought the abductions had something to do with Thomas and me," Alex added. "The first two women had a connection to my family. Diana was pursuing Thomas and Susan worked for Deveraux Industries. There was another body found last night. This woman did not have a connection to us. Unfortunately another one of our employees has turned up missing. Tiffany Peterson has not been seen for five days."

"At this point," Dimitri continued, "I think we have to assume she is going to turn up soon as another victim. Paul has quietly been looking into her family and friends. No one has seen her since her disappearance. That brings the connection back to Deveraux Industries. We have no idea if the killer is a human serial killer with a beef against the company or if Radek is coordinating the attacks."

"Since Thomas is the prime suspect in the case, it also makes it impossible for us to investigate without drawing attention to ourselves. Anything we do is going to be discovered by McBride. He'll use that against us and solidify his belief that Thomas is guilty," Alex told the group. "We're open for suggestions. Something has to be done, I just don't know what. Abby is staying at the house to give Thomas an alibi, but I'm afraid that is just making her look like an accomplice."

Shadows

The room was silent. Nobody seemed to have a solution to this particular problem. Tala was the first to speak. "Cornelia, I didn't realize the situation here was that serious. If I had, I would have talked to you about this in private," she studied the girl for a reaction. "But I have a suggestion if you are willing."

Cornelia was sure she knew what Tala was going to suggest. It wasn't necessary for both of them to work on the problem with Atticus. One of them could stay here and help out in the city. She took a deep breath. Could she stay in New York for that long? She felt like getting involved in the situation with Thomas was playing with fire. She would be taking on the police, and what if she ran into her father? But these people seemed desperate. If that's what Tala wanted to do, Cornelia could help out for a while. If things got too hot, or she felt threatened she could find an excuse and leave. She nodded, signaling Tala to proceed.

"It sounds to me like you have two threats that need investigating," Tala began. "My proposal is for me to take Atticus and investigate the threats on his life. Cornelia can stay here in New York and work on the murders. Nobody knows her. There is no way this detective could make a connection between her and the Deveraux family. If Cornelia is careful she can make it look like she was hired by a victim's family. That will give her a lot of leeway with McBride and the department won't get in her way. The last thing they want is negative publicity on a crime they haven't been able to solve."

"I agree," Cornelia said soberly. She really hoped this was not a mistake. "I'll need a contact other than Thomas or Abby though. It can't be Alex or Dimitri either. McBride will be suspicious. Once I start snooping around he's going to check me out. I'm sure he'll pull my phone records. I need a roundabout way to communicate with Thomas. Also, I won't be able to come to the house again. I just hope my being here today has gone unnoticed."

Tala smiled. "I can make sure those men outside don't remember this visit," she sobered a little. "If that's okay with you that is. I know you don't like me messing with your minds," she glanced at Victor and then Atticus.

"Our minds...no," Victor smiled. "Mess all you want with the cops."

Kylee looked at Victor in shock. "What do you mean by that?" she exclaimed. "How are you messing with their minds and will it do permanent damage?" She was disappointed in Rand. They'd been friends for a long time. He was usually more reasonable than this. But she didn't want someone messing with his mind and damaging him permanently.

All eyes were on Kylee. "Uh, well...I just don't think it's a good idea to cause permanent damage to a cop," she paused. "Detectives need their brains to do their jobs. I don't think I can be a part of someone losing their livelihood over this."

Sam narrowed her eyes. "Wait a minute," she glared at Kylee. "Detective McBride?" she asked. "Did you say Detective Rand McBride was the guy harassing Thomas?" she asked Alex.

"Yeah, why?" Alex asked curious now.

"Because that's the same detective Kylee tried to get me to talk to when I was showing up at her ER injured. She said he's a friend of hers," Sam turned an accusing look at Kylee.

Shadows

"He is a friend of mine," Kylee admitted. "That's one reason I don't want you to harm him," she paused. "That doesn't mean I would tell him anything if that's what you're thinking. Rand is very passionate about his work. He was also raised in a very religious family. I don't think he would take knowing about the supernatural world I've entered well. I'm on your side. I hope you believe that," Kylee practically begged.

Alex studied the woman intently. She seemed to be sincere. Had they made the right choice when they agreed to include her? This was not a welcome twist.

"Look," Kylee argued. "I know this might make you nervous and you may not let me stay now. I hope it doesn't change your minds though. In fact, it might be beneficial. I know Rand. I realize to you he seems very unreasonable right now. He's really not. I don't know what's gotten into him. He's typically more observant. It's hard to explain but Rand usually has a sixth sense about things. I don't know why he's being so dense about this. But if things get worse, maybe I can talk to him. If he knew I was associated with your family it might make a difference," she shrugged. "I don't know. I'm only hearing your side, but this doesn't sound like Rand at all. Something had to set him off. There has got to be a reason he's so focused on Thomas. Did you guys try to hide something from him?" she asked, knowing she needed to tread lightly.

Abby thought back to their first meeting. Of course they tried to hide something. Thomas was upstairs connected to a bag of blood. "We may have," she said softly.

"Then that's what started it," Kylee said abruptly. "Rand would have picked up on that," then she paused wide eyed. "Oh, you said Thomas was poisoned. He didn't see Thomas hooked to an IV full of blood did he?" she said terrified of their answer.

"Of course not," Abby said defensively. "However, that is what we were hiding. When McBride demanded to see Thomas we couldn't point him to the room and hope he would understand."

Kylee considered the problem. "Rand won't stop until he can rule Thomas out absolutely and completely. Like I said, he has a sixth sense. He would have taken your initial reaction to mean Thomas was hiding something. That you were all hiding something. He won't let that go easily. I'm afraid you guys are right. Once Rand makes up his mind about something it's almost impossible to change it. He is going to pursue Thomas relentlessly until he catches him in the act. For Rand there will be no question Thomas is guilty. Now he just needs proof," she closed her eyes. Why did Rand have to be so stubborn? "I'm sorry. I wish I could help, but under the circumstances I don't think I can. In fact, if I told Rand I was associated with your family I think it might make things worse," Kylee paused. "If Rand knew I was out here, he'd do exactly what you're worried about. He'd be pounding on the door as soon as it was humanly possible to get here. We need to keep him away from the fort."

The room was silent. If Cornelia helped they might be able to solve the murder but the situation somehow seemed more urgent now. Kylee would never forgive Rand if he cost her this opportunity. After everything she'd done to try to gain their trust her association with a cop was going to ruin everything. How ironic.

"I think for now Kylee can stay," Alex finally said. "I know it's dangerous but I still trust her. I hope you don't give me any reason to regret my decision Kylee. I'm putting an awful lot of lives in your hands."

"Thank you," Kylee said sincerely. She would not do anything to make them regret this. She knew Alex was putting a lot of trust in her. She wasn't sure she deserved it, but she was going to do her best to earn back their trust.

Tala watched, interested in the proceedings. She was even more impressed with the queen now after that last exchange. She wouldn't have trusted Kylee if the decision was up to her, even with her mind reading ability. "So Cornelia will stay in New York and work on the murder and Atticus and I will continue to work on his mystery," she looked around the room. She wasn't sure what role her daughter and Tony would play in all of this. "Cornelia will still need a contact. How is she going to keep in touch?"

The group sat silently thinking about a solution to that particular problem.

Thomas finally spoke up. "Jake and I paid Susan Jones' family a visit. They are not happy with the police, especially Detective McBride. Apparently her mother worked for dad for a while. They are convinced I'm innocent and have complained to the Commissioner about the direction the investigation is going. I think I should stay out of this, but Jake could pay them another visit."

"What are you thinking, Thomas?" Alex asked.

"I'm not sure on the details but if the Jones family knew we were willing to provide a PI to look into this, but it had to come from them, I think they'd cooperate. Once we set things up initially I don't think the police would look into it that closely. The Jones' have been causing a stink, in fact they've been very vocal about it. Hiring a PI to look into their daughter's death would seem like a natural progression at this point. I'm confident they would cooperate. It doesn't solve the contact problem, but I think we could at least point the police in the wrong direction."

"That might work," Abby agreed. "I'll call Travis and have him push things from his end. Phone records won't be a problem if everyone believes the Jones family hired Cornelia. Plus, I can hang around a little more and make sure they're not looking our way," she added.

Alex didn't like Abby hanging around the police station, but at this point she didn't really have a choice. Abby was going to do whatever she wanted to do. Alex knew she didn't have the authority to stop her.

"If Tala takes care of the thugs outside, I think Jake and I should visit the Jones family together," Cornelia turned to Tala. "Do you have to leave immediately?"

"We could probably stay a day but no longer," Tala said hesitantly.

"Tony and I are staying with Thomas. Our cover's blown anyway. What do you want from mom, Cornelia?" Megan asked.

"I was thinking once Jake and I met with the Jones family, Tala could make a casual suggestion to McBride. You know, plant the thought that the Jones' hired me. Maybe she could even make him feel annoyed about it. Something to keep him from looking into my activities or employment. He's really the only one we're worried about, right. It doesn't sound like anyone else will question the cover," Cornelia asked.

Shadows

"I can do that," she looked at her mother. "Mom doesn't have to stay for something that simple. She and Atticus were planning on heading up to the Dillinger's old farm after this meeting. Don't change your plans for this," Megan told her.

"Were you planning on sticking around for a while?" Thomas asked Megan. "I don't want you to change any plans on my account."

"Sure," Tony said with a friendly smile. "If you can put up with us for a few more days."

"Okay. I think this might work," Dimitri said feeling a little better about the situation. "Alex and I need to stay in New York for now. Alex is still having problems at work and I think Kylee can take care of any medical emergencies that surface out there. I'd like to keep Alex here just in case we have problems."

Everyone voiced their agreement. "Let's break for now. But we may need to call another conference if anything changes."

The group disbursed. Thomas clicked off the television and surveyed his guests. He was thankful for the help, but felt a little overwhelmed by it. These people were putting their lives on the line to help him. Thomas thought he was very blessed to be surrounded by so many great people. "I don't know what to say," he finally admitted. "There's no way we can ever repay you for your kindness."

"Then don't say anything," Abby told him. "We all know you'd do the same for us."

He would, Thomas thought, but that didn't detract from his gratitude.

Cornelia stood. "I'm going to go track down Jake and arrange a meeting with Mr. and Mrs. Jones," she paused. "Until Megan takes care of the mind tricks I'm going to be extra cautious. I really can't be linked to you in any way, Thomas. It's the only way I'm going to get answers. Even then, the police aren't going to want to give me much."

"I can help with that," Abby told her. "Tell me what you need and I'll get it for you."

"How?" Cornelia asked curiously.

"I'm a shifter," she reminded her. "I can get into the precinct anytime night or day. I've seen where McBride keeps his files. All I have to do is sneak in at night and copy whatever you need. Getting it out is a little more difficult, but I'll manage." Abby was thinking, trying to come up with a solution. "Hey, do you need actual hard copies or could I just take pictures with my phone?"

"Pictures would be fine," Cornelia assured her.

"No problem then," Abby grinned at her. "Dad has an office in the building. I'll have him take my phone and leave it in his desk. Then, I can sneak in at night, grab the file and record everything in it. I'll just leave the phone back in the desk for dad to bring home the following day. He's working on a case for Special Victim's so his presence won't seem suspicious. It might take a couple of days, but you'll have everything McBride has."

"Handy," Cornelia said impressed. "I agree with your previous assessment, having you on our team is going to be very useful."

Shadows

"Why don't you head out first Cornelia?" Tala suggested. "Atticus and I will be right behind you. That way I can make a quick stop at the car for a little mind alteration before we head for the Dillinger's farm."

"Sounds good," Cornelia turned back to Abby. "Let Jake know when you have the phone back. I'll get it from him."

The group left to start working on their respective projects.

Atticus hesitated before heading out the door. "Thomas," he said gently. "Hang in there. I know how it feels to be unfairly accused. You have a lot of good people on your side. Let them help you. I was too proud to let the warriors help me. I've often regretted that. My stubbornness caused a lot of unnecessary pain for me and Victor." He silently slipped out the door.

Chapter Six

Thomas looked at Abby, Megan and Tony. "I guess it's just us, now. Are you interested in breakfast?" he asked no one in particular. "I think I have bacon and eggs."

"Sure," Tony agreed, "I'm starved."

The group headed for the kitchen. Everyone helped and breakfast was on the table in no time. "I appreciate all of you staying on here but I hope you don't get bored," Thomas was concerned. "I spend a lot of time at work these days. There's been a few problems with our managers since dad died."

"I heard they are testing the waters to see what they can get away with," Tony told him. "Victor said Alex is fed up with the games. Are things starting to improve yet?"

Thomas wasn't sure how much to confide in these two, but Tony was close to Victor. They could be trusted. "Not yet. Not

Shadows

really," Thomas admitted. "We haven't had to fire anyone for a couple days. I guess that's something. Maybe word has spread. I hope so. It's difficult to fire good people. It's also difficult to find new ones, good replacements that is. I never would have guessed this could happen. I thought dad's managers were happy and content. Apparently that was only partially true."

"Do you need my help?" Megan inquired. "I could drive around with you all day and plant happy memories in their minds. Visions of sugar plums and beautiful fields of wild flowers. They'll be dancing around joyfully for years to come."

"No thanks," Thomas grunted. "I think I'd prefer the problems to dancing and sugar plums."

Megan laughed. "Well, you passed that test. I'm not like mom. I only use my gift when I have to or I think it's important. Mom tends to use hers as a matter of routine. It helps a lot in her line of business, but I just can't get past the feeling I'm being rude somehow."

"But you and Tony communicate don't you? I'm pretty sure I've witnessed a few private conversations in the past couple days," Abby asked.

"We do," Tony agreed. "But that's different. We do it on purpose and I know when Megan gets in my head. She knows she's welcome any time."

"That makes sense," Abby agreed. "I guess it is different between spouses."

For the next hour, the group chatted casually. Thomas cooked enough bacon and eggs for an army. They inhaled the food and cleared the dishes as they discussed the multitude of problems facing them on so many fronts. Abby moved to the sink to start washing dishes when the doorbell rang.

They all reacted to the sound of the bell. Abby's heart sank. This couldn't be good. It was too early for company. Nobody would be visiting anyway, they just had a long video conference.

"I've got it," Thomas told the group. "Why don't you stay out here? I'm sure this isn't going to be pleasant."

"Not on your life," Tony stood and followed Thomas out of the room. "I want to meet this Detective McBride for myself. I have a feeling we're going to be seeing a lot of each other in the near future."

"I'm coming too," Megan stood to follow. "I need to know who he is in case I need to alter a memory or something."

Abby set the plates in the sink and took up the rear. She wanted to know why McBride was here. She thought she already knew. Alex and Thomas had been so worried about Tiffany Peterson. She assumed the police had finally located the body. Thomas wasn't going to take this well. He already felt guilty about Susan Jones. Adding another victim's body to the list was going to make things worse.

Thomas opened the door and stared at the detective. It suddenly hit him that Jake wasn't here. He knew the man had been warned not to contact him without his attorney again. Was he that cocky to disobey a direct order from his chief? Apparently he was because there he stood on the front door step.

"May I come in?" McBride asked coolly.

Shadows

Thomas didn't respond verbally, he just stepped back and made room for the detective to enter. Then he turned and headed for the library. The rest of the group followed.

"I assume you know why I'm here," McBride asked.

"No. But if history is any indication, I have to assume you located another body," Thomas said without emotion.

"Tell me about your relationship with Tiffany Peterson?" McBride asked. He watched Thomas intently. There it was, the slightest glimmer of recognition in his eyes. Gotcha, McBride thought.

"She was one of my employees," Thomas said with regret. How was he going to face her parents? He had to pay them a visit, personally. Tiffany's family had been so hopeful when Regina's body was found. But deep down they knew it would come to this. There was no way Tiffany ran off without a word to anyone. Even Thomas knew that. He hadn't known the woman well, but he had dealt with her on occasion. She was smart and punctual and very attentive to her duties.

"Anything else?" McBride asked. He was going to catch Thomas if it was the last thing he did.

"No," Thomas assured him. "Isn't that enough? Why is it you immediately jump to the conclusion I was intimately involved with each murder victim?"

McBride shrugged. "I guess because you come across as a rich playboy to me. Someone who thinks he can break all the rules because he's wealthy. Not this time. This time I'm going to stop you. These women have value whether you think so or not." He stopped himself. If he angered these people he'd be answering to the chief again.

Thomas studied the man. He didn't understand Detective McBride. The guy had such resentment and hatred for the wealthy. Had McBride been poor growing up so he disliked anyone with money? Or was this personal? Thomas didn't know, but it really didn't matter.

"To put things plainly Thomas, you are a suspect," Detective McBride concluded. "I'm going to ask you not to leave town for any reason."

Thomas glared at him blankly.

McBride couldn't read any emotion, not anger, not resignation, not guilt. Nothing. What was Thomas thinking? He could usually gage people better than this. Thomas was good. Well, of course he was. He had brutally murdered at least four people. Thomas was a sociopath. He didn't have emotion. This only strengthened McBride's conviction. He had definitely found his man. Now, he just had to prove it. McBride turned to the rest of the room. "You might want to distance yourself from this man. He is my prime suspect in the murder of four people. If, during my investigation, I see you spending excessive amounts of time with Thomas, I am going to have to widen my investigation to include all of you," McBride finished bluntly.

Megan was debating with herself. She hated to intrude, but this man was obnoxious. She was studying him intently. Should she invade his privacy or let it go?

Shadows

McBride turned to Tony and Megan. "I just realized we have not met. I'm going to need your names and current addresses. I also need a number where you can be reached," he studied the couple.

Tony spoke before Megan could respond. "Tony and Megan DeLacy," he paused waiting for a sign of recognition. His family wasn't only famous among the fae. None came. "I'd say our current residence is here for now. We are visiting from Ireland but we'll be staying with Thomas until this situation is resolved. I guess you don't have the phone number here since you stopped by uninvited so early this morning. Maybe Thomas could give it to you before you leave. That way you won't have to be so rude next time someone dies."

"I have the number Mr. DeLacy," McBride narrowed his eyes at the new arrival. "You seem a bit cavalier about that young woman's death. When did you arrive in New York?"

Tony could tell Megan was getting upset. He answered the question before Megan could interject. "My wife and I flew into the city late last evening."

"And prior to that?" McBride requested, "Where were you last week?"

"We were assisting my mother," Megan answered coldly. "Maybe you've heard of her, Tala Fitzgerald." She watched as the man's face grew red with anger. So, he had heard of her mother. Most cops had. "She's working a case here in town and Tony and I thought we'd stick around to assist her. That's when we heard about Thomas and your relentless harassment. Naturally we decided to head right over and see what we could do to help." She smirked a little. The cocky detective didn't like that at all.

"With all due respect, ma'am," McBride said straining to maintain his cool. "You need to leave this matter to the professionals. Thomas may appear innocent to you, but history has demonstrated that sociopaths are good manipulators. Thomas is a dangerous man. Go back to Ireland where it's safe and take your mother with you."

"I'm afraid we can't do that Detective McBride," Megan began. "You see, Thomas is innocent and as such, he is going to need all the help he can get. While the police are focused on him, the real killer or killers get to run around causing havoc throughout this large city. While you focus on Thomas, we will focus on justice."

McBride knew he had to stay calm. He wasn't supposed to be here in the first place but this woman was really pissing him off. And to top off everything he was going to add Tala Fitzgerald to the mix. Things just kept getting better and better. How was he supposed to do his job, prove his case and arrest Thomas when all these obstacles kept getting in the way? "Mrs. DeLacy," McBride began. "I am warning you to stay out of my way. Stay away from Thomas and by all means stay out of my investigation or you will find yourself in jail." McBride glared at the woman. "I am advising you for the last time, go home. Go back to Ireland and have a tea party or something."

What an arrogant prick. "With all due respect detective I'm about as likely to have a tea party as you are," Megan paused.

Tony snorted. Detective McBride had no idea who he was dealing with. He really did enjoy watching his wife at work. She always made him so proud.

Shadows

Megan shot a loving smile at her husband then slowly walked across the room. She stopped in front of McBride, but made sure she invaded his space just a little. "My husband and I, again that is Megan and Tony DeLacy, as well as my mother, Tala Fitzgerald, will be staying here in New York until this mystery is solved." Her closeness was only partially for effect. She could usually get a better read if she was close to her subject. Megan slowly pushed her way into the Detective's mind. What was he up to? Resistance. She hadn't felt that for a long time. Not with a human anyway. No problem, she'd just push a little harder. Not too much, she didn't want to cause damage to this one. Megan concentrated, a little nudge and she was in. Now to see why he had focused so intently on Thomas. Wait, what was that? A hidden compartment? Why had he suppressed something so deeply? She didn't usually pry but under the circumstances they needed everything they could get. Another slight nudge, nothing. He was closed up tight. She could force her way in, but it was sure to cause permanent damage. She wasn't willing to go that far yet. Wait! What was that? Are you...? Hum, now isn't that interesting? Megan quickly exited McBride's mind.

McBride pushed his way past Megan. "Suit yourself," he said trying to sound casual. "Just remember you've been warned. If you get in my way, I won't hesitate to arrest you for obstruction of justice. You might want to warn your mother as well, I don't care who she is. This is my investigation. Don't cross me," he warned, looking from Tony to Megan. "Thomas, I mean it. Don't leave town. I'm not impressed by your money or your influence. I'd love to throw you behind bars, please give me a reason." He silently stalked out of the room and through the front door. Thomas, Megan and Tony listened as the detective's unmarked car sped out of the drive.

Megan turned her attention back to the room. Abby hadn't said a word throughout the entire exchange. She addressed her first. "He's afraid of you," Megan began studying Abby until she looked up. "He knows he shouldn't be here and you have such a connection to his boss. It pisses him off, but he's afraid of you. I think we might be able to use that if we need to."

"I kind of assumed that, but it's nice to have it verified," Abby looked at Megan in wonder. What a cool gift she had. Abby immediately thought of Thomas. If only she could get into his mind and know what he thought of her. Or if he thought of her at all. Don't be stupid Abby. He doesn't think of you. Stop fantasizing about something that could never be.

Megan turned to Thomas. "He doesn't have anything concrete on you," she smiled at his annoyance. "Okay, I know he couldn't because you didn't kill those women, but I'm just saying there is not one ounce of evidence that points to you. He just didn't like the way this family acted the first day he arrived. He also has some religious conviction about money corrupting or some nonsense like that. He got it from his parents. All of which has him obsessed with you as his only possible suspect. He's pretty determined to bring you down. He saw something in your eyes today, some sort of recognition when he mentioned Tiffany. Whatever it was, reaffirmed his conviction all over again. He's not going to stop harassing you. This will only get worse unless we can track down the real killer," she shrugged. "I just thought you might want to know where you stand."

"Thanks," Thomas said gloomily. "Like Abby, I sort of already guessed that but at least now we know for sure."

"There's something else," Megan said hesitantly.

Shadows

"What?" Tony asked curiously.

"It was difficult for me to get in. More so than it should have been. Humans are typically easy targets for a shadow. Anyway, once inside I found a hidden compartment so to speak. A place McBride hides a very dark secret. Or at least he thinks of those memories that way. I'm not sure what he is but, after my experience in his mind, I can say with certainty he is not human."

"What?" Thomas asked surprised. "Then what is he?"

"I don't know," Megan said shaking her head. "I didn't have enough time, plus I pushed as hard as I was comfortable with. Any more and I could have done some serious damage. Whatever the secret is, he thinks it's evil and unnatural. Again, something his parents taught him. I get the impression they are very, very religious. Fanatically so. Anyway, he could be anything. Shifter, fae, warrior even. I just don't know. I know he's not a vamp if that helps. I can't even get into a vampires head. Maybe they don't have minds," she smirked. "Most of them are pretty stupid."

"We'll save that discussion for another day," Tony told her. "So our pesky detective is something supernatural," he mused. "That's very interesting. It might also explain why he's so focused on Thomas."

"How so?" Thomas asked.

"Megan says he's hiding what he is. It's a secret and it's bad. His mum and dad told him the supernatural world is evil and unnatural," Tony paused. "Are those the words you used, hon?"

"Those are the words I extracted from his brain, yes," Megan corrected.

"We are all supernatural," Tony concluded.

"And?" Abby pressed.

"And," Tony continued, "I think he would have sensed that. Maybe not consciously, but everyone in this room knows you can sense another supernatural being. I knew Abby was a shifter immediately. Thomas, there is no way you could hide the fact that you're a warrior from me or Megan or Abby. If McBride is one of us, he's going to sense what you are. You too, Abby. As well as me and Megan. I didn't do anything, but he immediately began questioning me about my whereabouts. Like I was a new suspect. He sensed I'm different and went on the offensive. I think Megan might be right. Detective Rand McBride belongs in our world. He doesn't like it, but he's one of us. The thing that intrigues me the most is that we didn't sense him."

"I need to talk to Dimitri about this. We need to keep an eye on McBride. Could he be a shadow?" Thomas asked Megan, concerned.

"No," Megan assured him. "That is one thing I am sure of. If he was, he would have known I was in there immediately and I would have sensed he knew. I think it's more likely he's either some kind of shifter or he's fae," Megan guessed. "I'm almost positive we can rule out warrior," she paused. "It was difficult to get in, but not the way it is on a warrior. None of us can enter the mind of a seasoned warrior, not even mom and there's nobody better than she is at gaining access when she's determined. No, I'd be very surprised if he was a warrior even with his denial," she said confidently.

Abby needed to talk to her father. Was it possible to be a shifter and not know, or to hide it completely? Shifters could identify each other. They had a distinct smell. But so did the fae. If McBride was supernatural, she had missed it completely. That didn't sit well with her. That shouldn't even be possible. "Uh, I need to go home and pack a few things and do some laundry. Anyone mind if I head out?" she asked casually.

"No," Thomas said. "Go ahead, I need to head to the office anyway," he turned to Tony and Megan. "You two going to be okay here alone? I probably won't be back until late this evening."

"We're fine," Tony answered. "I wanted to show Megan around town anyway. It seems like a nice day, maybe we'll go sight-seeing."

The group split up, each eager to start their day.

* * * *

Atticus and Tala walked quietly through the old farmhouse. The kitchen was a mess. There was rotting food in the refrigerator. The Dillinger's hadn't lived here for at least twenty years. Atticus believed Lawson must have been staying here until recently. They left the kitchen and headed for the living area. One bedroom was empty, but the second room was furnished. Again, Atticus assumed that was Lawson's doing. Foster had cut his older brother off financially a while ago. Lawson would believe this place belonged to him since he was the oldest son. He wouldn't think twice about taking up residency.

"What a pig," Tala said under her breath. "How can they live like this?" she asked in disgust.

"I think Lawson's probably been staying here. He never did have what you would call high standards," Atticus said with a grin.

"High standards? This guy doesn't have any standards at all," Tala corrected.

The two of them reached another door. Tala assumed it led to a basement. She tried to turn the knob, but it was locked. She jiggled it again, nothing. "That's strange," she turned to Atticus. "What could he possibly have down there that he wants to keep secure?"

Atticus shrugged. "Why don't we go see?" he said reaching in and playing with the lock. Tala took a step back to give him more room. She had lock picking tools, but she wanted to let Atticus give it a try first. She was a little surprised when the door flew open and Atticus held out a hand for her to proceed. Tala pulled a small flashlight from her purse and took a cautious step forward. Nothing. She took another, still nothing. The basement looked dark. She slowly proceeded until she was standing on the landing at the bottom of the large staircase.

Tala swung her flashlight around, searching for any sign the place had electricity. She felt Atticus' arm brush hers as he casually reached behind her and flipped a small switch on the wall. The dingy basement immediately filled with light. "Apparently you've been here before," she observed, hoping he wouldn't notice how breathless she sounded after such a simple touch. Why her body found the man so potent was a mystery, not to mention annoying.

"Unfortunately I have," he said studying the large open basement. Nothing had really changed. George Dillinger, his former father- in- law, spent a lot of time down in this dungeon of a basement. George thought he was a master chemist. In reality, he was just a crazy old man that didn't want to work for a living. Atticus heard that after Dannica's death, George had become obsessed with his potions. That's how he eventually blew himself up. Atticus was surprised he hadn't blown up the farmhouse as well. From what he remembered George rarely worked in the barn. He preferred the comforts of this dark, dirty basement.

"I think I lost you somewhere back there," Tala observed.

"Maybe a little," Atticus smiled. "Lost in unpleasant memories, that's all. So, where do you want to begin?"

"You knew these people, do you have any suggestions?" Tala asked.

"George, that's Lawson and Foster's father, spent most of his free time down here. This was his workspace," Atticus looked around. "But it looks like Lawson has taken over while he's been living here. Maybe we should call Ty and see what we should be looking for," he suggested.

"Ty?" Tala wracked her brain trying to remember who Ty was.

"Yeah," Atticus said heading towards the long work bench. "Ty's an expert in explosives. I'm wondering if this is where Lawson built his bombs. Ty would know what we should be looking for."

"Oh," Tala vaguely remembered hearing about a warrior that worked in explosives. To be honest she was thinking about adding him to the suspect list. "Maybe we should do this on our own," she suggested. "At this point, Ty should be on your suspect list. Is he in the close friend column or the acquaintances column?" she inquired without emotion.

Atticus spun around and stared at her. "You think Ty is a suspect?" he demanded, offended at the very thought. "Ty saved my life. He's risked his own life every time one of those bombs has been planted. Ty is not a suspect. You can just get that out of your head right now," he told her stubbornly.

"I'm afraid I can't take your word for it. If it was up to you, two thirds of the people on that list would be eliminated. That's not the way I solve cases, Atticus. Ty stays," she said with finality.

"Ty might stay on your list, but he's not on mine." Atticus turned and pulled out his phone.

Tala approached him and saw Atticus was scrolling through numbers. She realized it must be his address book but before she could stop him, he pressed an entry and moved the phone to his ear.

"Hey Ty," Atticus said cheerfully. "It's Atticus. I'm sorry to bother you. Are you busy?"

"Hey Atticus," Ty said enthusiastically. "No bother. What's up?"

"Well, Tala and I are out here at the old Dillinger farm." He paused when he saw Tala put her hands over her face in exasperation. He shook his head and continued. "I think this might be where Lawson was making his bombs, but I'm not sure what kind of evidence I should be looking for. Can you help us?"

"Sure," Ty said a little more seriously. "You are being careful, right? I mean, he could have the place booby trapped or something. You two are taking precautions to make sure you don't set anything off, right?" Ty pressed.

"Uh...yeah," Atticus said swinging around to see where Tala had gone. "Don't touch that!" he called out to her when she reached for a long handle fastened to the bench.

"Atticus!" Ty called. "Why don't you two go check out something else and I'll head up to the farmhouse and see what I can find?"

"No. That's okay," Atticus said relieved Tala had stopped when she did. He was now facing an angry woman, but that was better than getting blown up. "We're fine here. I just need you to tell me what to look for."

Ty took a deep breath then gave in. He was pretty busy today and if Atticus said he could handle it, Ty was going to trust his judgment. "How about I text you a list of items. Between the two of you I'm sure you can identify all of them."

"Perfect," Atticus agreed. "You send the list and if I have any questions, I'll call you back. Thanks kid," he said sincerely. "I appreciate your help on this."

"No problem," Ty assured him.

"Yeah. No problem because he knows what he left behind," Tala mumbled under her breath.

Atticus laughed. "I'm going to let you go. I'm in trouble with the boss. Tala thinks you're a suspect and I just gave away our location and our plans. Do me a favor, don't drive up here with a chainsaw and chase us around the house laughing sadistically, okay?"

"What?" Ty said in surprise. "She doesn't really believe that does she?"

Atticus laughed. "Not seriously, well I don't think so anyway. She's just being obstinate. I'll call you if I have questions. Thanks again for the help." Atticus slipped the phone closed and turned to Tala. "Now for you," he said heading her way. "Ty said to watch for booby traps. I can only assume that there handle is a booby trap," he smiled when Tala swung her head around and stared at the contraption.

Tala bent down and studied the handle closer. It *was* a booby trap. She glanced back at Atticus then circled around to get a better look from the other side. "That could have been bad," she finally admitted. "Look, you pull this handle and that little spring shoots that thing over there onto that contraption thingy," she paused.

"Please, slow down. Your technical terms are confusing me." He smiled as she narrowed her eyes at him. "I'm joking," he said defensively. "Lighten up a little. Are you always so serious about everything?"

Tala turned away. She was always serious. Why did his observation bother her so much? Why did she want Atticus Keisser to see her as fun and spontaneous? She was neither. "Okay, I'm all loose and jovial. Now that we've covered that, can we get back to work?" she asked shortly.

"Oh, yeah," Atticus laughed. "You're a barrel of monkeys all right," he glanced back at the bench. "Why don't I take this area and you can start over there," he paused. "Watch for traps. Lawson could have more of them around here."

Tala walked cautiously to the other side of the room. Her attention was immediately caught by a small stack of papers. She picked up the first sheet and studied it. Across the top was written "Paladin," then there were rows of scribbling. Something scientific that Tala didn't understand. She turned to Atticus. He was studying a small box. She rushed back over to him and stopped. "What's that?" she asked as she set the papers on top of the bench.

Atticus looked at her then studied the box again. "I'm not sure," he told her. "I can't access it from here. I don't have the right tools." He took a step to the side as Tala gripped the box and began playing with the lock.

"I don't think I can either. We'll have to take it with us." Tala sighed, she never liked to remove items from a scene. She was an investigator, not a burglar.

"I agree," Atticus spotted a piece of cord lying on the ground. "Do you have a bag or something for evidence?" he asked. He never took his eyes off the cord.

Tala reached into her purse and pulled out a large Ziploc bag. She pulled it open and looked around. "Right here. Why?" she asked still not seeing what Atticus thought was evidence.

Atticus pulled a pair of tweezers from his pocket. He crouched down, reached under the bench and pulled out the small piece of cord. He slowly stood and dropped the debris into the bag.

Tala studied it through the plastic. "I guess it kind of looks like det cord," she admitted, then she shrugged. "Can't hurt I guess.

Is there any way to know if that is the same cord that was used in the bombs?" she asked.

"Sure," Atticus assured her. "The council has several of them locked away in a safe place."

"What do you mean?" Tala asked. "Do they have unexploded bombs in their possession? If they've gone off, the det cord will be gone."

"Thanks to Ty they do," he said a little too cocky for Tala's liking but she ignored it. "Hey," Atticus said when he finally spotted the paper Tala had set on the large bench. "What's this?" He studied the diagrams then looked at the large writing printed across the top. "What's a pale-ladin?" he asked.

"I think it's Pal-a-din," she corrected. "And I don't know, I was hoping you could tell me. I've never heard of it."

"Nope," Atticus admitted. "I have no idea. Do you think that's a real word or something George made up?"

"I don't know," Tala admitted. "We'll check when we get back to the room," Tala continued studying the large space.

They both jumped when Atticus' phone beeped. He pulled it out and studied the screen. Then he handed it to Tala. "Here's our shopping list," he said as she took the phone. "I know what most of that is. Let's see how many items on that list we can find in this workspace," he looked around the area. "Keep that bag handy. Here are a couple more things we should take." Before moving on Atticus slipped the mysterious paper into the bag as well.

"Why is that evidence?" Tala asked skeptically.

Shadows

"Because I need Bastian to look at it," Atticus said simply. "He can't look if we don't take it."

"I'm not a thief," Tala objected. "Curiosity isn't a valid reason to walk off with Lawson's personal property."

"Actually, that's George's personal property," he corrected. "I recognize the hand writing." He grinned at Tala's frustrated look. "Don't worry. I have just as much right to those documents as Lawson or Foster. I personally believe that particular sheet is part of Victor's rightful inheritance. If Lawson or Foster disagrees, they can file a petition with the council to have me turn it back over to them immediately. Even if the council rules against me, it's not criminal, it's a civil matter. The same holds true for anything else I decide to take from this property," he paused. "Relax Tala, you're not going to get arrested for burglary."

How did he know what she was thinking? She was the shadow, not him. She did relax a little at the news though. She'd never stolen anything in her life. She was very careful when she agreed to take a case. That wouldn't change just because her current client was the most attractive man she'd ever met.

The two worked for several more hours, occasionally placing items into the bag. Once that one was full, Tala pulled out another. By the time they left, they had three bags full of potential evidence. They were both satisfied they would not need to return to the property again.

Atticus sat in the passenger's seat perplexed by the woman at his side. He'd finally begun to relax around her. Oh, he still blocked her from accessing his mind, but even that was getting easier. They seemed to work well together. He had no doubt the bombs had been made in that basement. What he didn't know was if Lawson had developed them himself or if Foster had some part in all of this. Then there was Patricia. What was her role in the whole thing? They still had a lot of questions to answer. But at least he was beginning to trust Tala. She seemed to know what she was doing and they were already further along than he had really hoped for. He just hoped he could keep his attraction to the complex woman in check. She didn't seem like the type that would welcome personal feelings into her investigation.

* * * *

Thomas and Abby sat in the cozy study playing card games. Abby was surprised at Thomas' good mood. He seemed relaxed and playful this evening. After their early morning visit that was the last thing she'd expected. Once she left the house, she'd tracked down her father. They had a lengthy discussion about the recent developments, but she hadn't gotten a definite answer to her question. Mason had explained that if a shifter never shifted or hadn't shifted for years, he may not put off the shifter scent. Or the scent might be very faint. He told her not to worry about it. She was young and as she got older even dormant shifters would be obvious. Mason wasn't convinced McBride was a shifter, anyway. The sticking point was Travis Monroe. Travis was very old, older than her father. As a pack leader, a dormant shifter shouldn't be able to avoid detection by Monroe. Abby's father agreed to talk to his old friend about the situation but told her not to get her hopes up. If McBride was supernatural, he was probably fae.

Thomas cleared his throat. "Earth to Abby," he said jokingly.

"Sorry," she smiled, shaking off the confusing thoughts rushing through her head. "I was just thinking about my

Shadows

conversation with dad this morning. But I'm finished, I'd rather not talk about unpleasant things right now." She picked up a card and smiled. Then she laid down her hand triumphantly. "Rummy," she said as she grinned enthusiastically across the table.

Thomas groaned. "Not again," he set his cards down face up so Abby could see his hand. One more card and he would have won. "You have better luck than anyone I know." He glanced down at their glasses and realized they were both almost empty. "You ready for another soda?" he asked.

"No thanks," Abby declined. "If I drink anymore Coke I'll be wired all night. I'll never get to sleep."

Thomas started to respond then stopped when the doorbell rang. He glanced at the clock, knowing a visitor this late could not be good news.

"I'll get it," Abby rose and started for the door.

Thomas put a hand on her arm. "No Abby," he stopped her. "This is my problem. I'll handle it." He gave her a little smile. "You can't protect me all the time."

Abby studied Thomas for a short moment then nodded once in agreement. She watched with mixed feelings as he exited the room. Her arm was still tingling from his touch. As Thomas disappeared around the corner Abby sighed. She knew she was in love with him. Spending time with him like this just made her love him even more. The naïve optimist in her wished they could do this every night. She closed her eyes and sighed again. Daydreams were going to have to wait. He may not allow her to protect him, but she was going to stand by his side and assist him.

Abby exited the study and stopped. She'd expected McBride, but it was Alex and Dimitri. "Oh," she let out a soft gasp. She relaxed a little until she saw Alex's face. It was bad news after all. Then it hit her, someone they knew was missing.

"Who?" Thomas asked, also reading his sister's grim expression. "Who is it this time?"

"Let's go into the study, Thomas," Dimitri ordered.

The group walked silently back into the room. Abby couldn't bare the contrast between the jovial mood a few minutes ago and the somber atmosphere of the moment. When would this nightmare end?

"I know it's bad," Thomas said immediately. "Just tell me who it is, Alex. We're going to have to deal with it sooner or later. It might as well be now."

Alex took a deep breath then began to cry. "Angela's missing," she whispered. "Her mother just called. As soon as I got off the phone we headed over," she looked up at Thomas hating to see the pain in his eyes. "I'm so sorry, Thomas. I wish it was anyone but her."

Who was Angela? Obviously she was somebody important to Thomas. Abby would never forget this moment as long as she lived. Pain radiated in his eyes and an agonizing look of torture quickly spread across his face. The tangy odor of despair instantly filled the room. It was so thick, Abby's throat hurt. She reached out and silently swallowed the last of her soda.

Thomas slowly sank into the chair behind him. He was in shock. Not Angie. He closed his eyes and lowered his head into the palms of his hands. How could this happen? He'd left her to protect her and now she was going to die because of him. He wanted to scream, he wanted to lash out. Mostly, he wanted to cry.

Alex walked across the room and knelt in front of Thomas. She was still sobbing. Angela was such a sweet, energetic woman. She'd spent a lot of time at the house during Thomas' teen years. Alex didn't know what happened between Angela and Thomas, but she had always liked Angie. Now she was going to die. Alex couldn't deny it. They all knew they couldn't save her. She was mostly worried about Thomas. How was he going to take this? He was already feeling so guilty. Thomas had loved Angela. Just because they ended their relationship a long time ago, didn't mean he had forgotten her. She pulled Thomas into a tight hug. "I don't know how to help you with this," she whispered softly.

Thomas tried to comfort Alex. He rubbed her back as she held him. She couldn't help him with this. He needed to be alone. He was suffocating. "You can't help," he finally told her. "I need time. I hate to be rude, but I'd really like to be alone for a while."

Alex lifted her head and studied him. She knew Thomas, she'd grown up with him. He was going to lock himself away and avoid everyone even remotely close to him. Then he'd convince himself this was all his fault. The guilt was going to eat away at him until he was completely destroyed. She wasn't sure he was going to pull out of this one. She wished her mother was here. Marlena could always give Thomas what he needed to work through a problem. Alex wanted to scream. She felt helpless. Every day she felt like more of a failure. "Okay," she nodded. "I'll give you time tonight."

"Thanks," Thomas said sincerely.

"But only for tonight Thomas," Alex warned. "I'm not going to let you shut yourself off and wallow in your guilt. If I sense, even a little, that you are blaming yourself for this, I'm moving back here. I won't let you take responsibility for something that's not your fault. I know you, the burden will destroy you. I'll move back in and I'll pester you every minute of every day until you snap out of it." She stood and walked to Dimitri. "Let's go home," she told him.

Dimitri studied Thomas. He walked across the room and stopped in front of his friend. "Alex is right. I understand grief for a friend. But if you take this on yourself, even for one minute, you are going to answer to me," he smiled. "As much as I like the idea of Alex tormenting you, I'm not going to be happy if she moves back to the mansion."

Thomas stood and gripped Dimitri's hand. "Thank you for coming over so quickly," he paused. "I really appreciate it. I'm fine. You two go home. I'll be okay here."

"I'm coming back to check on you tomorrow. Don't think you can fool me. I know you too well," Alex warned.

Abby didn't move. She sat motionless as Alex and Dimitri left the room, wondering what she should do now. Once the door shut Thomas turned toward her. "I'm sorry, Abby. This is a shock. I really do need some time to myself. Will you excuse me?"

Abby could see Thomas was suffering. He was putting on a good face, but she'd gotten to know him over the last few weeks. It broke her heart to see him hurting like this and not be able to comfort him. She stood and moved forward until she was standing directly in front of him. "I assume this Angela is somebody you are close to. I'm sorry, Thomas. I wish we had stopped this before it touched so close to home. I'll be fine. Go do whatever you need to do," she leaned in and gave him a quick hug.

Thomas turned and left the room. He didn't like bailing on Abby, but he couldn't pick up where they left off either. Angela had been abducted by a monster. Her days were numbered. He couldn't casually sit in the study and entertain company. He wanted to run out and search for her. He wanted to find the monster responsible and kill him, slowly and methodically. He wanted to do something. Thomas turned and punched a hole in the wall. He couldn't just sit here, but he couldn't leave either. He looked out the window and decided to head for the gym. Had Alex left any of her droids here? That might help. He'd fight one of them and imagine he was battling the killer. Thomas changed into his favorite workout clothes and headed for the basement.

Abby heard Thomas close his door and head downstairs. She listened to see if he left the house or if he was just going somewhere to hole up inside. She didn't hear the front door, so she assumed he was staying home. At least she didn't have to worry about his safety but still, it was going to be a very long, restless night.

* * * *

Radek sat in the dark finishing his dinner. He couldn't be happier. Everything was finally coming together at last. His plan was twofold, he had the secret weapon here in the city. That was working even better than he could have imagined. The warriors were preoccupied and scattered. The only downside was the fact that all his vampires were away trying to multiply his numbers. If he had enough of them here, Radek thought they could easily take out a few of the warriors. It was annoying, but that couldn't be helped now. He looked at Lilith. Since Hector's death their partnership had improved. That made him even more suspicious. It was a shame she was going to have to be eliminated. Radek refused to think about that now. He wanted to enjoy Lilith until the very end. He wanted to celebrate his success. Once he had hundreds of vampires under his rule they would attack. He'd need to develop a plan. They would have to choose their targets wisely. He glanced back at Lilith, she was watching him. She looked amused. He narrowed his eyes at her and scowled.

"Awe, don't get mad. I was just enjoying the sight of you so deep in thought. You looked content. I haven't seen you like this for a long time. This is going to work, isn't it?" she said enthusiastically. "Things are actually going our way this time. The warriors are divided and vulnerable and our vampires are building a monstrous army. In no time at all we are going to have the upper hand," she smiled with excitement. "I can't wait for the attack," she paused. "Have you thought about how you want to handle that? The final attack that is?"

Radek smiled. They were so alike. Too bad she couldn't behave. They really would have made a great pair. Lilith would have been the perfect vampire queen. He smiled at her. "I have a few thoughts. I think we should begin working on a detailed plan tonight. But first, I'm still a little hungry. Have Sammael bring me the girl. "

Lilith stood and walked to the door. Once she relayed Radek's wishes to Sammael she slowly moved toward him. When she reached the large chair, she climbed onto his lap. "Maybe we could celebrate first then get started on the plan. Sammael said the girl's pretty weak. It's going to take him awhile to get her here. I think we have enough time for a little fun," Lilith grinned mischievously.

Shadows

* * * *

Tony and Megan looked up when Thomas walked into the room. He looked terrible. He hadn't been himself for days. News of Angela's abduction had hit him hard. Alex was stopping in to check on him daily. Megan wondered if that was making things worse. He always seemed more depressed when she left.

"Hey," he greeted the couple. "Where's Abby?"

"She went out," Tony said casually.

"What do you mean?" Thomas glanced out the window, it was already dark. "Abby shouldn't be out this late at night. It's not safe," he was worried, which made him angry. Abby had more sense than that.

"Thomas," Megan said softly. "She's a shifter. She'll be fine."

Thomas took a deep breath. Megan was right. Abby was more than capable of taking care of herself. He just wondered where she had gone. He'd been looking forward to seeing her. The time he spent with Abby seemed to be the only thing these days that brought him pleasure. She had a calming effect on him somehow. After the trouble at work, the constant worry and the guilt he felt with Angela missing, he needed his time with Abby. Somehow she helped settle his tumultuous emotions each night.

Tony gave Megan a knowing look. They both thought Thomas had feelings for Abby, he just didn't realize it yet. They were rooting for the couple. Hopefully the current situation wouldn't prevent them from realizing what a connection the two had. All three of them jumped at the sound of the doorbell.

Thomas took a deep breath and turned to head for the door.

"No," Tony said pushing himself off the couch. "I'm going to get this one."

"Thanks but I've got it," Thomas took a step forward. "This is my problem, not yours."

"It's all of our problem," Tony corrected. "And I'm getting the door so sit down. I'm not asking."

Thomas stared at his guest in amazement. Tony was always so cordial and friendly. If it meant that much to him, Thomas guessed he should let him go. He sat in a nearby chair anxiously waiting to see who was visiting this time. He was terrified it was going to be McBride again. He hadn't heard from the guy in over a week. Angela had been missing for three days now. If the killer held to his pattern, her body would be found in the next few days.

Megan and Thomas were surprised when Tony walked in with Cornelia.

"Do you have news?" Megan asked anxiously.

"Not really. Sorry I haven't checked in for a while. I've been staying away to avoid detection from the cops. They're relaxing surveillance on the house though. I assume they can't afford the twenty four hour watch anymore. It's not helping anyway. So, I thought I'd come by and check in personally."

"If you don't have news, why did you want to check in?" Thomas asked.

Shadows

"I just thought you would like to know our cover is working. The police think I'm working for the Jones'. Susan's parents are also keeping the pressure on. I think the police have their hands full right now. The media is demanding answers. They want to know why the killer hasn't been caught yet. I knew this would happen and it makes things easier for me. People are viewing the local cops as incompetent. They're more than happy to tell me anything I want to know. Unfortunately, nobody really knows anything useful. None of the victims have similar patterns. The first victim, Diana, didn't work for Deveraux Industries and neither did Regina. It would appear the other victim's employment may be relevant, but I'm still not convinced of that."

"I am," Thomas said quietly.

"I heard about that," Cornelia said somberly. "Thomas, I know it's easy to personalize this. Anyone would have a tendency to think somehow all of this was their fault. It's not. Sure, you dated Diana a couple of times, but what about Regina? How do you explain her murder? How does that one have anything to do with you?"

"I haven't figured that out yet," Thomas admitted.

"You and me both. Until I find a connection that links all the victims, I'm operating on the assumption the murders are random. The only link is the fact that they are all women. You should do the same," she told Thomas.

Thomas studied her. The woman actually believed what she was saying. It didn't help Angela, but he hoped she was right. He hoped the women weren't being targeted because of him. He thought that was impossible, but for now he was going to hope Cornelia was right.

Cornelia lowered herself into a chair and began to fill the group in on her progress.

Abby silently entered the front door. She was tired and didn't want to visit with anyone tonight. She hesitated, debating. Go upstairs to bed, or stop in at the study? She heard voices and knew everyone was inside. She wanted to go to bed, but she couldn't do it. She couldn't avoid everyone like that. It just felt rude.

Thomas looked up as Abby stepped into the doorway. She looked tired. He wondered again where she had been. "Hey Abby," he greeted.

"Hey," she answered. "I just thought I'd stop in and let you know I'm here. I'm pretty tired so I'm going to head straight to bed," she glanced at Cornelia briefly then turned to leave.

Thomas stood and walked to the door. "Are you okay?" he asked softly. "You look exhausted." He reached out and gently brushed a wayward strand of hair from her face.

"I'm alright," she forced a smile. "It's just been a long day. I'll see you tomorrow," Abby walked out of the room and continued up the stairs. She wished that gentle act by Thomas meant something, but deep down she knew it didn't. He was just being Thomas, nothing more.

Thomas watched until Abby entered the guest room and closed the door behind her. That wasn't like her. He wondered if something was wrong. Was she really just tired or was something else going on? He hesitated momentarily, then reluctantly turned and rejoined the group.

Shadows

* * * *

Emma Miller sat on the edge of her couch studying the photos spread out across her coffee table. How had this woman gotten so close to Timmy? They paid for him to go to a good school because they thought he would be safe there. They paid a lot. But here were photos of this woman on the playground with him, walking him to the bus and there were even shots of the two of them in her own backyard. Emma was horrified that her child could be so vulnerable.

"Just speak to your husband when he gets home tonight," the woman suggested. "You know what I need and you know what's at stake. I really hope you won't let me down," she stood and headed for the door.

Emma didn't move. She continued to sit frozen, in complete shock as the woman silently slipped out the door. What were they going to do?

* * * *

Lawson glared at his mother when she walked into the room. "Where have you been?" He demanded. "I'm busy mother, I don't have time to sit around all day waiting for you."

Patricia hung her coat on the tree and turned to her eldest son. "I had things to do," she said casually. "I realize you and Foster think I sit around all day wasting time, but I do have a life. I have things that need to be handled. I was handling them."

232

Lawson realized he wasn't going to get a straight answer out of her, so he dropped it. She was probably having her hair done or something.

"Did you get me another girl?" Patricia asked casually.

"Actually," Lawson paused, "I got two. They're in the lab."

Patricia brightened with anticipation. "Two? How wonderful. But why? I thought you said more than one was too risky."

Lawson shrugged. "Because you insisted I get someone that's into exercise and she had to be at least thirty. I believe we will have more success with a young, energetic girl. I thought we'd try a little experiment. I picked one to your specifications. She's an aerobics instructor in her mid-thirties. The other is to my specifications. She is around twenty and works as a waitress at a busy restaurant," he smiled coyly. "We'll test them both at the same time and see who lasts longer," he told her. "If we're lucky, we were both right and we'll have two paladins instead of one. We can't lose either way."

Patricia liked it. A little competition and like Lawson said, they win either way. "It's perfect," she said, anxious to get started.

Lawson narrowed his eyes at his mother. "No cheating," he warned. "I'll know if you cheat. We treat both specimen's the same. They get the same formula, the same quantity, everything."

"Of course," Patricia said appalled. "I can't believe you think I would cheat at this. It's too important. The idea of bringing two girls along at the same time is fascinating and exciting. I want to see them." She turned and headed for the lab, Lawson following close behind.

Shadows

* * * *

Foster opened the door to the penthouse and froze. Lawson was here again. The smell of cigarette hit him first, then he heard voices in the back room. What were they up to now? He silently crept down the hall to eavesdrop.

Patricia felt giddy. "This is going to be so much fun, Lawson."

"Yes mother," Lawson agreed, amused at her excitement. "But don't get so excited you overdue it," he warned. "The girls are knocked out right now. I drugged them to get them here. Once they come around they're not going to be happy. We sound proofed the room. Make sure you always close the door." He glanced at the open door then back at his mother. "It can't be like the others. These two need to last."

She waved his disapproving look aside. "I'm not a child Lawson," she scolded. "I know we need to keep the noise inside this room. I was just so excited to see them. When can I start the experiments?"

Foster was horrified. His mother and his brother had two women locked up in that room. And they were planning on using them to experiment? Had they gone completely mad? He had to get out of here. Foster moved quickly down the hallway, careful not to make any noise. When he reached the front door, he looked around the room then silently slid it open and moved into the apartment's main corridor. Once he was out of that awful house he practically ran to the elevator and out the door. He needed air. Was his mother and Lawson responsible for the New York killings?

Were they the serial killers the police were searching for? For the first time in his life he didn't know what to do. He couldn't think. He couldn't focus. He walked to his car and mechanically slid inside, started the engine and drove to his new home. He needed to think. The business was going to have to make do without him today. He couldn't think about business. He needed to decide what to do about his family.

* * * *

Abby sat in the large study alone. She knew Thomas would be here soon. She couldn't avoid him forever. She was torn. She loved spending time with him, she loved him. But he had been so depressed and uptight ever since Alex told him that girl was missing. She still didn't know the extent of that relationship. Maybe Angela was Thomas' girlfriend. That would explain the way he was acting. If that was the case, she was doomed. She knew it was a long shot, but lately she'd thought they might have a chance. Until Angela's abduction anyway. Now she had to accept what she'd been trying to avoid. She and Thomas were only friends. They would never be anything more. The question now was what to do about it.

Thomas walked into the study and relaxed. Abby was here tonight. She still looked tired, but he thought her presence was a good sign. "Are you sure you're feeling okay, Abby?" he asked her. "You just don't seem like yourself lately."

Abby forced a smile. "I'm alright. I guess everything is just starting to catch up to me. I've been a little more tired than usual the last couple days. Don't worry, really I'm fine."

Shadows

"Can I get you anything?" Thomas asked as he walked to the corner bar and poured himself a brandy. He was exhausted himself. They still hadn't heard anything about Angela. The waiting was going to kill him.

"Maybe some wine," she told him. "Not much. It will make me even sleepier." Maybe the wine would give her enough of a buzz to help her relax.

Thomas handed the wine to Abby then sat down across from her. "So, you went to bed last night before I could tell you why Cornelia was here. She said the police are relaxing their watch a little. The community is putting pressure on them to find the killer. Maybe McBride has finally realized I couldn't have taken those girls," he said optimistically.

Abby hated to dash his hopes, but McBride hadn't given up yet. He was still focused on Thomas. She studied him, not knowing what to say.

"No?" he asked. "I assume you've still been tracking him. And I also assume your silence and that look on your face means he's still as stubborn as he always was."

"I'm afraid so," she said regretfully. "Monroe's not the only one putting pressure on him these days. The Commissioner isn't happy about the community outrage. He can't explain why his detective hasn't found the man responsible yet. McBride is stressed and as tired as we are, but he's still focused on you," she hesitated. "And me."

"I'm sorry," Thomas told her. "Why don't you get away from this for a while?" he suggested. "I don't have a choice, but he's focusing on you because you're here with me. Maybe a little space would divert his attention. Maybe he'd forget you and just focus on me."

"You don't want me here?" Abby asked before she could stop herself. She felt a little hurt by the suggestion.

"Of course I want you here," Thomas assured her. "I think your company is the only thing that is keeping me sane throughout this whole mess," he studied her. "I just thought you might need a break. I can tell you're tired and I'm not sure it's just a long day. I think the stress and constant pressure is taking a toll. I just thought maybe you wanted a break but didn't know how to back out gracefully. I'd understand if you wanted to leave," he told her. He hoped she wouldn't. What he said was true. She was the only one keeping him sane.

"I'm staying," Abby assured him. Why did she say that? He had just given her an out and she hadn't taken it. Was she masochistic or what?

Before Thomas could respond, the doorbell rang. The two took a deep breath at the same time and headed for the foyer. Thomas knew it wouldn't do any good to ask her to stay in the study. He pulled the large wooden door open expecting to find McBride but instead he saw a family of three standing on the doorstep. He knew the man, who was he? "Hello," Thomas said racking his brain trying to remember the guy's name.

"Mr. Deveraux," Jason Miller began. "I don't know if you remember me. My name is Jason Miller and I manage Sports Etc. for Deveraux Industries."

That's it, Thomas thought. "Yes, of course," he said as he motioned for the small family to enter. "You helped me pick out

Shadows

my first Yankee's t-shirt," he smiled at the man. "Come into the study and tell me what I can do for you." Thomas ushered the man, his wife and a small child into the large room.

Abby wasn't sure if she should follow or head upstairs.

Thomas turned to Abby, "This is my good friend, Abigail Cooper. Our families are close and she's been staying with me for the past few weeks."

"Hello," Jason said turning to shake her hand. "This is my wife Emma and our son Timmy," he introduced his family.

Thomas stood at the door, waiting for Abby to follow. He motioned for her to join them then followed her into the room. He trusted her. If this was confidential business Jason wouldn't have brought his wife and child. "Can I get either of you a drink?" Thomas asked.

"No," Jason said immediately. "We're fine," he glanced at his son uncomfortably. "Uh...I need to talk to you about something, Thomas. I'm sorry to bring business to your home, but this is important."

"Well, Alex actually runs the store these days. Should I call her?"

"NO!" Emma screamed. She was starting to panic.

"Emma," Jason said calmly. "We talked about this. Let me handle it. You have to calm down."

Thomas looked at the couple curiously. What was going on here? "Okay," he finally told them. "I won't call Alex. However, we run the company together. Anything we talk about here I'm going to share with my sister. Do you understand that? I won't hide anything that is going on in her branch of the company."

"We understand," Jason assured him. "In fact, I was counting on it."

Thomas relaxed a little at that. "Uh...if this is about business," he paused to look at Jason's wife and child.

"I didn't feel it was safe to leave Timmy with a sitter and it's actually my wife that needs to talk to you." He looked to Timmy again, clearly uncomfortable.

Thomas reached for the side of the large desk and a door opened in the far corner of the room. "Maybe Timmy would be more comfortable in the play room," Thomas suggested.

Abby felt out of place. "Why don't I take him in there?" she suggested. "We'll find something to play with while the three of you talk business."

Thomas smiled at Abby, grateful for the offer.

Emma hesitated only a minute. "Uh...is that the only way into the room?" she finally asked.

"It is," Thomas assured her. "Dad had it built for us kids. He wanted a place Alex and I could play freely that was also secure. He also wanted to be able to constantly monitor us so we didn't get into trouble. Timmy is perfectly safe inside that room. And I assure you he couldn't be in better company than Abby."

"Alright," Emma said softly. She walked to her little boy and whispered something in his ear. The child's eyes lit up and he ran for the room.

Shadows

Abby gave Thomas a reassuring smile and followed the small boy, disappearing through the open door.

"Okay," Thomas said to Jason. "Now I think you can speak freely. What brings you here this evening?"

Emma pulled a stack of photos from a file she'd been gripping in her hands. "These," she said directly as she handed Thomas the pictures.

Thomas studied them closely. They were all of their son and a woman. Thomas didn't know her. He was still confused. "I don't understand."

"That woman paid me a visit this afternoon," Emma began. "She supplied the photos so I would understand how completely vulnerable our son is." Emma blinked back the tears that were beginning to form in her eyes. "That one..." she pointed to one of the pictures, "is actually in my own back yard." Her voice raised a little.

Jason took his wife's hand and tried to comfort her. "We don't know that woman," Jason explained. "We've never seen her before in our lives," he paused. "So you can imagine our concern when we found out she'd been spending time with our six year old child."

Thomas sat behind the large desk. He didn't like where this was headed. He casually pressed a button on the inside panel. It was a recorder. He didn't want to try and relay this to Alex from memory. He wanted her to hear it for herself. Thomas still wasn't sure what this had to do with the business but he was confident the woman had made some kind of threats. "Of course," Thomas assured them. "I imagine any parent would be concerned if a strange woman showed up at their door and presented them with photos of their child."

"We send Timmy to an expensive school. We picked that school for safety reasons as well as the academic value," Emma supplied.

Thomas studied the couple. Was Jason asking for a raise or did they want help with the danger they felt their son was in? "If this is about a raise I'm going to have to get Alex involved," he began. "Jason, you have worked for the company for a long time. I'm sure we can work something out but I'm not comfortable doing that without my sister's involvement."

"No," Jason said abruptly. "You misunderstand. I can already send my son to that school because you and your sister pay me so well. Better than I deserve. Better than the job requires," he smiled. "I'm thankful for that. We're not here about more money."

"Okay," Thomas studied him. "Then why are you here?" he asked.

"This woman gave us these pictures because she wanted something in return. She thought threatening our son would ensure my cooperation. It does not," he said coldly.

"So..." Thomas was trying to guess what was going on here. "You want our security company to help protect your son?" he offered.

"No," Jason shook his head. "Please, I know I'm not explaining this well. When I got home this evening Emma was so upset. Almost hysterical. Then she explained what happened." He gently rubbed his wife's hand. "I told her we were going straight to

Shadows

Alex. Emma became even more hysterical and said that woman would harm Timmy if we talked to Alex. I ushered my family into the car and drove straight to you. I was pissed. I'm still so furious about this I can't think straight. Nobody threatens my family. Nobody tries to force me to do something against my will." Jason took a deep breath. "Sorry, but I haven't had a chance to calm down so I apologize for being a little confusing."

"I understand," Thomas told him.

"I can only assume that woman is some kind of competitor," Jason began. "She's gone to a lot of trouble to get my cooperation. She will never have it. Let me outline exactly what she wanted me to do." Jason proceeded to explain to Thomas the underhanded events Jason was supposed to put into place to sabotage the company.

Thomas was shocked. Is this why his managers were so out of control? Who was that woman? How many good people had been threatened in this same manner? He glanced back down at the pictures. There was something about her that looked familiar but he was sure he had never met her before. She had a look of wealth about her. Was she human or fae?

"I'm sorry you had to go through that," Thomas told Emma sincerely. "I can't even imagine the horror you have been dealing with while you waited for Jason to return home tonight." Thomas was thinking, putting a plan into place. "Since I don't know who that woman is, it's impossible to know if she's blowing smoke or if she is capable of making good on her threats," Thomas began.

Emma's head shot to the room where her son was playing joyfully.

"I'd like the two of you to leave town for a while," Thomas continued. "You will stay in one of our vacation homes."

"Oh, we couldn't do that," Jason argued. "It wouldn't be right to take advantage that way. Plus, I have so many projects in the works. I can't just pack up and leave. I won't do that to my employees."

"I appreciate your dedication, Jason, but I think protecting your family is more important than any project you might have at work," he said bluntly. "I am grateful you trusted me enough to bring this to me. You are a loyal employee. I can only assume this woman is responsible for a load of other problems Alex and I have been dealing with lately. I only wish some of the others would have trusted me as much as you did."

"I kind of came to that same conclusion on my way over here tonight," Jason told him. "We all know what's been going on. The managers talk. For what it's worth, the majority of your people are loyal. None of us could understand the actions of the other manager's. I guess I do now, but for me there was no question. I would have gone to Alex, but that woman said she would know right away if we did and my son would be in immediate danger. I couldn't risk it, so instead I came to you. I hope you can understand why I made the choice I did. And please, relay the situation to Alex. I really don't want her to think I didn't go to her because I don't trust her."

"Don't worry about that. Like I said, I'm very grateful you were willing to trust the safety of your family to me. I don't take that lightly. And I'm not going to let you gamble with your family's safety. I want you to pull your car around and park it in the back garage. Then I will arrange for a car to pick you up and take you to

Shadows

a secure location. In the morning the driver will transport you to the airport. From there your family will go to our vacation home in Cabo San Lucas. You will remain there until I am confident the threat has been neutralized."

"But..."

Thomas shook his head. "No. You can take work with you or leave it here, I don't care. The company will just have to manage without you for a few weeks. I know you work hard Jason, and I don't interact with you regularly. Let me and Alex do this for you. It's about time you had a nice vacation. Take your family to the beach and let us handle the problem here."

Jason still looked conflicted.

Thomas smiled. "It's an order," he told him. "You may technically work for Alex, but we both own the company. I'm giving you a direct order. Are you going to disobey?"

Emma spoke up. "Somehow, someday we will find a way to repay you for this," she promised. "Jason, I think we need to accept his generous offer. Not because we are going on a luxurious vacation. I'd want to go if they were sending us to an igloo in Alaska. I want to take Timmy and get away. I need to know that woman can't find us."

Jason studied his wife. Finally he turned to Thomas. "Okay. But we need to return home to get some things. I need my laptop. If I'm leaving, I'm going to work on a few things while I'm gone."

Thomas smiled. "Workaholic," he accused. "No wonder we pay you so well," then he stood and held out a hand. "Thank you again for putting so much trust in me. I promise you won't regret it," he turned to Emma. "Do you have a purse?" he asked.

"Uh....yeah," she nodded. "I left it in the car."

"I'm glad you did," Thomas told her as a thought struck him. Could the Dillinger's be responsible for all of this? That's who the woman reminded him of. Lawson Dillinger. "Would you mind getting it for me? I want to check it for bugging devices."

"You think that woman bugged my wife?" Jason said, appalled.

"I can't think of any other way she would know if you took this to Alex," Thomas surmised. "Why don't you grab the purse Emma? Jason, you can pull the car around to the garage."

The couple left the room immediately. Emma returned a short time later. Thomas pulled Sam's bug detector out of the desk and turned it on. It immediately began to beep and turned red. Thomas lifted his finger to his lips and pointed at the purse.

Jason walked in just in time to realize his wife's purse was bugged. He stalked to the desk and dumped the contents onto the flat surface. Thomas slowly ran the device above each item. It was fairly easy to isolate the target. The bug had been attached to the woman's wallet. Good idea. If Emma grabbed her wallet instead of the entire purse the woman would still get the information she wanted. Thomas removed the bug and slid it into the slot on Sam's brilliant device. The bug was immediately deactivated. Thomas switched it on again and all was quiet.

"Looks like you are now bug free," Thomas assured them.

Shadows

"Are you sure?" Jason asked skeptically.

"I am," Thomas told him. "Unfortunately, I am just as confident that more of these devices are planted in your home," he turned to Emma. "Did you invite the woman into your house today?"

Emma looked ashamed. "I did," she confessed. "While she was there, she also asked to use the bathroom. She could have put more of those bugs anywhere."

"That's another good reason you are not going to stay there tonight. I've called for a car. The driver will also be your bodyguard. I told him to take you home first and let you pack. He's going to escort you into the house and then take you to a safe place for the night. He will then escort you to the plane in the morning. Whatever you do, do not mention you are leaving while you pack. It would be best if you had a casual conversation. Maybe pretend like you are putting Timmy to sleep or something."

"I understand," Jason assured him. "We won't give anything away."

"If you don't mind, I'd like to have a crew go in and clean the bugs from your home while you're gone. I don't want you to worry about your space being invaded though. We could always wait for you to return if that makes you more comfortable," Thomas told them.

"No," Emma answered. "I'd rather they do it while we're gone. I don't want to know how many of those things that woman planted. We trust you to take care of it."

"Great," Thomas smiled at them. "Now, go collect your son and start preparing for a well-deserved vacation."

The couple loaded Timmy into the waiting car then climbed in themselves. Thomas watched as they pulled out of the drive then turned to head back into the study. Abby was watching him. "Thanks for your help with Timmy," he told her. "I'm not sure they could have been as honest and open as they were with him in the room."

"No problem," she told him casually. "He's a great kid."

Tony and Megan walked through the front door and stopped. "What's up now?" Megan asked hesitantly.

"I think I just caught a break," Thomas grinned. "I need to call Alex, but Megan do you know where your mother and Atticus are?"

"Uh..." Megan thought. "I think they are in Pennsylvania, why?"

"I need Atticus to look at some pictures. Do you have any idea when they plan to return to New York?" Thomas asked.

"A day or so I think," Megan told him. "What pictures?"

"They're in on the desk in the study," Thomas said absently as he quickly dialed Alex. Thomas moved into the study and began his explanation.

The three guests sat transfixed, listening to Thomas' end of the conversation. They were all shocked at the lengths this woman had gone to in an attempt to cause problems for Deveraux Industries.

Shadows

"How horrible," Alex finally exclaimed. Her mind was racing. How many of her managers had been put in the same position. Did this explain why good people were acting so badly? Why hadn't the others brought this to her or Thomas sooner? "What are we going to do?" she finally asked. "I'm just sick over the thought that I've fired good people because they were put in such a terrible position."

"We'll figure that out," Thomas assured her. "I don't like it either, but some of the blame lies with managers that didn't explain what was going on. They should have known we could protect them."

"True," Alex agreed. "I know they would have taken this to Luke right away, but Thomas we are new. Some of those guys barely know us. How could they be sure? I'm not angry with them, I'm just disappointed," she confessed. "So how do we find out who the woman is?"

"Well..." Thomas paused.

"You already know," Alex accused.

"Not exactly," Thomas disagreed. "But she has some of Lawson's characteristics. I wanted Atticus to see them, but he's not going to be back for a couple of days."

"I'll call Oberon," Dimitri told him. "He'll know who she is if it's a relative of Lawson's."

"Good idea," Thomas said a little surprised. He didn't realize Alex had switched to speaker. "By the way, I taped most of our conversation. If the culprit is fae, that's going to help. The Miller's left the photos with me and we can take those and the tape to the council if we need to."

"Good," Dimitri said soberly. "If Foster or any of his relatives had anything to do with this I want them to pay," Dimitri was angry. What the Dillinger's had done to the Keisser's was bad enough. He was not going to overlook the trouble they had caused Alex and Thomas. "I'm going to call Oberon, then I'll let you know what he says. He may just come over tonight to take a look for himself. If he wants to take the pictures, let him. Can you make copies? I'm sure when Atticus hears about this he's going to want to see them for himself."

"I can. Keep me posted," Thomas hung up.

The group sat in the study discussing the new developments. It didn't help with the murders, but at least they knew what was going on in the company. As soon as they knew for sure who the woman was, they could stop the harassment. Thomas was anxious to determine which employees had been threatened and which ones just behaved badly. He'd have to develop a plan with Alex, but he thought they should call in each person they fired and talk to them. If the behavior was a result of pressure and similar threats, they would get their jobs back. Most of the jobs were still open. Those that weren't would be offered one that was. He thought with time they'd be able to sort it all out.

Thomas jumped at the sound of the doorbell. These days he hated to open the door. There was always a good possibility bad news was waiting on the other side. He stood and walked slowly to the foyer. Oberon was waiting patiently on the large patio. He smiled warmly. "Thomas, I hear you have some photos for me to examine."

Shadows

"I do," Thomas agreed. "Come on in. They're in the study."

The two men entered the room and went straight to the desk. Abby, Tony and Megan relaxed. They had all been worried it was going to be McBride informing them they'd found Angela's body.

Oberon turned to Thomas. "This is Patricia Dillinger," he said confidently. "There is no doubt about it. The pictures are very clear. I assume she did that on purpose for effect when she threatened those humans, but it was stupid. Now there's no way she can deny her involvement."

Thomas sighed in relief. It was a Dillinger. "Patricia? Is that...?"

"It's Lawson and Foster's mother. You don't know her because she's basically a recluse. Has been since George died. She lives in the penthouse at one of Foster's hotels. From what I hear she only leaves to have her hair done. Otherwise, she keeps to herself," he glanced back down at the photos. "I guess she leaves more often than we thought," his face hardened. "She is not going to get away with this, Thomas. I assure you," he noticed the others in the room. "Oh, hello. It's Tony and Megan, right?"

"It is," Tony said standing to shake the man's hand. Oberon used to know him as Tank. Tony wondered how Oberon felt about his deception.

Oberon grinned at the couple. "I wish I had known you were Tony DeLacy instead of the vagabond Tank a few years ago. Had I actually met you, I would have. How this community missed the family resemblance is beyond me."

"Uh, yeah. I'm really sorry about all that sir," Tony said sheepishly. "I didn't know Ariel was in trouble or I would have returned to set things straight."

"No hard feelings," Oberon assured him. "Everything worked out just fine. I'm glad that's behind us, but now we have another problem to deal with. How are your parents these days?"

"They're doing well," Tony assured him. "In fact, they're a little worried about what's been going on here. I think they're considering a trip over."

"I'd hate to interrupt their busy schedule for this, but it would be a pleasure to see them again. It's been a long time. Too long." He studied Tony again then shook his head, grinning. "You really should have told me you were their son. But I have to admit I'm going to love it when the others find out. Please promise me you will reveal your identity to Mrs. Jackson and MaryAnn Saunders when I'm there to enjoy it."

"I'll do my best sir," Tony promised. "Now, Megan and I are a little tired. If you'll excuse us, we're going to hit the sack."

They were all surprised when the doorbell rang again.

"Now what?" Thomas said in exasperation. "He walked to the door and was more than a little surprised to see Foster standing on his doorstep."

"Foster," Thomas said flatly.

That got Oberon's attention. Had the Dillinger's already realized they'd been discovered? He stepped into the foyer and studied the new arrival. Foster looked stressed.

Shadows

"Oberon," Foster said surprised. "Uh, well I guess that's okay. I mean, I guess maybe it's good that you're here, too."

"What can I do for you, Foster?" Thomas asked.

Foster sighed. "Okay, I know I'm not exactly welcome in your home," he began. He faltered when he noticed the hostile looks he was getting from both Thomas and Oberon. "I get it," he told them. "But I need to talk to you. It's important."

Thomas hesitated only an instant then stepped aside to give Foster room to enter. "We might as well take this into the library," he turned to Oberon. "Are you okay with that or do you need more time?" he asked.

"No," Oberon agreed. "I think that's an excellent idea." Oberon led the two men into the room and walked directly to the desk. He gathered up the photos and held one out to Foster.

Foster hesitantly took the photo and looked at it. Then he closed his eyes and handed it back to Oberon. "What has she done now?" he asked resigned. What else had his mother gotten herself involved in?

"Are you trying to tell us you don't know?" Oberon quizzed. "Do you know who that child is?" he asked more pointedly.

"I have no idea," Foster said. "Do you mind if I sit?" he asked Thomas.

Thomas studied the man carefully. He really didn't seem to know anything about this. "Go ahead," Thomas finally told him.

Foster walked to the couch and sat down. He covered his face with his hands in frustration. "Mother has been spending a lot of time with Lawson lately," he began. "I'm sure you know my brother and I do not get along. He wants a free ride, I refuse to give him one. He's been bumming money off mom and earlier today..." he faltered. "Well, we can get into that later. As far as that picture goes I have no idea what mom was doing with that child or who he even is."

Oberon walked over and sat in the large chair across from Foster. "Your mother is in a lot of trouble. If you know anything about that picture and the threats she issued to that boy's parents, I suggest you tell me now."

Foster's head shot up. "What?" he blinked once, then again. "Mother threatened that child's parents? With what?" He jumped up and began pacing. He didn't understand what was going on with his family. Sure, mother had been obsessed with that stupid project his father started and Lawson was lazy and good for nothing, but to take pictures and use them to threaten a small child's mother? Had she been taking the potion herself? He froze. No, she wouldn't.

"Foster," Oberon called. "Why don't you come sit back down? It seems we have a lot to talk about. I think you'd be more comfortable if you sat."

Abby stood. "Foster, would you like something to drink?" she offered. She knew it wasn't her house and obviously this man wasn't a friend, but he needed something to calm his nerves.

"What?" he asked, then seemed to snap out of whatever thought he was lost in. "Yeah, that would be nice. Maybe just a beer if you have one."

Abby moved to the bar and pulled a beer from the small fridge. "Anyone else want anything while I'm up?" she called.

Shadows

"No thanks," Thomas and Oberon said at once.

"Thanks," Foster said as Abby handed him the bottle. He sat back down on the couch and took a long swig. "Sorry. I don't know my mother anymore. Maybe I never did, I don't know. She's just so obsessed," he stopped. First he needed to know about the kid. "Who is the kid and why did mom threaten his parents?"

Thomas stepped forward. "The kid is Timmy Miller," he began. "His father is the head manager at Sports Etc." He watched Foster carefully for a reaction. Some kind of acknowledgment. Nothing was there.

"I still don't understand," Foster said honestly. "Why would mom threaten a kid whose dad works in the sports business?"

"Because the business belongs to Deveraux Industries," Thomas said flatly.

Foster was trying to make sense of this. Then it hit him. "She's trying to cause problems for Alex," he realized. "What did she threaten?"

Oberon was confident Foster wasn't involved in this. He'd handled too many of these investigations to be fooled. Foster was completely in the dark. "She ordered the Miller's to sabotage the company or she would harm their child," he stated simply.

"Oh mother," Foster groaned. "Why would she do that? I just don't see how she thought that would help," Foster was trying to understand, but it just didn't make sense.

"We were hoping you could help us with that part," Oberon suggested. "Thomas taped the conversation. It was reckless of your mother to leave the photos. She must be pretty confident. Do you know how many times she's done this in the past?"

Foster looked at Thomas in apology. "I have no idea. Have you been having problems with your managers lately?"

"That's an understatement," Thomas mumbled.

"I know mom has to be punished for this. I don't know why she would do that but I hope she hasn't caused too much damage," Foster finished reluctantly.

"I'd say she's caused quite a bit," Thomas said angrily. "Alex and I have fired several managers over the past few weeks. Some would have been let go anyway. However, I believe that most of the firings are due to your mother's antics."

"I'm sorry," Foster said.

"Somehow I don't think that's going to be enough for the families that are starving and trying to make ends meet now that they don't have a job. Now that they are unemployable because they were forced to choose between their family's safety and a paycheck." Thomas turned to face the window. He knew it wasn't Foster's fault but his family had gotten out of control.

"Thomas," Oberon said softly. "I understand your frustration, but I honestly don't believe Foster had anything to do with this. Your anger is justified but it should be directed at Patricia, not Foster."

"I know," Thomas sighed. "I know. It just makes me so mad when I think of what those families must have gone through. The decisions they had to struggle with. I'm not going to let this drop,

Shadows

Foster. Alex and I plan to file an official complaint with the council in the morning."

"I understand," Foster told him. "But the council might want to wait before they decide her fate."

"Why's that?" Oberon asked. There was something else. Something that had brought Foster here in the first place.

"You might want to do a little investigation to see if Lawson had a hand in it. He's had a hand in everything else," Foster said sarcastically.

"What does that mean?" Oberon asked again.

Foster sighed. "This is kind of a long story. Do you have time Oberon?"

"I can make time," Oberon assured him.

"My father was obsessed with the monarchy. I think everyone knows that," Foster began.

"Right," Oberon nodded.

"What they don't know is that dad believed he could make a new species. A group of men or women that could replace the warriors. He spent all his time trying to perfect his formula. His species was going to be stronger and more controllable than a warrior. In his mind the warriors would become obsolete and the community would embrace him as their hero. Naturally, he also believed the fae would welcome him back as their rightful king," Foster paused to take a drink of his beer.

"You're kidding, right?" Thomas exclaimed, the idea was ridiculous.

"I wish I were," Foster countered. "Mom got involved early on. They sat up nights dreaming and scheming. I was probably around seven or eight when dad got Lawson to try the potion. Lawson got deathly ill. I think it almost killed him. After that, mom was convinced the new species had to be all women. She argued that women could endure bodily changes better than men. They suffered through child birth didn't they? She insisted dad use Dannica as a test subject. Mom fantasized about her only daughter becoming the first new protector."

"Is that what happened to Dannica?" Oberon asked. "Did your parents use their potion on her? Is that why she became so paranoid and crazy at the end?"

"I don't know," Foster said honestly. "I think so," he admitted. "Not dad. Dad tried to protect Danni but mom was obsessed with her plan. One day mom snuck a sample of dad's potion and baked it into some cookies, then she made Lawson deliver them to Danni." Foster gulped the last of the beer and placed the bottle on the table. "I knew mom would be mad, but I loved my sister. I knew how sick that stuff had made Lawson. I knew he had almost died. So, I told dad. He was livid. He hurried over to the Keisser farm, but it was too late. Danni had already eaten some of mom's cookies. Atticus was on duty at the time. He wasn't due back for days and Victor was locked in the cellar. Dad stayed with Danni for three days, nursing her back to health. She was never the same after that. Dad never forgave mom for her betrayal, neither did I," Foster admitted.

Shadows

"Was that the only time?" Oberon asked. Maybe this explained Dannica's behavior.

"I have no idea," Foster admitted. "Mom was angry with me. She didn't speak to me for over a month. If she gave any more of that stuff to Dannica she hid it from me. I knew Danni had problems after that, but I still loved her. She was my older sister. Mom and dad blamed the warriors and Marlena for Dannica's condition," he confessed. "I'm starting to think that everything I was ever taught about the Deveraux's and the warriors was wrong. I think dad made it up to justify his experiments."

"I'm afraid you're probably right," Oberon agreed. "You have always had an unnatural hatred for the warriors, the Keisser's in particular, and Marlena. I don't think you got there on your own."

"I regret what I allowed to happen to Victor. I guess it took him saving my life to realize that. Dad told me, probably since birth, that the warriors were violent and selfish. He and mom made them out to be some kind of monsters. When I went to see Dannica she was always so sad and upset that Atticus left her to go fight. That reinforced the thing's dad said about them. I thought Atticus was selfish and that's why he left Danni alone all the time; because he didn't care. Then when they had Victor my parents went nuts. I guess I knew what she was doing was wrong, but I was so sure Victor was going to grow up to be another monster. I truly believed our community was better off without another warrior."

Nobody in the room moved. They were all too deep in thought.

"I'm sorry Thomas," Foster said quietly.

"I think it's Atticus and Victor you should be apologizing to," Thomas corrected.

"I owe them an apology as well," Foster admitted. "But I came here tonight to tell you that mom and Lawson have resumed their quest. They are determined to create these powerful women that will wipe out the warriors and give them back the monarchy."

Oberon was horrified. "Is that why there are missing women in New York?" he asked bluntly.

Thomas glared at Foster. Was his crazy mother responsible for the deaths of all those women? Did they have Angela?

"I don't know for sure but I think that might be the case," Foster admitted. "Like I told you, I cut Lawson off financially a long time ago. Mom wasn't supportive of that decision, so she continued to give him her money. Then she would insist I replenish her funds. A while ago I put my foot down and refused," Foster paused. It was difficult to air his dirty family secrets. "That night when I came home they tried to inject me with the serum. I got away and never went back," he paused. "Until today that is."

"What happened today?" Oberon asked.

"They don't know I was there," Foster assured him. "I felt guilty so I decided to try and talk to mom. When I entered the apartment I knew instantly that Lawson was there. He's picked up the human habit of smoking cigarettes. Well, to be honest that's not the only bad habit he's developed. Anyway, I smelled the cigarettes immediately then I heard voices. I decided to spy on them to find out what they were up to," he admitted a little embarrassed.

"Go ahead," Oberon persuaded.

Shadows

"I believe they have two women in captivity that they are using the potion on. Lawson and mom were talking about a contest to see which woman would last longer," he closed his eyes. He really hoped he was doing the right thing.

Thomas jumped up. "We have to help them," he demanded. "We have to try to save them."

"Mom was going to start her experiments earlier today. I'm afraid it may be too late," Foster admitted. "Even if they are still alive, a human's mind couldn't take that kind of shock. Look at what it did to Dannica. I don't know if she only had the one dose or if mom snuck her others. I just know that potion ruined my sister's life. There is no way a human could come out of that. Those women are better off dead," he said somberly.

"I don't care," Thomas argued. "Abby are you coming?"

"Hold on a minute," Oberon stopped Thomas. "I agree we have to try to help them, but we have to do this right," he turned to Foster as the phone began to ring. "Are you willing to go into seclusion while we try to deal with this?"

"Me? Why?" Foster asked. That wasn't what he had expected. Did they think he was involved in some way?

"Because I'm afraid for your life to begin with," Oberon warned. "Your mother and Lawson have already tried to inject you with their mad scientist formula. They want your money. Every minute you are alone, you are in danger. I have somewhere I can hide you."

"I can handle myself," Foster argued.

"Plus," Oberon continued. "I need to make sure you don't start to feel guilty about spilling the beans and run to dear mom and Lawson. You might warn your family we're onto them. I need to ensure our safety as well as yours."

Foster studied Oberon. It hurt that the man didn't trust him, but Foster understood. "Okay," he finally agreed. "I'll go with you."

Oberon turned to tell Thomas he was leaving and froze. Thomas was ghostly white. "Who was on the phone, Thomas?" he demanded.

"I don't know," Thomas admitted. "Someone that said I need to go to an abandoned Deveraux Industries warehouse if I want to save Angela's life."

Abby jumped up. "It's a trap, Thomas. You can't go."

Thomas swung on her. "It probably is but if there is the smallest chance I can help Angie, I'm going." He grabbed his jacket and headed for the door.

Oberon turned to Abby. "I hate to ask this of you, but can you please go with him?"

"I'm already there," Abby assured him. "No way am I going to let him walk into a trap by himself. You do know that's what this is, don't you?" she asked Oberon.

"I agree," he told her. "I can't go. I have to get Foster to a safe location. If that was Lawson, he may know Foster's been here. Foster could be in as much danger as Thomas. I'm going to call

Shadows

Dimitri. He needs to know what's going on. Go. Don't let him leave without you," Oberon gave her a little push. "I'll lock up here."

"Are you sure that's a good idea?" Foster asked. "Shouldn't we help him?"

"No," Oberon barked then picked up the phone and dialed Dimitri. "Get in the car. We need to go, now."

Chapter Seven

Thomas jumped out of the car and ran to the old warehouse. Abby was only a small step behind. She thought this was the most idiotic thing she'd ever seen Thomas do. It was obvious it was a trap. The murderer had already left, or he was hiding in the shadows waiting to pounce. Abby went on alert. If the killer pounced, he'd pounce her. She slowed a little. Maybe she should give Thomas a little space. If the killer jumped out, she could react.

Thomas rounded the corner and saw her. Angela's body was carelessly discarded on the cold warehouse floor. He ran over and crouched next to her limp, lifeless form. No! He wanted to scream. Not Angela. How could this happen to his sweet Angie? Thomas pulled the body into his arms and rocked it gently. This was all his fault. If Lawson had any part in this he was going to die a very slow, painful death. Memories ran through Thomas' mind. They were teenagers and in love. They were so carefree and happy. Then he remembered that last night, here in this very warehouse. Everything had gone so wrong that night. He knew, for her safety and sanity,

Shadows

she couldn't be a part of his life any longer. He gave her up to protect her and now here she was, lying dead on the cold concrete floor. Thomas sat transfixed. Rocking back and forth, holding Angela in his arms.

Abby's heart was broken. Thomas loved this woman. She'd been lying to herself. She never had a chance with Thomas. He was in love with someone else. And Abby was part of the nightmare. She slid back into the shadows trying to give him some privacy when she heard it. A very faint noise, something scraping across the floor. Then she smelled him. McBride was here. He was trying to be stealthy. He was on the hunt, adrenaline pumping through his veins. She wondered if humans realized the strong odor that was emitted when they got so excited. Probably not. But then again, McBride wasn't completely human. Was he aware of his scent or did he ignore that as well as his heritage? They would probably never know. If he continued to deny his destiny that question would never be answered.

Abby frantically searched the old building for something, anything to help her protect Thomas. That's when she saw it. A two by four. It was only a couple feet long, maybe even eighteen inches. That would be perfect. She quietly made her way through the shadows until she reached the small board. Then she moved into position. McBride would go straight to Thomas. He'd be so excited to finally catch his man red handed. She truly believed he'd block out everything else. She hoped so. She was going to need the element of surprise.

McBride stepped into the room and grinned. Finally a break. He didn't know who had called him, but they definitely saved his career. The brass was not happy he hadn't solved this case yet. Now he had. The man he'd been insisting was guilty was crouched on the floor saying goodbye to his last victim. McBride walked up behind Thomas then moved around the body so he was standing in front of them. "Put down the body and stand up very slowly. Keep your hands where I can see them," he ordered.

Thomas didn't budge. He just sat there, holding the dead girl, staring off into space.

Abby held her breath, not daring to move a muscle. She finally relaxed when McBride shifted and moved to stand in front of Thomas. His back was now to her, clearly he hadn't noticed her hiding in the darkened corner. Like she had hoped, he was too focused on Thomas to notice anything else in the room. She didn't hesitate, she had to make her move. Abby lunged and swung the board at the same time. McBride went down. He was knocked out cold. "Now what?" She mumbled to herself. She had to get Thomas out of here. Then she thought of Megan. Abby pulled her phone out and dialed the mansion. Ring, ring...no answer. "Come on...pick up," she begged. Two more rings. Just when she thought it was going to switch to voicemail Tony answered.

"Hello?" he said groggily.

"Tony!" Abby screamed. "I need your help. Actually, I need Megan's help."

"Slow down," he was wide awake and alert now. "Abby?"

"Yes," she said impatiently. "Thomas is in trouble. I need Megan and fast."

"What kind of trouble?" Tony asked, knowing he wasn't going to like the answer. He'd just convinced his father to give them a few more days. Maybe that had been a mistake.

Shadows

Abby quickly explained the situation to Tony and begged him again to bring Megan fast.

"We'll be there as soon as we can. See if there's something you can use to tie the detective up. Rope or twine or something. Hang in there. We're on our way," Tony assured her.

"Sounds like we're going out," Megan said, standing at the top of the stairs. Once Tony filled her in, Megan called Cornelia. "Sorry to bother you so late but I need you to meet us at this address. We may have caught a break. Someone called Thomas and told him to go there if he wanted to save the next girl. It was a trap of course, but the body is still there. Unfortunately, so is the detective but that's a long story. Can you meet us?"

"Of course," Cornelia assured her and hung up the phone. She glanced at the glass she was about to enjoy. Well not anymore, she gulped down the...'medicine' and headed for the door.

Abby didn't know what to do. McBride could come to at any moment. "Come on Megan. I need you, now!" Thomas was still out of it. She thought he might be in shock. He just sat there, rocking the dead body back and forth saying 'no, no, no'. Every once in a while he'd throw in a 'Not Angie.' Abby's heart ached. Thomas was devastated. If she could take the place of that girl, she would. If having that dead girl back would make his eyes dance again she'd be more than happy to make the sacrifice. But she couldn't. Angie was gone and Thomas would never be the same.

Abby jerked back when the detective began to moan. She didn't think, she just whacked him again with the two by four. Where were Tony and Megan? She couldn't keep hitting the man in the head. She might eventually cause serious damage. Abby heard a noise and slid into the shadows again. She hoped it was Tony and

Megan, but it could be the killer. She breathed a sigh of relief when Cornelia entered the room.

Cornelia took in the scene and immediately went to work. It would have been better had Thomas not touched the body, but she understood. She immediately went to the center of the room and examined the lifeless form the best she could. It was difficult with Thomas gripping the woman in his arms, but she did her best considering the circumstances.

Abby knelt beside Thomas and studied Angie closely for the first time. Another arrow shot through her heart when she saw how beautiful the girl was. She was far more attractive than Diana had been. So, this was the kind of woman Thomas fell for? Well, of course it was. Thomas was a warrior and a billionaire. The perfect match for such a powerful man would be a sophisticated beauty. Hadn't she already known that? No one as powerful and sexy as Thomas would settle for someone as normal as she was.

Abby continued to study the body then froze. "Cornelia?" she called.

"Yeah," Cornelia said looking up for an instant.

"Shine your flashlight over here. On her neck," Abby ordered.

"I need to see if I can find any fibers or hairs," Cornelia said with annoyance as she carefully ran the flashlight over the dead woman's body. "We don't have a lot of time here. I also need to make sure Thomas hasn't left anything that can implicate him."

Shadows

"I know what you are doing is important and we are running out of time," Abby insisted. "That's why I need to see her neck in the light."

Cornelia impatiently flicked her wrist until the light illuminated the side of Angela's neck.

"No, this side," Abby directed.

Cornelia shifted the flashlight and sighed. "Can I have my light back now?" she asked clearly irritated.

"No," Abby insisted. "Look, those are bite marks."

Cornelia was alert now. She moved in closer and examined the spot Abby was pointing to. "So our killer got a little sloppy," she mused. "Or all of the bodies have those marks and nobody noticed." She glanced back as Megan and Tony walked in. "You're girl here has a good eye."

"What did you find?" Tony asked curiously.

"Well, I assume you noticed there isn't a bloody mess around the body," Cornelia said taking pictures of the wound. "That's because our victim was drained by a vampire," Cornelia turned to Abby. "I realize he's in shock, but I need you to get him away from here. I can't examine the body while he's holding her like that. Plus, the longer he does that the more likely he is to accidentally leave evidence linking him to the scene."

Tony moved forward. "Here, let me help." Abby and Tony struggled to get Thomas to release his grip on Angela. Once free he just stood there, staring off into space.

Megan was crouched beside McBride. She slowly turned to face her husband. "Why don't you and Abby get Thomas back to the house? I'll stay here with Cornelia until she's finished. Once we're gone, McBride will discover the body. I've taken care of his memories. He won't remember a thing."

"Yeah," Cornelia agreed. "Go ahead. It's not going to take me much longer," she glanced at Thomas. "It might take you awhile to get him out of here in that condition."

* * * *

Abby sat on the bottom step watching the door. She was worried about Thomas. What if he didn't snap out of this? She looked over at Tony. He was standing next to the door, leaning against the wall. "We have to do something," she finally told him. "Should I call Alex?"

"I'll call Victor," Tony pulled his phone from his pocket and pressed a few buttons. Once Victor answered Tony explained the situation and then listened to his friend's response.

Abby was going crazy. Thomas was locked in the study. She was pretty sure he was getting drunk. She had no idea what Victor was saying and Megan and Cornelia hadn't gotten back yet. The night had turned into a complete disaster. She couldn't get the image of Thomas crouched on the floor rocking Angela out of her mind. She jumped when Tony called her name. "Huh?" she asked.

"We are supposed to expect company in a minute," he told her. "Victor said he's sending reinforcements. Whatever that means."

Shadows

Moments later two men walked through the front door. "Nick, Dante," Abby greeted. "We didn't know what to do. He locked the door and won't answer us. I think he's drinking."

Nick looked at Dante then the two of them kicked in the door. Abby gasped.

"Don't worry honey," Dante assured her. "I'm confident he can replace it." The two men studied their friend then Nick started to shut the door.

"Wait," Abby objected. "Is he okay?"

"We've got this," Nick promised. "You two can go to bed. Dante and I will handle things from here. We just need a little privacy." He gently closed the door and slid something in front of it to hold it in place.

Tony sat on the stair next to Abby. "I think we should trust them," he told her. "Victor said those three are best friends. Nick and Dante will know how to help him." He put an arm around her shoulder. "You look so tired. Do you think you could sleep?" he asked.

"I don't know," she admitted. "I am tired, but I'm so worried about Thomas."

"I think you should try," he stood and pulled her to her feet. "Go on. I need to wait for Megan but then we're going back to bed, too. There's nothing any of us can do for him tonight."

Abby nodded then headed for her room. She wouldn't sleep but she welcomed the solitude. She needed to be alone. Her heart was broken. All her hopes had been dashed. On top of it all,

Thomas was a mess. She also needed to think. It was all so confusing. Before that call, they had been so sure Lawson and Patricia Dillinger were responsible for the deaths. But they weren't vampires. Why would Angela have vampire marks on her neck? Why had she been drained and left in the warehouse. Clearly, her neck hadn't been sliced in the warehouse, someone had done that before they disposed of her lifeless body. That much Abby knew for sure. She needed to diagram it out, figure out the pieces in order to make sense of it all.

* * * *

The morning sun shone through the open blinds of the Study and woke Thomas instantly. He groaned. His head was killing him. He started to sit and realized Nick and Dante were still there. All three of them must have passed out at some point. Dante rolled over and moaned in protest. Nick stood and closed the blinds. As usual, Nick hadn't drunk himself stupid like the other two. Oh, he drank. But nothing like Thomas and Dante last night. Dante was a pro. It still amazed Nick how Dante could let loose and party all night long. Thomas on the other hand never got drunk. Nick thought last night was a first. He also hoped it was a last. But Thomas was suffering and Nick ached for his friend. So, if Thomas needed a repeat, he and Dante would be here to do it all again.

Thomas stood, slowly. "I'm going to shower and head to the office," he paused bracing himself on the large couch. His head was killing him.

"Are you sure that's a good idea? Maybe you should take a personal day," Nick studied Thomas closely. "How are you?"

Shadows

"I'm not taking a personal day. Within an hour my blood will take care of the hangover. I have a lot to do today. I need to get an early start," Thomas straightened. "Patricia Dillinger has hurt a lot of people. It's going to take time to sort it all out." Thomas let out a deep anguished sigh then quietly left the room.

Abby stood by the window, watching as Thomas walked to the car. So he was getting an early start this morning, too. She hadn't slept much last night. She was worried about Thomas so she had put that time to work coming up with a new plan of action. Her first priority was getting the police off Thomas' back. McBride's constant harassment was taking a toll. Thomas needed to be free. Abby was sure if Thomas could get back into a routine, a routine of hunting at night, he would slowly recover from the loss he experienced the previous evening. She was going to help him with that if it killed her. She knew, emotionally, that was a distinct possibility. She slipped on her jacket and headed out to begin her day.

* * * *

Tala and Atticus sat at the large kitchen table. They were only a few blocks from the old farm house. Atticus was still upset about his home. He was grateful Ken Brody had cleaned everything out. There was nothing left. Someone had come back and burned every building to the ground. Was Lawson responsible for this? Tala wasn't convinced yet, but Atticus was growing more and more certain.

"A penny for your thoughts?" Tala asked. That was amusing and ironic. She'd never had to ask that before. Other than that one time at the farm, when they first met, Tala had respected Atticus' privacy. She hadn't even tried to read his mind. Initially it was out of respect. Once she got to know him, it was because she cared. She'd been so worried when she initially saw the way her daughter interacted with the man. It didn't take long before she realized it was a good development, not a dangerous one. Atticus didn't seem to have any hidden agendas. As far as she could tell, what you saw is what you got with him.

"Nothing really," Atticus told her. "Just more of the same. I'm still upset about the house and I know you're not sure this was Lawson, but it just feels like a Dillinger to me."

"I know. We've gone over that a million times," she conceded. "I'm just not ready to rule everyone else out and focus solely on Lawson. Oh, he's an evil man and I have no doubt he's capable of this. I just have to limit my investigation to the facts. I can't decide we have our guy based solely on your feelings. Do you understand that?"

"I do," Atticus told her. "But there just seems to be a lot of evidence that points to Lawson. We found all those bomb making materials at their old farmhouse. You also have proof that Lawson is into explosives. He's been doing it illegally for years in the human world. I've been thinking, with his ties to the underworld it's plausible that Lilith sought him out to purchase his bombs. Then she used them to enact revenge on the shifter camp and the fae at the ballroom. From what I know about Lawson, he wouldn't care who the client is. He'd sell to vampires. In fact, if he knew Alex was going to be in ballroom, that would have been enough to make the risk worthwhile."

"You could be right, but it's still all supposition," Tala argued. "You're right, we have proof for some of it. We'll focus on proving the rest but we still have a lot of work ahead of us." She studied the man. She honestly didn't know what to do about him. They'd spent almost every moment of every day together for the past several weeks. She'd come to admire him. Okay, so she felt a lot more than that for Atticus Keisser. She was falling in love with the man. The realization terrified her. Her marriage had been so awful. She'd promised herself she'd never be vulnerable like that again. Now here she was, more vulnerable than she'd ever been in her life. Atticus could hurt her more than Joseph ever did.

She thought about her first husband. He was charming at first, but then the monster came out. After only a few months with the man, she knew she'd made a horrendous mistake. At that point, it was too late, she was already pregnant with Megan. Back then trying to survive on her own, pregnant in the human world, was impossible. She'd stuck it out with Joseph as a matter of survival. She also hoped once their child was born, things would change. It did, for the worse. Tala pushed aside the unpleasant memories. She had promised herself she would never think about that time in her life again. Her thoughts shifted back to Atticus. Did he feel the same or was he always this thoughtful to everyone? Her vulnerability was making her desperate. She needed to read him. She had to know if he was interested in her, too. Was it possible he was falling for her, the same as she was falling for him? There was only one way to find out.

Atticus reached for the pepper and froze. Tala was trying to probe his mind again. Blocking her was easy, but that wasn't the point. He thought they were past this. He knew he was falling in love with her. He had finally started to trust her. He was beginning to believe he may have actually found the real thing. What he had with Dannica wasn't love. Since her death he'd lived a solitary life, never believing he'd care for anyone again. Then he met Tala

Fitzgerald and for the past few days, he had honestly thought this might be real. Now he knew he'd been wrong, again. If she truly loved him, she would respect him. Trying to probe his mind was extremely disrespectful. He pushed himself up from the table and turned to leave, pausing in the doorway. "You can't get in unless I let you." he said quietly without turning to face her. "I never will. If you wanted to know something you should have just asked, Tala. By now you should know I wouldn't lie to you," he turned and stalked out of the room.

Tala sat at the table for the slightest moment then she jumped up and chased after Atticus. How did he know? She wondered. Both times he had instantly known. If she wasn't in so much trouble over this, that fact would have been intriguing. Tala was scared. She could tell Atticus was pissed. Her reckless use of her gift may have just cost her a relationship with the best man she'd ever known. She couldn't lose him. Not now. How could she be so stupid? Atticus and Victor were right, what she did was intrusive and rude. She'd never thought of it that way before, but now she finally understood.

Atticus entered his property and walked to the old tractor. It now had two flat tires. Whoever had burned down the place had also slashed them to shreds. Atticus kicked one, hard. How dare that woman behave with such callous disregard for others? Why did she think it was okay to just push her way in and take what she wanted? It wasn't and he would not tolerate it. She would never get inside his head, but the fact that she tried was so disappointing. He was surprised at how much the betrayal hurt. Oh, he knew he was falling for her but after what she just did, his feelings didn't matter. He didn't trust her. If he couldn't trust her, whatever had started between them was over. He wouldn't pursue any kind of relationship with a woman so...bullheaded, annoying, and downright rude as Tala Fitzgerald. He turned to lean against the tractor and froze. He'd been so angry he hadn't even realized Tala had followed him.

"I'm sorry," she began.

"For what exactly?" he asked skeptically. The woman was only sorry she'd gotten caught.

"For trying to invade your mind," she told him. "I'm sorry. You're right. I should have talked to you instead of trying to take the easy way."

Atticus raised one eyebrow. Did she really understand that or was she just trying to manipulate him?

"Atticus?" Tala asked desperately taking a step forward. "I know it was wrong to try again. I never should have done that. I'm sorry."

"Sorry you did it, or sorry you got caught," Atticus asked.

Tala studied him. She had to tell him the truth. "A little of both I guess," she finally admitted. "I don't understand how you knew. To be honest I don't understand how you can block me. I've lived a long time and nobody has ever been able to do that before," she studied him. He was still so angry. She was blowing this. "I know you won't understand, but my gift has been such an integral part of my life for so long, I guess it just seems natural to use it. I know that bothers you and I'm sorry."

Atticus didn't say a word. He wasn't sure how he felt about her apology. He only knew she had changed things. Nothing would ever be the same between them again. He looked around the farm.

It had been his sanctuary for so long. Working the fields had helped him get past the shame and the guilt after Dannica. It had given him something to love again. Besides Victor, he hadn't loved anything for the last several hundred years. This farm gave him purpose. Now it was gone. He took a deep breath. Well, he had built it once before, he would build it again. He looked back at Tala. A home for one. He closed his eyes and took a deep breath. He was shocked at how much that knowledge hurt. This time building his farm would help him deal with heartache it seemed. "I really don't know what you want me to tell you, Tala. If you want me to say it was okay, it's not." He surveyed the large expanse. "I'd like some time alone now. I have a lot on my mind."

Tala watched Atticus slowly walk away. She had to fix this. What could she do? Come on Tala, think. She knew if she let him go, things would never be right again. An idea hit her, but was she willing to do that? Was she willing to allow herself to become that vulnerable? What if he still rejected her? What if he rejected her because of what he learned? She continued to hesitate while Atticus took a few more steps towards the forest. She inhaled a long, deep breath then slowly began to follow in his path.

Atticus reached the edge of the forest when he saw it. He wasn't sure what to do. He didn't know how to handle evidence. This had been sloppy. Was Lawson really stupid enough to leave the gas can in the area? It looked new. Could they get fingerprints off the plastic? He had no idea. Maybe that's why Lawson left it. Lawson might know more about these things than Atticus did. He stood motionless, studying the object wondering what to do.

Tala caught up to Atticus. She was curious what had made him stop. As she stepped to his side she saw it. A gas can. "Don't touch anything," she said softly. "Let me take care of it." She walked to the can and studied it closely. There was still a sticker on the flat surface. If they were lucky, they might get a print off that. She knelt down and retrieved a kit from her purse. Then she expertly pulled prints from the shiny surface. Once she was done, she lifted the small can with a stick and placed it into a large bag then sealed the bag and stood.

"Now what?" Atticus asked.

"Now we take it to Bastian and see what he can tell us," she said casually. Tala stood and walked toward Atticus. She stopped directly in front of him.

Atticus studied the woman. How was he going to get over her? Life seemed so unfair right now.

Tala reached out and took his hand in hers. He didn't pull away, that was a good sign. She closed her eyes and focused intently.

Atticus silently watched Tala. He had no idea what she was doing. That's when he felt it. But he didn't know what it was. What was she doing to him? No, not to him. She was trying to give him something. He didn't understand.

"Don't block this," she requested. "It's the only way I know how to explain."

Atticus hesitated another moment then opened to her. He was shocked. Tala was letting him read her mind. He didn't know shadows could do that. He stood, mesmerized as his mind was filled with memories, thoughts, feelings, concerns. It was like transferring files from one computer to another. It was strange and intriguing.

Tala opened her eyes and studied Atticus. Her life was in his hands now. He knew everything. He now knew all about her past, her awful marriage, and worst of all, he knew how she felt about him. What would he do with the information?

Atticus was humbled. He finally understood. He still didn't agree with her tactics, but now he understood them. He took a deep breath and relaxed his mind. "Go ahead," he told her.

Tala looked at him, confused.

"I'm open," he told her, never taking his eyes off hers. "Come on, I'm going to let you in this time."

Tala shook her head. "No, that's not why I did it." A tear ran down her face. "I was just hoping if you knew, it would help you understand."

Atticus reached up and brushed away the tear. "I do," he said softly. "Now I want you to understand me." He pulled her close and held her tight. "I want you to read me. It will put us on equal footing. I also think it will explain why your attempts upset me so much."

Tala shook her head again and moved back a step. "I respect your privacy, Atticus. I don't need to read you. I finally understand what you've been trying to say. You'll tell me everything I need to know when the time is right."

Atticus leaned down and kissed Tala. At first, it was very gentle, then he deepened the kiss and pulled her closer against his chest. After a long moment he pulled away. "Please, do this for me. It's not disrespectful if I invite you in."

Shadows

Tala studied him, breathless from that first kiss. Her emotions were all over the place but she needed to concentrate. Why was he doing this? He hadn't even asked about her past. He seemed to really want this. Was he testing her?

Atticus brushed Tala's hair aside. "I really want you to do this, Tala. It's not a trap. I may have questions about what I just learned. I'm not comfortable talking about your past until you know about mine. Like I said before, I want us to be on equal footing. I'm in love with you too by the way. Let me give you this," he smiled at her. "I think we have more in common than you know. You just gave me a wonderful gift. Let me return the favor."

Tala took a deep breath and took his large hand in hers. She needed the contact. Not to read his mind, but for comfort. She closed her eyes and pushed inside. Tala stood, watching his life unfold before her eyes. She was shocked and horrified by what she saw.

Atticus watched Tala. He felt naked. He'd never allowed himself to be this vulnerable before, but she had done the same for him. She deserved to know what she was getting into. Once she finished, they could talk about where to go from here. He watched as tears streamed down Tala's face. What was she thinking? He didn't want sympathy. Not from her. He wasn't sure how long this was going to take but he was going to give her all the time she needed.

Tala pulled out of Atticus' mind and studied him. She loved the man even more now than she had before. He was such a strong, wonderful individual. She realized she'd been crying and reached up and brushed the tears from her face. "Thank you," she finally said. "Thank you for trusting me with that."

"You gave me the same trust," Atticus assured her. "I'm sorry for what you had to endure," his face hardened. "If he wasn't dead already, I would kill him myself," he told her. How could any man have such a wonderful woman and abuse her so relentlessly? The verbal abuse she'd endured was bad enough, but he never understood how a man could physically harm a woman. Especially one he was supposed to love and protect. He now understood her need to probe. After being treated that way, being so vulnerable, it would be impossible to trust a man again. No wonder she tried to read him.

Tala stepped forward and placed her hands on either side of Atticus' face. "I love you," she gave him a small smile. "You're right. We have a lot in common," she paused. "So I'm forgiven then?" she asked coyly.

Atticus leaned down and kissed her softly. He took her hand in his then lifted it to his mouth and kissed her fingers. "You're forgiven. Are you ready to head back to the rental?" he asked.

"Oh. I need the can," she started to turn to retrieve it.

"I got it," he casually picked up the large bag that contained the gas can and walked wordlessly away from his ranch, away from the home that had brought him solace for so many years.

The two remained silent, lost in their own thoughts as they slowly walked back to the old farmhouse they had rented. Atticus finally started a dialogue, quizzing her about her past, then broaching the subject of their future. They had a lot of options to consider. They both knew they were in love, real love this time. But neither one wanted to rush into another marriage. They'd figure something out. For now, they were just going to enjoy each other's company. They both wondered how their children would react to this new development. Hopefully they would be supportive. Tala was even more grateful for the connection Megan shared with Atticus. Atticus on the other hand was concerned about Victor. He and Tala had gotten off to a shaky start. He knew his son would come around, he just hoped it wouldn't take too long.

* * * *

Abby shifted and flew from the police station. She hadn't discovered much in McBride's notes. He was doing his best to put together a case against Thomas, but he really didn't have anything. It was all circumstantial and none of the pieces fit. She knew the DA would decline anything he took to them at this point. That was the good news, but she still hadn't figured out a way to change the focus from Thomas to someone else. It was going to be difficult. The police could never arrest a vampire. She'd considered framing someone else, but she just couldn't bring herself to do that. Not even if she could find an evil human criminal. Too many women had been killed. New York didn't have the death penalty but anyone arrested for this crime spree would spend the rest of their life in prison. They had the same problem with Lawson. If he was somehow involved, he couldn't go to a human prison. The whole human race would panic when their prisoner never aged. The tabloids would have a heyday.

Abby landed in the darkened alley and shifted from a pigeon back to a human. Once again, she realized how lucky she'd been to find this place. The alley was L-shaped and situated between two large buildings. Neither one had windows facing inward so there was no way anyone would see her. She casually strolled toward the open street enjoying the warm evening air. She liked this time of night and always had. She smiled as she rounded the first corner, she could see that foot traffic was light on the sidewalk ahead. Once she cleared the alley, her car was parked in the lot just a few feet to the left. She was alert, listening closely to the noises around her. New York was never quiet but night time was always peaceful somehow. That would make it easy to hear if someone approached unexpectedly. Vampires liked to hide in these dark alleys, but she wasn't worried. She could always shift and get away. She was almost to the entrance when a man jumped from a darkened doorway. She felt a prick to her arm and instantly felt dizzy. What was in the needle? Was it lethal? She started to panic, realizing it was impossible to concentrate. Until she could regain her wits, she was in danger. She was vulnerable. She couldn't shift.

"Don't fight it sweetheart. You can't win," the man laughed.

This guy was evil and sadistic, Abby could smell the dark stench all around him. They moved onto the sidewalk. Where was he taking her? As they walked under a street lamp Abby tried to study the man. He was definitely human. She inhaled. She wanted to remember his scent. If she could find a way to escape, she needed to know everything she could about this guy. She was determined to make him pay. Nobody attacked a Cooper and got away with it.

The man pulled Abby into Central Park. He leaned in and whispered in her ear. "I thought you'd be more challenging than this," he laughed again. "Thomas' first woman was a lot more fun. At least she fought back. That's why she died so quickly. I wasn't supposed to kill her that night, but she was a feisty one. I have to admit you are a disappointment."

What was he saying? This human was the one taking the women? How did he know Thomas? And why the vampire marks?

Shadows

She didn't understand, but she had to find a way to escape. They were moving towards a bench. Suddenly she had an idea. Hopefully it would work. Just before they reached the bench Abby let her legs go limp. The man wouldn't know she was fine. The idiot had drugged her after all.

"Stand up," he ordered.

Abby didn't respond. She pretended the drugs affected her more than they actually had. She was only going to have one shot at this.

The man grabbed Abby and shoved her onto the bench. "Listen to me now," he growled. "If you're up to something, you're going to regret it." He looked around and then kicked her in the ribs.

Abby screamed in pain. She hadn't seen that coming. She had to get out of here. Just a couple more seconds and she would be able to shift. She was pretty sure he'd just broken at least one of her ribs which was going to make things difficult, but she had to ignore the pain. She was running out of time.

"That's what I thought," the man narrowed his eyes at her. He grabbed the hair at the back of her head, wrapped it around his fist and yanked forcefully until he was staring into her eyes. Abby slammed her eyelids shut immediately. The man gave her head another hard, angry tug. "Look at me woman," he ordered.

Abby knew what he was doing. He wanted to look into her eyes to see if they were dilated. She kept them closed and hoped for a miracle. She had to concentrate. She needed to shift.

The man was furious. What was this woman up to? "I said open your eyes. Now!" he ordered. The girl didn't move. So, he had a stubborn one here. He pulled back his arm and punched her in the cheekbone. The girl fell to the side. Was she faking or had he knocked her out this time. He couldn't control his temper. He kicked her hard in the abdomen.

Abby's face was on fire. She needed to escape or she'd be doomed. She tried to take a deep breath, but she had such an intense burning pain under her left rib cage. She gave up and took short shallow breaths, hoping to calm her mind enough to concentrate. She was only going to have one shot at this. Abby forced herself to ignore the intense pain trying to consume her and finally shifted into a hawk.

Kahn was taken by surprise. He'd never seen anything like this before. Women couldn't just change into birds. He pulled out a knife and swung wildly at the animal. He knew he'd gotten in a good swipe, but the bird flew higher anyway. Kahn was pissed. He flung his knife into the bench, frustrated as the blade sunk deep into the weathered wood. Another freak had gotten away from him. Well, not for long. Maybe he'd just found the challenge he'd been hoping for. He smiled. It had been a long time since anyone had given him a challenge. Things just got interesting. He'd leave her alone tonight. If she survived, he could track her tomorrow.

Abby couldn't see. Her vision was starting to blur, she felt dizzy and her breathing was becoming even more shallow. She couldn't go into shock now. She had to get to the mansion. She was having a hard time flying and wondered how serious the wound on her wing was. She might have a chance if she could get to Thomas. He would call Alex. She took another shallow breath. Even as a bird, she could hear the loud wheezing in her chest. She was beginning to think that man had ruptured her spleen and her broken ribs may have punctured a lung. That was the only explanation for her condition. Abby was relieved when the mansion came into sight. She tried to glide closer to the ground without losing her balance. This was going to be tricky. She would need to shift back, but she knew she wouldn't be able to move once she landed. Her aim would have to be perfect.

Thomas sat in front of the fireplace drinking brandy. He and Alex had resolved a few problems at the office today. Two of the managers had been hired back into their original positions. They were both extremely surprised to not only be forgiven, but to get their jobs back. Beth was probably the most shocked. She'd felt terrible about her behavior, but didn't think she had a choice. Alex was relieved to find out Patricia had threatened Beth's family. That particular incident had been the hardest on his sister. Beth was supposed to be a family friend. At least the unexpected problems with Deveraux Industries were over. He and Alex had paid their head of security a visit first thing that morning and provided him a photo. It took Shawn less than an hour to distribute an alert companywide regarding Patricia. They were confident if she approached anyone else, Shawn would be notified immediately. His managers may not have confidence in him or Alex, but everyone knew Shawn was the best in the business. Patricia's games were over. Now if they could just resolve his other issues.

He looked at the clock. Where was Abby? This was the second time he'd found himself worried about his new friend. He really needed her tonight. She was the only one that could keep his mind off Angela. What could she be doing so late? He stood and poured himself another glass of brandy then returned to the chair and failed at keeping the memories at bay. He knew he would never forget that awful moment in the warehouse. Seeing Angie lying there motionless, her throat cut, her eyes vacant would be burned into his memory forever. He wanted to believe Cornelia, but now that they knew vampires were involved, the guilt was killing him. He had pushed Angela away to protect her from this world. Now she was dead because of it. He couldn't help but wonder if he'd made a mistake. Would Angie still be alive if he had continued their relationship?

If he hadn't pushed her away, they probably would have gotten married within a year. He could have kept their world a secret. Marlena had done it with Alex for almost thirty years. He felt selfish. Part of the reason he'd pushed Angela away was because he wanted a mate that would embraced their world. He wanted a marriage like his father had with Marlena. Maybe that was impossible. He told himself Angie would be happier with someone else. Maybe she had been, he really didn't know. But if he was completely honest with himself he had also pushed her away because he would be happier with someone else. Angela appeared to be happy. In fact Thomas remembered thinking on her wedding day how he'd never seen her glow like that before. When the invitation arrived he'd been surprised. Thomas went alone and left with the feeling he'd made the right choice. With him gone, Angela could have the life she always wanted. She had found a good, honorable man that was clearly head over heels in love with her. Thomas remembered how happy he had been that night. Seeing her happy like that was everything he could have hoped for. Now, she was dead because of him.

He looked at the clock again. Where was Abby? He jumped to his feet when he heard the loud thud. Thomas ran to the front door and flung it open. Abby was lying in a heap on the front porch. "No!" Thomas screamed. "Not Abby," he dropped to his knees and gently rolled her onto her back.

Shadows

Abby groaned in pain. She couldn't talk. She couldn't move. She knew she was going to black out, but she tried to fight it. Within seconds she lost the battle.

Thomas whisked Abby into his arms and rushed into the house. He grabbed the phone on his way to his room. He was grateful Marta had programmed Alex's number on speed dial. He impatiently waited as her phone rang once, twice, three times. She finally answered. "I need you here now," Thomas said anxiously.

"Thomas? What's wrong?" Alex said in a panic.

"Abby," Thomas answered. "She's in bad shape. I need you here. I need you to heal her." He gently set Abby on his bed and studied her face. One of her eyes was swollen shut. It looked like her cheekbone might be broken. He brushed back her hair and gently ran his fingers across it.

"I'm on my way," Alex assured him. "I'll be there as soon as I can."

Thomas shut off the phone and tossed it into a chair. He was worried about Abby. She was so pale and he was having a hard time finding a pulse. What could he do? He wasn't sure what was wrong. He gently lifted her shirt, sliding it gently over her head and froze. What had happened to her arm? She had a huge gash down the length of it. It was deep and bleeding profusely. How had he missed that? Thomas rushed to the bathroom and pulled out a towel. He wrapped her arm as tight as he dared in an attempt to stop the bleeding. Where was Alex? If she didn't get here soon Abby wouldn't make it.

Dimitri pulled into the drive and slammed on the brakes. Alex jumped out of the car before it even came to a stop. She threw the front door open and ran up the stairs. Thomas had been so panicked. That wasn't like him. Abby's injuries must be serious. "Thomas?" she called out. Where was he?

"In here," Thomas called back. "My room." He was putting pressure on Abby's arm, trying his best to stop the bleeding.

Alex rushed in and froze. What had happened to Abby? She looked terrible. Alex regained her composure and ran to the bed. "Which one is the worst?" she asked Thomas.

"I don't know. She must have some kind of internal injury and her arm's been sliced completely open. She's bleeding pretty badly," Thomas supplied. He glanced up as Dimitri walked through the door. He nodded in Dimitri's direction then turned his attention back to Abby.

Dimitri walked to Alex and put his hand on her shoulder. He studied Abby and cringed. He'd need to call her father. Mason wasn't going to like this. "What happened?" he asked Thomas.

"I don't know," he admitted. "I was in the study and heard a loud thud. I rushed out to investigate and found her lying on the front porch."

Dimitri nodded and left the room.

Alex pushed Thomas aside. "I need you to move so I can deal with her arm."

Thomas moved a step backwards. He didn't want to, he needed the contact. But, he knew Abby's only hope was Alex and he was in the way. He watched as Alex unwrapped the towel then held Abby's hand. The wound slowly began to heal. Thomas finally relaxed. Abby was going to be okay. He could feel it. Alex continued to concentrate on Abby's injuries. Thomas couldn't take the silence. He was just about to question Alex when he saw the swelling recede from Abby's face.

After a couple more seconds, Alex stood and turned until she was facing Thomas. "I've done all I can do," she told him. "She had a lot of injuries. Several ribs were broken and her spleen was ruptured. She was bleeding internally and one of the ribs punctured her lung. She's lost a lot of blood between the spleen and her arm. Her cheek was also shattered. I don't know what could have happened to her arm, but it was like it was sliced clean through. Who could have done this, Thomas?" Alex was worried.

They looked up as Mason and Jackie Cooper walked through the door. Dimitri followed behind them.

Jackie ran to her daughter. "What happened to her?" she asked. There was a lot of blood staining the sheets and blankets. Abby looked so helpless. Jackie sat on the side of the bed and felt for a pulse. She relaxed a little when she found it. It wasn't strong, but not as weak as she had anticipated.

"Nobody knows," Thomas said quietly. He ran through what little he knew for Abby's parents. Unfortunately it wasn't much.

Mason turned to Alex. "Thank you for saving my daughter's life," he looked at Thomas. "You too. If it wasn't for your quick actions she may not have survived this. Jackie and I will never be able to repay you." He sat on the bed next to his wife and took his daughter's hand. His little girl looked so weak and fragile. He hadn't seen her so vulnerable since she was a tiny baby.

Jackie looked at her husband. "She's still weak. We can't move her. She'll need to stay here for at least a day or two."

"I'll prepare a room," Thomas said immediately. "Tony and Megan are staying at the end of the hall. Abby was in the first one to the left, but the rest are open. Let me know which one you want and I'll prepare it for you. Feel free to stay as long as you need to."

"Thank you, Thomas," Jackie said sincerely. "We appreciate your hospitality."

Thomas sat on the back porch. How had he been so stupid? The fact that his life was a mess was no excuse. He rubbed his hands over his face. He was so tired. He looked up at the sound of the door.

Alex walked to Thomas and plopped into the chair next to him. "Will it ever end?" she asked. "I wish I knew how to fix this. Just when we find an answer to one problem a bigger one comes at us from another angle." The two siblings sat silently staring into the darkness, each lost in their own thoughts.

Dimitri finally walked out onto the porch. "It's late, Alex." He took her hand and pulled her to her feet, then he turned to Thomas. "We'll be back in the morning. You should try to get some sleep."

Alex pivoted to face Thomas and gave him a quick hug. "She's fine, I promise. She's just weak. I'm sure she'll be awake early in the morning. We'll be back first thing." Then she turned and the couple headed home.

Thomas didn't move. He just kept reliving the moment he opened that door and saw Abby lying there. No matter how long he

Shadows

lived he would never forget that moment. Abby could have died tonight. He wondered when he had fallen for her. Gradually maybe. He thought back over the past few weeks. Abby had such a calming effect on him. Each night as he left the office he found himself thinking about her. Even with all the trouble and the horror surrounding him, his mood lifted the closer he got to the house. He looked forward to their nightly visits. It didn't matter if they just relaxed by the fire or had a game night. He just needed that time with Abby. She rejuvenated him somehow.

When he opened the door and saw her there, it hit him like a freight train. Abby could be dead and he'd never kissed her, held her, caressed her. There were so many things he wanted to share with her. Abby was so sweet and kind. Could she ever feel the same about him? He'd been such a selfish, stupid clod the past few weeks. Had he ruined his chance with her? Well that's a bit arrogant, Thomas thought. What makes you think you ever had a chance? Someone like Abby may not be interested in all the baggage that comes with being a Deveraux. She was so beautiful and kind, but also a little innocent. Would she even be willing to take on a life where she'd be constantly scrutinized? Was it even fair to ask? He really didn't know.

Thomas reclined the chair and propped his legs on the ottoman. He didn't know where to go from here. He glanced to the side when he heard voices approaching. Thomas smiled a little. He should have known his friends would show tonight. Nick and Dante strolled around the side of the house and dropped into the comfortable patio chairs on either side of Thomas. "Hey," Thomas said in greeting.

"Hey yourself," Dante said shoving Thomas' to the side so he could prop his legs on the ottoman.

"By all means, don't let me get in your way," Thomas said sarcastically.

"I won't," Dante said casually. "Where's the beer?"

"In the refrigerator where it belongs," Thomas answered.

"If you were a decent host, you'd offer us one," Dante teased. "But considering the kind of night you've had, I'll cut you a little slack." He was trying to keep the mood light.

"How is she?" Nick asked softly.

"Okay," Thomas assured him. "Thanks to Alex," he added.

"We're lucky to have her around," Nick said seriously. "I'm not sure how this war would turn out if we didn't have her. Your little sister is going to save the day," he sobered. "She already has, several times."

"I know," Thomas agreed. "I knew she was special, but Alex is amazing."

"Are the Coopers still here?" Dante asked.

"Yeah, I offered them a room," Thomas told them. "I think they'll stick around for a couple days."

"Was Abby that bad?" Nick asked. "Bad enough that even with Alex she'll need a couple days to heal?"

Thomas closed his eyes and took a deep breath. Just thinking about her injuries made his stomach clench. "Yeah, she was," he let his legs drop from the ottoman and sat forward resting his arms on his knees. "If Alex had taken any longer to get here, I'm not sure

Shadows

Abby would have made it. She had a ruptured spleen. She was bleeding internally as well as profusely from a knife wound to her arm. And she couldn't breathe because her broken rib punctured her lung."

"Sorry man," Dante said sincerely. He knew Thomas and Abby had become close. He wasn't sure how close yet, but clearly Thomas was distressed over this. Which was the last thing he needed after the ordeal with Angela last night.

"Dimitri said nobody knows what happened to Abby, is that true?" Nick asked.

"Yeah, hopefully she can tell us when she wakes up," Thomas answered. "She's still out. Alex says she's just exhausted and weak. She lost a lot of blood."

"Internally or the arm wound?" Dante asked.

"She had a huge gash on her arm. It was deep, I think maybe a knife wound that ran from her wrist all the way to her bicep," Thomas said soberly. "Combined with the internal bleeding from the spleen she's lucky to be alive."

"This sounds different," Dante observed. "Do we have yet another threat to deal with now? Because if we do, that just sucks."

Thomas couldn't help but smile. He was grateful for his two friends. No matter what, he knew he could count on them. Just having them here made him feel a little better.

Nick was studying Thomas. He'd been worried last night. The pressure Thomas had been dealing with at work was starting to take a toll. Angela's death was an added blow that Thomas didn't need right now. When he and Dante heard about Abby, they rushed over wondering what condition he'd be in tonight. They had expected the worst. Nick was pleasantly surprised. Thomas was coping, better than either of them had hoped. Oh, Thomas was still beat and looked like the weight of the world was on his shoulders, but there was something different about him. Nick couldn't quite put a finger on it.

Thomas stood. "I guess it's time to get those beers," he turned to Nick, "I assume you want one, too."

"Sure," Nick said relaxing back into his chair. "Oh by the way, we ran into Tony and Megan. They said Atticus and Tala were back in town. The four of them were going to spend the night at Victor's apartments then head over in the morning."

"Hopefully Atticus and Tala have had better luck on that investigation than we've had on mine," Thomas said as he disappeared into the kitchen for the beer.

The three friends sat sipping their drinks and analyzing the situation. After a couple hours Nick turned to Dante. "It's late. We better head out. I've got an early morning and so do you."

"See ya man," Dante said to Thomas as he stood to leave. "We'll check back in tomorrow. Dimitri still doesn't want us to spend much time here but I figure if we get in too much hot water, Megan can just alter that morons mind," he smirked. "I wonder if I could convince her to follow my lead on a new memory for that guy." Dante grinned wickedly. "Oh, the fun I could have with that one."

"I doubt that," Thomas told him immediately. "I can only imagine what you're thinking. There's no way Dimitri would go for it. Stop fantasizing and get back to work," he watched as his two friends disappeared around the side of the house. Then he stood and headed for his room. When he reached the top of the stairs, the Coopers were just leaving.

"She's doing well," Mason told Thomas as they met in the hallway. "We thought we'd grab a couple hours sleep. Hopefully she'll be awake first thing and can tell us what happened."

"I'll stay with her tonight," Thomas offered. "That way you can relax and get some sleep. If anything happens, I'll be here. I don't think we have anything to worry about though. Alex assured me she took care of all her wounds," he glanced at Mason. "Uh, I was wondering if we should have reported this somehow. I didn't think of that before we let Alex heal her."

"To the police?" Jackie asked.

"Yeah," Thomas said hesitantly. "If the guy that's been killing those women did this, maybe it would get Abby off the suspect list."

"I'm not worried about that," Mason put in. "But now that you mention it, we might want to take a few pictures. You know, evidence. When it comes out that Abby was attacked, the first question is going to be why we didn't rush her to the hospital."

"I can provide an answer for that," Jackie supplied. "I'm a nurse. I'll just say I wanted to take care of my daughter myself."

"That might work, but we still have the same problem. If vampires did this, they can't go to jail for it. How are we going to clear Thomas if we don't have another killer to offer up?" Mason wondered aloud.

"We'll figure that out in the morning. First we need to hear what Abby has to say. Then we can decide what to do and how to handle her injuries," Thomas provided. "Let's go to bed. It's been a long night."

Mason nodded in agreement. "Goodnight, Thomas."

"Thank you for everything," Jackie said softly, placing a hand on Thomas' arm. "I'm so thankful you were here for our little girl."

"Me too," Thomas told her. "Goodnight then," he turned and walked into his room. He wasn't sure what Abby's parents thought of him sitting with their daughter all night, but they hadn't questioned his motives. Thomas pulled the large recliner next to the bed and studied Abby. She seemed to be resting peacefully. He hoped that was the case. He knew he wouldn't sleep tonight. He wouldn't be able to relax until Abby woke up. He trusted Alex, but he was still worried. He hated seeing Abby so weak and fragile. Thomas took her hand in his and sat back in the chair. The contact was soothing. He continued to wonder what to do about the situation. Would someone so kind and carefree ever want him? Or was he too uptight and complicated for Abby?

* * * *

McBride finally stood and walked to his car. What was this family up to now? He'd arrived just behind Alex and Dimitri. That wasn't unusual, Alex spent a lot of time with her brother. He had been surprised when Mason and Jackie Cooper showed up. They still hadn't left. Why would Abby's parents be spending the night with a killer? Maybe they were worried about their daughter's safety. He really took notice when the two large men casually strolled to the back of the house and stayed for a couple hours. He needed to find out who they were? If they were involved, that could explain how Thomas always had an alibi for the times the women went missing. Maybe his two brute friends abducted the women then Thomas killed them and dumped the bodies. It might also explain the left handed wound. Either of these two men had enough strength to manage it. Finally he had something to follow up on. McBride was grateful for the break. His investigation was growing cold. Rand turned the key and started the ignition. He'd catch a few hours' sleep then pick back up where he'd left off. He was going to catch Thomas and close this case if it was the last thing he ever did.

* * * *

Abby slowly opened her eyes and tried to orient herself. It took her a minute but when her vision focused she saw an unfamiliar ceiling? She continued to survey her surroundings, but the room didn't look familiar. Where was she? She tried to move and winced. She was sore all over and she still felt weak. At least she was alive. She shifted slightly and saw him. Thomas was sitting in a large recliner watching her. He looked tired. Had he been there all night? Her heart soared then plummeted when she remembered Angie. It didn't mean anything. Thomas was just being a good host.

"Good morning," he said softly.

Abby tried to sit up but was too weak. She started to lay back down but Thomas was instantly standing by her side supporting her weight. He propped up a pillow and gently maneuvered her against it.

"Better?" he asked.

"Thanks," she said self-consciously. She had to look horrible. How embarrassing. The image of Diana walking into the restaurant on Thomas' arm flew through her mind. Then another one of Angela, not the way she looked lying on that cold floor but how she must have looked when she was alive. Beautiful and vibrant. Abby wanted to cry. She wanted to hide under the blanket until Thomas left. Not only was she more average than his normal women, but her face still hurt and she knew it must be bruised and ugly. Her hand flew to her cheek. It wasn't as tender as it had been last night and the swelling was gone.

Thomas watched as Abby reached for her cheek. Her face was still bruised. Alex could heal the bones, but the bruising would have to dissipate on its own. There would be a constant, visible reminder of the horror of last night for several days to come. "Does it still hurt?" he asked curiously.

"No, not really," she admitted. "But I'm sure it looks atrocious."

Thomas grinned. Leave it to a woman to worry about how she looked at a time like this. "You could never look atrocious, Abby." He paused, he needed to tread lightly here. He didn't want to scare her away. "You're lovely, just like you always are. Just a little more...colorful." He laughed at her disgusted look. "Are you thirsty? Hungry?"

Abby's stomach growled right on queue. "I guess that answers your question," she said trying to make a joke of it. She was horrified. What must he think of her right now?

"I'll cook you some eggs. I think scrambled might be easier on your stomach. Alex healed you, but your body had a pretty serious shock. We better take it easy for a few hours. Do you want juice or coffee?" Thomas asked absently as he filled a glass with water then returned to the bed.

Did Thomas think she'd let him cook for her? He was a busy, important man. He didn't have time to play housemaid to someone like her. "No really, that's okay. I'll manage for an hour or so and then I can get something myself," she protested.

"Here," he said as he pressed the glass to her lips then waited for her to take a sip. "Don't be ridiculous, Abby," he scolded. "Coffee or OJ?"

Abby glared at him. "I'm sure you need to get to work, Thomas. Really, don't worry about me. I'll be fine."

"I'm not going to work today," he said simply setting the glass on the night stand. Then he turned to leave the room. "I guess you get both," he mumbled as he disappeared down the stairs. She didn't have the chance to say another word.

Abby sat in stunned silence. It felt nice having Thomas look after her. She wished it meant something. She wanted to fantasize about the two of them together, but she stopped herself. It would only make her more depressed. Her gaze began to wander around the large room. It only took a moment to realize this must be Thomas' room. It was very tastefully decorated for a bachelor. Abby closed her eyes. Thomas was a bachelor. A rich, powerful, desirable bachelor that could have any woman in the world. How many times had she seen magazines with Thomas' picture plastered across the cover, large bold letters screaming about the most eligible bachelor? Women all over the world would give far more than she would ever have, to snag a man like Thomas. He was completely out of her league.

She jumped a little when her parents walked into the room. "Mom, dad? What are you doing here?" she asked surprised.

"You didn't think Thomas, Dimitri or Alex would keep this a secret from us, did you?" her father asked.

"Well no," Abby said softly. "I guess not. I hadn't really thought about it."

Jackie sat on the edge of the bed studying her daughter. "You look good. I can see you're still weak, but all things considered I'm grateful for such a quick recovery."

"I'm sure that's Alex's doing," Abby said. "Thomas said she healed me. I'm still a little weak though."

"I know," Jackie said with understanding. "Thomas said he was going to fix you some eggs. I think that will help. It's not only the injuries, you also drained yourself when you shifted."

"Thomas shouldn't be cooking for me. He's a busy man. I'm sure he has more important things to handle this morning," Abby muttered.

"Thomas was very worried about you," Jackie scolded. "Let him do this. I think it will help him feel better. We all felt pretty helpless last night."

"Alex and Dimitri are on their way over," Mason told her. "We need you to tell us what you remember from last night," he paused. "But I think you should wait for them. That way you only have to relay it once."

Shadows

Abby nodded. She hoped they hadn't called Morrigan. He was happy at the fort and they needed him there. It wasn't necessary for him to waste time coming to the city.

"What?" Jackie asked. "Why the face?"

Abby smiled. "I was just hoping you didn't bother Morrigan with this," she answered honestly.

"I did call Morrigan," her father admitted. "He was about to shift immediately and fly home. However, I talked him out of that. I hope you don't mind, but I think he needs to stay at the fort for now. If Alex hadn't healed you, that would be a different story. But we all knew after a bit of rest you were going to be fine. Morrigan can see you in a few days."

"Good," Abby told him. "I agree. Morrigan shouldn't rush to the city just because I have a little injury."

Jackie narrowed her eyes. "Your injuries were not little," she corrected. "I will forever be grateful to the Deveraux's for their quick response. Those two saved your life last night. Just because you feel better this morning, don't minimize their actions. Without them you would have died, Abby."

Abby took her mother's hand. "I'm sorry I worried you mom," she said sincerely. "I know how serious I was and I'm sorry. I should have been quicker," she glanced at her father then back to her mother. "I know I've put you two through an awful lot the past few months. First the kidnaping, then this. I promise I'll be more careful from now on." She was a little worried they were going to order her away from the current murder situation. Especially when she told them a human had done this to her.

They all looked up when Thomas entered the room. He was carrying a tray of food. It was one of those trays with legs. Thomas walked straight to the bed and set the tray across Abby's lap. It smelled wonderful. There were scrambled eggs and fresh toast with orange juice and a cup of coffee.

"I wasn't sure how you liked your coffee so I brought the sugar and cream with me. You're going to have to doctor it yourself." He glanced at Abby's parents. "Are you two hungry? I have plenty of eggs. I also have ham," he looked at Jackie. "Do you think Abby's ready for something that solid?"

"I think we should wait," Jackie told him. "She's pretty weak and she lost a lot of blood. Her system is going to need food to recover, but I don't want to overdo it just yet," she laughed. "Be prepared. By lunch time my tiny Abby is going to be eating like a horse."

"Thanks mom," Abby grumbled.

They all laughed then glanced at the door. Alex and Dimitri walked in. They were followed by Tony and Megan, then Atticus and Tala. Wonderful, Abby thought. She had to look like death. Just what she needed, more visitors.

"You're looking much better," Alex said cheerfully. She was glad to see Abby awake and eating something.

"That's comforting," Abby said irritably. "I haven't had the pleasure of looking in the mirror, but I can only imagine the horror that's going to stare back at me when I do."

Shadows

Thomas scowled. He didn't like the way Abby was acting. She was too self-conscious about how she looked. She should be focusing on how she felt.

Dimitri stepped forward. "Abby, I know you're probably tired and you want to finish your breakfast, but we were wondering if you could tell us what happened last night."

Abby took a long drink of the orange juice. It tasted wonderful. The cold, sweet liquid was just what she needed. Her eggs were almost gone but she couldn't take another bite. Thomas must have cooked half the carton. "Actually, I think I'm done with the eggs."

Thomas stood and reached for the tray then hesitated as Abby grabbed the juice. He casually slid the empty water glass from the night stand to make room for her OJ when she finished.

"Thanks," Abby didn't look at him. She swallowed the lump in her throat and began to concentrate on last night. She needed to visualize the man in order to describe him accurately.

Tala straightened and studied the girl. "Kahn?" she asked. "Kahn did this to you?"

"What?" Abby asked, confused.

The whole room turned to face Tala. "I didn't intrude," she said defensively. "Not on purpose. It was like Abby was shoving a picture in my face. I couldn't help it." She relaxed when Atticus took her hand and gently rubbed his thumb across the back of it. He was trying to sooth her.

"Mama's right," Megan said in defense. "I saw him, too. I just didn't know who he was." She looked at her mother. "The same Kahn from a few years ago?" she asked concerned now.

Tala took a deep breath. "Abby, was that the man that attacked you last night? The man you were thinking about?"

"Yes," Abby said. She was perplexed by the reaction this had gotten. "I was concentrating as hard as I could to remember him so I could give a good description. I don't know him, but he's evil," she paused. "He also said he was the one that killed Diana."

"What?" Thomas said in shock. He'd been afraid of this. Whoever had been taking the women had tried for Abby. Was she a target because she was staying with him?

"Okay Abby," Mason said calmly. "I think you need to start from the beginning. This is all getting a little confusing," he turned to Tala. "Is this Kahn a vampire?"

Tala and Abby answered at the same time. "No."

"This guy was human dad," Abby said, ashamed. "I'm sorry, I should have been quicker."

Mason was surprised. He never thought a human would get the best of either of his children. "I'm not upset with you, sweetheart. Help me understand what happened."

"Uh..." Tala interjected. "I think you guys have the wrong idea. Just because this guy is human, don't underestimate him. Kahn is like no human I have ever encountered. He's vicious and sadistic, but he's also quick and he's good at what he does."

"Which is?" Dimitri asked.

Shadows

"He's a Columbian Drug Lord and a vicious killer," Tala told the group.

"So he is the guy you told me about?" Megan asked horrified. "That guy is here in New York?" Abby was lucky to be alive.

"Apparently he is," Tala said soberly.

"Okay. Maybe you should go first," Mason suggested. "Tell us about this guy. We need to know what we're up against."

"His name is Carlos Diego Rodriguez, but he goes by Kahn. I had the awful misfortune of meeting him a few years back. Like I said, he's a drug lord. He intimidates his way through life killing anyone that gets in his way. My client was a small business owner. Kahn wanted to use his storehouse as a front for drug operations. Donald told him to get lost. Kahn kidnapped his twelve year old daughter. He told Donald if he didn't cooperate, Susie would die a horrible death. Donald did what he was told and immediately came under the suspicion of the local police. They'd seen Kahn visiting the store and staked out the place. After a short time, they arrested Donald for dealing. That's where I came in. Donald's wife had moved to Dallas immediately following their daughter's abduction. Hiding out, really. I had just solved a highly publicized case a few weeks before all this happened. She tracked me down and promised me anything if I could help her. They were good people being used by evil. I took the case for free."

"Do I dare ask what happened to the daughter?" Dimitri wondered soberly.

"Surprisingly she survived," Tala told the group. "She'd been badly beaten. Kahn is not someone to cross. She was lucky. It could have been a lot worse." She looked at Abby then back to the group. "At least there wasn't any sexual assault. I don't think that girl would have survived if there had been."

"Why would Kahn be here, in New York attacking women?" Alex asked.

"I don't know," Tala said. "But my being here just complicated things."

"How so?" Mason asked.

"I don't know how Abby escaped that mad man, but he's going to be pissed." She glanced at Abby. "I doubt anyone has ever accomplished that particular feat before. You shouldn't feel bad, Abby. He's very tricky and slick. He almost got me once. If it wasn't for my uh...gift I might not be standing here today." She turned back to the rest of the group. "I suspect Kahn is watching the house. He'll be anxious for another shot at Abby. He'll view this as a challenge and he won't give up until he conquers."

"Well that certainly changes things," Mason said soberly.

"My being here is only going to add to the thrill," Tala admitted. "Kahn hates me. I bested him. He sent me a very personal message, making sure I knew no one has ever done that before. He also promised revenge when I least expected it. If he saw me enter this house, he's in competition mode. I'm sorry. I wish I'd known. Everyone in this room is now in danger. Anyone that Kahn sees with Abby will be in danger. He's smart and he's ruthless. Like I said, don't think of him as human, or an easy mark. He's not."

"Will you excuse me?" Tony said immediately. "I need to make a phone call."

Shadows

Megan's eyes grew wide. "Do you think you can catch them in time?" she asked.

"Who?" Alex questioned.

"My parents," Tony said dialing his father's number.

"Hello," Charles said cheerfully as he pulled off the road and headed for the mansion.

"Dad, where are you?" Tony said anxiously.

"Well, if you look out the window I believe that will answer your question," Charles teased.

"Don't ring the bell, just come straight in. We're upstairs," Tony said crestfallen. It was too late. He'd just put his parents in danger.

"What's wrong?" Charles said as he walked through the bedroom door. "You don't exactly sound happy to see me."

After introductions, Tony filled his parents in on the situation. "I was just trying to stop you before that madman spotted you and mom."

Charles studied his son. "I think it's my job to protect you, Tony. Not the other way around. I have to admit I'm not thrilled your mother is at risk, but I would have come anyway. That's why we're here after all." He walked across the room and took Alex's hand in his. "It is such a pleasure to finally meet you Queen Alexandria."

Alex winced. She still hated that.

Charles grinned. "So much like your mother." He smiled at his wife as she stepped in beside him. "I do hope you and Lizzy have a chance to talk before we have to go back to Dublin."

"I'd like that," Alex said sincerely.

Elizabeth stepped forward and pulled Alex into a hug. "Your mother was such a special friend. I am so happy we were able to schedule a visit, Alex. I can't wait to get to know you."

Charles cleared his throat. "So now that we understand the situation with that sociopath, maybe someone can fill us in on why we are gathered in this poor woman's bed chamber?"

"Oh," Abby exclaimed. "I guess that's my fault. Kahn attacked me last night. These guys are up here so I don't have to move to the library."

Charles studied the girl more closely. "Are you going to be okay?" he finally asked.

"Yes. Thanks to Alex," she admitted. "Otherwise, probably not."

"Abby honey," Jackie called to her daughter. "Why don't you tell us all what happened now? Then we can try to come up with some kind of plan to deal with this nightmare."

"Okay," Abby agreed. She proceeded to tell the group about the drugs and the beating and the confession from Kahn about being the one that took Diana. "I guess he's probably changed his mind about Diana being more fun than me now," she said confidently.

Thomas scowled. Abby was taking this all too lightly. The man had killed several women and he would have killed Abby too.

Shadows

But why? Thomas didn't know this Kahn and he hadn't tried to infiltrate any of Deveraux Industries. What was the connection?

"The part I still don't get is the vampire bite on Angela," Abby told the room. "I saw them. Hey, where is Cornelia?" Abby asked Megan. Cornelia had seen the bites too.

"She had some things to look into this morning. She's also hesitant to stop by the mansion again so soon. I promised to fill her in when we get back," Megan told them.

"Did she find anything usable at the warehouse?" Abby asked. She looked cautiously at Thomas and was surprised. He looked annoyed maybe even angry, not sad or upset because she mentioned Angela. What was going on with him?

"She thinks she might have," Megan affirmed. "There were foot prints in the dust and she found a piece of cloth that had snagged on a nail. She's gathered the evidence and is still putting it all together. I'm not sure what she has will help us, but having this guy's name and description may help Cornelia," Megan surmised.

"So where do we go from here?" Tony asked. "We need a plan. Clearly Abby is a target now. How are we going to protect her? How are we going to protect Megan? I don't like her being a target in all this either."

Megan rolled her eyes at her husband. "Tony is just as much a target as I am. This Kahn guy might decide to take out all the men to make the women vulnerable."

"But you're also my daughter," Tala said clearly upset. "By now he's going to know that," Tala worried. She knew she'd have to face Kahn again, but she didn't want Megan involved. "Kahn has resources. Within minutes of our arrival, he knew all about every one of us. Tony, you couldn't have spared your parents from this. The minute we walked in, Kahn knew about your entire family. I have no doubt he already knew Charles and Elizabeth were in town before they pulled up the drive."

"We can deal with this," Abby said a little disappointed in the group. "Why are we letting a human scare us?" she asked. "Mom and dad, you two can shift and disappear any time you want. Megan and Tala are shadows. They're not in danger so neither are Atticus and Tony. Alex and Dimitri have each other. Kahn can't take both of you out at the same time."

"We're not always together," Dimitri responded. "We both work during the day. There are too many work hours that we're alone to be confident of our safety."

"Well, like I said before," Abby repeated. "I don't understand the vampire bites, but having a human involved is good news."

"How so?" Thomas asked.

"We've all been trying to figure out how to deal with the human police. A vampire can't go to prison, neither could Lawson or Patricia if they are responsible for all of this. Now we have a human. Kahn can take the fall. He admitted to me he killed Diana. I can only assume he killed some or all of the others. Megan or Tala could convince him he was responsible for them all, even if he wasn't. We have our killer. Now we just need to lead the police to him," Abby suggested.

Thomas left the room and brought in chairs, one after the other. The small group continued to discuss the situation for hours. Several ideas surfaced. But there were still a few details to work out. Abby was refusing to run away and hide at the fort. Tony wanted Megan to join Abby, but Megan wanted to stay and help her mother. Well, more like help protect her mother from the madman who had vowed revenge.

"Thomas?" Alex said quietly. "Could I talk to you for a minute in the hallway?"

"Okay," Thomas agreed.

Once she shut the door Alex began. "I know you're not going to want to do this, but I think you should go to the fort with Abby," she hurried on. "No, just listen. Abby needs to be there. She's still recovering and this maniac is going to come after her again. She won't go if you stay here. I realize that's going to make Detective McBride go tilt, but I have an idea for that as well. We can use Monroe and Abby's attack as a cover. We tell Monroe where you're going and explain that Abby doesn't trust McBride. The police know where you are, so you're not on the run or hiding out and I believe Abby will go if you go, too."

"What about Megan?" Thomas asked. "She wants to be here to protect her mother."

"True, but I think Victor can get Tony to join him at the fort and Megan will go with him. Tala will be okay. It appears her and Atticus have a special connection. He won't let anything happen to her."

Thomas smiled. "I agree. Now you just have to convince everyone else in that room." He paused. "I have an idea. Let's get Dexter Cavanagh. He's in theater and can recreate some of Abby's wounds. Then we take photos and give them to Monroe for evidence."

"Great idea," Alex agreed. "I'll have Mara call. Dexter won't turn down the council leader's wife. I'd call myself but I'd never hear the end of it. Dexter would brag for the rest of my life about how he'd done the queen such a great personal favor. I never want to be indebted to that man." She shuddered at the thought.

They were both laughing as they entered the room. Alex took the lead and immediately began to explain their plan. Everyone involved reluctantly agreed. Megan, Tony, Thomas and Abby were going to head to the fort the following day. That would give Abby a day to relax before the flight. It would also give Dexter time to get the photos. Once at the fort, Abby would have plenty of time to recover. Tala, Atticus and Cornelia were going to focus on catching Kahn. They decided Tala was the best one for the job since she knew him and could easily pick him out in a crowd. Tala would coordinate the two cases with Cornelia. Alex, Dimitri, Charles and Elizabeth were going to work on the problem with the Dillinger's. Oberon was already involved in that, so it would be easy to bring him up to speed on the recent discoveries. Bastian was in New York so Megan was going to take the diagram and other evidence to him before they left. He could process everything and provide the council with whatever they needed. It was still a mystery how the vamps played into this. They just hoped by the time this was finished they'd have an answer.

"I think we've come up with a good plan of action, but can someone tell me what a Paladin is?" Tony asked.

Elizabeth answered. "It's a sort of hero or champion of a cause," she told her son. "The legendary knights of Charlemagne's court were called paladins because they were defenders of a noble cause."

313

Shadows

"That makes sense," Thomas told them. "It goes along with what Foster told me and Oberon. His parents were trying to replace the warriors. I can only assume they were going to call the replacement's Paladin's."

Tala's mind was reeling. She had a lot of information to compile. She had to admit Atticus had been right all along. Lawson was clearly behind the attacks. But he was behind more than that. She hated to turn Lawson and Patricia over to Alex and Dimitri, but it made sense. She could continue to gather and process the evidence against them while the queen and the council actually took them into custody. That part was urgent. They needed to find the girls while they were still alive and Tala needed to find Kahn before anyone else got hurt. "We need to go," Tala pushed the thought into Atticus' mind.

Atticus nodded in agreement then announced to the group that they were heading out. They wanted to get started. Finding Kahn was the priority. Everyone said goodbye as the couple left.

Alex and Dimitri also made their exit. Tony, Megan and Tony's parents headed down to the car to bring in Charles and Elizabeth's bags. They were going to spend the night here with the kid's then move to Dimitri's in the morning. The four of them would work with the council to deal with the Dillinger's. Foster was still in a safe house so at least they didn't have to worry about him.

* * * *

Thomas sat in the comfortable seat of the Learjet pretending to read a magazine. Every few minutes he glanced over at Abby. She'd barely said two words to him since the attack. Once their

314

group meeting was over she said she was tired and wanted to be alone. When he checked on her, she acted annoyed. When he attempted small talk, she said she felt like going for a walk. When he said he'd go with her, she wanted to be alone.

He was beginning to think he had missed his chance. If he ever had one in the first place. That's what bothered him the most. The not knowing. Had he blown his chance because he was stupid or was he out of luck from the start? He sighed and turned the page. The only explanation he could come up with for her behavior was the attack. He assumed she blamed him. Now, on top of the injury she was being relocated. He couldn't blame her for hating him. Everything that had happened to her was his fault. He still didn't know why? He'd never met this Kahn guy before. Tala had tracked down an old surveillance photo and distributed it to the entire group. She wanted everyone to know who they were dealing with so they would recognize him if he approached them. Thomas didn't know him nor had he ever seen the man before. None of this made any sense. And they still couldn't account for the vampire's involvement. There had to be some connection, but what. His mind continued to circle. He tried to keep it off Abby, but that was impossible. Abby was the foremost thing on his mind and he didn't think that was going to change any time soon.

* * * *

Tony and Megan sat at the back of the plane away from Abby and Thomas. He hated leaving his parents in New York while he went to the fort. They'd traveled all the way from Ireland to be here. He guessed it would be a good opportunity for them to get to know Alex though. He knew they wanted to spend some time with her.

Shadows

They'd been meaning to visit ever since Marlena's death, they decided it was more urgent after Luke died so soon afterwards.

"Stop fretting," Megan whispered. "We'll stay a few days and then head back. I know you want to spend time with your parents, but I think they really wanted to be alone so they could get to know Alex and Dimitri better."

"I know," Tony admitted. "I just feel guilty. They traveled all the way to New York and the next day I get on a plane and leave them alone in the city. With a killer on the loose no less."

Megan laughed. "I hate to break it to you, but I think there's always a killer on the loose in New York City. I know you're worried, but they're going to be fine. Plus, you didn't leave them alone. You left them with Alex, which is exactly what they wanted. They said once they got the Dillinger mess sorted out they wanted to get together with us and Victor. They want to meet Ariel. I'm sure they're going to be at the fort soon."

"I guess," Tony said in a noncommittal tone.

"I can't wait to see Victor and Ariel again," Megan continued. "It's going to be hard when we leave here. I feel like I've known them all my life. Maybe that's because you've told me so much about you and Victor and your many adventures," she grinned. There really was no telling what the two men would get themselves into when left alone too long.

Tony smiled. "I am excited to get back to Victor. We both get so busy. There's always too much time between visits." Tony was pondering something but didn't know if he was ready to talk to his wife about it.

"What?" she asked. "Don't try to hide it. You're struggling with something and you don't want to tell me. What is it you want?"

"Well..." he hesitated. "I was kind of wondering how you would feel about staying in the area for a while," he finally blurted. "I mean your mom and Atticus are obviously hitting if off pretty well. Victor's going to be floored when I tell him about that. Anyway, I thought maybe we could get a place in New York or stay at the fort for a while. Maybe we could help out with the academy or something."

"What about your family?" Megan asked. She liked the idea of sticking around for a while. That way she'd have more time with her mother but she also knew Tony was going to miss his family if they stayed too long.

Tony sighed. "I think it would be okay as long as we went back for frequent visits. I love my family and miss them terribly when I'm gone. But I don't think we're going to be welcomed by the community any time soon. This would also give them time to adjust to the idea there's a shadow in the royal family. Eventually we are going to have to move to Ireland, just like we talked about before. They won't love you until they get to know you," he grinned at her. "This way you can spend time with your mom before we make the big move to Dublin to be close to my family."

"I'm game if you're sure. I like the idea of spending time with mom. She's always so busy. I had just moved to Denver to be near her when you came along. This will give us more time together. She's going to need to take a break from the investigation business again anyway. This time she's had too much publicity. Cops everywhere have heard of Tala Fitzgerald. Atticus was going to help at the fort for a while. Maybe mom will stay on there too. If we offered to help, that would give us all time together. I realize Victor and Ariel will be going back to New York soon, but we'll figure something out." The couple continued to make plans for the rest of the short trip to Romulus.

Chapter Eight

It was just after noon when the group finally reached the fort. Thomas and Abby dropped their luggage at the farmhouse. Tony and Megan headed for their old apartment. Once Thomas unloaded his stuff in the guest room he stopped by the kitchen. He wanted a Coke, then he thought he'd wander to the fort and find Victor and Ty. He stepped outside just in time to see Abby walk through the large gate. So, she was headed to the fort as well. Thomas trailed behind, giving her plenty of space. Clearly she didn't want to be near him. He wasn't about to force her.

Moments later, Thomas spotted the group out on the field. Victor and Ariel were working on something to do with Ariel's gift. He knew that because Victor stepped back and Ariel concentrated then threw a fireball at a large rock. Thomas wasn't sure what they were doing. Victor was trying to teach something to Ariel, but she was just getting frustrated. Ty and Samantha were fighting in the far corner. Ty was ruthless with his moves. Sam was fairing pretty well, but she also looked annoyed. There were about a half a dozen

Shadows

kids spread throughout the field. They were fighting and wrestling playfully. Orin was sword fighting with Dusty. Thomas shifted his gaze again and spotted Morrigan. It looked like he was instructing a small group of kids. They must be talking about shifting. Thomas silently watched Abby as she approached her brother. Morrigan had his back to her so he couldn't see her coming. She was about fifty yards away when she shifted into a blue bird. Then she flew directly over Morrigan's head. Thomas sank down to the ground and continued to watch the interaction.

Abby suddenly shifted back and tackled Morrigan from behind. Morrigan laughed and flung her over his shoulder. That's when the game started. The two siblings began shifting. Abby was a cat, Morrigan a deer. As soon as their feet hit the ground they shifted again, Abby a monkey, Morrigan a lamb. And again, Abby a zebra, Morrigan a bull elk. The game continued, each sibling shifting as soon as their feet touched the ground. They had changed at least twenty to thirty times before both of them hit the ground and growled. The two black bears immediately began wrestling across the field. Finally, Morrigan pinned Abby and they both shifted back, laughing hysterically.

Victor studied Thomas as he approached his friend. Thomas didn't look well. He appeared tired and run down. No wonder Alex sent him to the fort. Maybe some time away from the city would do him good. He'd never seen Thomas so...off before. Not even when he had to deal with Luke's obsession with revenge and Marlena's death. Those times had been hard, but this was worse. "What's eating you?" Victor asked, settling in next to Thomas. His gaze shifted to Abby and Morrigan. They seemed to be having a good time.

"They're being reckless," Thomas grumbled.

"Looks to me like they're having fun," Victor corrected.

"Abby's not completely healed. Shifting like that is going to make her weak again. Morrigan should know better. Not to mention how vulnerable that makes them. What if we got attacked right now? How would either of them have enough energy to fight? They couldn't even protect themselves," Thomas deepened his scowl.

Victor laughed. He couldn't help it. Then he tried to put on a serious face when Thomas turned on him. He failed. "Sorry man, but are you listening to yourself? It's one thirty in the afternoon. There is zero chance we are going to be attacked by vampires anytime in the next few hours," Victor sobered. There was more to this than Thomas was letting on. "What's really eating you? I mean other than the obvious."

Thomas took a deep breath. "Nothing," he mumbled as he watched Abby walk away with her brother. They were still laughing and joking as they moved out of sight.

Victor was watching Thomas. "Does she know how you feel?" he finally asked.

Thomas jerked back around and faced Victor. "I don't know what you mean."

"Sure you don't," he said stretching out to make himself comfortable. He braced his weight on his elbows and studied the field. As his gaze hit Orin, he smiled. "Where's Tony?"

"Huh?" Thomas was surprised at the turn in the conversation. "Oh, um…maybe taking a nap." He glanced up as Tony joined them.

Shadows

"Megan's taking a nap. I wasn't tired," Tony corrected.

"Good," Victor's grin widened.

"What are you up to?" Tony asked. "I know that grin. You are definitely up to no good."

"I was just thinking Orin is getting a little too cocky for his own good," Victor looked back at the councilman. "I thought a little competition might knock him down a peg or two. You game?" he challenged his friend.

Tony studied Orin. The man was good with a sword, but Tony was better. His father had made sure of that. Charles was determined to find a way for his boys to defend themselves in a fight. When Tony showed talent with a sword, Charles jumped on it. Sure, there was bound to be someone, somewhere better than him, but it wasn't Orin. He looked back to Victor. "It might be fun," he admitted.

Victor jumped up and headed to Orin. "Hey, I was thinking it would be a good lesson for the kids if they were able to see an actual sword fight." Victor was trying to sound innocent. Ariel knew better, but she wasn't sure what her man was up to. Breena was alert now, too. She sensed Ariel's intrigue and wondered if she should be worried about her husband.

"I wasn't aware you knew how to use a sword Victor," Orin said coyly. A demonstration was a great idea, but he'd have to go easy on the warrior. Victor used ninja stars and daggers, not swords.

"Actually, I do. But that's not what I had in mind. I thought you could fight Tony," he glanced back at his friend. "He might be a little rusty, but I think it would be a good match."

Orin frowned. He wasn't sure taking on a DeLacy was a good idea. What if he hurt the man? Charles and Elizabeth wouldn't be happy. "Uh, I think it would be better if I fought you." Orin suggested.

Ariel understood Victor's game now. He was setting Orin up for a fall. Should she warn Orin or let him find out for himself? She glanced at Breena and decided to warn him but she had to be careful. She and Victor were already fighting. Well, it was worse than that, they were barely talking. She couldn't do anything to make matters worse. "Orin, I hear Tony's pretty good. Victor's right, it would be a fair match." She wouldn't betray Victor but she couldn't let Tony take Orin by surprise either.

Orin studied Ariel. She knew these guys better than he did. If Ariel thought it was okay, he could give it a try. "Okay. If Tony's game, I am," he finally said.

Victor slapped Tony on the back. "Go get 'em. Make me proud." He settled back in next to Thomas to watch the fun.

"You're definitely enjoying yourself," Thomas observed. "What are you up to? Nobody has ever won Orin in a fight."

"Not until today anyway," Victor shot a glance at Thomas. "Orin just met his match. You should feel lucky. Not many people have seen the master at work." Victor watched as the match began. As usual, Tony held back. He didn't want to reveal his talent too early on in the match. The kids were mesmerized by the display. Sure, Victor was having fun with Orin, but he truly believed a match would be a good lesson for the kids.

Shadows

Thomas was enjoying the fight in spite of his bad mood. Knowing Victor, that had been the point. The man always knew exactly how to pull you out of a slump.

"Now, back to my question," Victor said not looking at Thomas. "Does Abby know how you feel about her?" He paused to let out a whoop as Tony knocked Orin's sword from his hand. Orin was quick though. He dodged Tony's kick and came back up with his sword. "Or are you keeping your feelings a secret for some reason?"

"Was I that obvious?" Thomas asked. He'd have to work on that from now on.

"To me, but I recognize the look. Remember, I've been there. Oh!" Victor winced. "That one had to hurt." Orin had taken a hard kick to the back of his knee when Tony dodged his sword and maneuvered around him. Victor glanced back at Thomas. "Talk to me. I might be able to help."

"There's nothing to talk about," Thomas paused. "I love her, she hates me. It's simple really." Thomas shrugged and tried to sound flippant, but knew he hadn't pulled it off.

Victor studied Thomas. "Why do you think she hates you?" He asked thoughtfully. No answer. After a lengthy pause Victor continued. "Nobody hates you Thomas, it's impossible. I've tried, but even I couldn't pull it off." He grinned a little, trying for a laugh. He hated seeing Thomas this way. Didn't he have enough on his plate without the added frustration of a woman?

"I don't know," Thomas confessed. "The only thing I can think of is the attack. She knows it was my fault and she hates me for it."

Victor gazed in the direction Abby had gone with Morrigan. That didn't fit. Okay, so Victor didn't know the woman well, but they had spent a little time together in the forest after her rescue. He was certain she wasn't the type to hold something like that against Thomas. "I'm not buying it," Victor disagreed. "Granted I don't know her as well as you do, but you will never convince me that's what's going on here. If that was the case, she would have hated all of us because of the kidnapping. She didn't. She knew it wasn't our fault."

"That was different," Thomas insisted.

"How?" Victor asked. If Thomas didn't stop blaming himself for everything that was happening, the stress and guilt was going to kill him. It was starting to piss Victor off. Victor admired Thomas for his ethics and compassion but this had gone way too far. "Thomas, stop being an idiot and go talk to the girl."

Thomas glared at Victor. "You don't understand," he moved his gaze to Ariel. "You have the woman you want. Everything worked out great for you. That doesn't mean things work out for everyone. Abby won't even talk to me. Either she's mad at me for some other reason or she blames me for the attack. I can't think of any reason she'd be mad, so she must hate me. I don't blame her. It was bad. She almost died. We were lucky, Alex barely got there in time to save her. I'm sure that shook her when she realized she'd almost been killed because of me. I'd be more surprised if she didn't hate me and want to avoid me after that."

"You're really pissing me off," Victor said angrily. "Why do you think this is only your fault? Your personal problem?" he demanded. "The women worked for Deveraux Industries. How do you know this isn't all about Alex? She is the queen after all."

Shadows

Thomas blinked, shocked. He had never thought of that. Was this about Alex? Did Alex think it was about her? She hadn't mentioned that, but he really hadn't given her the chance. "Do you really think someone is trying to hurt Alex?" Then a thought struck him. Maybe she was in danger. Maybe someone was trying to get the rest of them out of the way so she would be unprotected and vulnerable. "Do you think Alex is the real target? The grand finale so to speak?" Thomas was worried. Was that how the vampires factored in?

That wasn't what Victor meant, but it was something to consider. "No, there's no reason to think that right now. And even if she is, Dimitri won't let anything happen to her. Don't even think about running off to New York now to protect your sister. We have a plan and we're going to stick to it."

Thomas was worried about Alex now, he needed to warn Dimitri.

"Stop it," Victor demanded. They both looked up as Tony knocked Orin to the ground and placed a foot on the councilman's chest. Victor laughed, "Good job, my man." He glanced back at Thomas. Then jumped up and swung Tony around in a bear hug. "I knew I could count on you."

Orin approached the two. "I guess I deserved that," he smiled at Victor. "But I plan to return the favor someday. Some friend you are." He slapped Victor on the back and walked to his wife. "You look tired, honey. Are you ready to go inside?" The couple left the field and headed for the apartments.

Ariel jumped up and ran to Victor. When she reached him she playfully slapped him on the chest. "You're cruel," she accused. Then she turned to Tony. "You too."

Tony smiled, "Never," he glanced at Thomas then back to Victor. He knew they were involved in a serious conversation. He turned to Ariel. "How about you come with me while I brag to my wife. You can be my witness that I'm not over exaggerating this time."

Ariel studied Victor and knew he wasn't finished with Thomas. "Okay," she said enthusiastically. She leaned in and kissed Victor softly. "Sorry I got mad at you. I know you are just trying to help."

Victor grabbed Ariel around the waist and pulled her close. "I am trying to help you babe. We'll figure it out," he kissed her hard then released her. "Now go help Tony brag. I'll be there in a while."

Tony and Ariel linked arms and headed for the apartments.

"You don't have to stick it out with me," Thomas told Victor. "I'm fine, really. Go enjoy the victory."

"I'm not finished here," Victor sat back down. "Okay. Let me try this a different way," he took a deep breath. "None of us like that you are blaming yourself for all of this. We're worried about you. It doesn't matter if someone is targeting those women because of you or Alex or because they don't like green cars or any other ridiculous reason. That man is targeting women because he's a sadistic maniac and he enjoys killing. Sure, he's using something as an excuse but the excuse is irrelevant. The man has been a killer for years. We need to stop him and I believe we will, but none of this is your fault and I wish you would stop blaming yourself. We all want Thomas back," he paused until Thomas looked at him. "I'd like my friend back."

Shadows

"I just can't help feeling guilty," Thomas told him. "Those women didn't deserve to die and the only reason they did was because they worked for my company. You'd be upset too if you were me. Don't try to deny it because I know you."

"I am upset and I'm not you. I want to hunt that guy down and kill him with my bare hands," Victor admitted. "I don't care that he's human and it's not allowed. I want to kill him for what he did to those women and for what he's doing to you." He paused and narrowed his eyes. "If Lawson had anything to do with this I will take him out myself. If that family has harmed one more person they're going to answer to me," Victor looked at Thomas. "But I wouldn't feel guilty, I'd be livid. I wouldn't internalize like you have. I would be out for blood," Victor told him honestly. "I wish you would do the same. I saw you deal with Hector. I was proud of you for the way you handled that," Victor grinned. "Frustrated but proud. You definitely took your time, but it was a lot healthier than this. That was personal, too. He killed your parents, Thomas. It doesn't get more personal than that."

Thomas considered what Victor was saying. He knew he was right. So why had he internalized this situation? Thomas didn't have an answer for that. He had a lot to think about. The bigger question was how could he handle this differently? "So what do you suggest I do? I can't track this Kahn down and cause him pain the way I did Hector." He was considering Victor's viewpoint. The more he thought about it, the more he agreed. He wanted blood.

"No, but together all of us can track him down and make him pay. We need to get you out of trouble with the police. I think Kahn is the answer to most of our problems. Oh, I think he should suffer substantially before we turn him over but I strongly believe we need to turn him in to the police. Unfortunately we're going to have to keep him alive. We need to make sure the police have an airtight case and ensure that Kahn is imprisoned for the rest of his life. I have no doubt he'll get the death penalty. Have you forgotten that a man died on my father's farm? A Pennsylvania farm? A state that does have the death penalty? Because I haven't. With a little help from us, everything is going to work out just the way it should," Victor smiled. "You're smart Thomas, help us nail this guy. Help us make sure he pays for what he's done. Stop letting him win. Take your life back."

"You definitely make a good case," Thomas agreed. "I particularly like the part about Kahn suffering substantially."

Victor sobered. "So you're willing to take back your life?"

"I feel a trap coming on, but yeah. I think I am." Thomas felt his life shifting. Victor was right. He needed to take control. He needed to do something. For the past few weeks he'd been completely focused on the murders and all the management problems. He had felt his control slowly slipping away and he couldn't take it anymore. He hadn't been himself ever since Diana had poisoned him. Maybe that was the first straw, discovering her plan had shaken him. If she had been successful they all would have paid for his mistake. Then his employees started to disappear. It was one problem after another. He finally broke when they found Angie's body. But that was nothing compared to finding Abby near death on his front porch.

"Good," Victor stood and pulled Thomas to his feet. "Start by telling that girl how you feel about her."

"I don't..." Thomas started.

Shadows

"Of course you don't," Victor gave his shoulder a little push. "But she deserves to know and what's the downside? She'll hate you? You said she already does. Talk to her, Thomas. You deserve to know firsthand how she feels. Learn from my mistakes. I thought I knew what was going on with Ariel and I couldn't have been further from the truth."

Thomas sighed. Maybe Victor was right. "So why didn't we have this talk weeks ago?"

"I've been busy," Victor joked. "Now, I'm going to go track down my woman, I suggest you do the same." He gave Thomas another push then walked toward the apartments.

Thomas started across the large field then stopped when he heard someone calling his name. He turned to see Ty running toward him. "Hey, what's up?"

Ty stopped when he saw Thomas. He looked so tired and worn out. "Um...never mind," he said realizing this might be a bad idea. Thomas didn't look like he was up to a physical fight.

"What is it, Ty?" Thomas pressed. "I know, you don't have to tell me. I look awful. But you obviously wanted something so spill it."

"Well, I'm trying to bring Sam along on the hand to hand stuff and she's doing pretty well but I'm making her mad. I thought it might help if she fought someone else. You know, before she decides she wants a divorce," Ty paused. "But you look pretty tired. Maybe we could do it another day."

Thomas turned and walked toward Sam. "You ready for a different opponent?" he asked her.

Sam glanced at Ty then back to Thomas. "Absolutely," she agreed. She knew Ty was only trying to help, but they were fighting all the time, physically and verbally. Maybe if she worked with someone else for a while it would help their relationship. If they continued the way things were going, she wondered if they would have a relationship much longer.

Abby and Morrigan walked into the house and headed straight for the kitchen. All that shifting had made them hungry. Abby pulled open the fridge and started naming off food. The siblings piled various items onto the table and dug in.

After a few minutes Morrigan spoke. "So you have the hots for Thomas?" he asked casually. "I didn't see that one coming."

Abby's head jerked up and she sat frozen, staring at her brother. How did he know?

"Don't look so surprised little sister. You smell like a dog in heat," he laughed at her disgusted face. "Why don't you just jump the guy already? He looks pretty stressed. Getting laid might help him relax a little."

Abby didn't move. She continued to glare at her brother for a long time. "Morrigan, just because you can turn into an animal doesn't mean you have to act like one all the time."

"Actually, Abby dear, I think it does," he grinned. "And don't tell me you're any different. Billy still hasn't stopped talking about that night at the beach."

Abby was even more annoyed now. "Billy's an idiot," she said in disgust as she pulled a chicken leg from a plastic bag. "We all make mistakes, Morrigan. Keep it up and we'll have a nice long conversation about Sally Perkins."

"Now that was a low blow," Morrigan studied his sister. Why was she so defensive about this? Then it hit him. "Oh shit," he mumbled. "You've fallen for the guy." The look on her face told him he was right. "So what's the big deal? I'd say that's even more reason to jump him."

"Very funny," Abby avoided her brother's gaze. He would never understand.

Morrigan sat back. "I saw Thomas' reaction to our game out there. He cares about you. So, I don't get it. What's going on with you?" He reached out and placed a hand on her shoulder, then waited until she finally faced him. "I can tell you're unhappy Abs, tell me what's going on here. I promise, I'll be serious." He crossed his chest with one of his hands.

Abby almost started to cry. She could never hide anything from Morrigan. They were too close. She wanted to talk to him, but he wouldn't believe her. "Yes. I've fallen for Thomas," she finally told him. "But the feeling isn't mutual."

"How do you know?" he asked.

"I'm not his type. I just know," Abby told him.

"Abby," Morrigan said gently. "What makes you think Thomas has a specific type?"

Abby looked straight at Morrigan. She might as well get this over with. "Look, I saw him walk into the restaurant with Diana, she was gorgeous and sophisticated. They looked good together. That's his type."

Morrigan sobered. He never understood why his sister had such low self-esteem. She was beautiful and all the guys wanted her. She was the one turning them down. "Um, I seem to recall hearing that she was also manipulative and psycho. Didn't she use men for their money and blackmail them. Well, other than her first husband. I'm pretty sure she just killed him for the loot," he studied her. "I think it's unfair to Thomas to claim that woman is his type. I know Thomas, he definitely has higher standards than that."

"I meant her looks and you know it. I know Thomas wasn't interested in her once he got to know her, but that's the point. He was attracted to her. That's why he dated her in the first place. Then there's Angela. She was movie star glamorous. That is Thomas' type. Not me."

"Do you think he's still hung up on the dead girl?" Morrigan asked. "Because that relationship has pretty much run its course. I don't think she's a threat."

"Sometimes you are extremely insensitive," she scolded. "No, I don't think he's still hung up on Angela. He hasn't talked to me about her, but from what I hear that relationship was over a long time ago," she paused. "But I can tell he really loved her. I guess that's my point. She's the type of woman Thomas wants. She was beautiful and smart and from what I hear, kind and sweet."

"I don't get your point, Abby. Maybe that's the kind of woman he's dated, but clearly he's looking for something else in a partner. Maybe he's looking for someone like you. Someone that is beautiful and courageous. Someone who can usually take care of herself." He glanced at the yellow and blue bruise covering her face.

"Don't start," she narrowed her eyes at him. "I know, I messed up. I didn't even see him coming until it was too late. I guess that's twice in the last few months. First the kidnapping then the attack. That doesn't sound like someone that can take care of herself. Thomas has to think I'm inept and stupid. Another reason I'm not his type. Those other women are...what word am I looking for?" She pondered, searching for the right word.

"Boring?" Morrigan supplied.

"Refined," she finally corrected. "They would never put themselves in the position to be attacked that way. Walking into a dark alley would be beneath them. Thomas needs a partner that will fit into his world. He's rich and powerful. He's respected internationally. His partner needs to be just as charismatic as he is. That's not me. Why would I want to put myself through that kind of heartache? I can do without the embarrassing rejection, thank you anyway."

"Then use him for sex," Morrigan suggested. "If you're not going to risk your heart, have a good time with him. Create memories then move on. Both of you could definitely use the release," he mumbled.

"You're disgusting and cold," Abby accused.

"What? Are you too refined for a one night stand?" he asked with a smile.

Abby didn't respond. He was trying to trap her and it wasn't going to work.

"Okay, don't answer that. It's redundant anyway, we both know I'm right. But listen to me, Abby. I'm being serious now."

He studied her until she finally looked at him. "I saw the look on Thomas' face this afternoon as we walked away. The guy cares about you. He was worried about you. That game was a little reckless. You are still healing. Look at you, even with the massive feast we just ate you still look weak and tired. If nothing else, the two of you have become friends over the past several weeks. If you are going to avoid him now, Thomas has a right to know why. I've never known you to be cruel. What you're doing right now, is cruel." Morrigan stood and kissed his sister on the top of her head. "Just think about it. I know you'll do the right thing."

* * * *

McBride slid into the shadows of the trees. What was this place? Who were these people? Abby and her brother Morrigan changed into twenty seven different animals in a matter of minutes. The blond threw fire. The sword fight had been unreal and then Thomas and the other couple engaged in combat like ancient warriors on a Hollywood screen. It was like they were preparing for battle. Were they planning on taking over the human race? He sat against a tree and pondered the situation. What could the others do? First, there was Alex and Dimitri back in New York. What about Tala Fitzgerald? Was she such an ace investigator because she had some kind of superpowers? If Abby and Morrigan were demons or something, what about their parents? Did Monroe know? He was close friends with Mason Cooper.

Rand needed more information. He could hide out in the forest and gather evidence. Then he'd decide what to do with it. He wondered what happened after dark. Did the werewolves come out? He was a little worried, but he had a gun. He was a cop. If he just stayed under the cover of these trees he could continue to observe this group undetected.

* * * *

Thomas watched curiously as Abby exited the farmhouse and walked to the large wooden railing that enclosed the patio. She leaned against the large frame and stared into the distance. After a few moments Thomas stood and moved in beside her. "I'm sorry Abby," he told her softly. "I'm so sorry that man hurt you. I don't blame you for hating me. Everything you had to go through is all my fault," he paused. His talk with Victor helped him to understand he needed to take control of his life again. He was now angry and determined to catch the man responsible, but he still felt guilty about Abby. This wonderful special woman had almost been killed because of him. He sighed. "I don't know what else to say. I just wanted you to know how awful I feel about all of this and I wanted you to know I understand."

Abby whirled to face him. She was pissed. "If you think I'm mad at you because some sadistic monster tried to kill me, you're an idiot." She turned away from Thomas and braced herself on the large rail. "How many times have I told you what this man is doing is not your fault?" she demanded shakily. She was losing control, that always happened when she got angry but right now she was absolutely furious. "A dozen or so?" she continued. "Every time another girl went missing and then again when that moron of a detective found their bodies and so many times in between I couldn't possibly count them all." She took a deep breath. "You honestly believe that after all of that, I could actually be mad at you because that man tried to abduct me and kill me?" She turned back towards him completely defeated. "I guess you really don't know me at all Thomas," she whispered regretfully. "If you did, you would never think I was that big of a hypocrite." She started to move away, she needed to get out of here.

Thomas stepped in front of Abby and placed an arm on either side of her. He gripped the railing with both hands as he studied her intently. She couldn't move, he had trapped her there on purpose. He needed to know how she really felt. Was it possible she was telling the truth? That she didn't hate him for this? Then what? Why had everything changed so dramatically since the attack? "You're right. I am an idiot." He grinned a little at her response. Emotion was flittering across her face. "I'm sorry for that too," he told her sincerely. He was a complete idiot for not recognizing his feelings earlier. "But before you go, I need to know why," he told her. "Please tell me why you have become so distant since the attack. I need to know what went wrong."

Abby closed her eyes. She didn't know how to explain this without humiliating herself. But Thomas was right, she had changed. It wasn't the attack on her that changed things though. It was the attack on Angela. "I guess I just realized I was going down the wrong path," she finally told him. "We've been spending a lot of time together lately. I realized I was starting to hope for something different. Something impossible. When I woke up after the attack I realized I needed to step back, that's all. Nothing happened Thomas. Nothing went wrong. For my own sanity I just need a little distance."

Thomas was afraid to hope, but did that mean she had feelings for him too? Had Victor been right after all? Well, now was as good a time as any to find out. He slowly moved forward until his body was pressed against hers. She didn't move, Thomas thought that was a good sign. He'd give her one more chance to react. He lifted his right hand and gently slid his fingers through her hair. It was so soft and beautiful. Being this close to Abby was intoxicating.

Abby remained frozen. She couldn't move, she couldn't think. What was Thomas up to? Was he going to kiss her? She closed her eyes as he lifted his hand and ran his fingers through her hair. She'd never been this alive before. Her body tingled all over. His touch made every molecule dance with pleasure. She waited with anticipation, not knowing how this would end, but in spite of herself hoping for more.

Thomas let his fingers glide downward until they reached the ends of Abby's hair. Then he reached back up and entangled his fingers in the soft locks again. This time, he maneuvered the palm of his hand to the back of her neck and forced her head upward. Her eyes were closed. He studied her, waiting for her to open them again. He needed her to look at him. He had to see what was in her eyes before he took his next step. It only took a moment. Abby stood there, gazing into his soul. He couldn't resist any longer. He slowly lowered his head and took her mouth with his. At first it was gentle, but then Abby deepened the kiss. He was a little surprised, but thrilled. The response she evoked in him was surreal. He'd never felt this way in his life. Both of them seemed to be experiencing some kind of desperate frenzy. Thomas gripped her buttocks and lifted her onto the railing. He needed to be closer to her. He needed to make love to her. That's when it hit him. Abby deserved better than this. He wouldn't attack her like a wild animal on the front porch. Thomas softened the kiss and pulled away, slightly.

Don't stop, she wanted to scream. Why was he pulling away? Had he changed his mind? Had she scared him? She sat on the thick wooden porch rail, watching him for a sign. Did he regret the closeness? She was confused. He was watching her, no he was studying her intently. She couldn't move, Thomas looked so relaxed. She realized she'd never seen him like this before. Thomas never relaxed completely. She honestly did not understand what was going on with him. She wished again for Megan's wonderful talent. She'd give anything to read Thomas' mind right now.

Thomas placed his hands on her waist and gently set her on the ground. Then he took her hand and led her to the bench. He casually sat down, pulling her with him. "I think I got a little carried away back there." He admitted as he took her hand in his and gently traced the top with his thumb.

Abby didn't think so. She thought things were pretty much perfect before he took a step back. But now that her body was relaxing again, her brain kicked into overdrive. This didn't change anything. Thomas wasn't hung up on Angela or her death anymore. She knew that wasn't the problem. The big, glaring unavoidable problem was that Abby was not Thomas' type. He fell for glamorous, sophisticated, worldly beauties. Abby didn't have a sophisticated bone in her body. She wasn't glamorous nor was she beautiful. She was down to earth and normal in every way. She could never hold someone as rich and powerful as Thomas Deveraux. He deserved better. He deserved a woman he could be proud of, a woman he wouldn't be ashamed to walk into one of those important social events with. He deserved someone like Angela. Her stomach clenched in pain as she realized this was still impossible.

Thomas frowned. Something had changed. Abby was pulling away again. He moved in a little closer and rested his arm across the back of the bench. "Will you please explain to me what's going on?" he asked softly. "Abby, please talk to me." He reached up and pushed a lock of hair away from her face then gently brushed his finger across her bruise. Seeing it there still made his stomach twist in agony.

Abby moved away from him. She continued until her side hit the arm rest. Then she swiveled and pulled her legs onto the bench. She wasn't sure what to do here. She wrapped her arms around her legs for protection as she rested her head against the back of the bench. Thomas deserved an explanation, but she didn't know where to start.

Thomas didn't move. She was pushing him away again, but he didn't know why. How was he supposed to fix this if he didn't understand what the problem was? He waited for her to explain. Nothing. Just when he was about to give up and retreat into the house, she spoke.

"I've been attracted to you since the moment I laid eyes on you," Abby began. She knew she'd leave this patio humiliated, but Thomas deserved an explanation for her behavior. She didn't know how to be anything but completely honest with him. "You stepped into the doorway of that horrible cave and I was mesmerized," she admitted. "I watched as you tried to comfort Ariel then I stood in amazement as you systematically killed Hector."

Thomas closed his eyes now. He'd forgotten she'd witnessed that scene in the cave. He'd been obsessed with punishment and revenge that day and had risked the lives of everyone for vengeance. All of them could have been killed because, even back then, he'd gotten caught up in his problems and shut everyone else out. Only now did it hit him, the realization that he was selfish. Somewhere along the line he'd become so absorbed in his own problems that he could shut everyone and everything else out completely.

Abby's voice abruptly brought him out of his thoughts. "I don't know what it says about me but as I stood there watching you, I was elated. I could see you weren't just trying to kill that monster, you wanted him to suffer and pay for everything he'd done. At the time, I believed you were doing it for yourself. But I think I understand you a little better now. Hector had to pay for the pain he'd caused your family, sure. But you also did it for me and Lakeisha. You wanted him to pay for it all. He had to pay for the deaths, the torture, the fear that man instilled in so many. A sudden death was too good for him. He needed to suffer before he died. You gave me that Thomas and I thank you for it. I enjoyed being a witness to it. I guess that makes me less of a person, but I can live with that. I can accept that about myself," she paused.

Thomas didn't think that made her less, he actually thought that made her perfect. How was it possible he had found a woman so perfect for him and he was about to lose her? He sensed that coming. He had been too stupid to recognize his feelings and now it was too late. He was trying to come up with something to say when she continued.

"I also understand that you can't. That you would never be able to want someone like me. Someone as flawed as I am," she whispered, blinking back tears. This was so hard. She didn't know how she was going to get through it.

Thomas' head shot up. What was she talking about? He started to move towards her, but she held up her hand to stop him. He sat there, frozen in shock.

Shadows

"No," Abby said holding up her hand. She couldn't get through this if he came any closer. "I understand that someone like you needs a certain kind of mate. Someone far more glamorous and special than I could ever be."

"Abby," Thomas interrupted. "I don't..."

"No," she begged. "Please, just let me get through this." She swallowed hard, took a deep breath and tried to continue. "The entire way home, that awful walk with Victor and Ariel, was so tense. I felt bad for them, but I was also feeling sorry for myself. You had made such a profound impression on me but I could tell I hadn't made the slightest impression on you. You didn't even know I was alive. It was disappointing, but not surprising. The surprise was that someone like you would come after me in the first place," she swallowed. "Anyway, I went back to my life and you went back to yours. I assumed we wouldn't cross paths again. Then came the night of the bombings. You spent the entire evening at the shifter camp helping Ty defuse those bombs. Once again I realized what a wonderful man you must be. You have power and tons of money. You're father used to be the warrior leader, your sister is the Fae Queen. The reality of that hit me all over again. I didn't even try to talk to you that night, what would have been the point?" she shrugged.

"Then you walked into that restaurant, Diana on your arm and I knew I'd been right. I'm too normal for you. There is nothing about me that a man like you would find the least bit interesting. I didn't plan to get involved in this. I planned to leave you alone. I'm sorry that my backing away made you think I was angry with you. None of this is your fault, Thomas. I really wish you could accept that. You've spent so much time feeling guilty and responsible for something that's beyond your control."

Thomas moved a little closer to Abby. It felt like there was such a huge gulf between them. How had he messed this up so badly? She was wrong about everything. "Abby?" He said softly. "You know I didn't have the slightest interest in Diana. I guess she may have seemed glamorous and sophisticated from a distance but..."

"I know you didn't care about Diana," Abby interrupted. "But you were very much in love with Angela." She paused, studying the confused look on Thomas' face.

"I don't understand," he finally admitted.

She gave him a forced smile. "Thomas, you were in love with Angela. She was also gorgeous and refined. I could even see that in death. Angela would have made the perfect wife for you. She's the kind of woman you could be proud of. Someone you could walk into one of those fancy socials with and know, without a doubt, that your wife was the most beautiful woman in the room. That's the kind of woman you deserve, Thomas. I am confident that's the kind of woman you will eventually end up with. Like Luke and Marlena. When they walked into a room, everyone stopped and stared."

That's when it hit him. Abby reminded him of Marlena. Maybe that's why he was so attracted to her. Marlena, the real Marlena, was the most down to earth and loving woman he had ever known. There wasn't a woman in the world that could stand up to the competition. Except Abby, that is. Abby was just as good and kind and poised as his mother. "Angela was all of those things," Thomas agreed. "She was beautiful and refined. And I admit I did love her once, a very long time ago. I'm not still in love with her if that's what you think," he argued.

Shadows

"I don't," Abby assured him. "I just know that's the type of woman you will love. I also know I could never be that woman," she paused. "That's why I need distance. I just need a little time to sort out my feelings. Maybe someday we can be friends again Thomas, but not now. Right now it's too painful for me to be around you. I'm just asking you to give me some time and space."

"I'm sorry. I can't do that," he told her seriously.

"What do you mean?" she asked. If he didn't stay away she'd never be able to get over him. She'd never deal with the disappointment if she had to see him all the time.

Thomas slid in a little closer until his leg was touching her foot. She looked down at the contact then back into his eyes. "I can't give you space Abby, because being away from you is too painful for me." Thomas studied the woman. How had he missed her beauty? He should have noticed how stunning she was the first moment they met, but instead he was focused on the danger they were in. He had been completely oblivious to everything else around him, except Hector. The same had been true the past few weeks. He'd grown close to her, loved every minute they were together. In fact, he'd secretly begun to long for those quiet moments the two of them shared each night at the end of a long day. But, he hadn't noticed how utterly beautiful she was. Apparently, neither had she. Not if she believed the nonsense she'd been muttering. He reached up and brushed away a tear.

Abby didn't know what to do now. Was he serious? How could being away from her be painful for him? She didn't understand.

"Abby," Thomas began. Then he gently lifted one foot after the other and placed them on the ground. He needed to be closer.

He wanted her in his arms…forever. Thomas took a chance and leaned in to press his lips against hers again. At first Abby didn't move, then she wrapped her arms around him and kissed him with just as much passion as she had the first time. As much passion as he had for her. Thomas hoped that was the case anyway. He gently shifted Abby so she was nestled under his arm, her head resting on his chest. "I think maybe I should explain something to you," he began then stopped. "I honestly had no idea you were that shallow and judgmental."

Abby pushed away from Thomas and glared at him. What did he mean she was shallow? She wasn't in the least bit judgmental and she wouldn't even allow Thomas to make such an accusation.

Thomas laughed. "I thought that would get to you," he said pulling her back down and forcing her head onto his chest. "Okay, you're not shallow or judgmental, but you are certainly acting like it. I'm not sure where all that nonsense about you being too normal for me is coming from but I don't like it," he scowled. "There is nothing normal about you, Abby. You are the most special, unique woman I have ever met."

Abby tried to shove him away so she could look him in the eye, but he pushed her back down. She was the one to scowl now. He might get away with that once, but not again. If he wasn't running his fingers through her hair right now she'd be able to think. She knew she should get up, force him to stop, but she didn't want him to stop. Having him this close felt so good, she never wanted this moment to end.

"Now for the explanation," he began as he stared out into space. "Angela was my high school sweetheart. We met and instantly had a connection."

Shadows

Abby pushed herself up this time and tried to move away but Thomas wouldn't let her. "Thomas, I don't need to hear this," she paused to catch her breath, "I don't want to hear this. I already know how deeply she impacted your life."

"Angela did impact my life," Thomas agreed. "But not nearly as profoundly as you have, Abby. I think you need to hear this and I need to tell you. Please, just give me a minute," he studied her, waiting for an answer.

Abby didn't know what to think about all this. But, if Thomas needed to talk about Angela, she would listen. Then she'd make a run for it. "Okay. Go ahead," she said as she laid her head back against his chest. She'd enjoy the moment now and suffer the consequences later.

"So," Thomas continued. "Angela and I began spending time together. I thought she was special. I thought eventually, if things continued as well as they had been going, I could share my secret with her. I guess deep down I knew that would never happen. I think that's why I never actually told her about my family and their lineage. I realized somewhere along the line that she wouldn't understand and she wouldn't accept it."

"You can't know that," Abby argued. "If you never told her, you can't know how she would have reacted."

"I do know," Thomas disagreed. "You're getting ahead of the story," he paused. "I shared a lot of firsts with Angela. First girlfriend, first kiss..."

"I get the picture," Abby interrupted. She really didn't want to think about all his firsts.

Thomas laughed. "We were rapidly approaching the end of our senior year when things became undeniably clear to me," he sighed. "Angela's sister was having a party. It seemed that's all Angie wanted to do anymore. I've never been big on parties or alcohol so I begged out. I told her dad needed my help. Dad took me hunting that night. He said I needed to start learning the trade. You know, the warrior side of things. I'd been training all my life, but I'd never actually been out hunting with dad. I was shocked and elated. I couldn't wait. Dad and I entered a dark alley and located a small group of vampires milling around. We were well into the battle when a group of girls exited a popular club by the side door. I was only vaguely aware the girls were even there. As you've probably noticed I tend to get tunnel vision," he smiled. That was an understatement. "Anyway, I had just finished off the last vamp when I saw her. Angie was standing at the end of the alley. The only way to describe the look on her face is horrified. I started towards her and she stepped back. Then she immediately became hysterical. She ordered me to stay away from her and called me every name she could think of. Bottom line, she thought I was a monster."

"But eventually she came around, right?" Abby asked pushing herself off Thomas' chest and shifting so she could watch him.

"No," Thomas said flatly, "she didn't. Dad tried to talk to her, but that only made things worse. Eventually Dante and Nick entered the alley and pretended to be Good Samaritan's. I was shocked by the fact that Angie wouldn't come near me, but she'd willingly walk out of a dark alley with two strange men."

"Wait," Abby stopped him. "How did she not know Dante and Nick? You guys are best friends."

Shadows

"They were part of a world I kept secret. She never met anyone from our world except my family." Thomas explained. "Nick and Dante took Angie to an empty warehouse," Thomas paused. This part was difficult. "It was the same building we went to that night. The night we found her body."

"I'm sorry," Abby whispered softly. That building obviously held some significance to Thomas and Angela, even before her death.

Thomas closed his eyes and continued. "Dad called Marlena then we headed to the warehouse. When we walked in the building, Angie began to scream. No matter what I tried, she wouldn't come near me. That's when Marlena and a friend of hers joined us. The guy was a shadow. Dad explained everything to me and then we turned the man loose on Angie. After a few moments he looked at my family in sorrow. It seemed there was no hope. He had read Angela's mind. She was too horrified and disgusted with what I was to ever be reasonable and accepting about it. He assured me that her love for me was real, but he was just as confident she could never accept our world. Marlena instructed the man to change her memory."

"That's how things ended?" Abby asked in shock.

"Not exactly," Thomas assured her. "The guy gave her a memory of finding me and dad on the street just outside the club. She thought I had broken off from dad and the two of us had come to the building to be alone. I tried to talk to her and act like everything was normal, but I was devastated. I know it's not what you want to hear, but I did love Angela. I had hoped the two of us could spend our lives together. Then, it was over, in an instant everything had changed." Thomas paused to gather his thoughts.

"How could you be sure?" Abby asked. "Wasn't your love for her worth fighting for?"

"If I thought there was a chance for us to be happy of course I would have fought." He looked out into the darkness again. "But I had firsthand experience with this. My mother felt the same way about dad and our life as Angela did. I watched mom and dad struggle for years, trying to balance two worlds. Mom hating the supernatural and resenting dad for bringing her into it. Dad depressed all the time because he was making the woman he loved so miserable. I couldn't live that way, Abby. But mostly I couldn't force Angie to live that way. I had one last night of intimacy with her before I began to sabotage our relationship."

"What do you mean?" Abby asked, curious now.

"I didn't want to hurt her. I wanted our breakup to be her idea. I thought she needed to leave me in order to have a normal, healthy life and give another guy a fighting chance. So, the following day I told her I had decided not to go to college after I graduated. I explained to her that I wanted to get involved with dad's business. I didn't need college for that. In fact, going to college would be an unnecessary delay. She tried to convince me to change my mind. When I stuck to my guns she broke things off. She went to college, met a nice guy and married him a year later."

"What?" Abby exclaimed. "How is that possible? You said she loved you."

"She did," Thomas said confidently.

"No way," Abby disagreed. "You can't love someone one minute and just move on the next."

Shadows

Thomas studied her. Wasn't that what she'd planned to do? How was that any different?

"No. It's not the same," she argued seeing his thoughts reflected in his eyes. "I never had you. She did. You were never in love with me, you loved her. The situation is totally different."

"Not so different Abby," Thomas disagreed. "Anyway, I'm glad she moved on. I would have felt much worse about the situation if she hadn't. Angela went to college and then she moved back to New York with her new husband. Eventually she got a job working for dad and I think you pretty much know the rest." He didn't want to talk about her death again. He'd gone through all that with Dante and Nick the night they found Angie's body.

"I didn't know Angela was married," she finally told him. "How did her husband take it?" She was sure she already knew the answer, but she had to ask. What had Thomas done for this man to help him deal with his loss?

"I didn't have to take on that particular horror," Thomas confessed. "I have to admit I'm grateful for that."

"Why not?" Abby asked, confused.

"Angela's husband was in the military. He died a couple months ago in Afghanistan. I think it was a car bomb," he admitted.

Abby was silent for only a minute then she turned to Thomas. "I'm glad," she said then hurried on at the strange look on his face. "I'm sure it was difficult for Angela to deal with the loss, but now they're both together again. They both experienced something horrific but now they have each other. Angela's story has a happy ending after all," she said confidently.

Thomas was amazed. Abby always had such a different outlook on life. She was optimistic and uplifting. So why did she have such a low self-esteem. He still didn't understand how she could think any woman alive was more beautiful than she was.

"You're staring," Abby told him uncomfortably. She looked down at her lap and waited to see what would come next.

"I can't help it," Thomas said not taking his eyes off her. "You're beautiful," he said then sat back in surprise at the angry look on Abby's face. What did he do now?

"Stop it Thomas," she said through gritted teeth. "I wasn't looking for a compliment. Don't patronize me. I am what I am," she took a deep breath. "I think you have gotten the wrong idea. I'm fine with who I am. I'm just realistic about it," she glanced away. "Most of the time." She hadn't been realistic lately. She'd allowed herself to dream of Thomas. She had pushed her way into his life, trying to force something that simply was not there.

She still didn't get it. Well, Thomas thought, he'd just have to be more direct. He reached around and placed his hand on the small of her back and pulled her to him at the same time as he placed his other palm on the back of her head. Then he kissed her. Not a gentle dainty kiss. A hard, passionate, intimate kiss. When he eventually had to come up for air he leaned in and whispered into her ear. "I am hopelessly, passionately and irrevocably in love with you Abigail Cooper." He smiled as she looked at him in wide eyed disbelief. "I would be honored to walk into any room, anywhere, at any time with you on my arm. And..." he continued, "I happen to believe you would be the most beautiful woman in the room. Never doubt that." He smiled at her then raised one eyebrow. "Now I'm just wondering what you plan to do about it," he asked.

Shadows

Abby was speechless. Was it possible, how could it be? "Please Thomas, don't joke about this."

"Who's joking?" he asked seriously.

"You," she said unsure of herself.

"Abby how can you be so astute about some things and so dense when it comes to yourself?" Thomas asked a little annoyed.

Abby glared at him not saying a word.

"Okay, sorry. I guess I could have used a little more tact. I just don't get you. I give you a compliment and you look at me like you want to bite my head off."

"I could. All I have to do is shift," Abby said without emotion.

"Yeah, but you wouldn't," Thomas said confidently.

"What makes you so sure about that?" she countered.

"Because I know you. You're too kind to cause anyone harm," Thomas paused. "Especially someone you love," he said hopefully.

Abby paused. "What makes you so sure I love you?" she asked hoping she sounded more casual than she felt. She did love Thomas, but the idea he loved her too was preposterous.

"Actually," Thomas gazed at her intently. "I'm not. It's just wishful thinking."

Abby couldn't lie. She was staring straight into his eyes and she couldn't lie to him. "I do love you, Thomas. But the idea that you love me is ridiculous. You're just under a lot of stress right now and I don't know, maybe you're afraid to be alone. Or you've gotten used to our friendship and you don't want to lose that right now." She knew she was babbling and she needed to stop herself.

"Or…like I said, I am in love with you." He studied her. Why wouldn't she believe him? "Abby, why did you recognize right away that I had strong feelings towards Angela but you won't accept my feelings for you?"

Abby shrugged. She was starting to waiver on her conviction that she was right.

"I did love Angela once. When she came up missing I knew right away what the outcome would be. I was devastated and I felt responsible somehow. When we got the call from that maniac I knew it was too late, but I had to go anyway. You understood that and you had to go too. You had to go so you could protect me. I understand that now. At the time, I wasn't thinking about why, I was just glad you were going." He stopped to study her. "Abby I know I've been selfish. I've been so self-absorbed," he looked down at his feet. "I'm truly sorry about that. I'm sorry I didn't realize I was falling for you until it was almost too late. I don't know, maybe it is too late. But I want you to know what I felt when I saw Angela lying on that floor, the horror, the guilt, the anger, that was nothing compared to the feelings I had when I opened my front door and saw you lying there. Seeing you crumpled in a ball like that almost killed me. I was so afraid, almost too afraid to investigate further for fear you were already dead. I knew in that instant how much I loved you and how much I needed you. When I realized you were still alive I could finally breathe again. If it weren't for Alex, I know you wouldn't have survived. I owe my sister a great debt. One I could never repay. If you can't trust that I love you, at least give me time to prove it. Please don't push me away. Let me spend some time with you. Let me show you how I feel. Maybe then you can love me, too."

She already loved him. But she liked the idea of time. If she gave this a chance, she'd know how he felt once this was all over. Her heart was going to be broken anyway, maybe Morrigan was right. She should jump in with both feet and enjoy the ride. She continued to study Thomas, then she smiled at him. "Okay," she finally said.

"Okay, what?" Thomas asked.

"Okay, we will spend some time together, getting to know each other. I like the idea of time. The more you can spare the better," she told him.

"Why?" he asked skeptically.

Abby frowned.

"Don't," he protested. "I like the smile better. I just want to know why you agreed. Is it because you believe me or because you think you need to stick it out until this is over?"

"Both I guess," Abby finally admitted. "I know this has been hard on you. I guess I have also realized that my being here for you has somehow helped you get through it. I'd like to continue to be there for you until this nightmare has ended," she paused. "It seems too surreal to believe you could actually love me, Thomas. But you sound sincere. I also like the idea of you proving it to me. I wonder, what does a rich and powerful man do to prove his love to a woman anyway? Mostly I like the idea of more time with you. If you break my heart I'll find a way to deal with that later. For now, I think I'll enjoy the ride."

Not exactly what he had hoped for, but it would do for now.

Abby rested her head back on his chest. "Thomas?"

"Yeah," he answered.

"It would kill me if you just used me as a one night stand. Please promise me you will never do that," she requested.

Thomas stood, walked to the railing and stared into the darkness. He was a little angry and extremely hurt by the request. He'd just told her how much he loved her and she thought all he wanted was a quick fling. He turned around and studied her for a long time before he spoke. "I don't think I deserved that, but maybe I do. I'm not the wealthy playboy the magazines portray. I don't know where that came from. Maybe you made that judgment when you heard about Diana or maybe you already believed it. I don't know."

"Thomas," Abby tried to interrupt.

"No. Now it's my turn," he cut her off. "I want to make love to you more than anything in the world. But, I'm not going to."

"What? Why not?" Abby protested.

"Because you don't think I'm serious. Because you don't believe me. I won't share that kind of intimacy with someone that thinks I'm just using them for a one night stand. The fact that you could suggest that means we're not ready for that kind of connection. When you are sure of my love, then we can consider it. But you

Shadows

will have to initiate the contact. My only request is that you don't do that until you know. I love you. As soon as you understand and accept that, we can be together. Not before."

Now Abby was upset. She knew she'd hurt Thomas and that was the last thing she wanted to do. She didn't know what to say or do. She didn't know how to fix this. She stood and walked to him. "I'm sorry," she said softly. "I didn't mean to hurt you." Abby wanted to cry. She had hurt him deeply, she could see it in his eyes.

Thomas reached out and wrapped his arms around Abby. She was sorry for hurting him, but not for suggesting he had less than honorable intentions. They both stood there, wrapped in each other's arms thinking about their future. Mostly wondering if they had one.

* * * *

Thomas looked up when the screen door opened and Victor walked out. Abby tried to pull away, but Thomas tightened his grip. He didn't want her to move yet. He shifted slightly so she could see it was Victor. "What's up?" he asked trying to sound casual.

"I really hate to interrupt this, but I need you in the security room. It's important. I hope you know I wouldn't have come out here if it wasn't." Regret was written all over Victor's face.

Thomas took Abby's hand and walked toward the door. When he reached Victor he put a hand on his shoulder. "Don't worry about it. I think we said about all there was to say for now." The three of them walked up the stairs and into the security room. Dimitri had set it up similar to the one at the Deveraux cabin. Computer monitors were spread out across the room showing various angles of the fort. Victor took a seat and began pushing buttons. An image popped up on the monitor directly in front of them.

"McBride," Abby and Thomas said at the same time.

"That's what I was afraid of," Victor sighed. "Now what do we do?"

"How long has he been there?" Thomas asked. "Rewind it and see when he arrived."

"Good idea," Victor said pressing buttons. The image fluttered across the screen as the recording went back, one hour, two hours. Victor finally stopped at one o'clock that afternoon. "Shit," he said kicking the chair next to him. It flew half way across the room.

"He knows everything," Abby said, shocked at the realization. They were all in trouble. "We have to detain him," she insisted. "We have to stop him. He'll ruin all of us if we don't."

Thomas ran his fingers through his hair. "I don't like the idea of bringing him into our home, but I think Abby's right. I've been dealing with him for weeks. He won't let this go. We have to detain him," he looked at Victor. "I'll do it. This is my property, legally. He's trespassing on government and private property. And he's way out of his jurisdiction. Let me take care of this on my own. I don't want anyone else targeted over this."

"We're all a target now," Victor corrected. "He saw Ariel," he turned to Abby. "He saw you and Morrigan playing your shifting game. Thomas and I will get him back to the house. Abby, you tell the others. We need everyone to agree on where we go from here."

Shadows

Abby brightened. "The others! Megan's here," she took off out the door and down the stairs before anyone could say a word.

"You two work things out or did I interrupt too soon?" Victor asked. He was worried about his timing.

"We didn't exactly work things out, not completely but don't worry. Like I said, I don't think there was anything left to say tonight," Thomas said evasively.

"What does that mean, exactly?" Victor asked as he headed for the front door.

Thomas wasn't sure what he wanted to tell Victor. He knew he could trust him, but this was personal. Abby had hurt him. He took a deep breath and followed Victor out the door. Once they were outside Thomas decided to confide in his friend. "She doesn't believe me," he finally said.

Victor slowed. "About what?" he asked, curious now.

"She doesn't think I'm in love with her. She thinks I'm just looking for a quick fling. A one night stand," he confessed.

"What!" Victor asked wide eyed. "You?" he was dumbfounded. Did the girl know Thomas at all? Then he began to laugh.

"I'm glad you find my life entertaining. I personally found it insulting," Thomas grumbled.

"Look, I'm sorry." Victor tried to regain his composure. "You have to admit it is kind of funny. For those of us that actually know you anyway," he paused. "Okay, in all seriousness, the girl is whacked. I thought the two of you spent a lot of time together. How could she possibly think you would want a one night stand?" Then it hit him. "The tabloids. You know I used to be jealous of you. I tried for centuries to gain the rep you have with women. No matter how hard I tried, I never could catch up."

"I'm so glad you're getting such a kick out of this," Thomas mumbled.

"Thomas, Abby might have doubts because of the papers and magazines, but she'll come around. Deep down she knows you. Give her a little time. Things have been just as hard on her as they have been on you lately. She's a suspect too and then the attack. Let things settle awhile. I know it's insulting, but keep it in perspective."

They reached the forest and both men immediately became silent. They wanted the element of surprise when they encountered McBride. As they approached the tree where he'd been holding surveillance all day, they slowed. Victor took the right, Thomas the left. Both men spotted him at the same time. Each nodded to the other as they pounced. The cop didn't have a chance.

McBride sat against the tree debating. He was just about to leave when two men jumped from the shadows. Before he knew what was happening, he was pinned to the ground. There was no use fighting. He couldn't get free if he tried. The men tied his arms behind his back and forced him to his feet. McBride instantly recognized Thomas. He didn't know who the other man was, but they were going to regret this attack. "Assault on a PO. Not your usual MO Thomas, but still against the law," he smiled. "I've got you now. Bad move. Now you get to rot in jail while I finish putting the case together on the killings. You will never see daylight again."

"I think you've forgotten something very important," Victor said casually. "You're the one in custody, McBride."

Shadows

"Good, that's all the proof I need to show you knew who I was when you jumped me," McBride sneered. "My case keeps getting better by the minute. Anything else you want to confess while we're at it?"

"Uh, again I think you've forgotten something. Aren't you supposed to give me Miranda before you question me?" Victor taunted. "And here I thought we had a smart cop on our hands. Move it," Victor shoved the detective.

"Getting someone else to do your dirty work, Thomas?" McBride asked. He couldn't get free, not yet. The large man had tied the rope too tight. He was securely bound, but he wasn't going to give up.

Thomas didn't take the bait. "McBride, you are being detained for unlawfully trespassing on government property. And please don't pretend like you didn't see the signs. You can't walk two steps without encountering one. We are going to detain you until such time as the military decides what to do with you. This is a highly classified military operation. It's a matter of national security. You have no jurisdiction here McBride and you know it. So keep spouting off about assaulting a PO and intent. You're the one that's going to find yourself behind bars."

The group left the forest and headed for the farmhouse. Ty and Tony joined them and escorted McBride through the front door and into the library. The rest of the group was waiting inside.

Kylee jumped up at the sight of him. "Rand McBride, what are you doing? Have you completely lost your mind?"

"Kylee, why are you here?" He glanced around the room then settled on Thomas. "Don't tell me you've abducted Kylee, too."

"Don't be ridiculous Rand," Kylee answered. "I work for the Deveraux's," she studied him. McBride didn't look good. "When was the last time you slept?" she demanded.

"Kylee it's okay to tell me the truth. If they threatened you, I can protect you. Why did they capture you? Are they forcing you to conduct scientific studies or something?" McBride speculated.

Kylee sighed and shook her head. "You are further gone that I thought. If you don't stop this nonsense I'm going to perform a scientific study on you," she turned to the rest of the room. "I'm sorry. He's usually more observant and astute than this. His obsession with Thomas has clearly muddied his mind," she sat back down and glared at McBride.

"Don't give me that look Kylee. I know you never would have quit the ER on your own. These people are monsters. I've seen it. Do you have any idea what you've gotten yourself into?" Rand argued.

"I did quit the ER and I know exactly what I've gotten myself into. These guys are not monsters. They're a lot like you. They're fighting evil and protecting society. If you'd stop to think for about half a second you'd figure that out for yourself. But not Rand McBride. No, you have to be stubborn and bullheaded about everything. Well, this time your inability to give in is going to hurt a lot of good people. If you hurt them, you're going to hurt me."

"Kylee," Rand begged. "Let me help you. You know I can."

"Enough," Victor cut in. "Kylee I realize he's a friend of yours, but there's no reasoning with him. I assume Abby filled you in on the situation."

Shadows

"Yes," Kylee said sighing. "I'm afraid it's worse than you might think. Rand comes from a very religious family. I have no doubt what he saw shocked and disturbed him. He's not open minded like me. He won't stop until he destroys everyone here and anyone else he's convinced himself is involved." She glanced at McBride, he was scowling. "He means well, but I'm afraid with him everything is black and white. He's not going to be able to distinguish between good and evil. To him good is human, supernatural is evil. I wish I could help both sides; you guys and him, but I'm at a loss."

"Megan?" Victor asked. "Do you have any ideas?"

Megan shook her head. She was trying to get in but just like before it was very difficult. "Let me think about it for a few more minutes," she said cryptically hoping they understood.

Orin didn't like the situation they were faced with. They had to detain the guy, but he was a detective with the NYPD. This could turn out worse than any of them suspected. "There's a jail facility in the basement. For now, let's put him in there. I assume it was the brig or something when this was still an active military base. Or maybe a private prison from years ago. Who knows? Right now I'm just grateful it's down there. Thomas, we'll wait for your contact with the State Department to get back to us before we make any other decisions," Orin bluffed.

Megan stopped Victor before he and Thomas left the room. "He needs to be watched. Don't untie his hands yet. I need to talk to everyone before we go forward. I got in, but only momentarily." She began to pace the room, agitated.

"Okay, he's behind bars and his hands are still secure. What did you learn?" Thomas asked as he and Victor stepped back into the room.

"I only had a second. It was difficult to get in," she took a deep breath. "He's a shifter," she admitted.

"What?" Kylee and Abby said at the same time.

"He can't be left alone," Abby said, slightly panicked. "I'll watch him. If he can shift, he can escape," she turned for the door.

"Wait just a minute," Megan stopped her. "I agree we can't leave him alone for long and he can't stay in a jail with bars. Eventually he's going to give in and shift," she looked at Abby then Morrigan. "He's fighting it. Like Kylee said, his parents were very religious. McBride first shifted when he was very young. His mother caught him in the act. She freaked. I got that memory loud and clear. He's struggling. He wants to get away, but his mother convinced him shifting was bad. She said he had a demon inside him. If he gave into the demon, he would eventually turn completely evil. He's never shifted again. He believes his mother's assessment. He thinks if he gives in and shifts, he will have a harder and harder time controlling his dark side."

"He honestly believes that?" Morrigan asked. "Wait, you said his parents were religious and told him shifters were demons. If he's a shifter at least one of his parents also shifts."

"I don't think so," Megan told him. "Maybe he was adopted or something," she turned to Orin. "Can you send someone to investigate that? Maybe have a couple guys pretend to be a salesman or repairman or something? I honestly believe they are going to learn the two of them are one hundred percent human though."

"Are you sure about this?" Kylee asked. She'd known Rand for a long time. She was having a hard time believing he was a shifter.

"Positive," Megan assured her. "Like I said, he's only shifted once in his life and he was very young at the time, around four I'd say. He's afraid of the consequences. He has a lot of respect for his mother. He believed she was right. The problem he's having, is he needs to escape. He's having a very difficult struggle. Should he give in to the demon and escape or be imprisoned by us. He also believes we are evil, just as bad as the demon. In fact, he's using Abby and Morrigan as an example of why he shouldn't give in." She smiled at the siblings. "He believes you two have given into the demons. That's why Abby is okay with Thomas being a serial killer."

"Is he going to give in to his need to escape?" Morrigan asked.

"I believe so, yes. It's going to take time, but not much. We're going to have to find another place to detain him. Somewhere he can't escape once he shifts," Megan admitted.

"What if we move him to one of the bunkers? They're supposed to be air tight. We have that one near the edge of the fort that we outfitted for the workers. It already has a bed and a table. He'll be comfortable there but secure," Victor suggested.

"I want to check it out myself," Morrigan told him. "Give me a few minutes and I'll let you know. I'll need someone to come with me. You'll have to lock me in and see if I can escape."

"I'm coming too. It will be faster if we both shift and try to get out. Two minds are better than one and all that," Abby smiled at her brother. "Who's going to lock us in?"

"I will," Victor told them. "That way I can work on a locking mechanism for the door while the two of you test the inside."

The three of them left the room. Abby was uncomfortable. Victor kept watching her. She felt like he wanted to say something but he was holding back. They walked in silence to the bunker. "If you can get out, then he can," Victor deduced. "If it's really secure, bang on the door and I'll let you out. You have twenty minutes. If I haven't seen or heard you by then I'm opening the door."

"Okay," Morrigan agreed. He and Abby entered the bunker and watched Victor close the large door. Morrigan turned to Abby. "We don't have much time. Spill it. What happened between you and Thomas? I was sure once you talked the two of you would work things out. Things between you are still strained. Why?" he asked as he walked the long wall looking for openings.

"I messed everything up," Abby confessed. "I offended and hurt him. I'm not sure he'll ever forgive me for it. I opened my big mouth and stuck my foot in it."

"What did you say?" Morrigan asked as he pushed on the corner of the wall.

"I suggested he only wanted me so he could have a one night stand," Abby said.

Morrigan turned around immediately. "You what?" he asked astounded. "Of course he's offended. What did he say? What in the world could have made you make such a ridiculous accusation?"

Shadows

"Uh..." Abby hesitated. "It's private," she finally told him.

"Abigail Cooper. What are you not telling me?" Morrigan demanded.

"Okay fine. He said he's in love with me. I didn't believe him. So he said he wanted to spend time getting to know me. That's when I told him I wouldn't be a one night stand," she said coldly. "You satisfied? Now you know all the sordid details."

"Abby," Morrigan shook his head and took a deep breath. "You're not going to get out of this easily," he finally told her. "Men rarely admit they're in love. He opened up to you. He let himself become vulnerable for you. If Thomas told you he was in love with you, it wasn't easy for him. It was bad enough you didn't believe him. Then, for you to suggest he was only after sex...I'm sorry, but that was cold. It was cruel and insulting. Maybe with time he'll forget it, but it's not going to be easy for him. No wonder there's tension between you two."

"You're not telling me anything that will help," she scowled. "I can't see any holes over here. How is your side?" she asked.

"Fine. I think the walls are secure. We'll need to shift into something small and study the seams, but I think we can detain McBride in here," he paused. "Abby I don't know how to help you. Why exactly did you decide Thomas was lying when he said he's in love with you?"

"I didn't say he was lying. I said I didn't believe him," she corrected.

"That's the same thing," Morrigan argued. "Why don't you believe him? He didn't sound sincere?"

"No. He sounded sincere," she admitted.

"Then what?" Morrigan asked. "I don't get it."

"It doesn't make sense. How could someone like him love someone like me?" she told him.

"So, Thomas bared his soul and confessed his love for you and you rejected him simply because of your ridiculous insecurities?" Morrigan said angrily. "Thomas didn't deserve that. You owe him an apology. I don't know that it will matter, but you still owe it to him."

"I already told him I was sorry I hurt him," she said angrily.

"But not sorry you doubted him. Not sorry you offended him. Not sorry you questioned his intentions?" Morrigan asked.

"Well no," Abby said. Was she sorry for doubting him? Was this all about her own insecurities not Thomas' intentions? She sighed. She had to admit it was. She just couldn't see Thomas loving her. She wasn't powerful and charismatic like he was. He was in control of the largest, most successful company in the world. She didn't even have a job. Not a real one anyway. She was insecure because, what could she possibly bring to the relationship?

"If you're not sorry for any of those things, you're right. You don't deserve him." He was upset with his sister. He knew she didn't believe in herself and he hated that, but now her low self-esteem was hurting others. "We're running out of time. Do you want to shift into a bird or a mouse?"

Now her brother was angry with her, too. She sighed. "I'll shift into a mouse and take the bottom. You take the top." She

Shadows

immediately changed and tried to find a way to escape. The bunker was solid. She couldn't find a single flaw. No escape route from the bottom. She shifted again to check the walls. This time she changed into a large lizard. She climbed the first corner seam, then scurried back to the ground and ascended the second seam. Once again she slid back down and moved to the third section, then the fourth. Once she finished, she changed again. This time into an elephant and charged the wall. Nothing, all the walls were secure. She changed once again, this time into a gorilla and leapt upwards grabbing a large ceiling beam. She swung her enormous body and kicked the door as hard as she could. Nothing. The door didn't budge. She was just shifting back when the entryway swung open.

"What was that?" Victor asked. He caught a glimpse of Abby as a gorilla then as Abby again. Morrigan had been doing more of the same. He finished before Abby and was just waiting for her to be satisfied.

"It's secure," Morrigan assured him. "I couldn't find any way out of here no matter what I changed into. Abby and I have had more experience than McBride. He won't escape. I'm confident of that."

"Good," Victor smiled. "Finally something we can count on."

Morrigan walked out of the bunker and headed for the house. He didn't say another word to his sister. He was becoming more and more livid by the minute.

Victor furrowed his brow at Morrigan. Something had changed while they were in the bunker. He turned to Abby. She was just as upset. "Are you sure it's safe to lock the guy in there?" He asked Abby. "I mean the two of you walked in there as normal contented people and you both walked out disgruntled and unhappy."

"No. It's me, not the bunker," she confessed.

"I see," Victor studied her. "Does this have anything to do with Thomas?"

She sighed. "I guess he told you about our talk?"

"No. Not really," Victor said casually as he turned and headed for the house.

"I don't believe you. He told you what I said, didn't he?" Abby persisted.

"Abby," Victor stopped to face her. "Thomas is an honorable man. He wouldn't brag or gab about a private conversation. As a friend he did confide in me. I convinced him to tell me what was bothering him. After a lot of persuasion, he finally did. I don't think I have to tell you what part of your conversation that was. You know how you treated him. He confessed his feelings for you and you threw it back in his face. He told you he loved you and you treated him like a rich playboy. So, if you and Morrigan were fighting over the way you treated Thomas, I'm happy about that. At least Morrigan understands Thomas even if you don't." He turned to head for the house then stopped. "You know, it's not easy for Thomas and Alex. They are constantly in the spotlight. Nothing they do is private. Unfortunately, the two of them rarely give the tabloids' anything to talk about. They are good, honorable, honest people. So the magazines have to make things up. Gossip and scandals sell after all." Victor shook his head at her. "Never mind. If you don't understand I can't explain it to you. If you honestly believe Thomas could declare his love just to get you in the sack, he's better off without you." Then he turned and walked quickly to the house.

Abby stood there, stunned. Victor thought she believed the tabloids. That meant Thomas thought so too. She sat on the ground and laid her head on her knees. What had she done? Morrigan was right. She was insecure and she was hurting people because of it. She thought back over her conversation with Thomas. He had seemed sincere. No, he was sincere. She knew that. Thomas was being honest with her. She felt his love in his kisses, all of them. He was gentle and loving and open and honest about his feelings. Abby began to cry. Thomas had offered her everything she'd ever wanted. The man of her dreams had offered her the world and she'd accused him of wanting a one night stand. How could he ever forgive her? She wasn't sure she'd forgive him if the tables were turned. If she ended up alone for the rest of her life, she had no one to blame but herself.

Thomas watched as Morrigan walked through the door. He seemed angry. Where was Abby? "So?" Thomas asked. "Are they secure?"

"Uh...yeah," Morrigan answered. "I couldn't find a way out neither could Abby. McBride's not going to escape if we couldn't." He started to head for the kitchen then stopped. "Thomas?" he paused. He was ashamed of his sister but he wanted to fix this. He just wasn't sure what to do. He was treading on thin ice here. He didn't want to embarrass Thomas, but he needed to apologize.

"Yeah?" Thomas answered studying Morrigan. The man was nervous and clearly upset.

"Can I talk to you for a minute?" Morrigan asked.

"Okay. It looked like you were headed for the kitchen. You want to talk in there?" Thomas asked.

"Sure," the two men headed in that direction. Morrigan pulled out two Cokes and sat next to Thomas at the table.

"I'm not sure how to put this," Morrigan confessed. "Abby was upset, so she talked to me about what happened with you two." He paused, but didn't get a reaction from Thomas. "I'm sorry," he finally said. "I could strangle my sister. For such a smart person, Abby can be so dense sometimes."

"Morrigan, don't worry about it," Thomas told him. He didn't need an apology from Abby's brother.

"I am worried," Morrigan told Thomas. "Abby is in love with you. And I'm afraid her low self-esteem may have offended you to the point you won't give her an honest chance."

Thomas smiled a little. This was starting to sound like a recent conversation he'd had with Dimitri. "Morrigan, I don't know if things are going to work out between me and Abby. I know I love her, but I'm not sure she understands me." He closed his eyes. How could he explain this?

Morrigan cut Thomas off. "I think the problem is more complex than that." He studied Thomas. "Abby is insecure. I'm not sure why. I think it might have to do with her late start."

"What does that mean?" Thomas asked.

"When Abby was little she was more interested in learning about animals than turning into them. She spent hours studying the different kinds of animals, their habits and characteristics. The knowledge has helped her tremendously now that she does shift. Her choices are far more diverse than any of the rest of us. We have to think of the animal to change into it. The more animals you know, the better your choice. Especially in an emergency. Anyway, Abby got a late start when it came to shifting. The other kids teased her a lot. Some of them were extremely cruel. She seemed to handle it well, but I think it's had a lasting impact. I realize I'm biased, but I think any guy would be lucky to have her. She disagrees. She doesn't think she's good enough for you. I'm sorry you finally told her how you feel and she couldn't believe it. I hope you will give her time. She really is worth the wait."

"I'm not going anywhere," Thomas said sincerely. "Morrigan, I love your sister. I'm not going to walk away from that. She agreed to give me time. I'm going to take it. Sure, she pissed me off. Her assessment of my character was insulting. But it's not the first time someone misjudged me because of a tabloid story. I want your sister in my life. Now it's up to her. She needs to decide if she wants me in her life, too. Unfortunately she's going to have to accept all of me. That includes the media, the lies and constant attacks on my character. It's not easy. I wouldn't blame her if she walked away. But it's her call."

"You think she believes the magazines?" Morrigan was shocked. "Then you got her all wrong too," he assured Thomas. "I know it's none of my business, but can I make a suggestion?" Morrigan asked.

"Sure," Thomas shrugged.

"I think the two of you are starting in the middle and it's causing a lot of confusion for both of you," Morrigan began.

"I don't follow you," Thomas admitted.

"You need to go back to the beginning. Most people meet, they go on a date, or hook up for drinks. Then they talk and get to know each other. Little by little they decide if they are compatible and then move to the next step. You and Abby were thrown together during an intense time for both of you. She basically moved in and you jumped to love. It doesn't seem like either one of you really knows the other one. You're both jumping to conclusions because you haven't had time to get to know each other. You're both wrong by the way. Abby wouldn't believe a tabloid story any more than you would use her for a quick night of fun. My suggestion is to go back to the beginning. Ask Abby out on a date. Talk about your hobbies, your likes and dislikes. Take some time to get to know each other. I guess I'm saying take a step back. I know you love her and she loves you. That's not going to change if you slow down. Your love is real and it's based on attraction and character but that's not enough. Do you understand what I'm trying to tell you?"

"I do," Thomas considered what Morrigan was telling him. It made sense. Maybe they should try to take this a little slower. Morrigan wasn't completely correct though. He'd had several nights getting to know Abby. The nights were always interrupted by something bad, but they did know each other. "I'll think about it," he told Morrigan. "By the way, do you know where Abby is?"

"Sorry, I don't. We kind of got into a fight. She disappointed me and I expressed my distaste in her lack of manners. I also told her she owes you an apology. She does. If she won't give it to you, I will. I'm sorry," Morrigan sighed. "I know that's not enough, but I am."

Thomas stood and placed a hand on Morrigan's shoulder. "Thanks. It's enough." He walked out the front door in search of Abby. He found her sitting by the bunker they were going to use

Shadows

for McBride. As he approached, he realized she was crying. He silently continued and sat beside her. She didn't move. Thomas pulled her into his arms and held her tight. He hated seeing her like this. Was it his fault?

"Thomas?" Abby sniffed as she straightened. "I am so sorry," she wiped the tears from her eyes. "You offered me the world and I offended you. I'm such an idiot."

Thomas smiled. "Then I guess we make a good couple. I've been an idiot for weeks now. I'd say you were pretty patient with me. I'm sure it's only fair that I forgive you, too." He moved back until he was leaning against the bunker. "Come over here," he pulled on her hand. Abby started to slide towards him when he put his hands around her waist and pulled her onto his lap. "I need to feel you close." He wrapped his arms around her and held her as she laid her head on his shoulder.

"Can we stay here forever?" she asked. "Sitting here in your arms feels so perfect. I never want to leave," she yawned. She was so tired.

Thomas kissed the top of her head. She looked so vulnerable and worn out. "We can stay for a while," he promised. "You're so wiped out, Abby. Why don't you go inside and go to bed early tonight?"

Abby hesitated. She wanted Thomas to hold her all night long, but she didn't know how to ask.

"What?" Thomas asked. "What is it you want?"

"I want you to hold me," she admitted. "I feel so safe and content in your arms."

374

Thomas laughed. "If you haven't noticed, I am holding you."

"I noticed," Abby said softly. "I meant, I wish you could hold me all night."

It was going to be hard to hold her and not take it any further but for her, he would do anything. "Then I will," he said softly.

Abby lifted her head so she could study him. "Really? You would do that for me?" she was surprised.

"I would," he told her.

"Thank you, Thomas." She was touched by his tenderness and love, she realized. No wonder she had fallen for Thomas Deveraux so quickly.

* * * *

Megan stood in the dark hallway waiting. She'd probed McBride's mind again, but it was getting more difficult. She assumed that was significant. He was going to shift any minute now. It was always harder to read the minds of the supernatural. Mom could do it easy enough, but she'd been using her gift all her life. Megan only used hers when it was necessary. She watched McBride. He was pacing. Megan knew the instant he made up his mind. She pressed her back against the wall a little harder and sent a warning to Tony. McBride was about to act. She needed to concentrate. If they were all going to get out of this without getting hurt, she had to get into his head at just the right moment.

McBride paced the small cage. Was his mother right? If he allowed the dark side out, would it consume him? Could he ever go back to being normal if he released the demon inside him again? He didn't know, but he had to get out of this cell. He'd done it once before when he was a child and then suppressed the darkness. He could do it again. But that was the problem, he never really felt like the darkness was suppressed. It was right there, all the time itching to get out. He'd struggled with this before but his conscience always won. If he used what he had inside him for personal gain, would he be able to squelch the desire in the future? He continued to pace, debating his options. But that was just it, he didn't have any. He could either change and get free or remain at the mercy of these...what? Not people? He had no idea what this group was or what they were capable of. He had to get free. He was going to do it. He'd use the evil inside of him one more time then turn his back on it forever.

Rand took a deep breath and changed into a cat. He easily slid through the metal bars then stopped, staring at the small enclosure on the other side. It felt good to use his powers. It felt exhilarating. He wanted to run outside and romp and play like a frisky kitten. He caught himself. That was the demon talking. He needed to change back and fast. He needed to put this whole thing behind him and never, ever do it again. He shifted back to a man and silently headed for the door.

Megan stopped McBride with her mind. "Tony," she called. "Hurry, I don't know how long I can hold him."

Tony rushed forward and tied McBride's hands again. Then the couple quickly escorted him to the library.

Morrigan sat in the big chair watching McBride. "Why won't you listen to us?" he asked in frustration. "You have a gift. It's genetic. It's what you are. Join us and let's go after the real threat. Work with us, not against us," he pled.

McBride didn't say a word. He would not join forces with these monsters. He would not turn his back on the human race. Mother was right. The demon inside was trying to take over. He needed to fight it.

"Fine," Morrigan said in exasperation. "We have no other choice. Let's take him to the bunker," he stood. He, Tony and Megan escorted McBride to his new cell. He was going to have to call his father as soon as they got back to the house. He hated this, but he knew dad would be more upset than he was. Shifters were never imprisoned. They didn't handle it well. As they approached the bunker he saw Thomas and Abby. They were cuddled together on the lawn next to the metal building.

Thomas and Abby stood as the group approached. "That didn't take long," Thomas observed.

"No," Megan said sadly. "But he's throwing off all kinds of conflicting emotions. Get him inside and I'll explain it to you."

"Wait," Abby said. "Let me try to talk to him. Maybe I can explain things. Maybe I can help him understand."

"I already tried," Morrigan told her. "Go ahead if you want, but he's not budging. He thinks we're evil monsters and he doesn't want to be one of us. I don't think we have any other choice."

"Don't waste your breath Abby," McBride said angrily. "You're an evil demon like your brother. If there's anything I would pay less attention to than that, it's the girlfriend of a killer."

Shadows

Abby sighed. "You're right," she told Morrigan. "There's no use trying, it's hopeless."

* * * *

The group locked McBride in the bunker and headed for the house. Abby was starting to feel weak again. Then she remembered, she hadn't eaten after that last shifting episode. She took another step forward and faltered. She would have been okay if she hadn't played that game with Morrigan earlier this afternoon.

Thomas felt Abby stumble and immediately reached out to steady her. "I knew you shouldn't have played that stupid shifting game. You're too weak to walk back to the house," he grumbled.

"Morrigan said you were annoyed at that. I didn't believe him at the time," she laughed.

"I'm glad you find it funny," Thomas said angrily as he lifted her into his arms and continued toward the farmhouse.

"Thomas," Abby said, she was surprised at his strength. She knew she shouldn't be, he was a warrior, but he lifted her up like she was nothing. "I'm not weak because of the game. I'm weak because I shifted several times in that bunker to make sure there was no way McBride could escape. I just need a glass of milk or something and I'll be fine."

"Yeah, after you shifted about thirty times out on the field earlier this afternoon." He glanced at her bruised face, "Which came after a maniac tried to kill you." Thomas inhaled a deep breath. Thinking about how close Abby had come to dying always twisted his stomach into a tight knot.

"Well, it sounds like you won't believe me but you're wrong. That game Morrigan and I play is what saved me from that madman. It takes a lot of concentration for most people to shift. Because of that game, for me and for Morrigan it's almost automatic. Oh, I had to concentrate because I was injured but if I hadn't played that game with Morrigan a million times since I was a child, I probably wouldn't have gotten away. It's a harmless game and it gives me stamina. Morrigan said it was reckless too. But I was so happy to see my brother it just came natural, automatic. Don't be mad at me for it," she paused. "And we're almost to the house so put me down. You're going to scare everyone if you carry me in like this."

Thomas studied her then grinned as he flung her over his shoulder and marched through the door and up the stairs.

"Thomas Deveraux you put me down this instant," Abby ordered as she slapped him on the butt.

Thomas laughed. He kicked open her door and stepped inside. "As you wish," he laughed as he dropped her on the bed.

"Very funny," she pouted.

Thomas leaned down and kissed her gently. "I'll go find you something to eat," he smiled. "That should give you plenty of time to get ready for bed. I'll be right back."

Abby watched Thomas leave the room. Was he really going to stay with her tonight? If so, she wanted to look her best. She rummaged through the drawer until she found what she was looking for. She rushed to the bathroom, brushed her hair out and slid on the silky nightgown. It was her favorite. She always thought it made her look good. She pulled down the blankets and slid into bed. Then she positioned herself on her side so she could see Thomas as soon as he walked into the room.

Thomas slid into Abby's room and closed the door behind him. He'd made Abby a protein shake. She might argue but he was sure the events of the past two days were taking its toll on her. She hadn't completely recovered from the attack when they boarded the plane and headed to the fort. She had to have jet lag, then she immediately jumped into that game with Morrigan. After the shifting they wrestled around on the ground like children. He'd been worried sick that she was going to injure herself again. Then she and Morrigan had to go secure the bunker. It was too much for anyone to take in such a short amount of time. He turned to face Abby and froze. There was a full moon tonight and the light was glittering through her hair making it look magical. She looked so enticing lying there in that...thing. He tried to swallow the giant lump in his throat. Was she trying to drive him completely insane? The skimpy silk and lace nightgown hugged her body, accentuating all of her curves. The woman was making this difficult. He walked to the bed and handed her the shake then turned to undress.

Abby was studying Thomas. She liked the impact her attire had on him, just what she'd been aiming for. The look in his eyes told her everything she needed to know. She accepted the glass from Thomas and took a sip. It was good. "You didn't have to go to this much trouble," she said as she quickly gulped it down. "But thanks. It was delicious."

Thomas undressed down to his underwear. He turned in surprise. "You drank it already?" he asked.

"Uh...yeah," she shrugged. "Not too lady like I know, but I needed the boost. And you make a mean shake." She held out the empty glass, studying him as he casually walked across the room and deposited it into the sink. So, Thomas wasn't shy but he was definitely hot! Abby continued to watch him and realized he was grinning as he climbed into bed.

Thomas considered sleeping in his jeans, but that would be uncomfortable and anyway two could play at this game. If she was going to sleep in sexy lingerie, he was going to sleep in his underwear. Once he was in bed, Abby moved forward and brushed her body against his as she kissed him gently.

"You're killing me, Abby," he said closing his eyes and trying to maintain control.

"Whatever do you mean?" she asked innocently as she leaned in and gave him another kiss, this one not so gentle and definitely not innocent.

Thomas grabbed her around the waist and flipped her over until her back was to him. He pulled her close and held her firmly in place. Then he leaned down and kissed her shoulder, trailing kisses up her neck. Once he reached her ear he gently took her lobe between his lips. Then he leaned closer and whispered softly. "Go to sleep. At least one of us should get some rest tonight. You need it."

Abby couldn't move. Her entire body was tingling. She wanted Thomas, but she knew that wasn't going to happen tonight, thanks to her big mouth. She didn't want to think about what that monumental mistake had cost her. Unfortunately, she couldn't stop thinking about it. She pressed her body as close to Thomas as she could. He felt so good. His rough hand was gently rubbing the soft silk across her stomach. As good as it felt, she knew it would feel even better minus the silk. She tried to turn to face him again, but he wouldn't let her.

Thomas was losing control here. If Abby didn't stop, he was going to break his promise. He didn't want that. He needed her to be sure of his love before they took this to the next level. When she tried to turn back to face him, he had to stop her. He pushed himself up on one elbow and studied her in the moon light.

Abby watched Thomas, he was positioned above her watching her but not saying a word. She recognized the love in his eyes. She hoped he could recognize the same in hers.

"Goodnight princess," he said softly as he leaned down to kiss her.

"Goodnight Thomas," Abby whispered. "I love you." Then she settled back and tried to drift off to sleep.

Thomas didn't move. He knew she loved him. He could see it in her eyes. Why couldn't she see the same in his? He really couldn't understand it. He reached down and brushed her hair away from her face. She was finally asleep. She looked so peaceful and lovely lying there in that damn nightgown, the moon glittering through her hair. The only flaw was the brown and yellow bruise covering her face. Kahn was going to pay for that, Thomas vowed angrily. That man was not going to attack the woman he loved and get away with it. He couldn't kill the guy, but he could hurt him. Thomas took a deep breath then silently whispered, "I love you too, Abigail Cooper." He gently kissed her temple. "One day you are going to accept that. One day you will feel my love so deeply and so passionately you will never doubt me again." He slowly laid back on the pillow and tried to get some sleep.

Abby laid motionless. She didn't dare open her eyes. The moisture trapped inside would escape and Thomas would know she was still awake. How had she been so stupid? How had she not seen how much Thomas loved her? She wanted to jump up and somehow convince him that she did know. She accepted it now and she would never doubt him again. But he wouldn't believe her tonight. She fought off the tears and silently vowed she would never hurt Thomas Deveraux again. Somehow she was going to fix this. She didn't know how, but she was determined to find a way.

Thomas opened his eyes and immediately saw Abby, watching him sleep. "I guess I got some rest after all," he studied her. "You look better today." He gently brushed a finger over her bruise. "Even the bruise is a lot lighter this morning," he told her as he pushed himself up and leaned against the head board.

Abby climbed on top of him and straddled his lap. "Good morning," she smiled. "You look pretty good yourself."

Thomas stared at her, not moving an inch. He was struggling with himself. He wanted her so badly he ached. But he'd told her she was going to have to decide. He would stick to that if it killed him. Then she kissed him. She tasted like mint. He narrowed his eyes at her. What was that all about?

"What?" she asked a little worried. She wanted to seduce him and she couldn't do that with morning breath. Obviously he'd picked up on the mouth wash. What was he thinking anyway?

"Nothing," he said softly as he rubbed his hand down her back and pulled her in for another kiss. "You just taste good, that's all."

Shadows

Well, Abby thought. It's now or never. She reached down and pulled her nightgown over her head and let it fall loosely to the ground.

Thomas was studying her face. He needed to know if there was any hesitation at all before they continued. She was so beautiful. How could she possibly think she wasn't good enough for him? He wasn't good enough for her.

Abby was waiting for Thomas to touch her. He was just sitting there, not moving. What was he waiting for? Then it hit her, he was waiting for her. He told her it was going to be up to her. He had insisted she would have to make the first move. "Thomas, I want to make love to you." She slowly ran her fingers down his chest, playing with the dark hair covering his broad torso.

"Be sure Abby," Thomas could barely speak. "I don't want you to regret this. I never want you to have any regrets with me."

"The only thing I regret is doubting you. I love you and I know you love me. I want to show you," she smiled at him. "I want you to lose control. You are always so controlled. I want to see what it's like when you're not, and to know I'm the one that did that to you."

"Abby dear, I haven't been in control for the past forty eight hours. And you *are* the one that has done that to me." He flipped her over and trapped her body with his. Then he kissed her. He hoped she could feel his love and his passion. He hoped she was feeling as desperate as he was. He'd never wanted anything the way he wanted Abby.

There was a soft knock on the door. Thomas and Abby ignored it, they were too caught up in each other to care.

"Abby," Morrigan called softly. "I'm sorry, but dad's downstairs. He's not happy about the way we handled the McBride situation. He wants to talk to us in the library."

Abby closed her eyes and moaned. "My life is so unfair!" she protested. "As much as I absolutely hate to say it, can I have a rain check?" she wanted to scream.

Thomas stood and pulled on his jeans. "Give me five minutes to change and then we'll go down together."

"Uh, dad wants to talk to me and Morrigan. We're the ones in trouble here, not you." Abby reached down and snatched the nightgown off the floor. She immediately covered her chest with the thin garment.

Thomas laughed. He reached out and snagged the gown then tossed it across the room. "I like you better this way." He pulled her close and kissed her long and hard. "I do love you, Abby. I love you with all my heart. I can't wait to finish what you started." He grinned and left the room shutting the door behind him.

Abby sighed. Her father had such terrible timing. She stood and found a sweatshirt then pulled her hair into a ponytail. Finally she rummaged around and found a pair of old jeans. Once her tennis shoes were tied she opened the door and saw Thomas leaning against the wall. He looked fresh and wonderful. "No fair," she grumbled. "Life is just not fair. I came this close to having sex with the most gorgeous man in the world but got interrupted by my father. Then, you show up looking like a guy off the cover of GQ while I look like a frumpy teenager. Where's the justice?" she sighed.

Shadows

Thomas ignored her and backed her up against the wall then kissed her passionately. "I missed you already." He kissed the tip of her nose. "Let's go see what your father has to say."

"Okay, but don't be surprised if he kicks you out of the room. Now that we know McBride is a shifter, this is shifter business. The warriors and the fae are not responsible for him or his consequences."

Thomas realized instantly she was right. McBride didn't fall under their control or their laws. The shifters would have to determine his fate. He didn't know how they would handle someone like Detective McBride. "What's going to happen to him?"

"I don't know. That will be up to dad or Monroe maybe. We don't know which pack he belongs to, so the two local pack leaders will have to come to some kind of an arrangement." She reached the library door and hesitated. She wasn't sure how her father was going to react when Thomas walked in with her.

Thomas reached down and took Abby's hand. "Would you prefer it if I waited outside?" he offered. "I understand if you're not ready for your father to know we're involved."

Abby tightened her grip on his hand and flung open the door. She was more than ready for her family to know about Thomas. The two entered the room then stopped just inside.

Chapter Nine

Mason Cooper stood staring out the large window. He was angry with his children. How could they lock up one of their own? They knew how captivity affected their kind. He heard a noise and turned to see Abby and Thomas Deveraux standing just inside the door. "Good morning Thomas," he paused. "It's good to see you again, but I hoped I could have just a few minutes alone with my children. We need to have a family meeting."

Morrigan was watching Thomas and Abby. It looked like they may have worked out their problems. He knew Thomas spent the night in his sister's room. The last thing he had wanted to do was knock on that door this morning, but it couldn't be helped. Dad was furious.

"I'd like Thomas to stay if that's okay," Abby requested. She placed an arm around his waist.

Mason raised an eyebrow but didn't speak.

Shadows

The moment was a little tense, but Thomas wanted his feelings to be clear. He reached around and locked his hand around Abby's waist. Then he gently maneuvered her in front of him and wrapped both arms around her, pulling her against his chest as he casually leaned against the wall. He was going to protect the woman he loved and everyone in the room knew it. They all recognized the manly gesture.

"I see," was all Mason said. "Morrigan do you have any objections to Thomas being here?" he asked flatly.

"None," Morrigan assured his father. He knew dad wouldn't hold back, but he was also sure Thomas had been here a time or two with his own father.

"I'm very disappointed in both of you," Mason shifted a hard look towards Abby then Morrigan. "You know better than this. How could you lock a shifter in a cage? I trusted you." He demanded, glaring at Morrigan.

"With all due respect father, I don't think you did. Or do, for that matter," Abby pushed away from Thomas then took his hand and led him to the large couch. The two of them sat.

Thomas placed an arm around Abby's shoulder. He wouldn't interrupt. It wasn't his place. He was surprised she was taking on her father so directly. He never would have done that with his own dad. Luke would have blown a gasket.

"Abby, I came here for a family discussion, not an argument. Don't push me right now. I'm furious with you and your brother," Mason continued to pace. He wished Jackie was here with him right now. She always knew how to calm him. That's when it hit him. Thomas was doing the same for his daughter. She was so much like him, but today she was confident and relaxed. He moved his gaze to Thomas. He too was relaxed, but somehow alert at the same time. He was ready to defend Abby at any moment. Mason smiled inwardly then remembered why he was here. "I need an explanation, Morrigan. How could you lock a shifter in a bunker? You know how our kind reacts to captivity. It only makes things worse. Shifters can't concentrate when they're locked up. They can't think or reason," he took a deep breath.

"I know of one exception to that rule," Morrigan said glancing at his sister. "Abby seems to deal with captivity very well. Maybe that's a myth," he shrugged.

Mason whirled around to face him. "Nonsense," he barked, narrowing his eyes at his son. Why was he so confident about this? He should be ashamed of himself. "You're not even going to apologize for your behavior?" he finally asked.

"There's nothing to apologize for," Abby insisted. "I wish you trusted us dad. I wish you had faith in our abilities but clearly you don't," she sighed. "Before you go any further, go see for yourself. Go talk to McBride. Then come back and explain to your inept children what they could have done differently."

Mason was surprised at his daughter. She was a lot like him, but not usually so direct and disrespectful. Maybe Thomas wasn't as good for her as Mason originally believed. "I think I'll do just that," Mason said turning to walk out the door. He needed some space and time to calm down before he dealt with his daughter.

"Whew," Morrigan said clearly relieved. "What's gotten into you this morning, sis?" he asked amused. "I've never seen you handle dad like that before."

Shadows

"He's wrong," she said angrily. "He knows nothing about McBride but he walks in here and immediately begins chastising us when we did nothing wrong. You tell me, what choice did we have? None. I didn't want to lock that man up any more than you did. But we didn't have another option. Clearly he doesn't trust us or he would know we didn't have a choice. For dad to stand there and act all disappointed in us was unfair. I guess I just couldn't handle one more unfair event this morning," she was a little surprised at herself. Her dad was going to be angry with her. She couldn't decide if she owed him an apology or not. Maybe, she decided. She'd taken her frustration and disappointment out on her father, maybe that was a little unfair too.

Thomas pulled her close and kissed the top of her head. Then he whispered softly in her ear. "I'm proud of you, but don't be too rough on your father. We'll finish what we started, I promise."

Abby leaned in and kissed him. "I'm sorry you had to be a witness to that," she winced. "I don't suppose you were ever that hard on your own father?"

Thomas laughed. "Oh, don't bet on it. Dad and I got into plenty of arguments. We handled things differently, but the results were pretty much the same. Sometimes I was right, sometimes he was. It always worked out for the best in the end," he paused to look at Morrigan. "He's going to see you didn't have a choice. I'd guess it will take about two minutes, tops." He thought back to his father and then thought about Mason. His father was far more composed. He never would have paced the room nervously when taking on his children. Luke wanted to intimidate. It worked for a while, but dad was a softy. He had a big bark, but he loved his kids too much. Any punishment he gave was just as hard on dad as it was on him and Alex.

All three of them came to attention as Mason walked back into the room. "It seems Abby was right. I should have trusted you. I'm sorry," he said sincerely. "There's no reasoning with that man." He sat in a large chair, defeated. "Promise me you won't go near that bunker until I speak to Monroe and we can decide what to do with him," he ordered. "Morrigan, Abby, do not open that door for any reason," he said with more force this time. "He's vowed to kill you both. Me too, and he hasn't decided about Monroe yet. He believes we are all evil demons that need to be exterminated for the safety of all mankind." Mason sighed and ran his fingers through his hair.

"Abby's worse than that," Morrigan told his father. "She's also the girlfriend of a killer."

Mason's head shot up. "I'm sorry, Thomas." He was truly distressed over the situation. "I'm sorry McBride is so stubborn and disrespectful."

"There's no need for you to apologize for that man's behavior," Thomas assured him. "It's not your fault."

"But it is, he's one of us. He's a shifter, which makes me responsible for his behavior," Mason surmised. "I'm truly sorry for all the trouble he has caused you over the past several weeks," he stood. "I need to get back soon. Abby before I go, could I have a word with you?" he glanced at Thomas. "Alone, please."

Thomas stood. "I need to call Alex. She should know about the new development. I'm sorry Mason if we stepped on any toes here. It didn't occur to me that with McBride being a shifter, this is out of our jurisdiction." He turned and gave Abby a warm smile. "Your daughter had to point that out to me before this meeting."

Shadows

"No apology necessary," Mason assured him. "You haven't stepped on any toes. But can your people accept that McBride's fate will be determined by me, or Chief Monroe?" he asked. "No matter what we decide?"

Thomas nodded. "We can. I don't know much about your laws. McBride's fate is now in your hands. We won't interfere. We'll keep him here as long as you need us to. The bunker is secure. He can't escape."

"Thank you," Mason walked towards Thomas. "Once again I'm grateful for our alliance."

Thomas nodded then left the room.

Mason turned to his daughter. "Abby, let's go for a walk."

* * * *

Kahn sat in the dark, dingy cave watching the vampire behind the desk. The guy wasn't happy. Well, that wasn't Kahn's problem. "Since the mark has disappeared it's time for me to move on," he said again. "It would be counterproductive for me to tag another girl. The last thing you want to do is provide the police proof that Thomas is innocent. He disappeared, which means the abductions and killings need to stop for now as well."

Radek wasn't happy about it, but the man was right. If they continued, the pressure would immediately be off Thomas. Where could he have gone? "Find him then. Start immediately," he told the human.

"No way," Kahn shook his head. "I agreed to do your killing and put pressure on Thomas Deveraux. I never agreed to track him. That's not what I do. Anyway, I've had something come up myself. I have a personal problem that needs my full attention. I just came here to tell you I've finished the deal and I'm moving on."

Radek was seething. How dare a human tell him when the deal was done? He was in charge, not this madman from Columbia. If he didn't need the guy, he'd kill him right now. "For now, I agree. While Thomas is missing you're free to work on your personal problem. Once we locate Thomas, you will finish what you started," Radek insisted.

A small warning bell went off inside Kahn's head. He knew if he was smart he'd disappear right now. Head back to Columbia, put things in order then disappear completely. But he couldn't do it. He couldn't walk away and let that girl win. Her escape was bad enough, but when he saw Tala Fitzgerald walk into the house he knew this wasn't finished. Not by a long shot. First he would take care of the freak that could change into a bird then he would focus on that busy body Fitzgerald. "We'll see how things play out," Kahn said not committing to anything. "But for now I've gotta go."

Kahn stood and quickly left the cave. He missed the old days. The days when he didn't know about such things as vampires or freaky girls that changed into birds. Life was much easier living in the dark. This place gave him the willies. He couldn't wait to get away. He exited the cave and inhaled deeply. He was not coming back here, ever. He wanted to put as much distance between himself and these vampires as humanly possible. As far as he was concerned his debt to Lilith was paid in full. He knew she might not see it that way. Eventually he may have to hide out for a while.

Shadows

But for now, he needed to get started on locating the girl. That was his first priority.

Radek glowered at Lilith. "That man is out of control." He picked up a lamp and threw it across the room. "You brought him into this, you take care of it. I need you to watch him. It's up to you to make sure he finishes this. Once Thomas is located, Kahn has to be there to ensure his demise. I want Thomas out of the picture for good." He stalked to his chair and plopped down in the seat. "What about Felix? Have you located him yet?"

"Not yet," Lilith admitted. "I can place him in Mexico three weeks ago. But nothing after that. There are several reports of missing persons though. His group has to be large. From what I'm hearing it sounds like he was more successful than we could have hoped. I'm just worried he was killed by the Mexican drug cartel. If that's the case there are probably hundreds of vampires wandering aimlessly. They're not going to know where to go or how to return to New York. They may not even know they should return to New York," she paused. She was hesitant to pin Radek down, but she needed to know what he wanted from her. "Do you want me to track Kahn or continue to search for Felix and his nest?"

That was a good question, Radek thought. He needed to keep track of Kahn. He was worried the man would try to disappear. But he also wanted to know what happened to Felix and the rest of his vampires. That was his answer. He needed Kahn. He knew from the start he might lose the Mexican vampires. Losing Felix was a calculated risk. If they were gone, taken out somehow, he'd make do without them. But he couldn't risk losing Kahn. "Track Kahn," he finally told her. "We need him to finish the job. I want Thomas out of the equation," he smiled wickedly. "One warrior down. Then we'll move on to the next one. Once Alex is unprotected, she'll be mine. Her empire is weakening. We won't lose ground now. Keep Kahn under control. He's your problem Lilith." Radek stood and walked to the door. "Sammael!" he called.

Lilith knew that was her cue to leave. Radek wasn't in the mood for her tonight. Things had been so perfect just a few days ago. Now this. Kahn was off dealing with personal business and Thomas had completely disappeared. It was up to her to get things back on track. Radek was too irrational. If they were going to prevail, it was up to her. She slid into her room and pondered the situation, pacing from one end to the other. She still had Lawson. Her ace in the hole. As she slowly sat on the edge of her bed, a plan began to fall into place. She could handle this.

* * * *

Abby approached the small building that would eventually be a bakery. She walked to the patio and sat on a large bench. "Dad I'm sorry," she began.

"Hold on," he stopped her. "I was just about to tell you how proud I am of you. Don't ruin it with an apology," he smiled. "It's about time you and your brother stood up to me. I keep forgetting you're adults. Sometimes I need a little reminder."

"That's true," she agreed. "But I should have been more respectful. I guess I've had a couple difficult days. I took it out on you and I'm sorry for that. Don't get me wrong, you were out of line. But I could have been more...tactful I guess."

Mason laughed. "That's my girl," he put his arm around her. "I love you, baby." He kissed the top of her head. "I am sorry I

Shadows

didn't trust you and Morrigan. I'm proud of you two. I couldn't be more proud of my children," he smiled at her. "Morrigan didn't let me get away with my criticism either. He was just more subtle than you were. He gets that from his mother. I'm afraid you take after me, my dear."

"Yeah, I caught that," she told him.

"Morrigan wasn't just telling me how great you took it in captivity. He wanted to remind me that you knew what it was like to be locked up. McBride had to be out of control for you to agree to his imprisonment. I knew that, but still somehow I let myself question your judgment. I have no excuse. I guess you were right. I want to trust you and Morrigan, it's just difficult. I still think of you as my kids. Be patient with me. I'll try to do better."

Abby kissed her father's cheek. "I'll cut you a little slack, but not much. Otherwise you'll never catch on," she grinned. They sat in silence for a few moments.

"So, is it safe to assume this thing between you and Thomas Deveraux is serious?" Mason finally asked.

"I think so," Abby said softly.

"Before I say anything else, I want you to know that I approve," he smiled at her. "Thomas is a very good, honorable man. I'd be thrilled to welcome him into our family if that's what you want."

"Thanks," she said sincerely. "We haven't gotten that far, yet. But that's good to know."

"Having said that, I hope you realize a relationship with Thomas is a huge responsibility." He paused.

"How so?" she asked.

"Thomas isn't just rich. He's a public figure. His life is an open book. I've always been amazed that Luke could hide his secrets so completely. We didn't know Luke and Marlena but we all knew who they were. We knew of them. Thomas and Alex have picked up where their parents left off, but it takes a lot of work," he paused. "You are very spontaneous Abby. I've always loved that about you," he grinned. "You've been through so much over the past few months but still, you are somehow innocent and optimistic."

Abby cringed. She really wasn't that innocent. Maybe it was natural for her parents to view her that way though.

"Don't get upset. Maybe innocent isn't exactly the right word. But you are also spontaneous and sometimes reckless. You get that from me. You see something that needs to be fixed and you rush off to handle it on your own. I'm afraid that's how you got injured. You were determined to fix this thing with Thomas. I'm just saying you need to curb that impulse if you're going to be with Thomas. That means as a girlfriend, a wife or even just a friend."

"I understand," she told him. She had thought about these things. Her father wasn't telling her anything she hadn't been pondering on her own.

Mason smiled at his daughter. "Thomas is good for you," his smile widened at her surprise. "I noticed it this morning. I watched the two of you sitting on the couch. You should have been nervous, but you weren't. Thomas gave you strength. His love and support

Shadows

relaxes you and gives you confidence. Your mother does that for me. I depend on her more than you know. The connection you have with Thomas is special. I hope you will cherish that. I'm not trying to scare you away from him. I just want you to understand what you're getting into. I respect Thomas. I never want you to do anything that will hurt him or cause his family trouble. Just be mindful of the situation. Know that the media is constantly watching the Deveraux's. If you get involved with one, they will also be watching you. No more shifting games with Morrigan unless you know for sure you're in a secure location."

"Okay, I guess I shouldn't have done that. Thomas and Morrigan have already told me it was reckless. But honestly, Ariel was practicing her fire throwing and Ty and Sam were practicing their warrior moves. How could I have known we were being watched?" she objected. "I missed Morrigan and I was in the mood for a little fun."

"You couldn't have known McBride was there," he assured her. "That's not what I was saying. I'm just saying in the future, that could be a photographer trying to get the big shot. When you and Thomas go public, you're going to have to be very careful. Eventually the frenzy will die down, but until then you can't be reckless or impulsive. That's all. Don't get angry or frustrated with me. I'm only trying to help."

"Dad, you're not telling me anything I haven't already thought of. I'm sorry," she paused. "I'm worried that once people find out I'm seeing Thomas, you and mom will also be in the spotlight. Morrigan, too. They are going to try to tear my life apart. Do you want me to lie? Tell them I'm an orphan or something?" she asked jokingly.

"Of course not. They'd only find out and it would make things worse. Don't you worry about us. Abby, I can see Thomas makes you happy. Give this relationship your all. Don't hold anything back because you're worried about how it might impact your mother and me. We can handle ourselves. It won't kill me to be a little less impulsive for a while, too. I do have some self-control you know?" Mason sobered. "Now, I need to talk to you about something more serious."

"What?" she asked curious about the change in her father's tone.

"McBride," he said flatly. "I'm not sure he's going to come around."

"What are you going to do?" she asked.

"I don't know yet. But you need to prepare yourself for the worst. If he continues down this road we won't be able to let him go. Once he's free, he'll do his best to ruin Thomas and Ariel and Victor," he paused. "He's vowed to kill me and my entire family. Monroe's also on his list. We can't risk that. We can't let him expose the shifters, the warriors or the fae. Do you understand what I'm saying?"

"He might have to die," she sighed. "We can't keep him imprisoned forever, but you will give him a chance to accept his gift before you destroy him, won't you?"

"I will," he promised. "But don't get your hopes up. McBride may have to die in the line of duty," he told her.

"How does Monroe feel about that?" Abby asked.

Shadows

"It was actually his idea. I've been resisting, but I'm beginning to think that might be our only option. I just want you to be prepared, that's all. Thomas and the rest also need to know it's a possibility," Mason warned. "Are you comfortable talking to them about that?"

"If I need to. I'm not sure it's necessary. I still think there's hope for McBride. If you give him a little time I think he'll come around," Abby argued.

Mason stood and pulled his daughter to her feet. "Like I said, my little optimist." He put an arm around her shoulder. "I hope you never lose that. I love that about you. Now walk your old man back to the house. I need to get back to the city."

Thomas watched Abby and her father approach the house. He hated to interrupt, but he didn't have a choice. "Uh, Mr. Cooper?" he called. He cringed, that sounded so formal.

"It's Mason," Abby and her father stopped directly in front of Thomas. "Mr. Deveraux," he said grinning.

"Okay, point taken. Please, never call me that again. I hate to detain you, but Dimitri has called a meeting. He wanted me to ask you to stay. I know you have a busy day but it sounded important," Thomas said apologetically.

Mason looked at his watch then back to Thomas. "Give me a minute to call my secretary and I'll be right in." He pulled his phone from his pocket and punched in a number.

Abby looked at Thomas in question. "What's up?" she asked.

"I don't know yet. Dimitri is gathering everyone he can. He said there's a problem." Thomas looked up as Mason joined them. "I can give you an hour, but no longer. The rest of my day can't be altered."

"That should be plenty," Thomas said taking Abby's hand and leading them into the library. The rest of the group was already there. Dimitri and Alex were on the big screen.

"Mason," Dimitri greeted him. "Thank you for joining us. I know this is an inconvenience."

"Like I told Thomas, I only have an hour then I need to head back. I have a busy day ahead of me," Mason advised.

"Then let's get started," Dimitri suggested. "I'll get straight to the point. With Foster's help, Oberon and Tighe searched the Penthouse," he glanced at Alex. "Lawson and Patricia are missing."

"What do you mean missing?" Victor asked. "Where could they be?" He was worried about his father. Tala had enough evidence to prove Lawson was responsible for the trouble at the farm. Lawson had already tried to kill his dad once. They needed to find him soon.

"We don't know. Foster has checked all the obvious places. We think they became suspicious when Foster went into hiding. Until then, they couldn't get close to him, but we think they were keeping tabs during the day. Foster secretly built himself a house. He's confident they don't know about it but both of them would have known his regular routine at work. That's changed. Foster hasn't gone into work for over a week now. Once Lawson and Patricia realized that, they must have fled to a safe location. We're working hard to find them, but so far we're not having any luck."

Shadows

Dimitri turned to face Ty and Samantha. "We would like the two of you to get started on that. Sam is phenomenal with a computer. Alex and I are confident you can find the trail if they've left one."

"I'll start immediately," Sam assured them. "If there's a trail, I'll find it."

"We'll find it," Ty corrected smiling. He could see Sam wasn't thrilled about the partnership. Since they'd started training, things had been strained between them. He had considered stepping back, but he couldn't. He had to know she'd be safe if they were attacked again. Sam had to learn to fight. They could work everything else out later.

Dimitri continued. "Tala, Atticus and Cornelia are actively trying to find the Dillinger's," he assured them. "I'm asking for help because Foster hasn't been able to come up with anything. There's more. We have evidence that Lawson has made additional bombs."

Ty was alert now. "Do you think Alex is the target?" he asked anxiously. He couldn't protect her if he was at the fort.

"I probably am," Alex told him. "But we need you out there Ty. We need you to work with Sam to locate Lawson. Dimitri also needs you to work on security at the fort. We need to make sure those kids are safe and he can't get away right now. We have to focus on things here. Tony, your parents are staying with us. They've been a big help. I don't want you to worry about them. Dimitri has the house decked out to the limits. Nobody can get within a hundred yards of the place without us knowing."

"But..." Ty began.

"No," Alex said shaking her head. "Those missing girls are in danger. I can't have you rushing back here to try to prevent something that might or might not happen. We need to find those women," Alex emphasized. "Bastian's been studying that formula Atticus and Tala found. Even if we find them, they're going to have a lot of damage. They may have too much damage to ever be normal again. The longer it takes us to find them, the worse their condition is going to be. If it takes too long, they might die. Forget about me, Ty. I'm taking precautions."

"Sorry, that's not possible. I could never forget about you. You're my hero," he smiled.

"Okay enough," Dimitri grumbled. "That covers the Dillinger problem. We have another one. One that I think is even more pressing. Kahn is also missing. Tala is convinced he has set his sights on Abby. If he tracks her to the fort you are all in trouble. Remember, those bodies had vampire marks. If he has somehow joined forces with them, he could be heading your way with reinforcements. Everyone there needs to be prepared for a battle."

Abby was shocked. Was she putting everyone in danger? What about the kids?

"We have a number of issues and they are coming at us from all directions. I'm sorry, we need to do our best to work on multiple threats simultaneously," Dimitri told them. "That seems to be the new norm for us."

"Uh…I think this may all be connected," Mason disagreed.

"How so?" Dimitri asked.

Shadows

"Kahn has been linked to the vampires through the bodies. We know that. I agree, Kahn's most likely target is my daughter. She escaped him. I've generated quite a file on him. A man with an ego like Kahn's won't walk away from that. I also agree he may have vampires with him. But I think Lawson is also connected to the vampires. We know Lilith used several of his bombs in her attack on us and the fae. Then, Patricia has been causing trouble for the Deveraux's in their company. What if Lilith is driving all of this? Or Radek. Everything seems to be directed towards Thomas and Alex. Lilith could be encouraging or even helping the Dillinger's. Maybe you can't find them because the vamps are hiding them," he suggested.

"No way," Ariel disagreed. "I'll give you the connection with Lawson and Lilith. We know it's there. Those bombs were planted by Lilith and we know they were made by Lawson. He would join forces with the vamps without a second thought. But Patricia Dillinger would never associate with a vampire. She's obsessed with the monarchy, but that's why your theory is so wrong. She's too devoted to her people. She vehemently hates the vampires and could never think of them as anything but an enemy. There is no way Patricia Dillinger would come within miles of a vampire."

"Oberon and Foster also agree with Ariel's assessment," Alex said. "We asked. We hadn't put it all together the same as Mason. I have to admit your theory is something to think about. We only asked because of the connection with the bombs. We know Lawson made them and Lilith used them. It was a pretty easy jump. Foster says no way. His mother detests vampires. She wasn't happy when she learned about Lawson's connection to Lilith."

"Bastian is on his way to the fort. He should be there within the hour," Dimitri continued. "He has some additional security items. Victor and Ty I need you to get those up and running immediately. Bastian will explain the system. I'm confident the two of you can get everything in place. It's important we keep those kids safe. If Kahn attacks with a group of vampires I want everyone out there to be prepared."

"Breena?" Alex called. "I know you're not going to like this, but I think you and Orin should come back to the city. You can stay at my house. If vampires attack out there, you're in no shape to fight."

"So let me get this straight," Orin immediately surmised. "We basically have two choices. Stay here and face a possible battle with who knows how many vampires and a crazed killer or we can head back to the city and hang out with you, Alex. Where you think Lawson may place his bombs and try to blow you and your house up? Is that about right?"

Alex sighed. "I know the choice isn't ideal, but Breena can't protect herself out there. I'm not there. If she gets hurt I can't heal her. I can't heal the baby," she argued.

Mason was studying the couple. The pregnant woman didn't look well. It must be a difficult pregnancy. "Why don't the two of you come back with me?" he offered. "You can stay at my house. My wife's a nurse. Jackie will know what to do to help with the pregnancy."

"That's a wonderful idea," Abby exclaimed. "It's perfect. Nobody's after you. I'm not there so your house is probably the safest place on earth right now. Orin and Breena, please say yes. I couldn't stand it if something happened to you or the baby because of me."

Shadows

"Are you sure?" Orin asked Mason. "We don't want to impose."

"Absolutely," he assured them. "At this point, Breena doesn't need to be worrying about her safety or the safety of your child. She needs to relax. She can do that at our house."

"Okay," Orin finally agreed. "I feel a lot better about staying with you than our other two options," he admitted.

"Kylee?" Alex continued.

"No way," Kylee shook her head adamantly. "I'm not leaving."

"Kylee, be sensible about this," Alex begged.

"I think I'm the only one being sensible. You are in New York. If something happens there, you can take care of the medical emergencies. That leaves a lot of people vulnerable out here. I need to be available to take care of them. If there's a vampire battle there could be a lot of injuries. I'm not leaving. These guys need me," she said stubbornly.

"We'll protect her," Sam assured Alex. "I think she's right. If we have an emergency we need a doctor. Kylee should stay here and you need to stay there. If we're strategically dividing our assets, Kylee is right where she should be. She knows the risks and it sounds to me like she's willing to accept them."

"I am," Kylee assured them. "I won't leave, please don't try to make me."

"Okay," Alex conceded. "I hope you know what you're doing."

"Now that we have that settled, let's move on," Dimitri said abruptly. "We're going to continue working on this end. Tala is trying to track Kahn. If we find anything we'll let you know. Sam, work fast. We need to find those women. The rest of you get started on security and developing a plan to keep those kids safe. Alex and Thomas have gotten good at tracking down money trails over the past few weeks. She's going to sift through Foster's business records and see what she can find. I have Nick and Dante scouring the streets to find clues and try to locate Lawson."

"Send me some of the records," Thomas requested. "Like you said, we've both been doing this for weeks. Foster has a lot of hotels. The more eyes on the books, the better."

"Victor?" Dimitri called.

"Yeah?" he immediately responded.

"I'm putting you in charge out there," he studied the warriors. "I can handle things here. We'll coordinate and keep each other posted but I need you to develop a plan and oversee security. Ty's going to be busy with Sam, and Thomas is handling the books. I need Bastian to continue his work on that formula. Like I said, those girls are going to be in bad shape. They've been gone a long time. I have no doubt that Patricia and Lawson have given them several doses of that toxin already. We're fighting against time here," he paused. "Oh, I forgot to ask, any update on McBride?"

"Don't worry about McBride," Mason said soberly. "He's my problem now. He's a shifter. I'll meet with Monroe later tonight and we'll decide how to handle things with him. You have enough to worry about. I'm counting on you to keep my daughter safe," he said more than a little worried about his children.

Shadows

"Thank you," Alex said. "We'll do our best. I'm sure Morrigan will help out with the Abby situation," she smiled at the group. "As always, you guys are great. Thank you so much for your willingness to help out. I couldn't handle all of this without each and every one of you."

"Alex, is Oberon still with Foster?" Thomas asked.

"Yeah," she affirmed. "He and Tighe are helping him sort through the company records. They're researching all their properties to see if Patricia has checked into a hotel under a slightly different name. Foster is sure he'd recognize it immediately."

"Have Foster check financial records. Not in the last couple months. Go back a couple years. Highlight anything that's even slightly off. Remember the problem dad had in Paris? Joe wasn't taking large amounts of money. The amounts were large enough to make it worth his while, but small enough to avoid detection. The withdrawals were written off as mistakes for a long time before we figured out what was going on. Lawson may have been doing the same thing. It might lead us to him if he's trying to grow a nest egg."

"That's true," Alex agreed. "I'll get him on it right away."

"Once he identifies the companies, have him pass the info on to Sam. She can take it from there," Thomas directed.

"Good idea," Alex told him. "Everyone get started. We have a lot to do in a very short amount of time."

* * * *

Kylee stood from the metal lab stool and headed for the door. "It's lunchtime. I think I'm going to take a quick break," she told Bastian then disappeared out the door.

Bastian watched her leave and smiled. He'd be finished with this test in a few minutes then he'd follow her. Ten minutes later he pulled two sacks from the small refrigerator and headed for the large mat room. Kylee was inside, fighting with one of the droids. He leaned against the wall and waited. She was improving at a faster rate than he'd expected. He knew she'd been doing this for several weeks but he'd only given in to his curiosity last Thursday.

Kylee was determined to win this time. She needed to improve if they were preparing for a battle. She was disappointed in herself. She thought by this time she would be taking on two of the droids. She ducked a little too late and landed hard on her butt. The droid immediately shut down. She'd lost again.

Bastian straightened and walked toward the mat. He stood over Kylee and held out a hand. "Not bad. You're improving quickly," he said casually.

Kylee was shocked. How long had Bastian known about this? She took his hand and allowed him to pull her to her feet. "I'm sorry," she began. "I mean, I know I didn't have permission to use the equipment. I won't do it again, I promise. I'll find some other way to work out." She was terrified Bastian would send her away.

Bastian studied her. Why was she so afraid of him? They worked so well together in the lab, but the minute they walked out that door Kylee changed. "Nobody cares if you use the droids Kylee," he began. "In fact I happen to think it was a brilliant idea. We all knew you were vulnerable. I like knowing you can protect yourself. You still have a long way to go, but I think you could hold your own until one of us can step in and help," he said proudly.

"Thanks," Kylee sighed. "I thought I'd be better at this by now. At this rate I'll never be able to protect myself."

"What are you talking about?" he asked confused. "You almost won that droid today. That's a lot harder than a vampire. Why are you so glum?"

"Are you serious?" she asked. "I thought I'd need to fight two or three of them at a time before I was ready to take on a vamp. When they injured Ty they attacked in a group."

"Alex can handle three droids at once, but I've never seen anyone else do it," he paused. "Where did you learn to fight like that anyway? Most women aren't as talented as you are."

"Mom made me take lessons. We had a private tutor come to the house once a week. At first we both participated, but later mom left it to me. I was pretty good. I surpassed her right away. I've always worried that's why she gave it up," Kylee was lost in the memories for a moment. She was surprised to see Bastian had set up a little picnic on the large mat. "What's this?" she asked.

"Well, learning to fight is only half the battle," he told her as he began pulling lunch items out of the two bags. "The other half is proper nutrition. You've been neglecting one half to focus on the other. So I thought we could have lunch together today," he handed her a plate. "Dig in," he said proudly.

Kylee was surprised. She didn't think Bastian even liked her. But here he was making sure she had lunch. "I don't know what to say," she confessed.

"How about...Bastian, you are so considerate. Next time I'll make lunch," he suggested.

Kylee stared at the man. She hadn't realized he had a sense of humor. "Okay," she finally answered.

Bastian laughed. "Kylee lighten up. I just thought we could enjoy a nice lunch together before we got back to that potion business. We're dealing with a lot of ugliness here," he sighed. "I just hope they find those women soon. This stuff is going to do a lot of major damage." He handed her a bottle of water then laid on his side with his food arranged in front of him.

Kylee picked up a sandwich and took a bite. It was good. "Thanks," she said sincerely. "I actually was starving." She relaxed a little. This was nice. They seemed to work well together in the lab, but once they finished their business she didn't know what to say to Bastian. He was so smart and good at what he did. She was a little intimidated by him. Maybe this was the start of an actual friendship. She liked that idea. The man was hot. All the warriors looked like they belonged on the cover of a magazine. She'd never seen men as rugged and built as these guys. She grinned, this wasn't a bad gig. Okay it was great, she admitted. Kylee smiled as she took another bite.

Shadows

Sam strolled into the kitchen. She was starving. She needed a snack and a break. She rounded the corner and froze. Ariel was rummaging through the contents of the fridge mumbling to herself. She didn't sound happy. Sam took one silent step backwards before Ariel poked her head over the refrigerator door. Again, Sam froze. They hadn't had a conversation since the incident with Ty and the blood. Sam assumed Ariel was still angry with her for the poor way she handled the discovery.

Ariel raised one eyebrow. "What are you waiting for?" she asked. "I assume you came for food. Don't let me stop you." She pulled out two bottles of water and an apple. "It's all yours," she lifted her arm in invitation.

Sam slowly, cautiously walked to the fridge and studied its contents.

"The pie looked really good, but since I only have two minutes before General Patton comes after me, I had to pass," she rolled her eyes.

"Honeymoon's over for you too, huh?" Sam asked hesitantly.

Ariel laughed. "I guess you didn't see the fireball this morning?"

"Actually I did," Sam confessed. "Victor must have done something awful to piss you off like that. I never thought I'd see the day you threw fire at him. You two used to be so happy together."

Ariel sat deflated at the table. "I actually feel really guilty about that," she confessed as she rubbed her hip. "But I guess he got even with me." She knew she had a huge bruise, but she couldn't tell Victor. He felt bad enough already about losing his temper. If he knew she had actually gotten hurt, he'd never forgive himself. Plus, she deserved it.

"I realize it's none of my business, but exactly what is Victor trying to teach you?" Sam asked. "I can tell you are just as frustrated with him as I am with Ty."

Ariel looked at Sam surprised. She thought everyone knew what they were doing. And that she was a failure at it. "I thought Ty would have told you about it by now," she finally answered.

"We aren't really talking much these days," Sam confessed. "Other than him telling me I'm doing it wrong and stop acting like a sissy, that is." She sat at the table next to Ariel. "Sometimes I wish I could break his nose or something. He is so aggravating."

Ariel laughed. "I'm not sure men were meant to be teachers. Not to women anyway," she relaxed a little. It was nice to have Sam to talk to again. She missed their interaction. "Victor is determined to get me to split my fire. Mom throws ice daggers. She can conjure three or four of them at a time and throw them at multiple targets. Victor believes I should be able to do the same with my fire. I can't. He thinks I'm not trying hard enough, but that's not it. It just doesn't split once I have it in my hand. It's like once I create it, I no longer have control over it. Victor doesn't understand that. I don't think he believes me," Ariel said defeated.

Sam studied Ariel. "I'm new to this. Would you mind explaining to me how it all works?" she asked. "How do you conjure the fire in the first place?"

Shadows

"I don't know. I just envision it in the palm of my hand. First I concentrate on my palm getting warm, then hot, then the fire beginning to build until I have a large ball." She paused to look at Sam. "Does that make sense?"

"It does," Sam nodded. "Uh, obviously I don't know what I'm talking about so if this is a stupid idea don't get mad." She prefaced her next thought.

"I'm finished being mad at you Sam," she said honestly. "What are you thinking?"

"Well, what if you envisioned the fire coming from your fingertips instead of a large ball in the palm of your hand," she suggested. "I don't know, maybe try it with one finger then think of it growing until it's the right size to do a vampire damage, but not as large as the fireballs you typically throw. Once you can make it materialize from one finger move on to another one. Then maybe try with both index fingers at once. If you could make two smaller balls instead of one bigger one at least you could take out two vamps at a time," she shrugged. "I don't know if that would work, but it might be worth trying."

Ariel studied Sam seriously. "You know, that might work. Instead of trying to split it after the fact I'd be funneling my energy in different directions. That actually might work, thanks Sam." She jumped up and ran out the back door.

Sam watched her leave then gathered her lunch and returned to the library. She still had a lot of work to do. So far, she hadn't found a thing that would help locate those girls.

Megan and Tony escorted McBride to the kitchen. "You have two minutes to fix yourself a plate then we're going back to the bunker," Tony directed. "Don't try anything funny. We're ready for that," he warned.

McBride paused at the library. Thomas and the two fighters were concentrating on something. It looked important. He continued to study them, wondering what they were doing. Tony gave his shoulder a little push. Rand looked at the man. "What's up in there?" he asked. "They haven't even noticed I was here." That struck him as strange.

Tony hesitated, then decided it wouldn't matter if McBride knew what was going on. "There are two additional girls missing. They're trying to locate them. Now move," he said impatiently.

"Why don't they just ask Thomas where he took them?" Rand asked sarcastically.

"You know, your one track mind is beginning to sound like a broken record," Tony said annoyed. "Don't try that crap with me. I don't have the patience for it. Get your food, I have things to do," he grumbled.

McBride studied the contents of the fridge. He filled a plate and turned to the couple. "I guess I'm ready," he grumbled. The last thing he wanted to do was go back to that bunker. He was curious about the activity in the library. As he headed back towards the front door he studied Thomas. Was it possible he really wasn't the killer after all? Rand had been so sure he was guilty. Once McBride was back in the bunker he set his plate on the table and paced the large room. Things could be worse. This thing was huge and he was actually pretty comfortable. Why were they treating him to such plush accommodations? Nothing really made sense any more.

Shadows

Ariel ran into the library and pulled Sam into a huge bear hug. "You are a genius!" she declared, swinging Sam around the room.

Sam grinned. "I take it that worked?" she asked when Ariel finally released her hold.

Ty was watching the two women in amazement. Ariel hadn't said two words to Sam in months. Maybe they had worked things out. He wouldn't know, he and Sam were barely talking these days. He hated it. He wanted his wife back. He just didn't know how to fix things and still teach her to fight.

"Like a charm!" Ariel grinned.

"I agree with you, my wife is a genius, but what exactly did she do this time?" Ty tried to sound casual.

Ariel turned to Ty but rather than tell him, she decided to show them. She focused on the fireplace and threw fire daggers with both index fingers at once. Then she decided to show off a bit. She threw one after the other each one flying from a different finger, hitting a different spot on the large log. She turned to Sam, excited. "Come on, now it's your turn. I have a few pointers for you."

"What?" Sam asked confused. "Uh...Ariel I can't throw fire," she reminded her.

"Of course you can't. Come on. Mark your place or whatever you need to do. We're blowing this joint to do some real training," she glanced over her shoulder at Ty. "Sorry honey, you're fired. Sam's training with me now." She grabbed Samantha's arm and pulled her toward the door.

Sam laughed as she stumbled and tried to keep up. "Ariel, you really don't need to do this," she paused. "Uh, I kind of like that you're speaking to me again. I don't want that to change so soon. Ty's made it perfectly clear that I'm terrible at this."

Ariel ignored her protests and continued to pull Sam onto the field.

Megan finished securing the bunker and noticed Sam and Ariel headed for the training area. "Um, honey, I want to see if they're going to practice fighting. Do you mind?" she asked.

"No," Tony said immediately. "I haven't had a chance to talk to you about the possible battle heading our way. Do you know how to fight?" he asked hesitantly. "If not, don't worry about it, just stick close to me."

"I'm not as good with a sword as you, but don't you worry. I can hold my own in a fight. I'm just a bit rusty. I thought it might be fun to work out with Ariel and Sam," she assured him.

Tony studied his wife. "You'd tell me wouldn't you? If you couldn't fight, you'd let me know?" he asked skeptically.

"Tony," Megan sighed. "My father was a tyrant, but he was an egotistical tyrant. It just wouldn't do for his daughter to be killed by vampires. It was imperative that I knew how to fight so dear old dad didn't have to suffer that kind of inexcusable embarrassment. Ironic isn't it? After ranting incessantly, he was the one killed by a vamp. I can fight, better than most. Don't worry about me." A particularly bad memory surfaced. She was so caught up in it she didn't realize she had shared it with her husband.

Shadows

Tony pulled Megan into his arms. "I'm so sorry Megan. I'm sorry you had to grow up with such an awful man for a father."

Megan pulled away. "I didn't do that on purpose," she said embarrassed. "I guess that's the trouble with getting so close to another person. I throw thoughts your way when I have no intention of sharing."

"Hey," Tony lifted her chin so she had to look him in the eyes. "I'm glad you are that comfortable with me. I want to know everything there is to know about you. We're partners, remember? We share everything, good and bad. I can't relate to what your father put you through, but I want to be there for you when you're trying to deal with it. Please don't shut me out. And never be embarrassed that I know something," he smiled. "Hanging with Victor you've learned some less than flattering things about me recently."

Megan smiled. "True," she laughed then sobered. "I won't try to hide things. Thanks for understanding." She kissed him quickly then headed for the field.

Tony watched his wife walk away. He wanted to trust her, but he needed to see for himself. He sauntered around the large field and hid under a tree where he could get a good look. Then he sat down in the shadows and observed the women at work.

Abby saw the other women out on the field and decided to join them. With one more, their numbers would be even.

Ariel called out when she noticed Abby approaching. "You game, shifter? We could use another fighter."

Abby smiled. "That's what I was hoping for." She jogged to the group happy to be included.

418

A short time later, Ty and Victor joined Tony in the shadows. "They're an awesome sight, aren't they?" Victor observed.

The two men sat on the ground admiring their women. Not long afterwards Thomas joined them. He stood quietly behind the group studying Abby. She hadn't shifted. She was holding her own in human form. She looked tired, but he was proud of her. Ariel and Megan were amazing. Even Sam was holding her own against the other women. "Ty?" Thomas called softly.

Ty jumped a little. He had been so enthralled with Sam he hadn't noticed Thomas approach. "Yeah," he finally answered.

"Sam's good. What's all the arguing about?" he asked confused. "You made it sound like she couldn't hold her own against a single vamp. I think she's ready for almost anything."

"It's Ariel," Ty admitted. "Less than two hours with her and Sam's a pro. I couldn't get her to move like that after weeks of instruction," he admitted gloomily. "You fought with her yesterday so you know that."

"Don't be too hard on yourself. Ariel and I have been working on the fire thing longer than that. She didn't show any sign of getting it until she spoke to Sam this morning. I guess the women should stick together. They seem to be better at problem solving as a group than with our help," Victor said.

The men remained silent for a long moment. Each of them transfixed by the talent of their women. Tony finally stood and spoke. "They're erotic like that aren't they?" He laughed at the look on the other men's faces. "Oh, come on. Don't act like you haven't been thinking the same thing. I can't stand it any longer. I want my woman." He pushed a particularly seductive thought Megan's way. He knew the instant she caught it.

Megan heard Tony's thought, turned his way and smiled. She ducked just in time to miss a punch from Ariel. She took off at a dead run, just before she reached her husband she leapt into his arms. Tony caught her as she wrapped her legs around his waist and kissed him passionately.

"See you girls later," Tony laughed. "I have a much better offer." He shifted Megan around, piggyback style and headed for the apartments.

"I guess one of us is going to have an enjoyable evening," Victor laughed. He sobered when Ariel stepped in front of him. He was so proud of her, but he didn't know if he was forgiven yet.

"I think my work here is done," she grinned at Ty. "Sam's a pro."

Ty was watching his wife approach. "Thanks to you," he said gloomily. "All I succeeded in doing was making things worse and pissing her off. I did successfully cause my wife to despise me."

Sam stopped in front of her husband but didn't say a word.

"Actually, you taught her the basics. Those moves are yours. They just needed a little feminine tweaking, so to speak," Ariel told Ty honestly.

"What does that mean?" Ty asked.

"It means you were trying to force Sam to fight like a man. She's got the talent, she just needed to act more like herself," Ariel smiled. "Sam's more feminine. The moves need to match her personality, not yours."

"I still don't get it," Ty said confused. "She's a warrior. I was just trying to teach her to fight like one."

"Ty, Sam's a woman," Ariel said bluntly. "She moves like one. Forget the warrior junk. Just be happy with the explanation that you taught her the moves and I showed her how to apply them as a woman. Problem solved," she glanced at Victor. He still hadn't moved. Ariel stepped in close until their bodies were touching. "I'm sorry I tried to hit you with a fireball this morning," she batted her eyes. "Will you ever forgive me?" she asked playfully.

Victor grabbed Ariel and threw her over his shoulder. "See you guys," he too jogged towards the apartments. Ariel was laughing as Victor took the stairs two at a time.

Ty was still watching Sam. He didn't understand what he was doing wrong, but he was glad she'd caught her stride. If they were attacked, he wouldn't worry so much. He realized Sam's emotions were all over the place just like his. "I'm sorry I was so hard on you," he finally told her. "I've hated the way things have been between us for the past few weeks, but I didn't know how to fix it."

Sam didn't say a word. She just took Ty's hand and started for the farmhouse. Things were going to be okay between them now. She felt confident and ready to fight if she needed to. She would still need practice, but she thought she was off to a pretty good start. "I owe Ariel a lot. I don't ever want us to be like that again," she sighed. "I know you were only trying to help, but you were making me so angry. I couldn't stand to be around you. And I knew you didn't want to be around me, either. I could feel it. I guess our connection can push us apart as much as it brings us together," they had reached their room.

Ty lifted Sam into his arms and pushed open the door, then kicked it closed behind him. "I love you," he said as he gently set her on the bed. "I wanted to be around you, I just didn't want to fight with you anymore. Now, I just want to make up. I want you to feel how much you mean to me," he gazed down at her sprawled across the bed. "If we didn't have this connection, I don't think I could have made it through the last couple weeks. As mad as you were at me, I still knew you loved me. I can get through anything as long as I know that," he laid on the bed and pulled his wife into his arms. "I'm sorry I failed you," he whispered.

"You didn't," Sam said softly. "Like Ariel said, we only needed to tweak what you taught me for everything to click into place. If it wasn't for you, I wouldn't be this far along," she leaned in and kissed him. "I don't want to talk about that anymore. I want to make love to my husband."

Thomas and Abby slowly walked hand in hand toward the house. "You're tired again," he observed. "I wish you wouldn't push yourself so hard."

Abby sighed. "As much as I hate to admit it, that attack took more out of me than I originally thought. I shouldn't be this worn out." She leaned her head on Thomas' shoulder. "Maybe you're right. I need a little more rest before I'm back to a hundred percent."

Thomas looked down at Abby. She could barely hold herself up. "Will you slow down a little for me?" he finally asked. "I hate to see you like this. You're exhausted."

"I'll try," she promised.

Once they stepped inside the house Thomas paused. "You go up to bed. I'll get you a snack."

Abby hesitated then nodded. She needed a snack. Maybe he'd make her another one of those yummy shakes. She slowly climbed the stairs and slipped into the room, anxious to feel the comfort of the large bed in front of her.

Thomas finished making the shake and headed upstairs. Abby had liked the one last night so much, he decided to make her another. Plus, the protein would do her good. He pushed open her door and stopped in surprise. Abby wasn't in there. He walked to the bathroom, but that was empty too. Where could she be? His room, he wondered? He walked down the hall and stepped inside then smiled. She was there alright. Passed out on his bed, still fully clothed.

Thomas walked to the bed and set the shake on the night stand. She couldn't sleep like this. He thought for a moment then pulled out one of his t-shirts. Once he had stripped her and gently pulled on the shirt, he sat on the edge of the bed and lifted Abby onto his lap. She needed the shake. "Abby," Thomas said softly. "You need to drink this before you sleep."

Abby kind of woke up. She was coherent enough to guzzle the contents when Thomas gently pressed a glass to her lips. She had a vague thought about how wonderful and fruity the shake tasted. Then she was out again. Thomas slid Abby into bed and undressed himself. He studied her in the moonlight. Apparently fate was against them. He hoped this wasn't a pattern for the future. He wasn't built for a life of abstinence. He climbed into bed and pulled Abby's body against his, holding her close. She felt so good

Shadows

in his arms. He realized this was something he'd like to repeat every night for the rest of his life, while he drifted off to sleep.

Abby woke and wondered where she was. Oh yeah, she was in Thomas' room. She rolled over and realized Thomas was still sleeping soundly next to her. She slowly slid from the bed and quietly tiptoed to the bathroom, chastising herself the entire way. Stupid, stupid, stupid, she chanted in her mind. How could she have been so stupid to fall asleep? Thomas promised to finish what they had started yesterday morning. If she wasn't so stupid they could have had a wonderful night together. She opened the drawer and pulled out the toothbrush she'd hidden there last night. Well, they were going to have a wonderful morning. If anyone interrupted, she'd kill them. She turned on the water just enough for a small stream to come out and began to brush her teeth. Hopefully she'd make it back to bed before Thomas woke up. She rinsed off the brush and set it aside, cupping her hands to clean off the paste then reached back to find the towel and froze. The towel found her. Abby slowly stood and saw Thomas standing directly behind her.

Thomas was amused. He didn't have to brush his teeth so the ritual intrigued him. Abby was adorable with white paste covering her lips. Once she rinsed it off, he couldn't resist. He grabbed the towel and stood behind her. When she straightened he moved in close pressing his body against hers. She was still in his t-shirt and he found that amazingly sexy.

"You caught me," Abby said breathlessly. The feel of Thomas pressed up against her in only his underwear did strange things to her body.

Thomas leaned down and took her mouth with his. Then he gently lifted her off the floor and set her on the counter. "Abby," he groaned as she linked her legs around his waist and pulled him closer. He couldn't wait any longer. He picked her up and walked back to the bed. "I need you," he said softly as he lowered them both onto the sheets.

Later that morning, Abby was wrapped around Thomas, exhausted and happier than she'd ever been in her life. She studied him closely, was he sleeping?

"You're staring," he said as he slowly opened his eyes.

"I am," she said smiling. "I can't help it. I love to look at you. You looked so peaceful."

"You mean exhausted?" He grinned as he pulled her on top of him. "You're a wild woman, Abby Cooper."

Abby froze. Had she been too wild? Maybe she should have gone a little easier on him their first time. She didn't want to scare him away. She knew the animal inside her was a little overwhelming sometimes. That idiot Billy had actually passed out it was so intense. It still annoyed her when that moron bragged about their night at the beach to everyone he saw. He's lucky she wasn't cruel enough to tell people the real story.

Thomas laughed. "That was a compliment," he said then pulled her mouth down to his. "I think I just hit the jackpot," his smile widened. "I'm the luckiest man alive. You might kill me, but I'm going to die a happy man." They both laughed, then got lost once again in the passion of the moment and each other.

Shadows

* * * *

Ariel climbed out of bed and headed for the shower. She turned too quickly and winced a little. Her hip was still really sore. She was beginning to wonder if she'd broken a bone. She'd missed a dose of tea last night. She didn't want Victor to ask questions. If he knew she was injured, he'd just be upset and blame himself. This was her fault, she didn't want him taking the blame or feeling guilty.

Ariel climbed carefully into the shower and turned on the water. She had her eyes closed, lathering her hair when a masculine body slid in behind her and placed his hands over hers. After a moment, she lowered her hands as Victor continued to gently massage her scalp.

Ariel moaned, the massage felt good. "As much as I'm enjoying this, you might want to be careful," she smiled. "My boyfriend's in the next room and he's a little possessive. If he catches you, I'm afraid you might not live much longer."

Victor ran his hands over Ariel's shoulders and down to her waist then he gently turned her around to face him. He wrapped his arms around her and pulled her close, then kissed her passionately.

Once he released her, Ariel smiled at him. "Oh, it's you," she pretended to be surprised. "Well, that's good. I wouldn't want some random guy to die because of me."

"You're wrong," he told her, still studying her face. "I'm more than a little possessive, but you are right about the dying part." He smiled as he picked up the soap and began to lather his hands. He started with her shoulders, gently caressing her soft skin as he slowly washed her luscious body.

Ariel leaned her head against the wall and closed her eyes, enjoying Victor's rough hands as they caressed her wet skin. She knew the exact moment he saw the bruise. She sighed and opened her eyes. He was staring up at her. Pain and regret written all over his face.

"I did that to you, didn't I?" he choked out.

"No," Ariel corrected. "I did that to myself."

Victor sat on the long bench that ran across the shower wall and put his face in his hands. "Why did you hide it?" he finally asked. Then a thought struck him. He jerked his head up in shock. "Ariel, did I hurt you last night? Did I make it worse?" He hated himself for what he had done.

Ariel crouched down in front of Victor. He looked so miserable. "This is why I hid it from you," she said softly. She ran her palm down the side of his face. "Baby, this was my fault. But I knew you'd blame yourself so I didn't want you to know," she paused. "And no, you didn't hurt me. I'm pretty sure you could tell the only thing I was feeling last night was pleasure." She smiled at the memory then climbed into Victor's lap. "Victor, don't do this to yourself. I caused this, it was an accident."

Victor stood and carried her to the bed. He gently placed her on her side and sat down to study the bruise more closely. He was so angry at himself for losing his temper with her. He pressed slightly on her hip and she winced. His head shot to her face. "Have you been taking tea for this?" he asked even more worried now.

Shadows

"I have, but I missed a dose last night," she smiled. "I was a little preoccupied."

"Ariel, this isn't funny." He looked back at the bruise. "I think you may have broken something. If you've been drinking the tea, you should be healed by now."

Ariel sat up and pulled Victor into a tight hug.

Victor wrapped his arms around her and rubbed her back. "I am so sorry," he said softly. "I'm never going to forgive myself for this. I love you, how could I hurt you like that?"

Now Ariel was getting mad. She pushed Victor away and glared at him. "Stop this right now," she demanded.

"I can't," Victor told her. "Ariel, I love you more than life itself. Yet, I shoved you across that clearing and probably broke your hip. How can I stop feeling guilty and miserable about that? How can you not be furious with me for that?" he asked.

"Because this is my fault," she said raising her voice for the first time. "Victor. I think you're conveniently forgetting that I lost my temper, not you. I'm the one that threw fire at your face." She stood and pulled on Victor's large shirt, then she began to pace. "Do you have any idea how guilty I feel about that? How ashamed I am of my behavior. When I think of what that ball of fire could have done to you if you hadn't deflected it with your dagger, I can barely live with myself. But even that didn't snap me out of my rage. It pissed me off even more. So I stalked over and shoved you. What did you do? Nothing," she answered her own question. "You just stood there and took it. So I shoved you again, harder. Again you stood there patiently taking my abuse. It wasn't until I took a swing at you that you got pissed and shoved me away. So I landed on a rock and injured myself. So what!" she yelled. "I deserve this," she pointed at her hip. "I deserved worse. This is the consequence for my bad behavior. Nothing more. Having you sit there hating yourself because of something I did, makes me angry. I already feel guilty enough. Please don't blame yourself for this. I can't take it. I can't bare the pain I'm causing you because I was so reckless and out of control." Tears began to roll down her face.

Victor stood and walked over to Ariel. He pulled her into a tight hug. "Please don't cry baby. I can't stand it when you cry. It breaks my heart to see you upset like this."

"I am so sorry Victor," Ariel choked out. "I am so sorry I tried to hurt you."

Victor walked to a chair and sat down, settling Ariel on his lap. The two sat silently clinging to each other for a long while. They both needed to feel the comfort of the other's love. "I'm going to try to stop dwelling on the pain I caused you, but you have to promise to do the same."

Ariel studied him, not saying a word. She wasn't sure she could do what he was asking. She didn't know if she could ever forgive herself for what she tried to do.

"Ariel," Victor said sternly. He gently wiped the tears away from her face. "I pushed you on purpose. Clearly I pushed too hard. I crossed the line and you got angry," he smiled at her. "I'm proud of you. You worked so hard and finally found the secret to expand your gift. We both behaved badly. Neither one of us handled the situation like we should have. If we had, we wouldn't have been so divided for so long. It almost killed me, being at odds with you all the time. Let's just put the whole thing behind us. We'll just remember it as an extremely bad experience. One I never want to repeat. I need you baby," he leaned in and kissed her. "I need to feel you close like we are now," he laid his forehead against Ariel's. "I think the part I hated the most was not being able to hold you every night, not feeling you close to me as I fell asleep. Having you so close, but so far away was unbearable. I promise I will never let things get that bad again. Will you please promise me the same?"

Ariel shifted and straddled Victor's naked body. "That I can do," she said wrapping her arms around him and pulling him close. She pressed her mouth to his and kissed him gently at first, then she deepened the kiss.

Victor reached under the large shirt and caressed Ariel's back. All he wanted to think about right now was their love.

Ariel stood and took Victor's hand leading him back to the bed. "I vaguely recall you telling me that when I was bad, I had to make it up to you with sex." She climbed onto the bed and motioned for him to join her. "I think I'd feel much better about the whole situation if I paid my debt." She smiled at him seductively. "It hardly seems fair though." She moaned as Victor climbed on top of her and stretched her arms above her head. "My debt always feels more like a reward."

Victor took Ariel's mouth with his and the conversation abruptly came to an end.

About an hour later, Ariel and Victor were sprawled out on the bed. Ariel was on her side, her head resting on Victor's chest. Victor gently touched the bruise. It was in almost the same place Ariel had been shot as a teen. "Did you change your mind about the tattoo?" he asked curiously.

"No," she admitted. "We've just been busy and I didn't think it was a good idea to do it until things calmed down a little. If we end up getting attacked, I want to be prepared. You said getting a tattoo is very painful. I assumed it would take a while to heal. It's waited this long, it can wait a little longer. I was thinking I could get a smaller version of yours. Kind of like his and hers," she smiled at him. She thought that would somehow bind them together even more tightly.

"I'd like that," he told her kissing her temple. "I guess it goes back to that possessive thing you mentioned earlier. Does that bother you?"

"No," she said looking at him. "It might sound strange, but it makes me feel loved."

"You are loved," Victor kissed her again. "I love you more than anything in the world. You are my world, Ariel. I hope you know that."

"I do," she said softly. Her stomach growled. Ariel laughed. "I'm starving," she started to sit up. "How about I make you breakfast?" she suggested.

Victor also sat. "How about we make breakfast together," he countered. The couple climbed out of bed. Moments later they were headed to the kitchen.

Victor immediately made Ariel some tea. Then they went to work on breakfast. The two decided if they were cooking, they might as well make enough for the whole group. They were halfway through when Thomas and Abby showed up.

Shadows

"Something smells wonderful," Abby declared. She was starved.

"Pull up a chair, we're almost finished," Ariel told them. "Have you seen Ty and Sam or Tony and Megan this morning?"

"Nope," Abby said pulling up a chair and resting against Thomas.

Victor smiled. He was glad the two of them had worked things out. Thomas could use a little happiness in his life.

Ty and Sam walked in. "I knew I smelled bacon," Ty said sitting at the large table then pulling Sam onto his lap. "I told you babe. All we had to do was wait and someone would provide a great meal."

"Yeah, I think it's your turn tomorrow buddy," Victor called from the stove. "You got lucky this morning, I was in a good mood and decided to be nice."

"What does my getting lucky this morning have to do with your good mood?" Ty asked casually.

Sam slugged him.

"Oh, sorry. I guess that was a secret," he kissed Sam gently. "I'll do better next time."

"I don't think that's possible," Sam said climbing off Ty's lap and sitting in the chair next to him.

"Okay stop," Victor begged. "We get it, you two made up. We don't need the sordid details." He set two cups of coffee on the table in front of Sam and Ty then returned to the stove.

Ariel set the pancakes on the table. "Dig in," she told them. "The eggs and bacon should be ready in a minute." Ariel walked to the fridge and pulled out milk and orange juice. Just as she kicked the door closed, Victor pressed her back against it and kissed her passionately. Ariel pushed him away and laughed. "Behave," she scolded.

"I guess we're not the only ones that made up," Ty said to Sam. "If I can't talk about it," he called to Victor, "you can't demonstrate."

"Unfortunately for you Ty," Victor said as he placed a large plate of bacon on the table. "I don't need your permission to show affection to the woman I love."

Ariel set a large platter of eggs on the table and sat next to Sam. "I guess we're even," Ariel smiled. "I'm glad."

"Me too," Sam said as Ty reached under the table and placed a hand on her knee. Sam looked around the room. It seemed like all was right with the world this morning. With all the ugliness and trouble looming, it was nice to enjoy a nice breakfast with friends.

Within minutes Kylee joined the group then Bastian and Morrigan followed. Tony and Megan never showed. The group assumed they were having a private meal in their room.

* * * *

Ty, Sam and Thomas were all in the library again when Megan and Tony escorted McBride to the kitchen. Rand studied the group on his way out the door. When they were almost to the bunker he decided to make his request. "I was wondering if I could help," he said quietly.

"With what?" Tony asked.

"With the investigation," he continued. "I know you won't give me a computer, but if you would give me a map and a marker and whatever info you have on the missing women, I might be able to help narrow things down."

"We'll see," Tony said nonchalantly.

"Please," McBride asked, stopping to face the man. "I'm going out of my mind in there and I want to help. Why not let me try, isn't it worth it if I can help save those girls?" he pressed.

"I'll talk to Victor. If we decide to let you help, I'll bring you the things you asked for," Tony agreed. "Now eat your breakfast," Tony waited while McBride entered the bunker.

"What do you think?" he asked Megan.

"I didn't get any vibe that he was up to something. I think he really just wants to help. Plus, it will give him something to do. I'd go crazy in that bunker alone all day without any freedom. He has my vote. Like he said how can it hurt? There's no downside if he helps to find those girls," Megan told him.

"I agree. I'll talk to Victor, but I think he'll like the idea." They headed back to the house to talk to the others. Everyone agreed to let McBride in. When Megan checked on him at lunch time, he had already narrowed things down.

"I know I'm probably not welcome in there, but it might help if I explained my findings to those guys working the problem," McBride suggested.

"Go ahead," Tony said glancing at Megan. She gave him a slight nod. She had to concentrate. If McBride tried something she wanted to be ready. He was getting more and more difficult to control.

Sam studied the map. "It seems logical," she finally said. "I'm willing to go this route if you are Thomas." She handed him the map.

Thomas studied it for a minute then looked at McBride. "Okay. We'll try it your way. We can always expand the search if we don't find them." He picked up the phone to call Dimitri. Once the plan was put into place Thomas studied McBride. "Why?" he asked.

"Why what?" McBride answered.

"Why would you help us? You think we're the ones responsible," Thomas told him.

"I'm not sure what I think anymore," McBride said honestly. "I decided early on you were guilty based on the reaction I got that first morning. You were hiding something. Abby acted guilty, so did Alex. You...I couldn't get a fix on you, Thomas. That seemed suspicious somehow. Now I know you were keeping a secret. One I wish I didn't know, but I'm not entirely sure you killed those girls anymore. Don't get me wrong, I don't trust you. But if you really are trying to save two women, I guess we're working towards the same goal. I just thought I might be able to help, that's all."

"Thank you," Thomas said sincerely. "We don't trust you either but thanks for the information." He nodded to Tony and they escorted McBride back to the bunker.

McBride had narrowed the search area substantially. It seemed the two women lived, worked and played within a ten block section of the city. They had obviously been abducted there. What McBride didn't know was that Lawson and Patricia had also lived within McBride's circle. Foster owned several other hotels in the area as well. Maybe the detective had been helpful after all. Only time would tell.

Chapter Ten

Martinez walked with the large group of vampires headed back to New York. The longer they traveled, the more determined he was to leave. He needed to escape this group and head out on his own. He had refused to join the drug cartel as a human, he certainly wasn't going to conform now that he was a vampire, not that he knew what that meant. This particular band of idiots was beyond lacking when it came to useful information. And if they believed their attempts at intimidation would keep him submissive and compliant, they were in for a surprise. The drug cartel had made far more serious threats against him, his family and his friends but he would not be controlled. Not then, not now. Gomez always said 'Freedom is being you without anyone's permission.' Martinez planned to stay free. He sobered. He couldn't believe Gomez was gone. They'd been friends since they were four. They had fought together against oppression from the cartel and they had been turned into vampires together, which was bad enough. Then their new vampire leader, that Felix guy, went and got all of them killed. He

437

Shadows

couldn't care less that Felix was dead, but how was he going to make it without Gomez…and Zephrey? He'd barely met Zee, but the guy was cool and he seemed to know a lot about being a vampire. Now he was gone, too. Martinez glanced around and felt claustrophobic and vulnerable. He had never been so alone in his life and he didn't like it.

To pass the time, Martinez began to envision the world Zephrey had described so passionately. According to Zee, the Amazon was a place where vampires were left alone to live as they wished. He didn't know this Radek character, but he sounded a lot like the drug cartel. Crazy, egotistical and a control freak. Martinez was not going to die for a dictator like that. He wouldn't join up in life. He certainly wouldn't conform in death…or the undead…or whatever he was now. He looked around at the scenery then at the massive group of vampires traveling through the area. He couldn't help but think they were sitting ducks. Where exactly was Tyrone taking them anyway? He had no idea. All he knew was Felix had passed around that photo. The guy in the picture was huge and supposed to be their target. After Felix died Tyrone continued to pass it around every night, trying to stamp it permanently in their minds. He was not going to kill a guy just because some nut case told him to. He wasn't completely opposed to killing, he just needed a better reason. As soon as it was completely dark he was going to slip away. He could hide in the forest and escape to this Amazon world Zephrey talked about. He didn't know why, but instinct told him this group was headed for death. They might get their man, the guy in that picture, but if his gut was right most of them, if not all of them, would die in the process. He wasn't willing to give his life for someone else's cause.

The group hit the edge of the forest and Martinez immediately began looking for an escape. Was Tyrone really going to attack a military base? No wonder he had such a bad feeling about their mission. He took a few steps backwards then blended again. A few seconds later he paused, letting more vampires file past him. He needed to get to the back of the group. From there he would have a better chance of escaping. He could hear Tyrone giving instructions. They were to look for the man in the photo but attack and kill everyone they encountered. Good luck with that, Martinez thought. I'm out of here as soon as I get the chance. He took another step backwards, then another. He was almost free.

* * * *

All the alarms sounded at once. Thomas, Abby, Ty and Sam jumped up to their feet. Foster's paperwork would have to wait. They rushed out the front door and onto the porch just as Morrigan, Victor and Ariel ascended the stairs. Bastian and Kylee were running up the drive, Tony and Megan directly behind them.

"We got the kids gathered into the warehouse. The door is secure, but I don't want to leave them alone for long," Victor told the group. "Did you happen to check the monitors?" he asked glancing around.

"No. We rushed out to see if anyone was in trouble," Thomas admitted.

"I'll go," Ty dashed through the door and up the stairs. While he was there, he double checked the barn. His dogs were secure. He didn't want them involved in this, they wouldn't survive long against vampires. It only took him a minute to walk back onto the porch. "It's bad," he said soberly. "There are several hundred vampires huddled in the forest. They look like they're about to

Shadows

attack. We need to get to the kids, fast." He started down the front stairs, Sam securely by his side. The rest of the group was close behind. "Sam," Ty said quietly. "This is going to be bad. I trust you," he glanced at her. "I know you can handle this. But please stay close to me. For me, will you please stick close?"

"I promise," Sam assured him. "Don't worry Ty. I'm not going anywhere. I think we have a better chance at surviving this if we work together as a team. I'm not stupid enough to believe I'm ready for something this big. I know I need your help."

Ty stopped at the door to the warehouse and pulled Sam in close. "I love you," he kissed her hard and fast. "And I think you are ready for this. Well, as much as any of us are," he smiled at her.

"I love you too," she said taking his hand. "Thank you for pushing me so hard. If I am ready, it's all because of you."

The rest of the group reached the warehouse. Victor unlocked the door and they entered the large room that housed the kids. "I'm not going to lie to you. We're in trouble here. A large group of vampires are outside the forest. We expect them to storm the base any minute." He looked around the room. "Dusty?"

"Yeah," Dusty rushed forward. "I put everyone into groups. Most of them have a partner. A few of them are in groups of three. They know what to do."

"Good," Victor studied the group. "I don't want you to fight unless you absolutely have to. You came here to learn, not to get hurt. We're going to set you up in one of the bunkers. There are over three hundred of them out there so it should be difficult for the vampires to find you. If you stick together you have a better chance. Does everyone understand me?"

The group of kids nodded.

Victor turned back to the adults. "We need to split up, otherwise they might see us and head straight for the bunker," Victor announced. "Everyone gets a partner. Ariel's mine. Obviously Ty and Sam are together and Tony and Megan," he paused.

"Abby and I are together," Thomas put in.

"Kylee will stick with me," Bastian announced. He shrugged when the warriors looked at him in shock. "Someone has to watch out for her."

"Thanks a lot," Kylee said sarcastically.

"That leaves Morrigan," Victor said. "You need to join a group. I don't want anyone out there alone."

Dusty stepped forward. "I'd like to be his partner. I've put Nebi in charge of the others. She'll know what to do and can handle anything that comes their way."

Nebi stepped forward. "I can handle it," she affirmed.

Morrigan studied Dusty. They'd been working together frequently. The kid was good, but there were so many vampires out there. Morrigan looked at Victor. He could see the warrior was struggling with the same thing Morrigan was. How would they live with themselves if Dusty got hurt?

"Look," Dusty began. "Let me put it this way. I'm going to fight. I'm not hiding out in a bunker while you guys battle for your lives. I agree the rest of these guys should stay hidden. Most of them are new to this and aren't ready, but I've been here longer than anyone. I've already fought some of the vampires. I have experience on a small scale. I'm ready for this. Morrigan needs a partner. I'm available."

"I'm going to allow it," Victor finally said. "Past experience has told me Dusty is reckless and won't stay in the bunker like he's told," Victor narrowed his eyes at the boy. "I don't like it, but I'd rather you were paired with Morrigan than joining the fight on your own. And we both know that is exactly what would happen. Nebi?"

"Yeah," she answered enthusiastically. She was honored to be given the chance to lead the others.

"I've watched you, I know you're a good fighter. You're also quick and smart. You're going to need that tonight. We're hiding you out in the bunker, but if any of those vamps find you, they'll be on you before you know what happened. I'm counting on you to keep the group safe. Think fast and move if you need to. We're going to be busy so nobody is going to be there to help you. Do you understand?" Victor asked.

"Yes sir," she nodded. "I promise, none of these guys will get hurt on my watch."

"You may not be able to keep that promise. I won't hold you to it. All I'm asking is that you do your best," Victor turned to the group. "I'm sorry for this. If we'd had warning I would have removed you from the area. Unfortunately we have to accept the hand we were dealt. Listen to Nebi and watch out for each other. Tonight you will need to be a cohesive unit. Everyone make sure you take care of your partner."

The small group of kids acknowledged Victor's advice.

"Morrigan, I want you and Dusty to escort the group to the bunker. You know the one. Try not to draw attention to yourself. The rest of us will split up and try to cause a scene. We want the vamps to focus on us. Let's go."

They all split up and filed out. Morrigan and Dusty maneuvered the group around the bunkers, using them for cover. Once the kids were inside, Morrigan turned to Dusty. "I know you've fought vampires before, but this is different. You faced two or three. There are hundreds of them out there. We'll need to work together. The fae and the warriors use daggers or swords to attack the vamps hearts. Shifters work differently. Try to sever their heads. If you separate it from their body enough, they'll dissipate. Fight however you're most comfortable. At first I'm not going to shift, but if you are more at ease that way, you go ahead." He paused to study Dusty. The kid looked ready, a little nervous, but that was to be expected. "Ready?" Morrigan asked pulling a dagger out of a sheath.

"I'm as ready as I'll ever be." Dusty took a deep breath and followed Morrigan to the battlefield.

The battle had already begun. Abby and Thomas were fighting together. Abby hadn't shifted yet. She preferred to start off with hand to hand. If the numbers grew too big, she'd shift and continue in another form.

Ty and Sam were working together. Once they found their rhythm it was almost like a dance. They both immediately realized their connection was an asset. They didn't need to call out a warning. As soon as they saw their partner was in trouble the other one felt it also and was able to dodge the problem. Sam caught a glimpse of Ariel and Victor. They too were as one. She couldn't see Thomas or Abby but figured they were working in sync just like the others. Having a partner seemed to bring the group strength. She hoped Kylee was doing okay. She was Sam's biggest worry. Kylee was human. She shouldn't be involved in this. If anything happened to her, Sam was going to feel responsible. The only reason Kylee was here in the first place was because she'd followed Sam to the fort. As three vampires headed her way, Sam cleared her mind of everything but the fight. Losing wasn't an option.

Dusty saw them first. A large group of vampires was headed straight for the bunker where the teens were hiding. He realized their mistake too late. The rest of the buildings were opened. Closing one bunker drew attention to it. Dusty turned to Morrigan who was battling three vampires at the same time. "Morrigan," he called. "The group is in trouble."

Morrigan vanquished two vampires simultaneously. He was just about to attack the third when it disappeared. Dusty had taken care of it. He turned to the kid, trying to figure out what he was talking about. That's when he saw about fifty vampires headed for the bunker.

"Watch out," Dusty called as two more vampires came at Morrigan from behind. "You got this?" he asked as he turned and headed towards the problem.

Morrigan took out the attacking vampires and turned to follow Dusty. They weren't going to make it. He hoped Nebi didn't panic. She was going to need to think on her toes. Morrigan picked up the pace but he was forced to stop occasionally to defend himself and cover Dusty's back.

Thomas noticed the vampires heading for the bunker. The kids were in trouble. He grabbed Abby's hand and started that way.

444

Once he realized Morrigan and Dusty were taking care of it, he turned and darted towards McBride's bunker. It was the only other one in the lot that was closed. "I have to let him out," he yelled to Abby. "If anything happens it's on me, but I can't leave McBride in there to be killed like that. He won't know what's coming. He wouldn't be prepared for a fight."

Abby nodded in agreement. "It's on us," she corrected. "I agree with you. I don't know what his fate is going to be, but we can't leave him vulnerable like this."

Thomas swung open the door and called to McBride. Rand immediately stood and walked to the opening. He was surprised to see Thomas and Abby. Usually the mind controller came for him, but she was nowhere to be seen.

"Hurry up," Thomas ordered. "Do whatever you have to, but protect yourself." Thomas grabbed Abby's hand and started back toward the field.

"Wait," McBride called. He didn't understand what was happening here. Why had Thomas set him free? He slowly followed the couple toward the field.

"I can't," Thomas called back. "The others need us. If you come after me, I'll deal with that but for now leave. Get to safety," then he disappeared around the corner.

Rand still didn't understand. Was there some kind of emergency? He couldn't help himself, he slowly followed behind Thomas and Abby. As he got closer to the end of the row, he heard what sounded like fighting. He rounded the corner and froze. The scene was like nothing he'd ever witnessed before. What were those things? He had no idea, but clearly they were evil. They looked

Shadows

cold and violent. A memory hit him like a freight train. What had Mason said exactly? *We may be creatures of another world, but we were sent here to balance the scale.* There had to be a balance between good and evil. We were created by a higher being to ensure that balance. Rand hadn't believed him at the time, but looking at those things charging the small group convinced him Mason was right.

Dusty reached the bunker just in time to see Nebi go down. She had rushed forward to protect a girl that was huddled against the wall. Gerty wasn't even fighting. She just sat there, frozen, waiting for the vampire to attack. Nebi ordered the group out of the bunker. She told them to run to the warehouse and get back to the mat room. Then she flew across the bunker and shielded the girl with her body. The vampire hit her from the side. There was a large crack and Nebi sank to the floor. She knew several of her ribs were broken, but she needed to kill that thing. She pulled out a dagger and waited. Once he reached for her, she lunged, driving the knife into his mid-section. The girl behind her screamed.

Dusty darted in front of Nebi and began killing, one, two, three vampires before Morrigan arrived and helped with the rest. After they had killed about twenty vampires the remaining group fled. They ran for the field and the comfort of numbers. Dusty crouched over Nebi. He heard the crack and knew she had broken several ribs. He looked to Morrigan. "She's really hurt," he told him. "What do we do?"

"Nebi?" Morrigan asked. "Can you breathe okay? I know you're hurt. I believe you've broken a few ribs, but I need to know if you can breathe. We have to know if you've punctured a lung."

Nebi took several deep breaths. "No, it's painful but I can breathe fine. I think it's just the ribs," she started to push herself to her feet. "I told the others to run to the warehouse, back to the mat room. I need to get in there. They're not going to know what to do." She supported her body against the wall and tried to take a step.

Morrigan grabbed her arm and steadied her. He looked down at the girl still pressed against the wall. "You gonna stand up, or do you plan to sit there all night and hope another vampire doesn't find you?" he said angrily. If he had any say in it, that girl was going home. She didn't belong here.

Gerty stood up and glared at Morrigan.

"Good. I've made you angry," Morrigan paused. "Use that energy to get Nebi to the mat room. I want to use that as a make shift trauma center," he turned back to Nebi. "You are in no condition to fight. Don't try it. Get to the mat room and make yourself as comfortable as you can. Tell the others to split into two groups. There are two doors. Send one group to each door. They need to defend the room. Hopefully they won't have to fight, but if they do I want numbers on their side. We'll do our best to keep them away from the building. Do you think you can get back okay?" Morrigan looked at Dusty. The kid was worried about the girl. Obviously they had something starting there. "Never mind. Dusty, I want you to take her yourself. That way if any vampires approach, you can take care of them. Don't linger. I need you back on the field. Find me as soon as you can."

Dusty nodded then picked Nebi up and headed for the warehouse. "Come on," he told Gerty. "Try to keep up."

Shadows

Rand stood transfixed, studying the battlefield. The two fighters were working together, killing monster after monster. How was that possible? As soon as they plunged a dagger into their heart the monsters disappeared. It turned to dust right before his eyes. Victor and the fire thrower were just as amazing. Victor was throwing those little ninja stars, several at a time, each striking its mark precisely. The woman, Rand assumed it was Victor's wife or girlfriend was doing the same with fire. She conjured three, sometimes four flaming balls and killed multiple enemies at a time.

Rand shifted his attention to Thomas and Abby. They had rejoined the fight and were battling multiple attackers at once. What was Thomas and the others anyway? No human could fight the way they did. Then he saw the mind reader and her husband, Tony was it? Tony was swinging a sword like it was second nature to him. That may have been normal a hundred years ago, but nobody fought with a sword now days. The mind reader was fighting by his side, killing the things with a dagger. He turned and saw Morrigan running back towards the fight alone, single handedly taking out one of those things after another. As he watched the battle raging before him, Rand realized he'd been wrong. These people couldn't be bad. They weren't the ones that needed to be wiped from the face of the earth as he originally believed. His mother had been wrong. It wasn't a demon inside of him. Mason told him it was genetic, that he could change into animals because of a biological gift he was born with. Rand watched in amazement as the teenage boy joined Morrigan and they both shifted into grizzly bears and began tearing the monsters to pieces.

He realized the group of monsters was growing. The good guys were outnumbered. He watched as more and more things funneled in from the forest. There were hundreds of them. How would these people defend their fort? Rand couldn't believe such a small group could win against so many. As he studied the scene playing out before him he noticed two things at once. He saw Kylee standing next to a large man he'd never seen before, battling right alongside him. She was good. Not as proficient as the others, but she was holding her own. He also noticed a group of about twenty bad guys focused on Thomas and Abby. As soon as they saw the couple, they began to get excited. Then they started to move. They were slow and calculating but clearly focused on Thomas or Abby or both, Rand couldn't tell which. As the group proceeded forward, it began to grow. Now there were at least forty of them. Then fifty. Why were they singling out those two?

Rand turned back to Thomas and realized neither he nor Abby had spotted the group. They didn't know they were in danger. He didn't think. He just shifted into a lion and let out a loud roar. The noise thundered across the clearing. Rand marveled at the intense feeling of freedom he felt. Thomas spotted him first, then he spotted the approaching monsters. Rand darted toward the couple and leapt just before he reached them, landing hard by Abby's side. Letting his inner animal free was exhilarating.

Thomas was shocked. Why were so many vampires targeting him and Abby? He didn't hesitate, he shot forward and charged the group. He wanted the element of surprise. He knew they wouldn't expect that. Thomas kicked and jabbed and sliced through the crowd taking out as many vampires as he could. They just kept coming at him. His attackers were growing in numbers. He hesitated momentarily when he heard his name. Why did the vampires know his name? Were they here because of him? Had Lilith or Radek specifically sent this mob after him? Why would they do that? Alex! It hit him like a punch to the gut. They wanted Alex to be vulnerable. If they took him out, then maybe Dimitri,

Shadows

Alex wouldn't be protected the same as she was now. "Abby leave," he begged. "Go help the others. Leave these guys to me."

Abby looked at Thomas in shock. Was he crazy? There was no way she would leave him like this. That's when she saw it. One of the vampires pulled out a photo of Thomas. They were targeting him. Specifically sent here to take him out. Well, they were in for a surprise tonight. She would never leave Thomas.

"Go on, Abby. Please, for me?" Thomas asked again more urgently this time.

"I'm not leaving you," Abby told him calmly. "They're specifically after you. That one over there has your picture."

Thomas was surprised at that, but it just confirmed his suspicions. "This is a losing battle. You and Rand go help the others. I couldn't stand it if you got hurt because of me."

Rand shifted back into a man and glared at Thomas. "Do you seriously think I'm going to run like a scared chicken?" He grumbled as he picked up a dagger one of the vampires had dropped and immediately started fighting off the hoard. The cluster of vamps stepped back, they appeared to be trying to regroup. "We need a plan. And don't try that ridiculous run for your life bit again. I'm not leaving and judging by the look on Abby's face, neither is she."

Thomas gave up. Rand was right. "I don't have a plan other than fight. If they're all here for me, eventually they're going to swarm like flies. The others will figure it out and help us, but we might be on our own for a while." He glanced around the field. Everyone had their hands full. "The two of you stand on either side of me. I have the most experience fighting. Let me lead the charge. You two watch my back. We'll try to take out as many as we can."

"So, we're charging them again?" Rand asked. "You are a crazy SOB aren't you?"

Thomas smiled. "Maybe a little. Ready?"

Rand and Abby nodded and the three of them charged the group. Rand couldn't help but admire Thomas' talent. He was nowhere near that good even with a dagger. This wasn't working. He immediately shifted again. This time into a wolf. Maybe he'd be more limber that way. He remembered watching Morrigan and the kid ripping the heads off these things. He thought that would work better than him trying to fight as a man. He was good with a gun, but a cop never brought a knife to a gun fight.

Abby continued to fight by Thomas' side. Things were going pretty well until four large vampires charged Thomas at once. He took out three of them but the forth stabbed Thomas in the stomach. He went down hard, the wound was obviously deep and severe. She had to do something, the others were closing in on him. Abby was angry. She shifted into a gorilla and charged, swinging her knife with all she had. One of the vampires dissipated and she grabbed his dagger in her other hand. Now she could come at them twice as hard.

Rand was shocked. Abby was a force to be reckoned with when she got angry. He saw Thomas on the ground and understood. Abby was protecting her man. Rand shifted back and rushed to the injured man. He killed one of those things just before it reached Thomas. "What are they anyway?"

Thomas studied Rand, he might as well know the truth. "Vampires," Thomas told him.

Shadows

Rand looked at Thomas in surprise. "Vampires," he stated flatly. Well, why not? Thomas and his group were some kind of warrior fighters and then there were the mind readers and the fire throwers. He found it easy enough to believe vampires existed as well. He studied Thomas. "Can you stand up?" he asked. "Let me see how bad you're hit."

Thomas moaned in pain. He'd never been sliced through the stomach like this before, not even that night at the cabin. He was determined not to let it happen again. The wound was deep. He tried to stand, but the pain was too intense. "Just give me a minute. I'll be fine," Thomas hoped he was right. There were too many vampires for Abby to hold off on her own. That stopped him. He jerked his head up and saw her. She was magnificent. He'd never seen anything like her before. She was circling him, taking out two, sometimes three vampires with one swing. His heart swelled. He fell in love with Abby Cooper all over again. The pain was excruciating, but he thought he could finally stand. Out of the corner of his eye he saw a vampire charging toward Rand. Just before the vampire plunged a knife into McBride's back, Thomas reached out and stabbed him.

Rand jumped and looked back just in time to see the dust. "Thanks," he said a little shaken. "I think we need to get you out of here."

"No," Thomas objected. "Abby needs my help." Thomas began pushing himself up just as Rand let go and darted off in the opposite direction. Thomas heard McBride screaming as he ran. He wondered what had caused such an urgent reaction, but he couldn't worry about it now. Abby needed his help. He slowly pushed himself up and got back into the fight. It was difficult. He was slow and couldn't take out multiple enemies like usual, but at least he was doing something. Another vampire sliced his leg, but Thomas ignored it. That one would heal fairly quickly. Then one hit his arm. He had almost missed that one, it had come at him from the side and he didn't see it until it was almost too late. This couldn't go on for long.

Rand saw Kylee go down and panicked. Several of the attackers were closing in. He shifted as he ran and tackled one of the vampires in midair as it loomed above her. Kylee stood and thanked him. Her arm was bleeding and she had a slight limp, but she took a deep breath and got back into the fight.

Bastian felt Kylee's presence missing. He turned just in time to see McBride tackle a vampire that was about to bite her. He ran toward her and smiled as she stood, brushed herself off and got back in the fight. Her arm was bleeding and she obviously injured her leg but she was a trooper. He rushed to her side and ripped off part of his shirt. Then he tied the long strip around her arm to stop the bleeding. "You okay?" he asked concerned.

"I'll be fine," she told Bastian. "This is definitely harder than one of those droids," she admitted.

Bastian studied the field. At least they didn't have any new vampires flooding in from the forest. "Hang in there. I think we're almost finished," he looked up as Rand joined them.

"Thanks again for the help," she told him. Then it hit her, why was Rand fighting with them? "I see you decided to join in and help the good guys?" she couldn't resist. "It's about time."

Rand brushed a hand over her head. Then studied the field. There were still battles going on everywhere, but the numbers were more to his liking. "Thomas needs help," he told Bastian. "Those

Shadows

things had a picture of him." He glanced back at Thomas and Abby. "They're holding them off pretty well, but Thomas is injured and I think they could really use reinforcements."

Bastian took Kylee's hand and ran for Thomas. He needed to help, but he wouldn't leave Kylee alone. He had to stop and kill a couple vampires along the way, but he joined up with Thomas a few minutes later. "You okay?" he asked.

"I'll live," Thomas assured him. He jerked his head toward Abby. "My hero over there is protecting me. Until I'm back on my feet anyway."

They all watched Abby in awe as she systematically killed vampire after vampire. Bastian turned to Kylee. "Can you take care of Thomas until he's ready to fight again? I need to help Abby," then he turned to Thomas. "She's injured too. Keep her safe," Bastian turned and rushed to Abby's side.

"Sorry," Thomas told her. "I can defend our position, but I can't do much good just yet. You okay other than the arm?"

"Yes. I think I sprained my ankle when I went down, but I'm fine. Where are you hurt?" She could tell it was mid body somewhere because of all the blood. She also saw the cut on his arm and blood on his pants where his leg had been sliced.

"One of those suckers got me in the stomach," he admitted. "It hurts like a bugger. I don't think it hit any vital organs, but man does it burn."

Kylee lifted his shirt and studied the wound. It was already starting to heal. The bleeding had stopped and his body had already sealed the wound. She pressed on a couple spots and when Thomas didn't scream out in pain, she decided he was going to be okay. "You'll live," she ducked as Thomas killed a vampire over her shoulder. "If we can survive this attack anyway," she corrected herself. The vampires were flocking toward them. It seemed they had all realized Thomas was their target and they were rushing in for the kill.

Victor noticed the vampires were all swarming toward Thomas and Abby. He kicked out and knocked one vampire into another one as he swiftly threw a star killing the one on top. Then he grabbed the other one and plunged his dagger into his chest. He turned to check on Ariel just in time to see her fly through the air and strike a tree. She hit hard and immediately fell to the ground. "No!" Victor screamed as he rushed to her aid. He sliced through a vampire on the move and got to Ariel just in time. Two more vampires were charging toward her. Victor took them out and crouched at her side. "Ariel, baby. Talk to me. Where are you hurt?" He didn't dare move her. She was just lying there moaning in pain.

Victor knew he had to get her out of there. They were too vulnerable. He turned and defended himself against two more vampires then studied the field. The vampires were still heading for Thomas. He hoped the others realized what was happening because he needed to focus on Ariel. He turned his attention back to her. She had turned over and was trying to stand. She faltered and fell against the tree again.

"No," he gently lifted her into his arms. "Talk to me Ariel. Tell me where you're hurt? You hit that tree pretty hard," Victor said soberly.

Shadows

"I thought I got them all when one darted from behind that wide trunk. I saw him out of the corner of my eye, but it was too late. He charged hard and fast. He got me in the stomach and I went flying. I crashed into the tree, hard," she winced. "Victor, I think I shattered my hip," she gripped Victor's shoulder as she tried to control the pain. The movement was killing her.

"I'm sorry honey, but I have to get you to the warehouse. You need to lie down. Once this is over Kylee can help you but you have to hold on for a little while," Victor looked around. At least none of the vampires were coming after them. He didn't know what he would do if he had to fight one off.

Ariel focused on holding back the tears. She was in so much pain. She wanted to scream, but she wouldn't. She had to be strong. She could bare this. That's when it hit her. Where were all the vampires? "Victor why aren't we getting attacked?"

"I don't know. For some reason they all made a beeline for Thomas and Abby. As soon as they saw them, the vampires immediately turned and headed their way," Victor said perplexed.

"What?" she said shocked by that revelation. "You have to help him. Put me down and go to Thomas," she demanded.

"No way babe," he smiled at her. "I'll be sure and tell him you cared though. The others noticed it too and they all rushed to his aid. Thomas is going to be fine," Victor hoped he was right. Ariel would never forgive him if anything happened to Thomas.

Ariel tried to look back over her shoulder, but the movement hurt too much. The pain was so intense she actually saw bright lights and had to close her eyes to regain her composure. "He better be," she warned. "I can't tell Alex her brother is dead. She's lost too many people already."

"Shush," Victor told her. "Try to relax. Did you make any tea before all this started? You look pale and I know you're in a lot of pain."

"No," she admitted. "It all happened too fast."

They had reached the warehouse. Victor carried Ariel upstairs and noticed the kids guarding the room. "Good job," he said looking for Nebi. "Where's your leader?" he asked.

One of the kids stepped forward. "She's inside. She was protecting Gerty when the vampires attacked the bunker. One of them charged and Nebi jumped in front of Gerty to protect her. Nebi went down pretty hard and a few of her ribs are broken."

Victor sobered. "Looks like you have company," he told Ariel. "Can you get the door?" he asked one of the kids.

"What happened to her?" The boy asked, concerned.

"We think she shattered her hip," Victor walked to the mat and gently set Ariel next to Nebi. "I hear you're a hero," he told the panther.

"Nope," she said ashamed. "I'm sorry. I went down pretty quickly. They took me out from the start. I guess that's not a very good leader."

"Nonsense," Victor told her. "You promised none of those kids would get injured and you kept your promise. I would have preferred it if you included yourself in that promise, but I'm proud of you. Hang in there a few more minutes and I'll send Kylee up to

Shadows

help," he leaned down and kissed Ariel. "Hold on babe. I need to check on the others then I'll get Kylee in here. You going to be okay?"

Ariel tried to smile, but knew she failed. "I'll be okay," she told him. "Be careful. I'm not going to be around to save you," she was only half joking. She hated knowing Victor was going back out there without her.

"I think I'll manage," he grinned. "I survived a few centuries without you. I don't plan to go anywhere now that I found you." He kissed her gently again and then left the room. Victor paused just outside the door. "You have precious cargo in there boys. Take good care of my woman until I get back."

"Yes sir," the kids promised.

* * * *

"We're leaving," Dimitri told Alex as he walked into the room. She looked up from the paperwork and scowled. "Where are we going now? I thought we were done for the night. Lawson's in custody," she paused. "Did you find the other girl?" she asked hopefully.

"No," Dimitri sighed. "We're going to the fort."

"The fort? Why?" Alex sobered. "What's happened?" She studied Dimitri. Something was terribly wrong.

"There's trouble, it's serious. I think they need you. We have to get there as soon as we can." He pulled out a bag and started to throw a change of clothes inside. "The planes ready, we need to leave." He walked to the closet and pulled out another bag then tossed it to Alex.

Alex jumped up and threw a few things in the bag, then turned to Dimitri. "Let's go." The two of them rushed to the car and sped towards the airport.

Thomas sat on a large chair in the mat room. He refused to lay on the mat any longer. His stomach was slowly healing, but it still burned. It had been almost an hour since the battle had ended. He was worried about Ariel, she'd suffered the worst injury. Victor prepared some tea, which had helped a little. Kylee wrapped Nebi's ribs to help with her pain. They were going to have to heal the old fashioned way. Thomas had tried to call Alex, but there was no answer. He didn't know where they could be but he wished he could get in touch with her or Dimitri. They needed to know what had happened here.

Everyone was sitting around the room. Nobody was willing to leave until the injured recovered. They also wanted to be together if another attack was headed their way. Tony and Megan had made it out unharmed. Ty and Sam were fine, so were Morrigan and Dusty. Dusty wouldn't leave Nebi's side. He sat beside her, holding her hand while she rested. Victor had made Ariel as comfortable as possible. He had just finished helping her with more tea when Kylee moved to Ariel's side. "I want to x-ray your hip. We need to see if it's healing on its own. I have a portable machine, but this will still be painful. Let me know when you're ready. Then I'm going to wait a half hour and do it again."

"Go ahead," Ariel told her. She pretty much ached all over so they might as well see what was going on in there. It didn't feel like the tea was helping at all. She wished Breena were here. She'd know what to do to help with the pain.

Kylee rolled the machine to Ariel's side. Victor took Ariel's hand in his, she was so cold and clammy. "I'm sorry baby. I know this is going to hurt. I wish I could take the pain away." He gently ran his palm over her head, then he nodded to Kylee.

Kylee took the x-ray as gently as she could. She knew Ariel was in pain, but she didn't know how to help her. Ariel couldn't take pain killers and Kylee wasn't familiar enough with the herbs Breena used to help. "I'll be back in a few minutes."

Bastian approached Victor. "Give her this," he said handing Victor a small cup. "It won't help with the healing, but it should help with the pain."

Victor took the cup from Bastian. He didn't hesitate. He knew he could trust his friend. He glanced at Ariel and wiped a tear from the side of her face. "Honey, I have something that Bastian thinks will help with the pain. Can you drink just a little more?"

Ariel opened her eyes and sighed. She'd take anything if it would help curb the constant ache. She sipped from the cup as quickly as she could. Then she laid her head back and tried to relax. She was shocked. It didn't take long before the pain began to subside. "Will you thank Bastian for me?" she asked Victor. "It's already working. He's an angel."

Victor relaxed a little. He was glad Bastian's concoction was starting to help. He frowned as he spotted Kylee. She looked serious and unhappy about something. "What's wrong?" he asked when she stopped by his side.

Kylee handed Victor the x-ray.

Victor took it, but didn't know what he was looking for.

Kylee recognized Victor's confusion and moved to his side. "Here is the fresh injury." She pointed to Ariel's hip. "We were right, the entire hip bone is shattered. I think it is starting to slowly heal itself. If we keep up the tea, she should be a lot better by morning." She glanced at Ariel and immediately noticed she didn't seem to be hurting as much as she had been before. "What changed?" she asked looking at Victor. "She looks better."

"Bastian," Victor said simply. "He gave her something for the pain. It's working," he looked back at the x-ray. "You said the fresh injury. What am I missing?"

"There's another problem," Kylee sobered. "This, right here. It looks like an old injury. She has a lot of scar tissue around this area. This wound wasn't dealt with properly. Did you even go to a doctor?" she asked Ariel.

"Uh..." Ariel hesitated. "Sort of. It was a long time ago," she said vaguely. "What about it?" she asked.

"Well, if you had gotten proper care everything would be fine. But the scar tissue is a problem," Kylee paused. "It could be a problem if you want to have children," she said honestly. "It might not be, but I thought you should know," she looked at Victor. "The chances of her carrying a child full term is minimal."

Victor's stomach clenched. Ariel craved a baby more than anything. He realized that once Breena got pregnant. He studied Ariel, he was worried about her. She was already hurting physically, now she was going to hurt emotionally. He would love

Shadows

for Alex to take care of this, but Ariel would never ask. He felt so helpless. He wanted to give Ariel the world and something important to her had just been taken away. Something he couldn't fix. "Thank you Kylee. Could you give us some time alone?"

"Absolutely," Kylee told him. "I understand."

Victor laid by Ariel's side and took her hand in his. "I want to hold you, but I can't," he said frustrated. "I know this is a blow, but we'll figure something out. Don't give up. Maybe we can adopt or something."

Ariel couldn't take it. The tears began to flow freely. "No," she finally said. "I couldn't do that. I couldn't have a child knowing it would only live for a few years and then we'd lose him or her. That would be worse than not having a child at all," she wanted to be alone. She hated being here in this large room surrounded by people. They were all sitting around celebrating their victory. "Can you move me to our room?" she asked. "I know you don't want to, but I need to be alone."

That hurt. Did she mean she didn't want him around either? "How is your pain?"

"Better. Please just get me out of here," she begged.

Alex rushed into the house but realized nobody was there. "Where are they?" she asked.

"The fort maybe?" Dimitri guessed. The two walked into the large warehouse and studied the room.

Alex spotted Thomas first. He was obviously in pain. She rushed to his side and pulled him into a tight hug. "Tell me where you're hurt."

"No wonder you didn't answer your phone," Thomas told her. "You decided to go on vacation."

Alex lifted Thomas's shirt and frowned. "This was bad wasn't it?" she asked soberly.

"Bad enough that I'm very determined never to have a stomach wound again," he admitted. Alex pressed her palm to his abdomen. After a few minutes Thomas was completely healed. His leg and his arm weren't bad but the stomach wound was serious.

"I should have been here," she said upset at their delay. "Who else needs my help?"

"Ariel's bad," Thomas admitted. "She shattered her hip, but Victor just carried her out of the room. I'm not sure what that's all about."

Alex frowned then spotted the teenager. "How about her?" she asked.

"Broken ribs." Thomas supplied.

Alex walked to Nebi and introduced herself. "I want to help you," she offered. "I can heal you. I just need to place my hand on your side. Don't move," she said softly.

Dusty nodded at Nebi's hesitance. "You can trust her."

Alex placed her hand on the girl and within minutes her ribs were healed.

Shadows

Nebi was surprised. Her entire torso felt better. She looked at Dusty then back at Alex. "Can I take the wrap off?" she asked.

"You can," Alex affirmed. "You might want to take it easy for a day or so, but you're as good as new." She stood and went in search of Kylee. "Where is Ariel?" Alex asked as soon as she spotted the doctor.

"I think Victor took her to her room," Kylee admitted.

Alex realized Kylee had been crying. "What's wrong?" she asked.

"I gave Ariel and Victor some bad news," she admitted. "I feel terrible about it."

"What bad news," Alex asked.

Kylee handed Alex the x-ray. "I explained the x-ray to her," Kylee said soberly.

Dimitri walked up and looked at the black and white graphic. "I don't get it. What's the bad news?" He realized her hip was shattered, but that would heal.

Alex studied the picture. "The scar tissue is going to cause her problems, won't it?" she asked. She gave Dimitri a knowing look and saw his face sober.

"Yes," Kylee told them. "Why didn't she get proper medical attention when it happened?"

"She got the best care there was at the time," Dimitri supplied. "It happened a very long time ago. Don't put human time frames on this. I think you know enough about our people to understand."

"Oh," Kylee did understand. How old was Ariel anyway?

"I took care of Thomas and Nebi, is Ariel the last one?" she asked.

"Yes," Kylee told her.

That's when Alex noticed the wound on Kylee's arm. "What about that?" she asked.

"Oh, that's nothing. I'm fine," Kylee shook off the offer.

"Give me your arm," Alex ordered.

Kylee only hesitated a moment. She'd seen Alex heal before but it would be different actually being the patient.

Alex healed her arm then quickly surveyed the rest of Kylee. When she reached her ankle, she fixed that too. "Okay, you're all better." Alex stood and headed for the apartments. She needed to see Ariel. She knew her friend would be upset.

Dimitri followed Alex out of the room. He waited until they were outside to speak. "You still willing to keep that promise?" he asked soberly.

Alex looked back at Dimitri. "I am," she told him. "I made a promise to you, I plan to keep it. Don't worry. But I want to talk to Ariel about this first. Under the circumstances I can't just do it and tell her later. I want her blessing going in."

"What if she won't give it to you?" Dimitri asked, worried.

Alex stopped and turned to the man she loved. "Dimitri, I made you a promise. Trust me. I won't let you down."

Shadows

Dimitri pulled her into his arms. "I know this isn't easy for you either. She needs you tonight. Try to convince her this is what she needs. No matter what happens in there, just remember I'll be here for you when you're finished."

They entered the apartment and spotted Victor in the downstairs lounge. "Go ahead," Dimitri told her. "I'll take care of Victor." Alex headed up the stairs as Dimitri veered towards Victor.

Victor was drinking. Dimitri settled onto the chair next to his friend and pushed the liquid away. "That's not going to help," he put a hand on Victor's shoulder. "Don't get angry. Trust me. Alex will take care of it."

"She doesn't want that," Victor said soberly and placed his face in his hands. "I don't know how to help her. She doesn't want me either. She's trying to push me away. I'm not leaving," Victor said stubbornly.

"Good," Dimitri told him. "She doesn't really want you to."

Alex knocked on Ariel's door but didn't get a response. She knocked louder.

"Go away," Ariel finally yelled.

Alex opened the door and walked inside. Ariel was curled up on the bed, crying. "Not likely," Alex told her immediately and closed the door behind her.

"When did you get here?" Ariel asked.

"We haven't been here long," Alex walked to a large chair and sat down. "Do you want to tell me why you're up here alone and

Victor's downstairs drinking?" Being direct always worked best for her.

"No," Ariel said simply. "I don't need your help, please leave."

"I see," Alex said sinking deeper into the chair. "I suppose that's what you told Victor, too?"

"Alex, I'm not in the mood for this. I want to be left alone," Ariel closed her eyes and tried to ignore her friend.

"Too bad," Alex countered. "I'm not leaving until we deal with this."

Ariel sighed. "Then you talked to Victor. He had no right to ask for your help. This is my problem. I'll handle it."

"I haven't actually spoken to Victor," Alex paused to let that sink in. "Oh, I know Victor would like me to help you, but he'd never ask. He'd feel like he was betraying you. I'm sure you've made it clear to him that you don't want me to fix this. Victor is an honorable man. He wouldn't go behind your back like that. It's disappointing that you believe otherwise."

Ariel cringed. She knew Alex was right. Victor would never do that as much as he might want to. She remained silent hoping Alex would leave but knowing she wouldn't.

"I saw the x-ray," Alex finally admitted. "The scarring would be an easy fix. I plan to heal your hip anyway."

"I don't need you to heal anything. Go away Alex. When my hip gets too painful Bastian can give me another dose of that pain medication," Ariel said more forcefully.

Shadows

Alex didn't move. She was going to heal Ariel one way or another tonight. The question was whether she would do it with Ariel's blessing, or without it. "I never realized you were so selfish," Alex finally told her friend. "I'm surprised at you, Ariel. Surprised, offended and disappointed."

"I'm not selfish and you know it. Stop trying to goad me," Ariel said defensively.

"You are being extremely selfish," Alex countered. "Otherwise Victor wouldn't be down stairs, miserable, trying to get drunk while you're up here pouting about your condition."

Ariel shifted so she could glare at Alex. "Victor's upset tonight, but he'll get over it and he'll be better off in the long run."

"Oh, really?" Alex said sarcastically. "Maybe you could explain that one to me. Because I really don't see how that's possible."

"Victor deserves more," Ariel said defeated. "I've watched him with the kids at the shelter and with the teenagers here. He's great with kids. He'd make a wonderful father. He deserves that chance. He can't have that with me."

"You mean you aren't willing to give him that chance," Alex corrected. "He's not important enough for you to put aside your stubborn pride and ask for help."

Ariel was shocked. That wasn't it. She wouldn't ask because it wasn't fair to impose on her friend like that. Asking for Alex to heal her would be selfish. She wouldn't use Alex that way. "You're wrong. This is about right and wrong, not about pride."

"So it would be wrong for me to heal you?" Alex asked.

"Yes," Ariel said confidently. "I won't use you that way. It's inappropriate."

"Have you told Breena how you feel? Does she know you think it was inappropriate for me to heal her? How did she take it when she learned you didn't think she deserved the chance to have a child of her own?" Alex asked calmly.

"What?" Ariel asked in surprise. "That's not what I said. I'm glad you healed Breena. She and Orin deserved that happiness."

"But you and Victor don't?" Alex asked. "Why not? Victor is a wonderful man. Why doesn't he deserve the opportunity to have a child?"

"He does," Ariel almost screamed. "That's why I had to push him away."

"So it's you that doesn't deserve to be a mother?" Alex asked.

Ariel didn't answer. The room was quiet for a long time. Finally she sighed. "Maybe not," she admitted. "Maybe this all happened for a reason. Maybe I'm not cut out for motherhood so fate stepped in to make sure I couldn't mess it up."

Alex wanted to scream, she wanted to tell Ariel she was being stupid, but she could see her friend was serious. "I think you know that's not true," she finally said. "Fate doesn't work that way. If it did, Victor wouldn't exist."

Ariel couldn't argue with that, but she didn't understand why this had happened to her. She also felt guilty about losing her

Shadows

temper with Victor. What if she did that with a child, her child? She was capable of causing so much damage.

"What are you not telling me?" Alex asked. "What happened that you're trying to hide? Something has you convinced you wouldn't be a good mother?"

"It doesn't matter," Ariel sighed. Alex wouldn't understand. She'd just twist things around and rationalize them.

Alex stood. "Okay, I'll just go talk to Victor about it." She took a step towards the door.

"No," Ariel said desperately. Alex couldn't ask Victor. He'd blame himself for this, too.

Alex paused and studied Ariel. Something had definitely happened out here. What was it? "It's your call Ariel. Either you fill me in, or I ask Victor."

"Has anyone ever told you it's rude to meddle?" Ariel asked. She didn't have a choice. Alex would go to Victor if she didn't explain.

Alex smiled. "Not lately," she shrugged and returned to her seat. "Out with it. Whatever happened you need to get it off your chest."

"I lost my temper with Victor," Ariel finally said. "I got so angry with him that I threw a fireball at his face. When it didn't hit him, I got even angrier. I walked over and shoved him a few times, then I took a swing at him. That's when he got angry and pushed me away. I flew across the field and hit a rock. Victor already blames himself for my injury, don't ask him about it. It will only make him feel worse," she was almost begging.

"And because of that you decided you wouldn't make a good mother?" Alex asked.

"How could you possibly think I would be?" Ariel asked, annoyed. "I got mad and threw fire at Victor. What if that was my child? A child wouldn't be fast enough to deflect it like Victor did. I'm too dangerous. Like I said, fate stepped in to make sure I can't hurt someone that helpless."

"Nonsense," Alex said, angry with Ariel. "First of all, I get angry with Dimitri and do things I would never do to a child. That doesn't mean I'd be a terrible mother. We all have doubts about our abilities. I can't even manage a dog, how am I going to be responsible for a baby some day? Should I give up on the idea, too?"

"Of course not," Ariel told her. "That's different and you know it."

"Ariel, I agree you shouldn't have thrown fire at Victor. However, I also know that the men we love can push us and irritate us and drive us to behavior we never thought we were capable of. I know that because I've been there. Dimitri can infuriate me like no one else. I think that's part of the package. Everything has to have balance. Dimitri can also make me happier than I ever thought possible. He gives me more pleasure and makes me feel more alive than I have ever felt in my life. You know what I mean because Victor does the same for you. You can't transfer the feelings you experience with Victor to some child you haven't even given birth to yet."

Shadows

"But wouldn't that be true of a child as well?" Ariel asked. "Wouldn't a child give you immense pleasure and purpose? And conversely make you angry and frustrated?"

"Maybe," Alex admitted. "But I still don't believe it's the same. I think the love would be just as acute because the child would be part of yourself and a part of the man you love so intensely," Alex paused. "But I don't think the anger or frustration would be the same."

"Why not?" Ariel asked truly curious.

"Because the pleasure isn't the same. Your relationship with Victor is more intimate than it would be with your child. Just like me and Dimitri. That intimacy intensifies all of our emotions. I know it does for me. Dimitri is my partner in every way. He's my best friend, my lover, my confidant. As much as I would love my child, the connection would never be the same. Oh, it would be just as strong, but different."

Ariel pondered what Alex was saying. She finally realized Alex was right. She had a very close relationship with her parents, but she knew the love they had for her was different than the love they shared with each other. Not less, but different. Mom never got angry or frustrated with her the same as she did with dad. Oh, she got angry but it was different. "Maybe you're right," Ariel finally admitted.

"For what it's worth, I think you would make a wonderful mother. I've also seen you with the kids at the fort. They look up to you. They respect you. They trust you. The same at the shelter. You bring those kids joy. Something they haven't had nearly enough of in their short lives. I agree that throwing fire at Victor may not be the best outlet for your anger, but don't confuse that with motherhood. Deep down you know you could never do that to a child. Any child, but especially not one that belonged to you."

"You may be right, but the whole thing is mute anyway. I can't have a child. Kylee confirmed that. And I can't ask you to change that for me. I'm not being selfish, Alex. I'm trying not to be. I don't want to use you that way," Ariel explained.

"Why is that your choice?" Alex asked. "Why do you get to decide who I use my gift on? If I want to use my gift to help a friend, why do you get to take that opportunity away from me?"

"Because I'm the one that would benefit," she argued.

"So would I," Alex corrected. "I have a unique opportunity to do something for a person I happen to love and respect. Why do you think it's fair to take that away?"

"I guess I never thought of it that way," Ariel confessed.

"Ariel," Alex studied her friend. "I'm going to heal you today with or without your blessing. I'm going to do that for several reasons. Only one of which is to help my friend. I'd like your blessing, but I don't need it," she paused. "If that means you push me away, I guess I'll have to live with that. I know going in that's the way you do things. You shut Sam out, now you're trying to shut Victor out. If you shut me out, I guess I'll have to deal with that."

"What if I don't let you?" Ariel asked surprised at what Alex was telling her. Was she right? If Alex healed her without her consent would she shut her out the same as she had Sam? The same as she was trying to do with Victor? It seemed she had another character flaw to work on.

Shadows

"You can't stop me," Alex told her calmly. "You're injured. I know exactly what I need to do to fix both. Your hip and the scarring. It will take less than a minute. You could try to fight me off, but even if you're successful I'll still have enough time to fix the problem. I don't want it that way, but I'm willing to do that if necessary."

"Why are you so determined to heal me?" Ariel asked, truly perplexed.

"Like I said, several reasons," Alex began. "I already told you one of them. I care about you. Next to Dimitri I consider you my best friend. You were there for me from the start. You helped me get through a time when I was confused and insecure. You taught me to fight, you helped me understand my gift and you pushed me when I needed to be pushed with Dimitri. I owe you a lot and I care about you. I look at this as a small way to repay you for all the favors the past few months."

"You don't owe me anything for that," Ariel countered. "I did it because I wanted to. I did it because you were my friend." That's when it hit her, Alex was trying to tell her the very same thing. Alex wanted to do this because they were friends. "You said there were several reasons," she pressed.

"Yes," Alex said honestly. "The second reason is because I made a promise to Dimitri and I won't break that promise."

"Dimitri?" Ariel asked. Then she understood. Dimitri would want this for her. He would need this. She wasn't surprised that Dimitri asked Alex to fix this when he saw the x-ray. It would be a natural, instant reaction. "I see," Ariel finally said. "But Dimitri's reaction is a shotgun reaction to a set of x-rays."

"No, it wasn't." She studied Ariel. "Dimitri didn't ask me to do this tonight. He did ask if I was going to keep a previous promise I had made, but it wasn't a shotgun reaction."

"When did you make that promise?" she asked.

"As soon as we knew Breena was pregnant," Alex confessed. "I didn't know there was a chance you couldn't have children. You conveniently left that out of your original explanation. Maybe because Dimitri told me the story or maybe because you didn't want me to know. It really doesn't matter which one. But, Dimitri told me you didn't know one way or the other. He wanted you to have that chance. He asked me to check and make sure everything was okay if I ever had the opportunity to heal you. I promised him I would."

Ariel was floored. Dimitri had asked that for her? She shouldn't be surprised. He had always been like an older brother to her. He had always looked out for her, but she was touched by the gesture. She was speechless.

"I am also going to do this for Victor. He is a wonderful, honorable man. He doesn't deserve to be treated this way," Alex paused. "Victor doesn't care whether you can have children or not, Ariel. He loves you and wants to spend the rest of his life with you. That man has suffered enough. If you are going to push him away and cause him pain because you won't ask for this yourself, I'll take care of this for him. Not because it matters to him, but because it matters to you and Victor is the one paying the price for that."

"I'm not trying to hurt Victor. I just thought he deserved more," Ariel said softly.

Shadows

"You say that, but deep down you know that Victor is not going to move on if you end this. He would never recover from that blow. Victor loves you unconditionally. He's not going to move on and have a happy family with someone else. Not tomorrow, not next year, not a hundred years from now. He's not built that way and you know it," Alex said bluntly.

Once again, Alex was right. She was hurting Victor. She was being unfair to him.

"I am also going to do this because it's time you put the whole ugly affair behind you. For over three hundred years you have dealt with the unknown. You have wondered if one twenty four hour period so long ago was going to impact your life forever. It's time that ends. It's time it was all put behind you so you can focus on the present and the future. No more questions. No more consequences because a few evil men took advantage of a young girl. It ends tonight. I have the power to rectify a wrong and I'm going to use it. Now it's your choice. Are we going to do this the hard way or the easy way?" Alex asked. "Any one of those reasons would be enough for me to fix this but when you combine them all together, there is no way I'm leaving tonight without healing you."

Ariel considered the situation then thought about all the things Alex had said. "Before I make a decision, I need to talk to Victor. Would you mind getting him for me?" she asked.

Alex studied her friend, was she up to something? "Okay, but just keep in mind that you can't shut me out. If you're up to something I have Dimitri on my side."

"I'm not up to anything. I just need to talk to Victor. We should make this decision together. You said you and Dimitri are partners in every way. Well, the same is true for me and Victor. I think it's about time I started treating him like one," she sighed. "Thank you, Alex. If nothing else, you've helped me to understand that. If I want to have a real, meaningful relationship I need to share my life with Victor. That means all of my life and all of my decisions. The important ones anyway. We can still pick out shoes together," she smiled at her friend. She was grateful they had become so close.

"Wise choice," Alex said standing and walking towards the door.

Alex entered the lounge and silently moved to the large table where the two men were now seated. She placed a hand on Dimitri's shoulder. "Victor, Ariel needs to speak to you." He looked so unhappy. She could strangle Ariel for doing this to him.

Victor gave her a hopeful look. Was this finally over? Was the worry and the fear finally going to be behind them?

Alex walked toward Victor. He stood and she pulled him into a big hug. "Go talk to Ariel. She needs you just as much as you need her right now," she smiled at him. "I was a little hard on her. She could probably use some TLC." She pulled out a chair and sat next to Dimitri.

Victor left the room and headed up the stairs. Alex hadn't given him much information. He wasn't sure what to expect from Ariel when he walked through the door.

"Did you take care of everything?" Dimitri asked.

"No. Not yet," Alex confessed. "But I will." She proceeded to explain the situation to Dimitri. Then they waited for Ariel and Victor to work things out and come to a decision.

Shadows

Victor pushed open the door and stepped into Ariel's room. A room that used to be their room. He wasn't sure how he was supposed to act, or what to expect when he got there. Ariel was lying on the bed. Victor studied her intently. She was still injured. Why hadn't Alex healed her? He glanced around the spacious area then started for the chair in the corner. Ariel had made it quite clear she didn't want him around.

"Victor," Ariel said softly. "I know you're angry with me, but will you please come over?" she pled.

Victor paused, looking at Ariel. Then he turned and sat on the edge of the bed.

Ariel tried to sit up but she couldn't. "I guess I'm going to have to do this lying down," she finally said defeated.

"Why didn't Alex heal you?" he asked. Seeing her in pain like this annoyed him. Was she so stubborn she wouldn't even let Alex heal her hip?

"Because when she heals me, she is going to heal me completely," Ariel said flatly. "I won't let her do that until you and I talk."

"Then make this quick. What do we have to talk about?" he asked.

Alex was right, Ariel thought. She had really messed this up. "Well, first I owe you an apology," she began. "Then we need to talk about what we want to do."

"Do about what?" he asked.

"Victor," Ariel didn't know what to do. She'd hurt him and he wasn't willing to forgive her as easily as usual for this. "I need you right now. I know I hurt you and I'm sorry, but I don't know how to fix this."

Victor wanted to stay angry but he couldn't. He hated seeing Ariel in so much pain, physically and emotionally. He loved her too much to be angry with her. His expression softened and he took her hand. "I'm not sure how to fix it either but tell me what you need from me."

That was going to have to do for now. Maybe by the time she finished with her explanation he'd understand. She took a deep breath and began to describe the situation to him. Once she was finished she studied him. She couldn't tell if he was angry or frustrated or what.

"I see," he finally said. "So what do you need help with?" he asked again. He was furious with her. How could she possibly think she wouldn't be a good mother and didn't deserve that opportunity? And did she really believe if she left him he would just move on without a second thought? He loved her dearly, but she was so infuriating.

Ariel let out a frustrated yell. "Will you just talk to me already? Which part of what I told you is making you angry?" she asked. "The most angry? Is it my thinking I could push you away and you would move on? Because I know that was stupid. It just seemed like a good idea at the time."

"It's insulting to know that you think my feelings for you are that superficial," he finally told her. "That you actually believe that you mean so little to me that I'd just go off and find another woman to replace you without a second thought."

Shadows

"I don't believe that," she whispered. "I know you wouldn't. You wouldn't do that anymore than I would. If I lost you, I would spend the rest of my life alone. I would miss you terribly and I honestly don't know how I could go on without you. Have I lost you, Victor?" she asked as a tear rolled down her face. "Have I messed this up so badly that you can't forgive me?"

Victor reached over and wiped the tears away. "No," he told her. "I can't live without you, Ariel. I'm angry with you. I'm hurt, but I don't think it's physically possible for me to walk away from you. No matter what you do, I will always forgive you."

"I don't deserve you," Ariel told him. "I know I've been so stupid and difficult lately. That's the worst part of this. I know how much you love me. I don't know why you put up with me. Especially lately with the fire and then this, but I do know you love me."

Victor leaned down and kissed her lips softly. "You are in so much pain. What do we need to decide before Alex can heal you? I hate seeing you like this. I want to hold you, but I don't dare."

"Will you hold me?" she asked. "Will you please lay beside me and let me feel your body close to mine?"

Victor turned so he could lay down on the bed. Then he gently placed his hand on her face and brushed another tear away with his thumb. "I love you more than life itself." He leaned in and kissed her forehead. "What is it we need to decide? You said Alex was going to take care of this with or without your approval."

"I want to know what you think. I need to know how you feel about this." She took a deep breath. "Alex told me something else. She was explaining how throwing fire at you didn't mean I would do that to my child," she paused. "So that part made you angry, too."

"It did," he affirmed. "It's ridiculous for you to think for one moment that you wouldn't be a good mother. One doesn't have anything to do with the other."

"Well, that's pretty much what Alex said too," she paused. "But she helped me understand something else. I guess it's something I already knew, but I haven't practiced it lately."

"What's that?" he asked.

"That we're partners," she told him. "That we are supposed to be partners in every way. Kicking you out of here the way I did wasn't being a very good partner. This isn't only my problem, Victor. I understand that now. It's our problem. I want us to make the decision together. I want to know how you feel about Alex healing me. You were willing to sit back and do whatever I wanted before, but you've never even hinted at what you want. You didn't ask Alex to heal me because I told you I wasn't willing to do that myself. But you never told me how you feel about it. I need to know what you think and how you feel."

Victor sobered. Did she really want to know? What if she didn't like his response?

"I can understand your hesitation, especially in light of my recent behavior, but tell me what you think," she pressed.

"I've told you before, you are enough for me," he said hesitantly. "Since I've been with you, I've wondered what it would be like to have a child. Mostly because I know it's something you want. I know how important it is to you. I don't think you can be happy with just me," he finally concluded. "Don't take that wrong. I do think I make you happy. I just think, like most people, having at least one child was something you always wanted. It would be difficult to give that up. We've already had this discussion. It's never been something I've planned on. That doesn't mean I wouldn't like it. It just means I'm happy either way."

"I'm sorry I've given you that impression," she said realizing that once again she had been hurting the one she loved. "You are enough for me." She didn't know how to explain this.

"Shhh," Victor said softly. "I understand. I guess there's only one question for you to answer. Do you at some point in our lives want to have a child with me?"

"Absolutely," Ariel didn't have to hesitate. "I want to explain that, though," she continued. "I would love to have a child with you. Partially for me, yes. Because like you said it is something I always hoped for. But I'm a little different than Breena because I knew, from a young age, that I might not ever be able to have one. Plus, I've had so many emotional issues to deal with I've never felt I was ready for that kind of responsibility. But you make me want it. You are so kind and wonderful and perfect in every way. I want to have a child with you because I want you to pass on those traits to a child of your own. I've watched you with the kids at the shelter. I know that's enough for you and it would be enough for me too. But I guess I don't think it should be enough for you. Look at the relationship you have with your father. I want you to experience that joy. I want you to have a son you can be proud of. Someone you can brag about to your friends. Someone that you can teach to be as kind and giving to others as you are. I don't know. I guess I think our kid would be pretty great," she said shyly.

"Then I think we should give ourselves that opportunity," Victor said, humbled by her words. "It's not like we're going to have a kid tomorrow. But I think we deserve the chance when, or if, we decide we're ready for that responsibility. Don't you?" he asked.

She smiled. "I do," she loved him so much. She really didn't think she deserved him. "Do you want to get Alex now?" she asked.

"I'll send her up," Victor stood and started for the door.

"Victor?" she called.

"Yeah?" he stopped.

"You are coming back, aren't you?" she asked.

"Oh, if you're sure. I just thought you might want to do this alone," he confessed.

"I told you, I want to start being partners. I don't want to do this unless you are sitting here right by my side. I know that might sound silly but it's important to me," she told him.

Victor walked back to the side of the bed and knelt down so he was close to her face. "I love you," he told her. "I would like that. Thank you." He gently kissed her lips then headed out the door, anxious to retrieve Alex.

Once Alex was finished healing Ariel, she studied the couple. "I know the two of you would like some time together, but I can't give that to you. There have been several developments. I had to get out here to take care of the wounded, but we also need to have a meeting. Dante and Nick should be at the house by now. Once we adjourn you can have all the time you need."

Shadows

Victor stood and hugged Alex. "Thank you," he said softly. "Thank you for giving us such a treasured gift."

The three of them walked down to the lounge and were joined by Dimitri. He immediately pulled Ariel into a tight hug. "Are you angry with me?" he asked.

"Nope," Ariel said lightly. "I know you were just looking out for me like you always do." The four of them immediately headed for the mat room to gather the others.

* * * *

The large group sat in the library waiting for Alex to fill them in. She turned to the enormous screen and addressed the members still in New York. "Dante were you able to get Mason Cooper and Travis Monroe?" she asked.

"We're both here," Mason announced and came into view on the screen.

"Thank you so much for coming. I know it's late, or make that early, but this is important," Alex assured them. "The first thing we need to discuss is Rand McBride."

Mason sobered. "Travis and I haven't come to a decision on that quite yet," he said soberly.

"Good," Alex interrupted before they could say something they might regret. "Because the situation has changed out here."

"Oh?" Monroe said surprised. "How's that?"

"McBride, would you mind joining me?" Alex asked. McBride stood and walked to the woman's side.

"I see," Monroe said surprised. "Well, it's good to see you don't have to be locked up McBride. Does this mean you're not going to hunt down Mason's family and kill them like the dogs they are?" he smiled a little.

"No sir," McBride answered. "I've had a change of opinion on that matter."

Mason was studying the man. He seemed to be taking the situation much better. He wasn't sure he could trust McBride yet, but this seemed to be a good start.

"So," Alex continued. "As you can see things have changed. Detective McBride chose to stay and help our group fight off several hundred vampires. He was given the opportunity to escape, but chose to assist instead," she paused for effect. "I realize this is a shifter matter, but I would like to give McBride my support. He showed great courage in the face of danger. I for one appreciate his willingness to get involved."

Mason narrowed his eyes at McBride. "Does that mean you shifted to help with the attack, or that you joined the fight as a man?"

"Both," McBride admitted. "I started to help, but quickly realized I was better equipped to handle the situation in another form. To be honest, I guess I changed a couple times depending on the situation."

"So you no longer believe some evil demon is inside of you trying to take over?" Mason asked.

Shadows

"No. I don't," Rand said embarrassed by his original assessment. "I realized rather quickly that my mother was wrong about that."

Mason turned to Monroe and the two of them had a short, private conversation. "Rand?" Monroe finally asked.

"Yes, sir?" McBride answered.

"We're curious. What are your plans now? What is it you are going to do with yourself? What do you plan to do with the information on the shifters, the fae and the warriors?"

"Uh..." Rand looked around the room. "These guys really haven't filled me in on what's going on here. I understand the shifter part of what you said, but I don't know what a fae or a warrior is," he paused. "Well, let me correct that. Now that I think about it, I assume the warriors are the fighters. I guess the fae are the mind readers and the fire throwers?"

"Close enough," Alex told him. "You have a lot of knowledge about our people Rand. That's dangerous for us and for you. At this point you have to make a decision. Either you're all in or all out. There's no fence sitting here, no gray area."

Rand looked around the room. "I'm in," he said confidently. "I know I have a lot to learn, but I want to be in if you'll let me."

"Are you sure about that?" Mason asked. "You can't change your mind later on."

"I'm sure," Rand said confidently. "I get it now. Balance, like you said. I want to be part of the solution."

"Good," Monroe told him. "That makes things a lot easier," he turned to Alex. "Atticus and Tala have Kahn in a secure location. Charles and Elizabeth have Lawson under control. There's still no word on Patricia, but we'll find her. It's just a matter of time."

Thomas perked up. "You have Kahn? And Lawson in custody?"

"We do," Alex told him. "That's part of the reason for this meeting. While you guys were out here playing, Dante and Nick apprehended Lawson," she sobered. "There is bad news. They caught him disposing one of the bodies. Tina, the aerobics instructor, didn't make it. But as far as we know, Melissa is still alive. Foster is still trying to determine the location. Lawson won't talk and Tala can't get in without his consent."

"I knew it," McBride said slapping his hand on his knee. Everyone looked at him. "Sorry. I just realized Tala Fitzgerald must be a mind reader like her daughter. I didn't mean to interrupt."

"So do you have a plan?" Thomas asked. "I'd like to get the NYPD off my back as soon as possible."

"That depends on McBride," Monroe stated.

"What's the plan?" he asked the chief. "I assume you have one."

"Well, it's still developing. Now that you're involved I think we can simplify it," Monroe answered. "We had a few obstacles to overcome."

"Lay it out. I think between all of us we can come up with something," McBride suggested.

Shadows

Alex was the one to answer this time. "There are several things we know for sure," she began. "We have absolute proof that Patricia is responsible for the trouble at the company. She was dumb enough to leave a photo with each of her victims. I've been able to talk to the other managers and pieced together a concrete case against her. The evidence is now in the hands of the council. Tala and Atticus have gathered enough evidence against Lawson to prove he was responsible for not only the bombings and harassment against Atticus, but he also built the bombs that were planted at the panther and shifter camps as well as the ones used at the Fae Ball. We still think he sold those to Lilith, but it doesn't really matter. He was responsible. There is also enough evidence to prove he killed Atticus' neighbor in his attempt to get at Atticus. The council also has all of that information. They are just waiting for us to capture Patricia to move forward. The rest is a little trickier," she admitted.

"Who are Lawson and Patricia?" Rand asked Kylee.

"They are members of our community that want to cause trouble for me and Thomas," Alex answered. "They want to be in charge and they're apparently willing to do anything to achieve that goal."

"Okay," he had more questions, but he'd ask those later.

"We know Kahn is responsible for the attack on Abby," she continued.

Rand shot his head over to Abby in surprise. "You were attacked?" he asked. "That would have been good information for me to have. It also could have cleared Thomas of suspicion," he grumbled.

"Not likely," Abby argued. "And we didn't exactly trust you at the time."

"Point taken. Am I missing anything else?" he asked.

"A bit," Alex admitted. "So Kahn attacked Abby and he also had to be responsible for Angie. We've already established the Dillinger's wouldn't cooperate with vampires."

"Sorry, but I'm lost," Rand interrupted again. "What do vampires have to do with my victims? And who is Kahn?"

"Angie had vampire marks on her neck. We didn't get to see the other victims, so it's impossible for us to determine which of the others were killed by Kahn and which ones were killed by Lawson and Patricia," Alex answered. "Kahn is a Columbian Drug Lord."

Rand's mind was racing. "I think I can answer that. You're talking about those two small round marks on the women's neck. They were partially obscured by the knife wounds."

"Right," Alex admitted.

"Well," Rand was thinking. "Diana had them. So did Susan and Tiffany. Regina didn't have them. There were other issues with Regina as well. The ME insisted she was killed by someone else. Angela also had them. I don't know about Tina. You said vampires. How do they fit in?"

"We're not sure," Alex told him. "We think somehow Kahn is involved with either Lilith or Radek. He abducted the women, gave them to the vamps who drained their blood, then Kahn slit their throat to cover up the evidence and dumped the bodies."

Shadows

"Tala's working on him right now. I'm sure we're going to have a better picture of how he's involved in a very short time," Monroe assured them.

Rand's features hardened. This was getting worse and worse by the minute. "You said you had some complications. What are they? And who are Radek and Lilith?"

"Well, we obviously can't turn Lawson over to the NYPD. He's fae. He can't go to a human prison. So we have to have enough evidence to convince a jury Kahn did it all." Alex explained.

"Why can't Lawson go to prison?" Rand asked, he wasn't comfortable letting a killer go free.

"I'll explain that to you later," Mason assured him. "For now, just accept that it's impossible. Radek is the vampire king and Lilith is his girlfriend."

"So because this Lawson and his mother are fae, they get away with murder?" Rand asked. "Do you think that's fair?" He was trying to follow, but he had so many questions.

"They aren't going to get away with anything," Alex said firmly. "Trust me, they will pay for their crimes. They are going to pay more with our laws than they ever would with yours."

Rand studied Alex. He believed her. "That's good enough for me. But I still don't see the problem. Tala can make Kahn believe he killed those other girls. It wouldn't actually matter if he denies it. Once we prove he killed most of them it's easy to include a couple more."

"First, we have to find Patricia and Melissa. Melissa's body can't show up after the NYPD has Kahn in custody. That is our first priority," Dimitri explained. "Once that's resolved, someone needs to apprehend Kahn. Now that you're on board it would be best if that someone was you," Dimitri explained. "That was one of the obstacles."

"No problem," Rand nodded. "What else?"

"We need evidence. Kahn can never be allowed back on the streets. That's something else you can help with. Cornelia has the stuff from the warehouse. We can now turn that over to you. But we need to know what a jury is going to need to convict Kahn of the killings. All the killings, no doubts. He needs to get the death penalty. How do we make sure that happens?" Alex asked.

"What did you get from the warehouse?" Rand wanted to know.

"Cornelia has pictures of foot prints. She also has a small piece of cloth. We assume Kahn snagged his shirt on a nail," Dimitri explained.

"I have those ready to be booked," Monroe supplied. "Now that you're on board, you should be the one to book them McBride."

"I agree." McBride told him. "I can help decide what evidence will be the most damning in trial. But how do we explain where we got the evidence?" Rand asked. He was pondering the situation.

The room was silent. Each member trying to come up with an answer.

Shadows

"You said Melissa is still missing," Rand began.

"She is," Alex told him.

"It's hard to develop a plan until we find her, but I think I might have a suggestion," he began looking around the room. "If you can find out where Melissa is being held, I think we can plant enough evidence to hang Khan. We can set it up to look like Kahn's hole, the place he held the girls until he killed them. Everyone knows they were taken, then held for days then killed and disposed of. We find Melissa and plant enough evidence that no one could doubt Kahn housed all the girls there."

"What kind of evidence and where do we get it?" Thomas asked.

"Hair would work best," McBride told him. "That's easy to plant and it would make sense the girls lost a strand or two in the fight. If we could get into the girls homes and ensure we were taking their comb or brush or pillow we could get a strand from each one. We only need one for each girl. Maybe a couple from one of the girls so it wasn't obvious."

"I can take care of some of that. Cornelia should be able to help as well," Thomas offered. "Regina is out of my reach, I didn't have a connection to her. I don't have a connection to Tina either."

"I can take care of Tina," Monroe assured them. "She's still in the morgue. Leave that to me. I can also get some saliva on a glass that we could leave at the scene."

"Good idea," Rand smiled. "But how are we going to deal with Regina?"

Abby sighed. "You say you've accepted your gift, but clearly you haven't. How hard do you think it is to get into a house?"

"I don't know, how hard?" Rand asked.

"Easier than sneaking into the police station," she grinned.

"You've been spying on me," McBride accused.

"Of course," Abby shrugged. "We needed to know what you were up to and what you knew."

"I guess I would have done the same," Rand conceded. "So, Thomas you work on collecting as much evidence as you can. What you can't get Abby and I will supply. We'll hold on to it until we find the hide out. It would be nice if we had a bracelet or necklace from one of the victims. Thomas, which woman was most likely to wear jewelry at the time they were abducted?"

Thomas thought about it. "Angie or Susan," he finally decided. "Angie wore bracelets frequently. I'll get one to plant in the room. I think that would be better than a necklace. It would be easy to lose a bracelet if she was trying to fight off her attacker."

"Let's go with that," Rand agreed. "We just need something, a plausible story that we can feed to the jury. We know Kahn did it, it's not like we're doing anything unethical," he turned to Megan. "Can't you just attend the trial and make sure the jury believes everything we feed them?"

Megan smiled. "As a last resort that might be possible. However, I'd prefer you present an airtight case instead."

"This might work," Alex told the group. "Monroe, Mason do you have any reservations?"

Shadows

"No. I don't," Mason assured her. "That man attacked and tried to kill my daughter. Regardless of his species, in my world that is an executable offense. Kahn is going to die. Normally it would be by my hand. Under the circumstances I am willing to allow the human justice system to facilitate his sentence. Like Rand said, there's no doubt about his guilt. In addition to the attack on Abby, Kahn has killed too many women in New York. Let's nail him. I want to make sure he can't get off on a technicality. We're going to have to find a way to tie that man from Pennsylvania in. Why would Kahn travel all the way up there and kill someone then try to murder Atticus?"

The group was silent. They needed a connection if they wanted the man gone for good. Prisoners, even those sentenced to life in prison, were frequently released on parole. If Kahn was ever released, Abby, Tala and Megan's lives were in danger. Maybe Atticus and Cornelia now too. Not to mention the numerous humans that came in contact with him daily. The case had to be plausible and there would need to be evidence backing up the story as well.

"The body at the farm would have been Kahn's first kill in the area." Mason began. "Obviously we have no idea where Melissa is being held but once we find her, maybe we can tie the Pennsylvania neighbor in that way. It would be easy to create fake documents linking the man to the hideout. We could just say the neighbor was killed by Kahn because he was the only person that could tie Kahn to the secret hideout where he took his victims. With Kahn's history, it would be easy to believe he was just tying up loose ends."

"That might work." Monroe considered. "We won't be able to finalize anything until we actually find that last girl. Once we do, we can see what Tala has tying Foster to the location and transfer some of that to Kahn. Don't worry, we'll come up with a plausible story and once Rand collects the evidence linking in Pennsylvania, he can turn that part of the investigation over to the locals. Believe me, they'll hit the ground running if for no other reason than to take the perp away from us."

"It's going to be a tightrope walk, but I think we can pull it off." Mason said soberly.

"I agree," Monroe told them. "McBride?"

"Yes sir," Rand answered.

"Will you please stop with the sir crap?" he said grumpily. "Save that for the office. We are putting a lot of trust in you. I can't help but think it may be too soon for that. Have you really accepted who and what you are? It just seems like a miraculous transformation. Why should we trust you with this?"

Rand understood where his boss was coming from but he could be trusted. "I don't know how to answer that. I don't think anything I say will convince you I'm on board one hundred and ten percent, but I am. I guess my only answer is because I want the man responsible for those deaths. This is my case, I want that man to pay. Forget all the other stuff if you need to. I'm sure you've looked into my record. You know my rep. Trust that I will do what's needed to ensure justice is achieved."

"I wish that were enough, but a lot is riding on your silence," Monroe pushed.

"Then all I can say is I won't change my mind. I was here during the battle. I saw the vampire's storm this compound determined to kill everyone inside. The first thing I thought of was

Mason's explanation. That we were created to ensure balance in the world. It may seem miraculous, but if you were involved in that battle, you would understand." McBride didn't have any other way to explain it.

Alex decided to speak. "I agree it seems like a quick turnaround but McBride learned about our world in an extreme way. I speak for my people when I say we're willing to put our trust in Rand McBride."

"Okay," Monroe agreed. He also believed in McBride, but he wanted the man to understand the gravity of the situation. A lot of people were counting on him. If he betrayed them, he was going to hurt more than just the shifters. "Then we're on hold until we find the other girl."

"Dante? Nick?" Dimitri called.

"Yeah?" Dante answered for them both.

"I just wanted to thank you publically for a job well done. You two were brilliant. Catching Lawson red handed that way will leave no doubt when this comes before the council. Thank you for all your hard work. You two haven't had much free time these past few weeks. Your sacrifice hasn't gone unnoticed. The same goes for the rest of you."

"Thank you," Nick said sincerely.

"Yeah, thanks. It does seem unfair that we missed out on the real fun but maybe the next battle will be here in New York," Dante grinned.

"Don't even go there," Alex warned. "You might jinx us."

Foster burst through the front door and ran into Thomas' library, clearly excited. Oberon followed closely behind him. "I think I found it," Foster said waving a handful of paperwork.

The entire group perked up. "What have you found Foster?" Alex asked.

Oberon explained. "We've been going through the records for those hotels in the ten block radius you provided. Foster found two things. First, he noticed a discrepancy in income. Basically it appeared someone was staying at one of the hotels for free." Oberon wanted to keep it simple. "So we dug deeper. He thinks he's identified the room his mother has been staying in. I agree. She's altered her name slightly, but it fits. The room shows as unavailable but not occupied. In the notes there is the name Trisha Diller. I have Tighe and Drake watching the place. We don't expect her to leave tonight. She's probably waiting for Lawson to get back. She doesn't know he's been apprehended."

"Mother's not the social type. She rarely leaves the house." Foster glanced at Alex then Thomas. "I'm sorry about the trouble she caused you two, but that was always during the day. She rarely leaves the house except to get her hair done and cause trouble apparently. Plus, she's obsessed with this project. I don't think she'll leave the girl alone at this point."

"That gives us time to get back to New York," Dimitri decided. "We'll be there in a couple hours. Make sure the hotel room is buckled down tight. We can't lose Patricia now. With Tina dead, we have to assume Melissa is going to be in bad shape."

"We're coming too," Thomas and Abby said at once.

Shadows

"Me too," Rand told them. "We need to secure the room and then immediately gather the evidence. The sooner the better. We can't postpone the discovery for more than a day. We need to get started on this tonight. Thomas, does that give you enough time to gather what we need? Once we get this Patricia woman out, we can plant the evidence. If I heard you correctly the hotel she's keeping Melissa in belongs to Foster."

"That's correct." Foster said, relieved they were nearing a conclusion.

"Then, with your help I think I can get a warrant and have the case closed before the end of the day. Chief Monroe, maybe you and Mason can come up with a connection between the hotel and the dead man in Pennsylvania while you wait for us to arrive. Finding that last missing girl in one of Foster's hotels may be a lucky break."

Bastian stood, "I'll pack some things. I need to be there to help with the girl. I think you should all be prepared for the worst," he sobered even more. "There's no way to know how many doses of that stuff Melissa has been given. If she's still alive, she's going to be comatose at best. She may have brain damage. Don't count on her as a witness. She's going to be lucky if she survives. I also want to look through any records or notes the two of them have recorded. I need to know all I can about this thing. It's our only hope of reversing the toxin."

"I agree," Dimitri told him. "Bastian needs to be closely involved." He turned back to the monitor. "Mason, with your connections at the police department can you get her assigned to you for treatment? That would help a lot. We could bring her out here to the fort and let Bastian and Kylee work on a cure."

Mason turned to Monroe. "I don't think that's going to be a problem, do you Travis?"

"No," he agreed. "I'll make sure of it. Let's get to work. We'll see you guys in a couple of hours."

Alex turned off the monitor. "We don't have much time, but I want to thank all of you for your hard work and diligence. The fort is coming along quicker than we had hoped. I can't say enough about the battle tonight. We had some casualties, but we didn't have any fatalities. That in itself is truly amazing. We have a long way to go, but thank you for everything." She took Dimitri's hand and headed for the door.

"Um, Alex?" Tony called. "Do you think maybe you have room for two more? Megan and I would like to join you in New York. For one thing we'd both like to see our parents. Plus, you might be able to use Megan's talents before this is all over."

"Sure," Alex told him. "We have room but we don't have a lot of time. Can you be ready in ten minutes?"

"Absolutely," Tony turned to Victor. "I'll give your love to dad."

"Not Elizabeth?" Victor joked.

"Her too," Tony assured him. "We're not going far. We'll see you in a few days."

"Will you do me a favor? Ask dad to stop in at Bojan Taverns and check in with Jack. I told him I'd be back days ago, but I haven't been able to make it," Victor requested.

Shadows

"We'll take care of it," Tony assured him. "If Atticus is busy, Megan and I will check in ourselves."

"Thanks man," Victor said taking his friends hand then bumping shoulders. "And don't let your parents leave until I get some time with them. I want them to meet Ariel."

"You know I can't control them, but I'll do my best," Tony said. "Gotta go. We need to pack a few things and I don't want to miss our ride."

Morrigan stood and walked to his sister. "You be careful, sis. I need to stay here a while longer. For one thing, I need to evaluate Gerty. As far as I'm concerned she's finished, but Dusty and Nebi are arguing to give her another chance. I want to deal with her personally."

Abby hugged her brother. "I'm so glad you got through that fight without getting hurt. I was too busy to keep track of you, but I was worried about you the entire time."

"Yeah, you were kind of the superstar of the night kiddo. All I can say is wow. Remind me never to piss you off."

Abby slugged him. "Stop it."

Thomas put an arm around Abby's waist. "He's right. I'm still in awe. Normally I wouldn't admit I was saved by a woman, but you are amazing babe."

* * * *

As soon as the plane touched down the group headed to the Deveraux mansion. They needed to finalize the plan. Foster was going to accompany them to the hotel and let them in. McBride and Cornelia were going to be there to get rid of any conflicting evidence. They didn't want forensics to find anything that could confuse a jury. They were going to hit the target at precisely eight o'clock. Thomas and Abby set out to collect evidence. What Thomas couldn't acquire, Abby took care of. They stopped at Angie's house last. It was locked up and secure, her parents hadn't arrived yet to clean out her belongings. Abby got in easily then opened the door for Thomas. They quickly gathered what they needed then locked up and headed back to the mansion to wait for an update.

Cornelia was waiting in the driveway when Thomas pulled in. He handed her the plastic bags through the open window.

"Were you able to get everything we needed?" she asked.

"It's all there," he assured her.

"Someone will call you when we're finished." Cornelia started the engine and shifted into drive. "Relax, this will all be over soon," she called as she headed back to the hotel.

Thomas opened the door and followed Abby into the library. They were both exhausted. The house was empty, but they knew that wouldn't last long. Thomas took her hand and led her to the large couch. He sat down and pulled her against him wrapping his arms around her waist. "I really am proud of you," he whispered.

Shadows

"You were so amazing during the battle and I couldn't have gotten that evidence without you today. You're pretty handy to have around," he teased then sobered. "I was so afraid you were going to get injured when I went down in that fight. But once you turned into that gorilla, words can't describe how amazing you were."

"They were coming after you, specifically. When I saw that vampire holding your picture I lost it. We just barely got together, there was no way I was going to let them kill you," she confessed.

Thomas laughed. "So give it a couple years and I'm on my own?" he asked.

"No. That's not what I meant," she sobered. She hoped they were still together in a couple years. Abby yawned. "I'm so tired. How can you even keep your eyes open?" she asked.

Thomas kissed the back of her head. "Go to sleep. I'll wake you when everyone else gets here. I promise. You look a lot better, but the last few days have been hard on you. Try to get some rest, babe."

Abby didn't hesitate. She couldn't have if she wanted to. She was so tired. She closed her eyes and immediately fell asleep.

Hours later Abby and Thomas entered the observation room of the police station and froze. Kahn was lying on the floor, writhing in pain. What was wrong with him? Thomas looked at McBride then to Megan and Tala. That's when it hit him. Megan and Tala.

McBride moved to stand next to Thomas. "Kahn's sister and his cousin stopped by asking to see him before the interrogation," he smiled. "I thought that was a wonderful idea." He turned to

Abby. "Tala's willing to take requests. Anything you want before we start the recorder?"

Abby was shocked. She looked at Tala then Megan. She'd never seen anything like this before. "Uh…no, that's okay. Just keep it general. The punishment can be for all of us, not one individual," she turned to Thomas. "You okay with that, or do you want to make a request for Angela?"

Thomas shook his head. He hadn't taken his eyes off Kahn. He wanted the guy to suffer for what he had done. It looked like he was. Thomas continued to study the man lying on the floor. He wanted him to pay for Angela, but even more he wanted him to pay for injuring Abby. Kahn screamed out in pain. Thomas jerked his head back to Tala and Megan. Which one of them had done that? Did it matter? Thomas was satisfied. Kahn was finally paying for his many crimes and he couldn't complain about it. Tala would take care of everything. Plus the guy would sound nuts if he claimed he'd been abused. He didn't have a mark on him. Thomas now understood why so many people feared the shadows. They were scary and ruthless when they wanted to be.

"You ready to go?" Thomas asked Abby.

Abby was staring at the man that attacked her. She thought back to the cave and Hector. She felt the same emotions right now. She was grateful the man was paying. He was suffering for the pain he had caused so many others, and her. She still didn't know what that said about her. Was she a bad person? Would Thomas still love her if he knew how she felt?

"Abby?" Thomas said again. "You ready to go?"

Abby jolted and focused on Thomas. "Uh, yeah. I'm ready."

Shadows

They walked out of the room and left the station. They didn't need to watch McBride's interrogation. Once outside Thomas turned to Abby. "Did that upset you?" he asked. "You seem okay, but are you? That was pretty intense. Can you live with his punishment?"

Abby looked at Thomas and decided to be honest with him. "Actually, it didn't bother me at all. Remember when I told you how I felt in the cave when you fought Hector? I was glad he was paying for tormenting others. I feel the same way about what's going on in there. That man is evil. Simply sending him to prison, even if he gets the death penalty, isn't enough. He killed a lot of innocent people for no reason. From what I hear, many of them were tortured. I'd be fine if they continued that for hours," she paused and looked at Thomas. "Does that bother you?"

"Not at all," Thomas said pulling her close. "I thought you were perfect for me. But you keep proving just how perfect you are over and over again." He leaned in and kissed her hard and fast. "I'm glad this is almost finished. Now McBride just needs to tie everything together so a jury can convict him. No loopholes for Kahn."

"Dad said McBride is going to spend some time with our pack and maybe Monroe's. Hopefully he'll find all the answers he needs in his personal life, too. He's coping better than I thought he would but he still has a long way to go," Abby told Thomas.

"What about his job?" Thomas asked. They needed him to make sure the case went as planned.

"Monroe is using that as an excuse to give him the time. It sounds like between McBride, Tala and Cornelia they already have the case prepared. But Monroe convinced the department to send

McBride to Columbia for a few weeks to follow up," she smiled. "He'll spend time with the pack and then return to the office with all kinds of information on Kahn's organization."

Thomas smiled. "I assume the information is complements of Tala Fitzgerald and her previous escapades?"

"One and the same," Abby grinned. "Everything seems to be falling into place perfectly." She sobered. "Any word on Patricia and Lawson?"

"They're securely in custody," Thomas told her. "They're not going anywhere. That case is locked up as well. The only question is their punishment. The council was inundated with evidence. It's going to take time to get through all the documentation Tala and Atticus gathered as well as the stuff from Alex and Foster. I think they'll have the trial in the next few weeks. Charles and Elizabeth have decided to stay until those two are sentenced. They have experience in this sort of thing. I'm grateful they're staying. Alex is worried, she feels like she's in over her head," he paused. "She's not. I'm confident Alex will do the right thing."

"I agree," Abby told him.

Thomas opened Abby's door then slid behind the wheel. "I hope Bastian can find a cure for Melissa," he said soberly. "Your family really came through for us with her."

Abby smiled. "It was actually pretty easy. Mom volunteers at the ER all the time. Nobody gave it a second thought when she showed up unexpected. All she had to do was keep herself busy until Melissa was admitted. Dad was the obvious choice. The hospital authorities called him immediately. Monroe agreed on behalf of the PD of course," she smiled. "Mom's documentation is going to help in Kahn's case but it also paved the way to release Melissa to dad so he could get her the special care she needs."

Thomas checked the clock. "Bastian should be touching down right about now. Between him and Kylee, Melissa will get the best care possible. If anyone can reverse the effects of that toxic formula, they can."

"Can you believe what the Dillinger's used on those women?" Abby said amazed. "How did they think anyone could survive multiple doses of that poisonous concoction?"

"Honestly, I think they're a little nuts," Thomas admitted. "I'm just glad we found her alive. Hopefully Bastian and Kylee can sort out the haphazard notes Patricia kept. But there are so many documents and most of them don't make any sense. It's not going to be easy, they can't just reverse the potion and fix the problem. It's going to be a long, hard process."

"I'm going to hope for the best," Abby told him.

"That's because you are the most optimistic person in the universe." He grinned at the annoyed look she gave him. Thomas pulled into the drive and shut off the engine.

"I thought you said you were taking me home," Abby said confused.

Thomas got out of the car and walked around to let Abby out. "I wanted to talk to you about that. Do you have time?" he asked hopefully.

"Sure," Abby said curiously. "But can we sit outside a while? It's such a nice night and it's going to be winter soon."

"Okay, I'm gonna grab a beer. You want anything?" he offered.

"Just a Coke?" Abby told him. She stopped to take a long deep breath of fresh air. It seemed like such a peaceful night. "It's like we've been carrying the weight of the world around for weeks and it's finally been taken off our shoulders," she smiled at Thomas. "It feels good to know we can finally relax a little."

"It does," he smiled at her. "I'll be back with your Coke."

Thomas walked onto the porch and saw Abby relaxing in the large wooden swing. He maneuvered her body so he could set her head in his lap. He instantly felt relaxed. He wanted to do this for the rest of his life. "Abby, I know my life is hectic and crazy a lot of the time."

Abby smiled. "I think that's an understatement." She didn't even open her eyes. She was too relaxed.

"Maybe," He agreed. "I'm wondering if you've thought about that."

"Which part?" she asked casually.

Thomas thought Abby was too relaxed. He was trying to have a serious conversation. He pushed her shoulders up to make her sit.

Abby took the hint, but was a little annoyed. She'd been comfortable. She studied him and realized something was up.

"Every part," Thomas finally said. "I live in the spotlight. The first time we go out on the town, there are going to be a million camera's following us. We're going to be plastered across every

Shadows

tabloid the following morning. I'm just wondering if you've thought about the complications."

"Well, I'll need plenty of notice?" she decided. "I don't want to hit the front page of Newsweek in sweats and a t-shirt."

"Abby, I'm being serious," Thomas said. "We've been sheltered so far because nobody knows you're staying here. Word hasn't gotten out about us. When it does, it's going to be a circus. The media is going to be asking you questions. They'll follow you to the grocery store, they'll climb into the neighbor's trees in an attempt to get a compromising picture."

Abby looked around wide eyed. "Do you think they got us relaxing on the swing?" She smiled mischievously then straddled his lap. "This might make an interesting intro." She leaned in and kissed him. It was soft and gentle at first, then long and passionate. Abby eventually leaned back and looked at Thomas. He looked conflicted. "Lighten up Thomas," she whispered. "I know who you are. I understand the situation. If you think I'm going to run away and hide the first time we're accosted on the street, you're wrong."

"I wish you would take this more seriously," Thomas told her. "I love you, I'm still not sure you understand how much. I don't want to lose you over this. I'm trying to make sure you're prepared. Sometimes the media can be overwhelming."

Abby kissed Thomas again. "I am prepared," she ran her fingers through his hair. "Thomas, the press will die down. They're not going to be focused on us forever. Not continuously anyway. I can handle it. I mostly worry about doing something to embarrass you."

"Abby, you could never embarrass me," he studied her. She didn't seem to be upset or taken off guard by what he was saying. "If it gets to be too much, will you talk to me? We can try to work something out if you can't take it."

"I promise," she grinned. "Now can we do something more interesting than talk about the paparazzi?"

Thomas frowned.

"I'm not trying to make you angry," she told him, pressing her body closer to his. "I know you think this is a problem, but I don't," she paused. "How is Dimitri handling things with Alex?"

"Fine," he told her. "But they're engaged. The story isn't as enticing."

"Well," she paused. "I guess we could get engaged. Would that solve the problem?"

Thomas grinned at Abby. "I can see you're joking but eventually, I will be engaged to you Abby."

She was serious now. She wanted that more than anything in the world.

Thomas laughed. "Not so funny now, is it?" He put his hand behind her head and pulled her closer. Then he gave her a quick kiss. "I will marry you, Abby Cooper," he said softly. "Am I scaring you, yet?"

"Not at all," she said softly. "Does that scare you?"

Thomas laughed and stood, cradling Abby in his arms. "No, but I do want to take this slow. There are two reasons for that. We started this under extreme circumstances. I'd like time to court you a little. I want to take you to dinner and buy you flowers. I want to sweep you off your feet."

"I think you just did," Abby laughed.

Thomas ignored her as he walked into the house. "The second reason isn't as important, but I think it would be smart," he continued. "Alex met Dimitri and rushed into an engagement. It worked for her, but I don't think it would work as well for us. First, the papers would assume you were pregnant or something. They wouldn't take us seriously, that would make things worse. I'm sure they'd invent some sordid and outrageous story to explain the quick marriage. I want to avoid that."

"Sensible," Abby told him.

Thomas reached the top of the stairs. "Your room or mine?"

"Yours," Abby decided.

Thomas placed Abby on his bed. He studied her for a long serious moment. Then he knelt in front of her. "I don't know anything about your customs, so I need your help to get this right. I'd like you to move in with me but I'll understand if you're not comfortable with that," he paused. "Abby, I love you. Publically we'll take this slow, but I want to start my life with you immediately."

Abby was happier than she'd ever been. "I'd like that too," she told him.

"So you'll move in with me?" Thomas said anxiously.

"Of course," she flung her arms around him. "This all seems so surreal," she looked around the room. "How many drawers do I get?" she glanced at the closet. "I've been in there, it's a little crowded already," she teased.

"Actually, I was thinking we could remodel the master bedroom," Thomas admitted. "I haven't moved in there yet. I was more comfortable in my old room, but I think it's time to clean it out and redecorate to fit our needs," he smiled.

Abby realized Thomas was talking about his parent's room. "Are you ready for that?" Abby asked seriously. "If it makes you uncomfortable I'd be okay in here."

"I'm sure," Thomas sat on the edge of the bed and studied Abby for a moment. "I love you Abigail Cooper. I want to begin a long, happy life together starting tonight. This house means a lot to me. I hope you can be comfortable here. But I want it to be our home. After I court you and convince you that no man alive could ever love you as much as I do, I want to marry you. I don't know about shifter customs so you might have to do all the planning when we get to that stage. Our wedding can be whatever makes you happy," he paused. "If it matters, I would be happy with something small."

"Thomas, that almost sounds like a proposal." She considered what he was saying. She liked the idea.

"Not even close. When I propose to you, it won't almost sound like a proposal. You will have no doubt what I'm asking," he grinned at her. "And if I do it right, you won't be able to refuse."

"Maybe you should pinch me," Abby grinned. "I want to make sure I'm not dreaming. It's not every day the world's most eligible bachelor makes such an offer to a small town girl." Abby grew serious. "You work so hard, you control the biggest company in the world and I don't even have a job. The media will capitalize on that. When they find out about us, my lifestyle is going to cause problems for you. I'm not bringing anything into this relationship. Are you ready for that?"

"They already say Alex and I are in over our heads. That we don't deserve the power and the wealth. That dad made a mistake by leaving his massive empire to a couple spoiled children. I'm ready, Abby." He pushed her down onto the bed then hovered over her. "What you bring to this relationship, can't be bought. I don't care what everyone else thinks. I know you are the only girl for me," he kissed her fervently.

Abby studied Thomas. He didn't seem worried. She grinned at him then rolled Thomas on his back and straddled his body. Her smile widened.

"What?" Thomas asked.

"Well, you said you wanted to start our life together tonight," she began.

"I do," he told her seriously.

"I was just trying to decide how to make it memorable," she mused. "We are both going to live a very long time. What could we possibly do to make this an amazing, unforgettable, earth shattering night?" She pretended to ponder the question.

"I'm sure we can think of something," Thomas pulled her down and kissed her again. His emotions were all over the place.

He felt so much love for this woman, but he was also amazed and excited that she was going to be his forever.

Abby slid her hands under his t-shirt. She loved to feel his hard muscles against her soft palms. She slowly leaned down and bit the side of his neck. "I have to warn you," she whispered. "I'm feeling a little frisky tonight," she paused. "We've been under so much pressure and now it's instantly gone. I haven't felt this good in years. In fact," Abby smiled, "the last time I felt this good, I got a little carried away. The guy wasn't man enough to handle my wild side. He passed out." She laughed at the look Thomas gave her then raised an eyebrow at him. "Do you think you're man enough to handle it?" Abby challenged.

Thomas rolled over and pinned her to the bed. "I knew I was the luckiest man in the world." He trailed kisses up her neck until he reached her ear, then he paused to whisper softly. "Give it your best shot, babe."

A slight breeze drifted through the open window and settled over the couple. The moon was full and their future was bright. Thomas and Abby blocked out the worries of tomorrow and focused on each other and their love. In that moment, nothing else mattered. Tonight was the beginning of a new life for both of them. A life full of possibilities. Everything else could wait for another day.

THE END